PRAISE FOR *THE FORGOTTEN HOURS*

"A deeply moving story about friendship and love, yearning and passion, memory and loss. *The Forgotten Hours* is a brilliant debut from a writer of uncommon grace."

—William Landay, *New York Times* bestselling author of *Defending Jacob*

"As fictional characters go, Katie Gregory seems not so much imagined as compelled into being by the unique forces of the times—the perfect envoy to accompany you into the red-hot cauldron of accused and accuser. That Katie is neither of these but bound by love to both makes her conflict more gut wrenching and the possibilities more terrifying. Add to this Schumann's gift for knowing—and conjuring—her character's heart, and you have a story that makes you feel it's *your* heart at risk, *your* life on the line. You may lose track of these hours, but you won't forget them."

—Tim Johnston, *New York Times* bestselling author of *Descent*

"*The Forgotten Hours* poses a super-timely question: In a #MeToo situation, who would you side with, your accused family member or your best friend, the accuser? A relevant, compelling, and compassionate look at the torture of conflicted loyalties and the slipperiness of truth."

—Jenna Blum, *New York Times* bestselling author of *Those Who Save Us* and *The Lost Family*

"With an elegance of style surprising in a first novel, Schumann shows how, when we seek truth about the past, the most treacherous secrets are those we keep from ourselves."

—Carol Anshaw, *New York Times* bestselling author of *Carry the One*

"*The Forgotten Hours* is a wise reminder that 'coming of age' stories aren't only for the very young. Katie Gregory's need to confront her own youthful beliefs and desires is something familiar—and compelling—to us all. There is so much insight in these pages, so much compassion, all woven into a mystery I couldn't put down."

—Robin Black, author of *Life Drawing* and
If I Loved You, I Would Tell You This

"*The Forgotten Hours* asks important questions about memory, adolescent understanding, the age of consent, and what men have gotten away with since time immemorial. Katrin Schumann has crafted a powerful tale for the #MeToo era which should resonate far beyond this cultural moment."

—Miranda Beverly-Whittemore, *New York Times* bestselling author of
Bittersweet and *June*

"*The Forgotten Hours* is a stunning novel about trauma and shame, loyalty, and truth. Ten years after an alleged crime destroyed her family, Katie Gregory returns to an abandoned cabin she prefers to forget. As memories of her last evening there bring conflicting emotions, she struggles to rediscover her ability to trust and her faith in love. Was her father guilty of the assault for which he was convicted? What part did she play in events of that night, and can she move beyond her own guilt? Trying to unravel the answers before the heart-pounding finish will keep readers up way past bedtime. A must-read for book clubs."

—Barbara Claypole White, bestselling author of *The Perfect Son*
and *The Promise between Us*

"For me, the best indicator of a good book is when you're thinking about the characters even when you aren't reading and wondering what's going to happen to them. This was definitely the case with *The Forgotten Hours*. I thoroughly enjoyed this well-written, compelling story."

—Marybeth Mayhew Whalen, bestselling author of *When We Were Worthy* and cofounder of She Reads

THE
FORGOTTEN
HOURS

THE
FORGOTTEN
HOURS

KATRIN SCHUMANN

Text copyright © 2019 by Katrin Schumann
All rights reserved.

Published by Lake Union Publishing, Seattle
www.apub.com

Amazon, the Amazon logo, and Lake Union Publishing are trademarks of Amazon.com, Inc., or its affiliates.

ISBN-13: 9781542040037 (hardcover)
ISBN-10: 1542040035 (hardcover)
ISBN-13: 9781503904170 (paperback)
ISBN-10: 1503904172 (paperback)

Cover design by David Drummond

Printed in the United States of America

First edition

To Kevin,
my love

For the want of a nail the shoe was lost,
For the want of a shoe the horse was lost,
For the want of a horse the rider was lost,
For the want of a rider the battle was lost,
For the want of a battle the kingdom was lost,
And all for the want of a horseshoe-nail.

—Benjamin Franklin

PROLOGUE

June 2007

Two girls—almost young women, but not quite—stand side by side on a dock in the shade of an old green boathouse. Their arms and legs prickle with goose bumps. Their skin is winter pale. One has a spray of purpling bruises on her thigh, and the other has forgotten to shave. They are laughing and laughing, their toes curled over the edge of the dock, splintered after months of snow cover. Below them the lake is chilly, not very inviting. The girls are eager to launch into their summer rituals, but neither has the courage to plunge in first.

The taller one, Lulu, is fifteen years old (or so she says). Over the past year, since Katie last saw her, she has grown two inches and let her black hair grow out so that it shifts in the wind, alive. There are hints of blue in it. Her body is soft and curvy; she has gained weight since last summer, and it suits her. When she's older, standing in dressing rooms blasted by fluorescent lights, she will curse her flaring hips, think they're ugly. And yet even now, men and boys—girls too—find their eyes drawn to her.

A man comes toward them, whooping loudly, and dares them to jump into the lake. His laugh bounces over the water, off the pines on the opposite bank, and then back at them. He's wearing faded pink-and-green swimming trunks, musty from being crammed in a drawer.

Lulu is almost as tall as he is, and her hair touches his shoulder as he stands next to her, eyeing the spring-fed water. He is stocky and muscular, the hairs on his broad chest darker than the closely cropped hair on his head.

"My beautiful girls," he says, though only one of them is his child. "Too cold for you?"

The other girl is his daughter, Katie—the slight one with the lank, midlength blonde hair. She feels as though she might burst when her father smiles at her. His approval is oxygen to her. It is always this way. Everyone wants to please him, make him laugh. She'd like to jump in to show him how tough she is, but she can't.

Her father's shoulders are hunched against the early summer breeze. He shoots them both a wide smile, the slight gap between his front teeth like an exclamation point on his good humor. Each summer, John Gregory's the first to swim out to the buoy and back. He's the one who braves the teeming ShopRite in Blackbrooke to stock up on all the best junk food, with some veggies and oatmeal thrown in for good measure. Early mornings, he'll take the kids bird watching, and late at night he'll make hot chocolate after they've been playing Marco Polo in the lake beneath the stars, cords of hair sending icy water dripping down their backs.

Now the sun, slowly gathering force, emerges from behind a cloud, and abruptly a thick ray lands on their cool skin. John yowls playfully, like an animal. He grabs Lulu's hand and propels himself into the water.

She lets out a scream. A second later, Lulu shoots up from the sparkle of the lake, sputtering. John races away from her toward the Big Float, leaving behind a trail of blocky whitecaps that peter out as they near the shore.

Katie watches the two of them. The wind whips her hair into her eyes. Seeing her friend in the flesh again always makes her a little shy. They said goodbye not far from this very spot last September, and now it is June again, an endless cycle. Each year Lulu comes to visit Eagle

Lake, and each year they silently catalog the infinitesimal changes that have taken place since they last saw each other. This year the changes in Lulu are more dramatic: longer legs, a rounder face—and her lips are fuller, her dark eyes more angled than before. A new tone to her voice betrays a hint of skepticism, a secret not yet shared.

Though she doesn't show it, Katie is self-conscious in the red string bikini she's had forever. Her body has changed, too, in ways she doesn't like. Heavier breasts, stronger muscles. That slight curve of her belly. She feels old and young at the same time. To her, the world is uncertain and wide open, full of unknown possibility. There is noise around her, and silence too—the silence of the woods, which to her seems almost loud as it hums inside her. Happiness laced with agitation, impatience. Contradictions everywhere.

Lulu is racing after John, though she has no hope in hell of catching him. He has swum into the darkness under the Big Float, which bobs high on eight empty oil barrels. All you can see from the shoreline are the shadows slung underneath the barrels, illuminated briefly by slivers of light, then plunged into darkness again as John tips the float back and forth. It is a dare: Will Lulu swim under there to catch him? When the girls were little, they were too afraid to swim underneath the float with its ropy, glistening spiderwebs hovering just above the shadowed water.

Katie sits on the grass by the pile of clothes they tossed to one side. She tilts her head back and looks up at the sky, inhaling the smell of ferns and mud and a lingering hint of her father's body odor. Above her, the clouds vanish, and the sky is a flawless blue, full of promise. This summer will be different; she can feel it in her bones.

PART ONE

1

June 2016

Katie had hated the sound of a ringing telephone ever since she was a teenager. Relentless, jarring—the way it broke into the moment, insisting that whatever the caller had in mind was more important than whatever you were doing. Today, when the phone jolted her awake, it wasn't even eight o'clock yet. A Saturday morning.

The sheets were warm, imbued still with the loamy smell of sex, and Katie smiled to herself, thinking of Zev. He'd been waiting for her at the apartment when she got home from work last night. Before she'd even shrugged off her suit jacket, he'd pulled her limp dress shirt out from the band of her skirt, placed his hands on the skin of her waist, and lifted her off her feet, carrying her to the bed (really just a queen mattress lying on the floor). She'd liked the way his gesture felt empowering yet also assertive—she gave in to it all. They'd tripped around, laughing, struggling to shed their clothes before falling to the floor, entwined. It was heady, this feeling of not being in control. The awkward fact that he had let himself in without asking—no text, nothing—was overshadowed by her pleasure at seeing him. The graying brown hair, the deep creases etched into his face, the thin T-shirt, worn out and yet somehow elegant. He was older, different from the boys she'd been with in college and the men here in the city.

Zev had left hours ago. He was mounting a show at a new gallery in the Village and had gone to meet the van carting two dozen carefully chosen sculptures and paintings from his studio up at Vassar. She turned her head into the pillow and grinned, remembering. Remembering. *God!*

Then another buzzy ring, but it must have been the wrong number—there was a click on the other end when Katie picked up, and she tossed the receiver aside. The warmth of the sheets was so lovely on her skin that it was hard to accept she was fully awake now and there was no point in trying to go back to sleep. She cast off the coverlet. The window over Hester Street was wide open. In the two and a half years she'd been in New York, she'd become immune to the howling sirens, drivers cursing at each other in Farsi and French, and mothers screaming in panic for their unruly kids, all before the sun even rose. The air had a spring chill to it, and she grabbed a tattered silk robe and headed for the kitchen. She was ravenous.

The apartment was in a renovated sewing factory on the Lower East Side, with crumbling redbrick walls and soaring ceilings. Insidious winds forced their way in through the window cracks during winter, ice creeping over the panes like a crystalline fungus. Her roommate, Ana, had moved out a year earlier to get married, and the silence still seemed fresh, the space no longer cluttered with her cast-off shoes and errant bobby pins. Above a frayed velvet couch hung an oil painting of a boxer in the ring, the canvas taped in the middle where Katie had snagged it on the edge of a dumpster as she'd hauled it out. On the wall near the kitchen was another oil painting, one of Zev's: an enormous, unidentifiable flower, colored shades of red and purple so deep it was almost violent. He'd told her it reminded him of her, whatever that meant.

In the fridge: some yogurt, skim milk, cheese *bourekas* Zev had brought over yesterday. At the sight of the food, her stomach tightened. Maybe coffee instead. Her cell phone, left in haste on the butcher-block countertop last night, showed two emails from the office (her boss was a total workaholic) and a text from Zev with a picture of the van in the gray morning light. The time stamp read 5:54 a.m.; he was an artist, but he sure wasn't a slacker.

When the apartment phone rang again, Katie hesitated, annoyed. She could count on one hand the number of times anyone had called her on the landline since she'd moved in—that is, anyone except her father. He was the only reason she even had a landline anymore.

"Hello," she said, reaching up to grab the coffee filters with one hand, tucking the receiver between cheek and shoulder.

"Katherine Gregory?"

Absolutely no one called her Katherine, and more importantly, she hadn't used the name Gregory for six years. No one had connected the dots between who she'd been before the trial and who she was after, when she'd adopted her grandfather's surname. "Who is this?" Katie asked.

"It's Marjorie O'Hannon, from the *Boston Globe*. You're John Gregory's daughter, is that right?"

Instantly, Katie clicked the off button. The coffee filter fluttered to the floor and tumbled around in the draft at her ankles. An image of her father came to her: his broad, cheerful face when she'd visited him a few weeks ago. His release date from Wallkill had finally been confirmed for June 23. He was ecstatic—he wasn't worried about a single thing. He had spent almost six years in prison, and now the nightmare was over, finally, truly *over*. He was dying to fire up a grill again, to stress over whether to buy skim or 2 percent milk, use teriyaki or steak sauce. He longed to play Angry Birds and try out Spotify. He knew so much about what was happening in the outside world without being able to participate, and now, soon, he'd be starting over. Neither of them mentioned, of course, that he would probably never be able to work in finance again, could never set foot in a school or live anywhere near where kids congregated.

The phone in her hand rang once more.

"What do you want?" Katie asked.

"Please, Ms. Gregory—listen," the woman said, her tone softer now, more conciliatory. "I want to hear his side of the story, your—"

"Who the hell are you, anyway?" Katie interrupted.

"I'm with the Spotlight team." There was a brief pause as the woman let the implications of this sink in.

"Just leave us alone, okay?" Reflexively, Katie turned to glance around the loft, thankful Zev was already gone. "Stop calling—"

"Your father has a right to tell his story, doesn't he? And we want to be fair—we want to understand your perspective, in particular regarding his long sentence."

Katie snorted. "And you're on my father's side? Right."

"No, that's what I'm telling you. We don't take—"

"And anyway, it's not a national story," Katie said. "The jurors deliberated for *five days*. There was nothing clear cut about his case. There was zero evidence."

"That's my point, Katherine."

The fake chumminess. The use of the wrong name. Panic began beating its ragged wings. "Why are you dredging this up, then?"

"Listen, we'd like to hear your thoughts. We've already spoken to your friend Lulu Henderson."

Her friend Lulu. Lulu had turned out not to be who Katie had thought she was. The nauseous sensation in Katie's stomach jumped to her throat.

"You're going to be getting other calls," the reporter continued. "Everyone's interested in these guidelines—the new sentencing guidelines. Whether public perception is influencing judges. We'd like you to tell Spotlight your story."

"I can't help you. And don't call me again," Katie said, hanging up.

She yanked out the phone plug. Outside, rain began to fall. She covered her face with her hands and started breathing in and out slowly. Time seemed to collapse in on itself. She was slipping into an adjacent world in which her memories of that summer were suffocatingly close, colors and shadows and smells emerging into spectacular focus—all the things she had been trying to forget.

What had Lulu gone and said now?

Her old friend loomed large in her mind, sucking up all the oxygen. Lulu, with her kinked dark hair. Curvy hips and blunt fingernails. Those eyes with their piercing gaze and array of fine black lashes.

Katie grabbed her cell phone and punched in her brother's number. Uncertain fingers, wrong number. She took another deep breath. Slowly this time she tapped in the digits, and voice mail kicked in. It was still early; David would be dead asleep.

"Call me back," she said, her breath hot in the receiver, sweat prickling her lip. "It's urgent."

Calling her mother wasn't an option. Charlie DuRochois—formerly Charlie Gregory, born Charlotte Amplethwaite—lived in Montreal now, ensconced in a house on the water with a man she'd met online a few years ago. His name was Michel (pronounced *Michelle*, like a girl's name), and he was about as different from Katie's father as you could get. Slim and wiry, fluid movements like a dancer's. A silky mustache on his upper lip. It would be funny if it weren't so painful: her beautiful British mother choosing this stranger over her own flesh and blood. Deciding she'd had enough and divorcing her husband while he was in prison, right when he'd needed her the most. Charlie hadn't had the patience to wait it out.

"I'm sorry," she'd said, staring at Katie and David, who was chewing on his fingers just as he had done when he was little. Couldn't her mother see how badly they all still needed her? She seemed to want to say more, but she didn't, and the children once again found themselves wordless in the face of her Anglo-Saxon reticence. "I just can't take it anymore. I'm done."

A mother, *done*? Done with being there for her family—was there a worse sin?

She didn't want to call her grandfather in England either; it didn't seem fair to drag him into all this, even though he never failed to cheer her up when she was down. She couldn't call her father; she'd have to wait until their scheduled call tomorrow. And she wasn't sure that he was the right person to talk to, anyway. He'd tell her something she couldn't quite believe—he'd tell her the reporter was right, that she'd listen to their side of the story, that Katie should talk to her, that it was an opportunity to be seized. Her dad always put a good spin on everything. Like the time her mother had returned from the hairdresser, tears in her eyes, her chestnut hair razored off in hideous chunks, and he'd told her it made her look like Mia Farrow. And when Katie had almost failed chemistry in ninth grade and he'd insisted it was for the best, that at least she now knew where her strengths lay.

Or maybe he'd tell her to just ignore the calls, that she should trust everything would work out—which she'd want to believe, of course, all the while knowing with a sick tug in her stomach that this wasn't ever going away. That no matter what she did or what the truth was, this would always be hanging over them, a multicell thunderstorm that only ever quieted down in order to build up energy for the next round.

The streets were damp, the sidewalks pocked with puddles that shone like oil slicks. The sun streamed down, the smell of wet garbage enveloping her as she ran across town toward the Greenway. At first she was chilled, but she warmed up quickly, running flat out until she could barely catch her breath. Baffled tourists stood in her way, clipped by a shoulder.

As she ran, she became lost in thought, remembering when she'd gone blueberry picking at Eagle Lake with her father late one summer. She had been maybe seven years old. It was before she had met Lulu. She'd been feeling cranky, and he was always up for an adventure. As they wove through the underbrush, he pointed out a pair of broad-winged hawks swooping and parrying in the air, courting. He held her hand, his fingers huge, palm warm and scratchy, telling her a story about a princess who felt lonely despite all her servants and the hustle and bustle of the court. Even though her father was always doing something or going somewhere, he was surprisingly patient when it came to his children. For them, he had infinite time. For them, he would do anything.

Her father's hair had been longer then, darkened with sweat, sticking to his forehead. He must have been almost forty—a little younger than Zev was now. After they filled their buckets with blueberries, he sat down on the moss and Katie perched on a rock, the gore of berries staining her lips, gnats buzzing around her drunkenly. Her thin brown shins were covered in scratches. She glanced over at her father after asking a question and getting no response.

Though Katie couldn't remember now what she'd asked, but she could feel the grit of the fruit's skin on her teeth, the pulpy burst on her tongue.

Katie asked her question again, and it took her father a long time to raise his face to her, and still he didn't answer. The look he cast her way was so distant, so alien, it was as though he were looking at someone he had never met before. Katie's white T-shirt was reflected in the blackness of his pupils, and she understood for the first time that her father, and therefore every grown-up, had an inner life. Hidden by default. She understood then that she was truly alone inside herself, as were all human beings on earth.

On and on she ran along the Hudson River now, one foot in front of the other, sweating with effort. How she missed him. For as long as she could remember, she'd been driven by the desire to be worthy of him, her choices calculated on a metric of his approval: Would his eyes light up—would she make him proud? She hadn't known it then, but when Lulu entered their lives, the family dynamic had shifted, slowly, until everything went belly-up. Why had her friend lied when Katie's father had taken such good care of her, when they all had? What the hell had happened?

All of a sudden, the sidewalk tilted upward under Katie's feet. She took a quick breath in—the sensation was like rocking on a swing, and yet she was no longer moving. Prickles began to form at the edge of her vision, and her stomach flopped; she thought she might throw up. Leaning against a lamppost, she squeezed her eyes shut and waited. When she opened them again, a woman and a young girl were staring at her, mildly curious. Two graying dachshunds were attached to a frayed leash on the woman's wrist, and another child, a boy, had stopped a few steps ahead of them to wait. Katie felt the urge to cry out: *I was a normal girl too—a girl with a father who took me blueberry picking and told me stories, a mother I could count on.*

I had a best friend I adored, and she betrayed us.

Was this true, this statement that had calcified in Katie's mind— had Lulu really betrayed them? Katie bent over and put her hands on her knees. She had believed this for so long, but the possibility that she had it all wrong insinuated itself into her mind. The possibility that, in fact, it was Katie who had been the betrayer, who had set everything off that last night of summer almost a decade earlier. After all, she'd been the one to screw around with the order of things, to mess with the unspoken rules between girls. She raised her head, pale and sweaty, and looked straight at the mother with her children. But the woman was just a stranger, and she walked away, yanking on the leash, heading off toward her separate life. Just like that, gone, and once again Katie was alone.

2

The thing about Lulu was this: she was brave and unabashed, and Katie was neither. When they were kids, Lulu stole eyeliner and pens from the five-and-ten in Blackbrooke and then managed to charm the Polish man with the stained teeth who caught her, while Katie cringed in the corner, cheeks flushed in shame. Lulu was unrepentant; she was always stepping out of bounds and being forgiven for it. When she was still a brand-new friend—could it have been the very first summer she spent at the lake, when she was just eight years old?—Lulu would get up before the sun even rose and pad from the bunk room the girls shared down to the kitchen. Hours later when the others started appearing, sleepy eyed and incoherent, there'd be flour all over the countertops, a dropped knife under the kitchen table among the dust motes. The smell of something burning coming from the oven. Lulu would be sitting at the counter, bright eyed, the corners of her mouth glistening with grease, her bony knees jiggling up and down. Smiling when you entered the room, happy for the company. But even though she had her own centrifugal force, she made space for Katie's brand of quiet. She would listen to her deeply, the bloom of unfettered curiosity on her face. The intensity of that kind of focus was an unexpected gift from a child with such energy.

These memories—they seemed to come and go, when in reality they were always a part of Katie's consciousness, simmering just under the surface at a constant, rolling boil. All it took was a smell, a refrain from some old pop song, or even the texture of something Katie brushed up against, and bang, they would return, fully present and in Technicolor. Gripping at her throat with meaty fingers. But Katie had become adept at distracting herself from them over the years. She could will her mind to move toward one thought and away from another, shutting out distractions. She used this skill in her adult life too: she'd become a dependable, focused, punctual woman. You could even call her predictable, though she wasn't sure that was anything to be especially proud of.

"You're not like any kid I've ever met," Tanisha from the office had once told her. They'd been at a bar in Chelsea during happy hour after working together for a year or so. It was funny to still be called a kid when she was almost twenty-five years old, but Tanisha was probably pushing forty. "You got that laser thing going on, that crazy-bitch focus." Tanisha laughed out loud, throaty and lighthearted, and Katie understood it was supposed to be a compliment.

After her run, she showered and, at a loss for what to do with herself, slipped back under the covers. The musky smell from earlier was gone, and the sheets were chilly, like the limp skin of a reptile. It took a long time for her to finally warm up. She begged off seeing Zev later, claiming to be coming down with a cold. She so badly wanted life to be simple, to move ahead steadily, and yet now she was being drawn in once again to the impossible question of why things had veered so terribly off course. In a matter of weeks, her father would be with her again, warm and funny and indelibly present. Life would not be the same anymore, and that was good. Wasn't it? The reporters' questions had stirred up feelings she didn't know what to do with. She tried calling her brother, David, again—still no answer. **Call me!!!!** she texted.

Fitfully, she dozed; she was afraid of dreaming, but the dreams didn't come. Instead there was a blank kind of panic that erased all conscious thought. It was a relief, really, and she sank into it.

Things looked different on Sunday morning. On her run along the Greenway, Katie reveled in the awesome power of her legs. Salty air blew over her face, cool and sharp, spurring her on. She was looking forward to her call with her father later that day. All her life, he'd made her feel like she was a priority for him. When she was younger, he'd been present at every parent-teacher meeting; he'd loved accompanying her on class outings or to buy a special dress for a bat mitzvah. During her brief flirtation with playing the violin, he'd sit and hold the notes up for her, encouraging her to keep sawing away, trying to persuade her she'd get better if she just kept trying. Even now—with unthinkable constraints reducing his life to a whisper—he focused on how he could help her. Not that long ago, she'd complained on the phone of sudden dizziness when rising, nausea sloshing unexpectedly in her stomach. During their next call he'd regaled her with advice about checking iron levels and having her thyroid looked at. He'd spent the hour allocated to him on the library computer searching for solutions to her problems.

"You've got to take care of yourself," he'd said. "You're my Amazon warrior, remember."

At midday when she entered the Gaslight gallery on Houston, Katie walked in with squared shoulders. Her jeans were tight fitting and flared, embroidered with vines along the side seams. She wore no makeup except scarlet lipstick. Zev looked up from a trestle table on which he was cutting up a sliver of wood with a handsaw. The overhead lights were turned up fully, bleaching the faces of the others milling around the gallery, unpacking crates and hanging art, but Zev's skin was dark hued, healthy looking. There was color high on his cheeks.

"You," he said. He smiled, and sharp creases sprang from the corners of his eyes. He was a striking-looking man, but it was his eyes that were hard to turn away from. They were so frank, startling, and there was something sad about them. "Come to spread your germs, huh?"

At first she didn't know what he meant; then she remembered her supposed cold. "Just the sniffles," she said. In the paper bag she was holding were twenty lemons from the market. Zev grew up in Tel Aviv, where his neighbor allowed him and his little sisters to pick lemons from her tree; he loved their scent and considered them good luck. Katie held the bag out toward him. "Brought you something."

He sank his nose into it and breathed in deeply. He swooned backward a bit and fluttered his lids as though he'd just taken a hit of something fabulous. "Yeah, baby," he said. With one arm, he pulled her toward him. "Glad you came. And thanks. We're slightly freaking out here."

The gallery was surprisingly spacious. The floors were wide-plank wood painted a high-gloss white and shimmering with reflections: blues and grays, the bright yellow of one woman's top. At the front of the space was a bank of large windows that sank almost to the ground. The walls were still mostly bare except for a few paintings hanging at the far end. Sounds echoed hollowly. "You're opening tonight, right?" Katie asked. "Isn't it tonight?"

"I know, I know," Zev answered, releasing her. "Better roll up our sleeves." His voice was deep and measured, with a singsong cadence that she'd originally thought was French but was in fact Israeli. He dropped his *h*'s and said "em" when hesitating, rather than the rounded, resonant American "um."

"Where's all your stuff supposed to go?" Katie asked, looking at the four walls, one of which was entirely made up of windows.

"Partitions," he said, picking up the saw and waggling it in the air. "We're figuring out a way to secure them to the pillars."

When they first met years ago, she had been a freshman at Vassar, and Zev an art professor. She hadn't known him all that well back then, but they'd developed a casual friendship over the years. She'd go to his studio with friends now and then, and he'd offer them cardamom tea with honey. His energy was so steady, so deep and calm. He was unlike anyone she'd ever met. When he looked at people, it was with a kind of forthrightness that wasn't accompanied by meddling inquisitiveness. Even when he engaged in conversation, that demanding curiosity she so often felt from others was entirely absent. This man seemed to want nothing from you, while at the same time thoroughly enjoying the fact of your presence. She loved to let his voice waft over her. Her father had been in jail six months when they'd met, and she didn't let on to anyone what was going on. Using her grandfather's name had allowed her to keep her story a secret in college and afterward, but she'd paid the price too. Nervous energy that kept her up at night, anxiety fueling ever longer, more punishing runs. During that time Zev's solidity, his easy silences, had been a great comfort.

Last October she'd bumped into him at a gallery uptown, at an opening for a sculptor friend she'd read about in the paper. They were standing across the room from one another, Zev surrounded by lithe women with shiny hair, clad in black leather. Katie was the awkward third wheel with a couple who were bickering incessantly. The place was packed, shrill with cocktail conversation, yet when she caught his eye, a silence seemed to fall over her. His look—the flash of recognition. When his smile landed on her, it contained something different than it had when they'd been at school, something startled, intrigued. She'd stared right back at him. Later that night they had gone back to her apartment together, falling onto the mattress on the floor, grateful her roommate was out. Now as she looked at him, she thought of her father, of the fact that these two men would be meeting soon, and she had to admit that it made her anxious. If she was honest with herself, she wasn't entirely sure her father would like him.

The girl with the yellow shirt came up to them. Her eyebrows were thin and severely curved, with a ring through each end. "Hey, can you help me back here?" she asked, gesturing. "I need some man power."

Ducking the low mantel of the doorway, they descended four steps and entered a back room filled with equipment, canvases, boxes, and a few paint-splattered tables. Against one brick wall was a long counter with a toaster on it and a sink. A single bed stood at the back near the door. The three of them wrestled with unpacking a wooden crate that had been stapled shut. Later, the girl, whose name was Janet, made them all toast, and an older man dressed entirely in jean material—pants, shirt, and even jacket—brought everyone Carling lager from the corner store.

The man turned out to be the owner, and the two younger men who had been installing the partitions for the last few hours were his sons, already home from college for the summer. They all sat on the empty crates and talked as everyone devoured toast. Just outside the back door was a tiny patio surrounded by towering, broken fencing and cascading ivy, tinged brown from winter, and Katie stepped out as the others got back to work. She allowed herself one cigarette, sucking the smoke in deeply. It had become a habit that was proving hard to break—a way to calm her nerves. Although now, as the ember burned down toward the filter, her stomach clenched, and she pressed out the butt into a forlorn planter. *I'm going to have to stop*, she told herself. *Soon.*

Zev was hanging a large painting on the partition closest to the front of the room. He had taken off his sweater and was wearing an old T-shirt underneath, frayed at the neck. His eyelashes were long and dark, casting spiky shadows on his cheekbones. "Hey, d'you get your messages?" he asked.

"Messages?" Katie cut her eyes to his. Nothing in his posture suggested that he was tense, that he knew anything about the reporter who'd called.

"Yeah," he said, pounding a nail into particleboard. "Your phone rang a lot when I was waiting for you, Friday. Forgot to mention it."

It was one of those interminable, distorted pockets of time: a thousand thoughts crowding her brain. This was her opening, the opportunity she'd been waiting for to tell him about what had happened to her family. She imagined that he'd probably already pieced together some facts about why her father wasn't around, why she rarely mentioned her parents, but she had never laid out the details. Words ricocheted through her mind like bits of gravel; they had a violent force of their own, sucking her further into herself. Together, those words didn't add up to anything cogent. It was impossible to explain any of this to him when she herself still understood so little about what had happened that night—and afterward. It was time to say something, to try—and yet. She wasn't ready; she couldn't.

"Oh, that," she said, slipping the fingernail of her thumb between her top and bottom teeth. "Nothing important."

Zev raised his arms high to place a painting onto a hook. He regarded it silently, then tilted the painting to the left. "I've decided to rent some studio space in Bushwick, or maybe Bed-Stuy," he said. "I was looking at places yesterday, and I think I've found something. Bare bones, but there's a toilet, at least."

"What about school? Teaching?" Katie asked. Zev taught three classes a semester at Vassar and had use of a large studio behind the maintenance garage. Years ago, that was where all the art students would hang out, smoking. That was back when Zev still smoked.

"Been there over fifteen years," he said, grunting slightly as he adjusted the painting again. "Time for me to do more of my own work, be more independent. And I'm feeling the city vibe. You know?" He flashed his eyes at her—just a second—and she understood he was asking her if she wanted to see him more often.

"Yeah, cool," she said, hating herself for her noncommittal tone, her childish vocabulary. She knew she should be happy, that this was a good thing, but she stalled. If Zev had a studio in Brooklyn, he'd be down in the city more often; surely this was good. This was nothing to be afraid of. As it was, they saw each other two or three times a month, and he stayed at her place for a few days at a stretch. When he wasn't with her, she counted off the days until he would be back. Didn't that mean she should want to see him more often?

"So, um. This straight now?" he asked.

"A little to the right. More." The painting appeared to be a rendering of a very large baby, pink skinned and bawling. At first glance it seemed literal, almost graceless, until Katie saw that Zev had painted flesh-toned weapons rendered in astonishing detail over the entire surface of the child's skin. Pistols, shotguns, brass knuckles, a cutlass, bullets, tanks. You couldn't tell from far away, but up close the weapons were delicate, almost photographic. He'd done a fine cross-hatching with a black pen that looked like an etching layered on top of the paint. The contrast between the initial assumption about what she was seeing and the reality of what was actually depicted was jarring; that must be the point, she figured. "Now to the left a bit," she said. "There, you got it."

Behind her, Janet, in the yellow top, was yelling at the boys to hurry up. The party would be starting in a few hours, and only about half the pieces were in place, though the partitions were finally up. Stepping down and taking a few paces back, Zev surveyed his work. He didn't seem fazed by the hubbub or Janet's frenetic tone—or Katie's reaction. When he finally turned around and looked at her with his blue, blue eyes, the washed-out blue of shallow water, his face registered surprise. "You are very pale, Katie. You all right?"

"I'm fine," she said, and right then it was true. When his attention was focused on her, his calmness was like a breeze on her skin.

"Good. Because I think I should move in with you." He cracked a smile, and the white of his teeth dazzled her, like the pop of a flash. "I think I should be based in the city and go up to Vassar when I'm teaching, not the other way around. What do you say? You've got space. Or we could find somewhere better, put our money together." He put his arms around her and stuck his face into her neck, his nose in the warm crook, his breath moist on her skin. "I want to be with you. And I think you want to be with me."

He was waiting for an answer, but he would not push her. And so she nodded her head slightly, bumping against his, and she squeezed him back, hiding her face, while inside there raged a blood-soaked battle between what she wanted, what she deserved, and what she could actually have.

3

Every Sunday evening, the phone in her apartment rang at the same hour, six thirty. Sometimes a few minutes later, but more often than not exactly on time. It never failed to startle her even though she was expecting it. An automated voice came over the line, asking Katie if she would accept the charges from Wallkill Correctional Facility.

Why her father insisted on doing it this way, she wasn't sure; it was inefficient. He wanted a landline, not a prepaid cell phone account. He claimed he could hear her better. He said it was easier for him. He liked knowing she was home. Maybe he wanted to be able to picture her sitting in the very same spot (on the edge of her couch) every single week, her attention centered solely on him. Maybe he didn't want to share her with a busy street corner or a rollicking subway train or another person in some friend's house, a friend he hadn't had the chance to meet. It was inconvenient to rush home every Sunday no matter what, but as soon as she heard his voice on the end of the line, she'd forget her irritation. The instant comfort she felt settled her down, reminded her what she cared about. Loyalty. Steadfastness. She was proud to be his one steady rock in a sea of shifting allegiances.

Katie stared at the receiver, off its base, the curled cord lying on the wood floor next to the trim board. The phone was still unplugged. In order to receive her father's call, Katie had to plug it back in, and whether she wanted to or not, she'd hear the beep beep beep of the answering service telling her there were messages waiting for her. It took her a few minutes before she felt ready.

Beep beep beep, she heard.

Her breath tightened, but she was too curious not to dial in. Marjorie O'Hannon had left a message on Friday, then restrained herself and only called twice more on Saturday afternoon.

"I wanted to let you know," her recording said, "that I covered the Duke case, and now Saint Patrick's, the boarding school? I, uh, well, I assume you heard about it—the boy was convicted yesterday. Statutory rape."

When Katie heard that word—*rape*—she stiffened. It never got easier.

A sigh was audible on the message. "So truly, I understand this . . . this he said/she said thing. Especially now, after the Stanford swimmer case, the extremely light reprimand. It's easy to get distracted from the truth."

Then a male voice on another message. Jules Forsythe from the *Baltimore Sun*. "Your father's case was under the jurisdiction of New York State, but of course statutory rape's not regional," he said. "We'd like to hear your opinion on issues related to consent, the age of consent. The girl in the Saint Patrick's case was fourteen too."

Each reporter mentioned having picked up on a reference to her father's case in the judge's summation at the Saint Patrick's rape trial, which had wrapped up the previous week. The last one, Cartwright—clipped tone, all business—paused breathlessly at the end of her message. "I know your community turned out to support your father, big-time," she said. "I think you should take this chance to stick up for him too." No one but O'Hannon mentioned anything about having contacted or having spoken to Lulu Henderson.

Katie hung up. As if she hadn't stuck up for her father! No one could pretend to know him as she did. They hadn't seen him in the middle of the night, fetching migraine medicine for her mother from the all-night pharmacy. They didn't know that he tipped the newspaper boy a hundred dollars at Christmas and invited a junior colleague to dinner every Sunday night after his fiancée died in a hit-and-run. That he happily gave his children his sweater when they were caught in the cold or a stubbled kiss when they awoke to a nightmare.

She moved about the room in a daze. Anyway, even if she were to talk to one of these journalists, what would she say? She had nothing to add to everything that had already been said—the jury had decided, and the sentence had been served. People thought whatever they thought. There was no changing people's minds now. Her father had been wrongly accused, but there was so much more to it than that fact. Though the truth was that all these years later, there were important things she had never come close to understanding: Why had Lulu accused him in the first place? What exactly had led to her father's conviction? It was beginning to eat away at her again, this realization of everything she didn't know. There was a part of her that wanted answers.

It would be time to head back for Zev's opening party soon, and she pulled a short black dress over her head. Green boots with sharp toes and cowboy heels. In the mirror, she saw hints of purple under her eyes. She applied concealer, pulled her hair up in a spiky blonde bun, and slipped on a pair of hoops. Tonight was important. The gallery owner, Hans, had invited some big collectors to view Zev's work. No one would be paying any attention to Katie, but she wanted to be there to share in Zev's accomplishment, to see the happiness spread over his face, to watch him work the crowd. Yet what she really wanted to do was retreat, curl up in bed again, turn her head into the fusty pillow, and dream herself into a different life. Could she pretend to be all right? Could she do it for him?

It was 6:33 p.m. when the phone rang. Katie waited for the recording to end and answered yes, she would accept the charges. The crackle on the line changed tone: the line was live.

"Sweetheart!" John Gregory said.

"Hi, Dad." Her throat was dry. "How's it going?"

As usual, they made small talk. The weather in New York (always a little different than upstate), her boss, a new book on neuroscience her father had just finished. He had been on a jag recently, reading everything he could get his hands on to do with brain science. This followed his Shakespeare period (every play the man had ever written, including *Cymbeline* and *King John*), his Norman Mailer obsession ("What a pig!"), and his earlier James Baldwin period. He was on good terms with the librarian, who let him order books from other library systems and take out as many as five at once. "But it's the last time I'll be going to this library," he told her, sucking in his breath. "Last time ever. Can't even finish the books I've already got before I'm out of here. Can you believe it, honey?"

"You know the exact time and everything? June 23, right?"

"Don't know about the 'and everything' part, but yes. Had my SORA meeting—"

"What's that?"

"Nothing, just means I'm all set to go."

She wanted to know what he meant, but this was like a game they'd been playing all her life, and she didn't know how to change the rules. The way it worked was that she'd be told whatever it was her parents wanted her to know, and she wasn't supposed to press for more. She thought then of the reporters and how they knew her father was being released soon. Could you look that sort of stuff up? Would they hound him, too, now that he was getting out, or would they have already crucified him in the press by then?

"You'll come pick me up, right? Would so love to see the Falcon out there, idling at the curb, waiting for me by the pearly gates of Wallkill Penitentiary," he said. He cleared his throat. "You think your mother might come too—just to say hello?"

"Oh, Daddy," she said. Something inside her slipped, a shifting of organs that hurt. Most often they talked about day-to-day things, what he ate, what he was reading, and he asked her about every detail of her week—but when he talked like this, as hopeful as a child, her thoughts always returned to when their roles had been reversed, when he'd been in charge and she'd been the kid. His voice as he read to her when she was little, her hand clutching his forearm, riveted. Conjuring up entire worlds that seemed so real to her. Now she had to be the one to guide him, to nudge him back into reality. "Mum's not going to come see you. You know that."

"No, Katie, listen. You never know. It's been a long time. Seeing someone in the flesh"—he hesitated—"I mean, no bars, no Perspex between us? She might be curious. If she still feels something. You know?"

Her parents had been divorced since her second year of college. While she and her father didn't discuss it, Katie assumed it had been that long since he'd actually seen or spoken to her mother. "She remarried, Dad. Come on, you know that. She's married to another guy."

He made a dismissive noise on the other end of the line. "Whatever *that* means these days."

"So the plan, Dad. The Falcon? I don't know how that's going to be possible."

"I'll need a car. Figured you could haul it out of storage for me, make sure it runs."

She smiled; this was just like him. "Because I'm such an awesome mechanic?"

"Ask your brother for help."

"Because *he's* such an awesome mechanic?" They both laughed.

"No, seriously, why not dust off the old lady and give her some respect?"

"And you'll stay with that friend—Alden what's-his-name?"

"Such a great guy, really solid," John said. "But he's got some sort of crisis; it's just one of those things. I don't want to be a burden. I told him it was no problem at all. I'm lucky to have two great kids, right? A whole backup team. Maybe I can stay with you a night or two, honey? Now your roommate's gone?"

She tipped her head to one side. He'd talked about staying with an old friend from West Mills, where she'd grown up. It had seemed like a decent-enough plan—after all, where else was he supposed to go? David was an acting student living in a dodgy rental in lower Brooklyn, and Katie lived in a one-bedroom with almost no privacy. And while her father knew about Zev, she hadn't told him yet that they were romantically involved. He'd gotten into the habit of calling Zev "the Israeli." He meant it playfully, but there was an undertone of suspicion to it, an intimation that there was no way a man with an artsy job and a background like Zev's could be entirely savory. Katie knew who her father wanted for her: a prep school boy her age, with a job at Goldman Sachs. John had been a commercial banker for Citigroup; he believed in careers that came with job specs and salaries, paid vacations and a decent-sounding title, something that had cachet. A career in which you could work your way up, slowly but surely, to the top. It was because of him that she'd chosen to go into consulting.

"Okay, well, sure—of course you can stay here," she said. Katie was beginning to understand what her father's freedom would mean: people would be taking sides again. It was easy not to talk about your father when he was in prison, but it would be different once he was out. There were reasons for everything, and at some point people wanted to know what those reasons were. She was sure Alden had had second thoughts, and it pained her. Of course her father could stay over if he wanted; she would figure out the Zev issue later. "Stay as long as you like; it's fine with me, Dad."

"Well, I'll be heading to the cabin, living up there for a while. Just until—"

"Really?" she said, looking up from the scuffed toes of her boots. He wanted to return to Eagle Lake? Her grandfather had bought the Big House and the cabin in the late sixties, back when he and Gram and their only daughter had left London. It was where Charlie and John had spent every summer vacation after getting married. They'd first taken Katie to the cabin when she was two weeks old, still shriveled and mewling. Her childhood had been measured in summers at the lake, until all that had stopped for good. She hadn't been back, not once, since the summer she was fifteen. "Is that . . . did you talk with Grumpy about that?"

"No, I did not talk to him. Your grandfather has no say in this, Katie. He gave the cabin to your mother when he sold the Big House and moved back to England, and she's got a bunch of our stuff in there. Your mother is letting me use it." He paused. "For a while, at least. Just till I get back on my feet."

So they *had* talked, her mother and father.

"You surprised?" he asked.

"Um, yeah," she said. "I guess so. I mean, Mum isn't exactly—"

"She's been very generous." John cleared his throat. "So, short notice, I know, but can you go there for me, check it out? Find out about the Falcon too? Your mother says everything's been locked up for years." In the background there was a bell, the sound of another man's voice. Katie knew exactly where he was, and she imagined him in that space, a man waiting to be released into his life again: He stood in a pale-green corridor with pay phones lining the walls. Fluorescent lights (they gave him headaches). The phones were next to the dining hall (he could guess what was for dinner by the smells saturating the air). When the line of waiting prisoners behind him got too long, he'd sometimes have to ring off abruptly. They had spoken nearly every Sunday, with only a few exceptions, for six years. Over two hundred calls.

"Dad . . . I can't," she said. "I don't want to go back to Eagle Lake."

"Look it, I'm not asking you for much. I just need the water to be running. Is the roof still up, that kind of stuff. It'll take you a day, max. It'll be no big deal."

"No, it won't, and that's not the point."

"Then what is your point?" he asked. There was silence while they both thought their private thoughts. Then he said, "And the car, it's in the Nicholses' garage. That's what Charlie said."

"I really don't want to." She poured herself a shot of warm tequila and drank it down in two gulps. "And I definitely can't get the car running."

"Get over it, hon; you'll be fine. It's the start of a new era. I still love that place, whatever happened there. Always will." They said their goodbyes and hung up.

Katie could not think of the cabin tucked into the feathered ferns without also thinking of her old friend. Did her father ever think about Lulu? she wondered. Did he see her caramel summer face, the electric teeth, and that smile, beguiling and brash? Did it not mess with his head to know that was the very same girl who had put him in prison? But he hadn't once brought up Lulu's name since the trial. It was almost as though she had never existed—as though, for him, every memory they shared had been erased or had never even happened in the first place. It wasn't like that for Katie.

She slipped on her jacket and checked the time. On her way to the subway, she kept thinking about the reporters' interest in her "perspective" as John Gregory's daughter. Did she have a perspective to offer them, when she had been in the dark for so long, shielded by others and by her own lack of gumption? It was pitiful, really. She realized it might no longer be possible for her to stay mired in her willful ignorance. If she wanted to understand what her role in all this had actually been, she was going to have to buck up and try to find out more about what had really happened.

4

The boys with their sunburned forearms, sinewy muscles pulsing as they move, each contraction casting shifting shadows on their skin. They are jostling for position. A rope hangs down over the water from an ancient maple at the edge of Eagle Lake, its reflection ribboning over the agitated water. It's afternoon, the middle of August. Kids, young and old, playing in the water, swinging on the rope, kicking out their feet, toes splayed. With the exception of Jack Benson, the boys at the rope are all a few years older than Katie and Lulu.

Jack. He is fifteen or sixteen, tall, hair bleached from hours on the tennis courts, the son of a Manhattan power couple renting the old McGuire house. Summer renters at the lake come and go, but this is the first time in the seven summers Lulu and Katie have spent together that a new boy around their age is in the mix. He thrills them with his searching eyes, his half smile. He spends every day at the dusty clay courts tucked away deep in the backwoods. At Lulu's insistence, the girls run past him, staring as he slams the ball against the backboard, again and again. They know his habits, when he practices. Sometimes they'll pass by twice in one day.

Years later, an image of Jack still comes to Katie at unexpected moments: eddies of dust at his shins, the broad swing of his arm as it arcs through the air until his racket meets the ball. The stunning relentlessness of the movement. Is Jack at the root of the problem? She can't shake the idea that this might be true.

The older boys: Kendrick, a sophomore at Ohio State. He is friends with Tommy, who's running the snack bar in the clubhouse. Two of the boys Katie doesn't know very well (she thinks they are the Hartney twins, from Pennsylvania), but the other one has been coming to the lake since he was little. Brad. His jeans are threadbare at the knees. He's probably eighteen years old, with the build of a backstroke swimmer, his bare shoulders bulging with well-formed muscles, clearly defined under freckly skin.

Brad points to the rope dangling over the water. "You don't think I can make that? You kidding me?" he asks Lulu.

"Said you were too *chicken* to jump for it, not that you couldn't do it," Lulu answers, not bothering to look up from her perch on the Adirondack chair.

Before she finishes her sentence, Brad stretches his arms out and makes a leap for the rope. His tanned feet drag on the water as he swings, head tilted back, and then he kicks to propel himself back onto the shore. He grabs onto the edge with his toes, and the other boys promptly start pushing him out over the water again.

Lulu refuses to look over at them. Instead, she studies her finger-nails. Chipped yet somehow lovely. Her skin is deeply tanned, her arms covered in the finest minky hairs. She's wearing jean shorts and a tight black T-shirt with a picture of Fergie from the Black Eyed Peas. It seems as though she doesn't care much what she looks like, as though the boys are of no interest to her. Katie knows this is not true. Earlier in the bunk room at the cabin, Lulu was almost in tears about the summer coming to an end. "I'll probably never see Jack again," she said. "This is it—this is my only chance." She needs to find a way to make him notice her. Katie's heart sinks, and she thinks, *Yes, I know exactly what you mean.*

"Hey!" Brad yells at his friends. "Traitors!"

The boys' energy pummels Katie. They are raucous, their laughter full bellied. The way they play with each other makes them seem younger than they really are. Jack sits on a chair nearby, watching them. It's hard to tell what he might be thinking. Is he one of them or not? To Katie, the college boys are like zoo animals: intriguing yet alien. Now as she watches them, she notices their big hands, the way their mouths open too wide when they laugh. The playful punching that is, at the same time, vaguely aggressive. For the first time ever, Katie feels part of the action, as though they are all the same species after all, recognizable to one another.

Lulu sits on the arm of the chair, one ankle angled over her knee. Suddenly she looks up. "Let's show them," she says to Katie, jumping up. "Round-robins! Okay, y'all, let the girls show you how it's done." She runs to the tree and beckons her friend, *Come on!*

The Adirondack chairs that line the lakeside are full of people sunning themselves. John and Charlie Gregory sit side by side reading paperbacks with water-stained pages. Katie's brother, David, just ten years old, is playing with much younger kids over by the sand. His hair is too long for his age, an affectation his parents can't get him to shed. He likes to let it hang over his eyes, thinking this makes him less visible. He's one of the in-betweeners, a kid who has no playmates his age, but this summer he's had fun ordering the little guys around, discovering his inner dictator.

The bigger boys start hooting at Lulu, as though playing with the rope is in some way daring or dramatic, when really it's totally run of the mill. Katie understands this is because of the heat, because of the late-summer energy; they all feel time running out. Each minute brings them closer to the end of the season. Each day that passes marks a win for winter, a loss for freedom.

The girls pretend to be warming up, stretching their slender arms above their heads, rolling their shoulders back and forth one at a time, touching their toes. They keep poker faces; Katie looks to see whether Jack is watching them and catches his eye. She's too scared to smile, in case Lulu notices.

Lulu lassoes the bigger rope that now dangles, inert, and pulls it toward her. After grabbing it, she takes a deep breath and begins running along the concrete lip of the lake. When she can't go farther without letting go, she holds on tight and flings herself out in a wide arc over the water, heading back in a half circle under the overhanging branches till she reaches the water's edge again and lands nimbly on the concrete where she started, completing the circle. Barely breaking stride, she slips the rope to Katie, who grabs it and runs, just as Lulu did, to the edge, swinging herself out over the water before landing again on the concrete.

Each time Lulu throws herself out over the water, her T-shirt lifts up and her tan belly flashes above her shorts. Again and again. All eyes are on them now—everyone's, even Jack's.

The girls are itching for more. Itching to do *something*, but what does that even mean? Katie and Lulu steal a bottle of Southern Comfort from the Big House. It's disgusting, but the warmth firing through their bellies is good. Katie is upset with her mother (years later, she won't remember why—isn't she always upset with her mother for one reason or another?), and Lulu has been listening to her, nodding with great intent. "I read somewhere about filial cannibalism," she says. "Heard of that?"

"You mean, like, parents eating their kids?"

"Yeah, animals, like fish and voles and spiders and things."

Katie laughs. Sometimes she wishes she could step into her friend's shoes and see the world through her eyes. The whiskey is creating a glow inside her, a growing ember that makes her want to run or shout or swim. She's lying on the grass near the boathouse. "So what are you trying to say? My mom hates me so much she wants to eat me?"

Lulu lies down on the ground next to her. "No, I'm saying parents are weird; everyone's parents are weird. I'm saying you're perfectly delicious. And I'm saying, let's go have some fun and forget about everything else!" She always knows what to say, Lulu, and what she says always makes Katie feel better.

The sky is covered in stars like powdered sugar. A few of the teenagers are lingering around the dock. It's a boring night, a weeknight. The minutes are ticking by steadily, but no one knows what to do. Katie can hear the bats swooping blindly overhead.

"Hey, listen," Brad says finally, running his hands through his reddish hair. "Let's take a ride in the Falcon. That's yours, uh . . . right?" He looks at Katie but seems to have forgotten her name.

"Hands off, big guy. That's her dad's car," Lulu says.

"Dibs on driving," some other boy shouts.

"Wait—he'll kill me," Katie says, sitting up straighter. Her father keeps the keys in the glove compartment, but there is no way she can let anyone drive it. He adores that car.

"Don't rain on my parade, man," Brad says.

"No way, José," Lulu interrupts. The smoke from her cigarette is gauzelike, diffusing around her lips. She won't let them bulldoze her, and she won't let Katie be bulldozed either. How many times has Lulu lightly placed an arm around her friend's shoulders, not in a possessive or domineering way but so that Katie becomes infused with a stronger sense of self, as though by osmosis? Over the years, Lulu's protectiveness has been both shield and sword. "That car's a stick shift, and I'll bet not a single one of you knows how to drive a stick. Am I right?"

Jack drains a water bottle filled with vodka and Gatorade. He chucks it on the ground by his feet. "Don't you wish summer would never end?" he asks no one in particular. "Like, what the hell good is winter?"

"You go skiing and stuff, don't you?" Lulu tugs on her T-shirt, stretching it over her rounded breasts. All summer she's been trying to trap Jack into admitting how rich he is. She pretends to sniff at it, but she's impressed. It's her way of flirting. Katie, on the other hand, flirts by ignoring him. Her face has eagerness written all over it, she's sure, whereas Lulu is so damn cool. "Don't you hit the slopes in Aspen or wherever?"

"Sugarbush," Kendrick says.

"That place sucks," Brad says. "You gotta go out west."

Lulu turns her head toward Katie. "You hear that? We gotta go 'west.'" She pantomimes quotation marks with her fingers. "Once we've got our pad in Manhattan and our big jobs, we'll take a ski vacation every winter. What d'you say? Head to Vale or Vancouver or wherever it is the rich and famous hang out."

"Nah, the Bahamas," Katie says, falling into her friend's reveries with ease. "We'll go somewhere warm." They've talked about their lives until their eyes were heavy and their throats dry. Katie's life is boring—what excitements have ever befallen her? But Lulu is full of stories she spins idly as they lie side by side in the woods or stacked on bunks in the cabin. She has a great-uncle who lives in Paris and cousins in the Deep South. Friends from school who hunt all winter long and clean and mount their own prey. She recounts high school intrigues that leave Katie short of breath, as though she's devouring the end of a romance novel. When Lulu talks, it's best to let her tales unwind uninterrupted. Her voice is a cashmere blanket of multihued scraps. And they talk about the future too. In Lulu's telling, the future assumes a promising pellucid shine: she knows exactly what she wants. To get out of Blackbrooke. To be a famous singer. To have a pair of shoes named after her. But she also listens as Katie half-heartedly tries on the various possibilities her future holds, showing no impatience with her friend's lack of certainty. Whatever Katie dreams up, Lulu believes it can come true.

"Tahiti," Jack says. "Or Bora-Bora."

Katie looks over at him and thinks he might be smiling at her. He kissed her a few nights ago—quickly, badly, in the boathouse. No one saw, and it almost seems as if it never even happened. The grass prickles her thighs. It is so hot, even at night. "Saint John's . . ." she says. She stands up and pats her backside to get rid of the itchy shreds. There's music coming from the clubhouse, some terrible eighties tune.

"We can take a yacht to Corfu. I'll be captain," says Lulu, standing up as well. "You and me, girl. You and me."

5

Katie is eight years old. There's a girl in the aisles at Walmart wearing a pair of dirty dungarees that drag on the floor behind her, trailing threads. But it isn't her clothing that catches Katie's eye; it's that she seems so completely happy all by herself, surrounded by teens with violet rashes on their cheekbones and old ladies dimpled with fat, leaning heavily on their shopping carts. Katie is both bored and anxious. Her mother is supposed to be buying conditioner, but she's gotten caught up looking for something else. This happens a lot. Her mother will often linger blankly while doing a chore, her open eyes strangely shuttered. For once she's taken Katie out to run errands in Blackbrooke, just the two of them, and yet where is she?

There is a long mirror in the cosmetics section near the hairnets and eyeliner, and this girl—with a solid, propulsive body, wearing this strangely boyish outfit—is looking hard at herself. She is wearing huge, sparkling rhinestone earrings and making faces in the mirror. When she finally notices Katie, the child puts her fingers to her lips as though they already share some sort of secret. The two of them stare at each other for a while, assessing each other in that frank way children do. There is something about not saying *hi* that makes it seem as though they already know one another. Then the girl yanks off her earrings, clip-ons, and comes close to Katie. Instead of handing the earrings over, she forces them on her clumsily, one by one, and Katie lets her.

Snap, snap; her fingers are tiny, pudgy things.

Charlie Gregory comes back before the girls have even said one word to each other. Katie notices her mother hesitate when she sees them together, but she doesn't realize till much later that it's because of the grimy pants, the air of neglect. Katie is entranced: when her mother asks the child what her name is and she replies, "Lulu Henderson," Katie thinks it sounds like a song—soft and pretty, not like *Katie Gregory*, with its hard angles. She asks if the girl can come play with her at the cabin, just a short ride from town. She often has to play alone or with her baby brother, who still pitches furious tantrums and tires almost instantly of her games.

They pick Lulu up the very next day, and in a way, she never really leaves Eagle Lake again.

That summer Katie treasures those earrings, wearing them over and over; she imagines being beautiful like her new friend. She keeps waiting for Lulu to ask her to give them back, but she never does. Summers come; summers go. Lulu often arrives at the lake with something special, something a little unusual. One year it's a rock she's painted black and covered in red hearts. Eyes big, the girls name it "the sacred stone." Another year it's a stack of old *Cosmopolitan*s they pore over (the sex tips as incomprehensible as Chinese). A thick macramé bracelet Katie wears for seven months straight until it rots against her moist skin. A pair of neon-orange hand-knit fingerless gloves. But the best gift of all is that she keeps coming back, as though she just can't get enough of Katie. As though she thinks Katie is someone special, worthy of devotion, and doesn't realize that Katie sees it the other way around.

About a dozen cars are still in the parking lot at the lake, including the red Falcon. The night is thick like coffee. Amber swaths of light from the clubhouse windows slice into the dark. The smell of rain. Only a few days of summer left now. Tick tick tick.

Lulu is playing Ping-Pong. Katie has stumbled outside to get some fresh air—and to get away from her mother, who is at the piano banging out a rendition of "Downtown." A few of the grown-ups are trying to sing along. Charlie is so embarrassing. Most often in the summertime, she's holed up somewhere with a book, sometimes not saying more than a few words in a whole day. Give her a few glasses of wine, and she turns into Petula Clark.

Oh, the cool rush of air on Katie's face! The boys are hanging out by the changing sheds, some perched on trash barrels, jumping up and down, trying to grab the branches of an overhanging tree. They are tireless, these boys, unable to stop moving, their laughter loud and possessive, as if they own the woods. Glowing cigarettes move erratically in the darkness. The air pulses with sounds—trancelike house music and shrieks from the lakeside, the high-pitched cries of grown-ups drinking and laughing.

It is hard to see much in the darkness, and it's Jack's voice Katie hears first; she strains to see where he is. Jack—she can't get him out of her mind.

"Hey, where's your friend Lulu?" Brad asks as Katie approaches the sheds. Last year, he'd barely said a word to her, but now he stares at her in a way that is both disconcerting and exhilarating. Suddenly she's become visible to him, and she likes it. On his wrists he wears a stack of thick string bracelets, like those braided together in craft sessions at summer camp. Kendrick climbs into one of the trees and dangles from a branch while Jack watches him, hands sunk in his pockets.

"Looking for you, duh," Katie answers. As soon as the words come out, she flushes. Stupid! It's as though she's trying on different jackets to see which one fits; she hasn't found the right one yet. She feels strangely like another person whenever Jack is around.

"That girl's turned into a total babe," Brad says. He has the bottled-up energy of a tiger or a pit bull. When he holds out a smoldering joint in her direction, Katie only hesitates for a second. She knows he'll tease her if she doesn't take it. The smoke is thick and spicy in her throat, and she suppresses a sharp cough. Peppery and exotic. Smelling slightly of decay. Earlier in the summer she'd tried pot and nothing happened, but now, after just a few minutes, she feels the sudden molten sensation of floating limbs, of a drifting mind. Her thoughts like dice bumping into each other. She is untethered from her body, and her limbs no longer seem so stubborn and gawky. A liquid sense of freedom courses through her, and she hands the joint back to Brad; he inhales deeply before passing it on to Jack and unleashing an enormous cloud of smoke that wraps itself around their faces and necks and makes them all burst out laughing as though at a secret joke.

Time passes. Clouds hang low in the sky, and Katie stares at them as they tumble around sluggishly. She lets the boys' murmurs wash over her; she isn't interested in what they have to say anymore, and she isn't thinking about Lulu either. It is a feeling she hasn't had all summer, a kind of looseness in her head and her body. The idea comes to her that she can say or do anything she wants, and nobody will stop her. It's her choice. Her life is hers to make happen—or not. Again and again the boys dive for the low branch, and some of them make it, swinging like monkeys.

Then it is just Jack and Katie. (What happened to the others? How had she not noticed them leaving?) He hoists himself up onto the edge of the shed, his feet in battered leather flip-flops. He doesn't need to say, *Come sit here with me*; she knows he wants her to, and so she does. In the shed, everything smells of overturned earth. It is so pungent, this forest smell, primeval. Jack leans toward her, and their lips touch. They begin to kiss. Katie falls into it as though her body is dropping through something viscous.

Her lips become raw. Only their mouths touch, and the kiss is unending. Is he too shy to touch her? At some point, she reaches up and places a hand on his shoulder, feeling the muscles moving under his polo shirt, and she thinks they might stay forever in this dank place, hidden just steps away from everyone.

There is a rumble, a distant clash that could be a plane or a trash can falling or maybe some faraway thunder. Her skin is slick with sweat. She opens her eyes, thinks of the cool lake water. She remembers Lulu, how upset she would be if she knew what was happening now. What Katie's doing—with Jack—and so she pulls away.

6

The night after Zev's opening, Katie was thinking about numbers as she rode the subway to her job at the Hamlin Consulting Group offices in Midtown. A single number was a solid, immutable thing; this Katie knew for sure. In and of themselves numbers were indisputable, even though they created new meanings when combined. The trick was making sure you found the right numbers and put them together in the right way: then you could achieve clarity. Then you'd have an answer to a question—not an opinion or a theory but an actual answer. She was turning over numbers in her head, over and over again.

Zev had been triumphant last night. He sold three paintings, which initially didn't seem like much, until he whispered in her ear that one had sold for almost $100,000, after commissions. Incredible. The Arts reporter from the *New York Times* had turned up (reeking of booze, accompanied by some wrecked kid wearing a purple bow tie) and promised to write a piece on him. Zev had mentioned to them that he was renting a studio, that he'd be showing his work more often in the city. That's what started Katie on the math.

If Zev could make more than $100,000 in one night, and she kept doing well at Hamlin (where she earned more than friends like Radha or Ursula—or any of her old college friends, actually, except those who'd gone into banking), then they'd definitely have enough money to get a new place together, maybe somewhere in Brooklyn, somewhere with a fire escape or a shared roof deck, perhaps a garden if they were really lucky. Katie missed the open air, the chance to sit on a stool in the breeze in the evenings or stare at the night sky before going to bed. Zev's finances were a mystery to her: he drove an old brown Datsun and dressed in jeans and T-shirts, a scuffed motorcycle jacket when it got cold. But he pulled out his wallet with no hesitation, chose restaurants impulsively, seemingly unworried about prices. It would be nice to have space to live, to have company, a life that added up to more than days piled on top of one another without accruing the additional freight of meaning or purpose.

If her father got out in nineteen days, then she had less than that amount of time to figure out how to explain to Zev why her dad might be staying in the loft. Maybe she had a week or two, maybe less. How many days would it take for him to absorb this news, make up his mind whether it mattered to him? Zev knew her parents were divorced, of course, that her mother was up in Montreal. She suspected he knew that her father was somehow banished, that he had done something to distance himself from them all. But Zev hadn't pried. He didn't know about Lulu, about the accusations and the trial and the conviction. It was a wound held together with dangerously loose stitches, but this was a problem that Katie wasn't especially eager to solve. It hadn't seemed all that urgent, at least not up till now. Somehow the two of them had avoided wading through the messy, confessional stage of new relationships—the endless admissions of weaknesses, the litany of regrets and bad behavior. They'd talked about old lovers; they'd talked a lot about work. But neither of them had dwelled on family—she didn't even know whether Zev's parents still lived in Israel. And what was she going to say to him: *Hey, we don't know each other all that well . . . but my father was convicted of raping my best friend?* There never seemed a good time to say those words, in any combination. She had a finite amount of time to solve that little problem.

And who knew when Zev would bring up the idea of moving in with her again.

If she had seven messages from four different reporters, did that mean they'd keep coming after her until she gave in? Her sweaty palm gripped the steel pole as the subway car lurched, and she did another kind of math too. Almost nine years since she'd been back at the cabin. Six since she'd last seen Lulu. More than two years for them to bring her father to trial and six years in Wallkill after that. What did *those* numbers mean? They did not add up to something logical, manageable. Shouldn't they, in the heft of their accumulated reality, mean an end to this uncertainty and shame? Surely it was time to start the clock from zero again, nice and neat, to begin counting forward in a linear way that would lead somewhere logical.

Hamlin Consulting Group was located in an unassuming block on Sixth Avenue. The lobby was spacious, decked out in stained marble and high ceilings that spoke of an earlier era, when gilded trim and gold elevators meant high class. Drasko sat behind the small reception desk. He smiled and raised a pudgy hand in greeting when Katie walked in.

"Good day, Miss Pretty," he said. His hair was so lush it looked as if a comb wouldn't make its way through the thicket. It shone under the overheads, giving off a faintly perfumed smell.

"Morning, Drasko," Katie said, pressing the up button. "Good weekend?"

Drasko was one of a small roster of security-guards-cum-receptionists and the only one who had been there since she'd worked as an intern the summer between her junior and senior years. Back then her hair had been very short, and the Serb had always looked a little alarmed when he saw her, as though thinking, each and every time, *Why would a woman choose to have hair like that?* The next summer on her first day back—as a paid consultant this time—she'd been growing out her hair, and he'd broken into a grin of instant recognition and approval. That's when he started calling her "Miss Pretty." It seemed like something Katie should be upset about (she noticed he never greeted other employees that way), but she didn't find it upsetting. She often wondered about that. Sometimes in those early months in the city, she'd been so lonely that Drasko's cheerful, soft face had been the only thing that made her feel connected to humanity. It had been wintertime; she'd graduated from Vassar a semester early, taken a tiny sublet in Queens. Those months, dark and frigid, while she'd hauled groceries to her walk-up so she could eat alone at a card table, Drasko's face would pop up in her mind periodically, the uncomplicated smile, the welcoming gesture, the predictability of it. *Miss Pretty.* It wasn't always bad or uncomfortable to be noticed.

On the fifty-second floor there was a real reception desk, above which hung a sign with blocky gold lettering that read **HCG**. The entire floor was studded with cubicles personalized with a plant or a light or family pictures, some piled high with papers and others pristine. The office itself was not all that important to Katie—during the workday she really only craved light, which she got plenty of, since she sat on the outer edge of the room near a window overlooking West Forty-Eighth Street. She liked the quiet studiousness of the place: everyone's head bent over spreadsheets, inches from a screen, absorbed by some presentation, banging out client reports with a focus unbroken by ringing phones or collegial chatter. She'd taken to the work quickly, even though she found spreadsheets boring and was, truthfully, only mildly interested in the problems the consultants were trying to solve. Since she was good with numbers, she was able to lose herself in the work; that was helpful. She tried to ignore the fact that it all didn't seem to amount to much, that it was soul deadening. Every problem they wrestled with seemed to end up in the same place: yet another slide in some endless deck showing how many people to lay off.

The morning went by quickly; she was researching the production cycle of various breakfast cereals. It was pointless work, since she wasn't currently assigned to a project. She was "on the beach," in consulting lingo. The other junior consultants loved being on the beach because it meant weeks of early nights and lazy mornings, but Katie far preferred being busy. At lunch she stepped out to stretch her legs. When she got back, one of the vice presidents was sitting behind the front desk, tapping into a smartphone. "Hey, Mr. Montague," she said. "Changed jobs, have you?"

Montague was in his late sixties. He was huge around the middle and had the disconcerting habit of sucking his teeth. "Filling in for Janis while she visits the ladies," he said. "Sometimes it's good to get a feel for what's happening out here in the real world." He frowned while not moving his eyes from her.

Katie stopped her forward movement. "Everything okay? Can I help with something?"

He held out a piece of paper. "You got some calls. I took messages for you," he said.

Before she even took the paper from him, her skin started to tingle. "Oh, thanks," she said. He had written in block letters: *Dennis Kanton, the Guardian*, and *Juliana DeVorgay*, from some unfamiliar online site. Montague's watery eyes bored into her, and she felt she had to give him some sort of explanation. "Some old business I need to deal with. Nothing to worry about."

"You're not in some sort of trouble, are you, sweetheart?"

His endearment put her on edge. "No," she said, "nothing to worry about."

"You're on the beach, right?" he asked.

"Yup," she said, "but just for the past week or so."

"Good. Why don't you take it easy for a bit?" He hesitated, his lips curling inward toward his teeth. "You're looking a bit peaked, if you don't mind my saying."

Involuntarily, her hand rose to her face, and she smoothed away some stray hairs. This morning she'd applied her makeup carefully, dressing in a new silk shirt and a dark-gray jacket and skirt, styling her hair in a low bun. It was a curse that people felt they could read her moods or her needs on her face, when she herself was trying so hard to appear decidedly neutral.

Smiling at him as naturally as she could, she said, "Maybe I'll do just that," and headed to her cubicle.

Charlie Gregory had spoken to reporters once, right after her husband's sentencing. The headline the next day read, "West Mills Wife Stands by Convicted Rapist" (especially ironic, of course, as it was soon proven to be untrue). For a few semesters at college, Katie had devoured a variety of seminal journalism books in a class that advertised itself as offering a fresh look at the modern media landscape: she'd read *Blur*, *Flat Earth News*, *The Death and Life of American Journalism*, and so on, all those doom-and-gloom books that cast a cold shadow over what was supposed to be such a noble profession. But what had stuck with her most was a book she couldn't remember the name of. It was slim and somewhat outdated, with a faded orange cover that curled at the edges, and it covered how data could be manipulated. As she'd flipped through the pages in the stacks at the library one day, it had seemed as though she were waking up to a world made up of rules she hadn't even known existed. She had already learned that people could not be trusted, but she had put her trust in numbers. Reading that book made her understand that there were no exceptions to the rule: human beings were *always* compelled to bring their own agenda to any endeavor. Juries, for example, didn't operate on mathematical principles: they didn't simply add up complex numbers and provide an airtight solution, presto. They came to their job as human beings, flawed and easily swayed. You could never truly be objective or dispassionate; your biases would always drive the way you saw reality and expressed facts. Returning to her cubicle at work, sliding into her chair, she thought again of that little orange book.

Too often, people who suffered trauma let themselves be defined by it, and she had been determined to avoid that fate. When she became Katie Amplethwaite—a name so alien, so liberating—she thought she'd freed herself from the past. She'd never told her first real boyfriend, Nate, about her father—or the next or the next, or now Zev. There was no reason for them to suspect anything. Her two closest girlfriends from college, Radha and Nicole, knew about it and had been sworn to secrecy, but even telling them had made her feel as though she were free-falling. Sometimes they would look at her and she could read the questions in their eyes like a data programmer reads code: the curiosity, the doubt, the desire to support her competing with the inherent pity they felt for Lulu.

Katie looked at the list of names and phone numbers she'd accumulated over the past few days: the *Baltimore Sun*, the *Milwaukee Current*, the *Providence Journal*, the *Boston Globe*, the *Arizona Republic*, the *Guardian*. Websites she knew and others she didn't. She wondered—with a genuine sense of curiosity but also some disdain—about the journalists trying to reach her, the ones who had now called her employer and would soon be calling her brother, no doubt, and maybe even her boyfriend. They'd probably already called her mother in Montreal, or maybe that was an old story not worth telling. Were they just in it for the scoop, or did they ever feel compelled by the stories they reported? Did they think about the people they were talking to, really think about them—the actual human lives they were disrupting with their intrusions and innuendoes? In times of quiet contemplation, did they ever wonder what it might be like if one of their own parents had been accused of some unthinkable crime?

Perhaps she was being cynical and these reporters believed in facts, the way people believed in what happened when you added chemical elements together, because they knew it to be true: hydrogen and oxygen made water. In this way one fact plus another equaled something new. As though the truth were some sort of pure, golden place that emitted an angelic chorus upon discovery, where everything had an order and a luster that could not be tarnished. But for Katie, that kind of thinking was treacherous: feelings were not facts, memories lied, and people were not who you thought they were.

7

"David? You there?" Katie called out, holding the buzzer down. It was early evening, and she'd trekked down to Red Hook after work, first a subway, then a bus, and then a ten-minute walk. The lights were on inside the apartment, and a vinyl jacket lay on a bench, some shoes thrown, helter-skelter, underneath. A sleeping cat stirred ever so slightly. She knocked on the window.

Finally, the door opened, and her brother stood in front of her. The nubs of his shoulders stuck out from his T-shirt, and a pair of white briefs hung from his hips. David shared a rent-controlled apartment in the basement of a brownstone next to a Con Edison power-exchange yard that took up two city blocks. His skin was sallow and drawn, his thick blond hair darkened as though he hadn't washed it recently.

"What the hell? I've been trying to call you," Katie blurted out.

"Ack," he said, yawning widely. His angular face was striking, with high cheekbones and a full, curving mouth. "Lost my cell. Sorry, sis. Come in."

She followed him into the apartment, watching his saggy briefs shift around as his muscles contracted. The catatonic cat opened one eye and shut it again. "Why don't you get a new one?" she said. "I've called you like a hundred times."

He raised his pale brows at her. "Something wrong?" He rubbed his eyes, digging at the sockets. "Just took a nap. I'm so beat."

"Are you going to school anymore?" Katie asked. Her brother was studying to be an actor, but she didn't really know what he did with his time. Whenever she called him, he seemed to have just woken up.

"Ha, you think I'm living *la vida loca*?" He flopped onto a beige couch and took a long slug from a glass that held an amber liquid and two small ice cubes. "I've got a job as an understudy at the Broadmore. Show starts in, like, two months. It's a ton of work."

The apartment was subterranean and dark, trade magazines and carryout cartons littering the floor and a dead spider plant sitting in a saucer of brown water. "You okay, Davey?" she asked. "I'm worried about you."

"Is that why you came? Sorry. I'm just tired is all. Kyle and I broke up, but it was a long time coming. I'm actually super happy."

"Okay," she said, stalling for time. "Sorry to hear about Kyle—I guess that's good, if you're all right about it."

"Yeah. I feel like I've been working so hard for years, you know? I want to just focus. It's all finally starting to make sense."

"That's a big deal—an understudy." Katie put down her leather satchel. Her brother had always been the odd one out, the quiet kid who'd stare at you with big, serious eyes. Once he took up acting, he'd still been the silent observer when among other teens, but when onstage, he became someone utterly different. It was amazing to her that he was capable of such total yet fleeting transformation. She pointed at his drink. "Is that whiskey? I'm going to get some, okay?"

She went to the sink in the galley kitchen and fished out a glass. The place was dingy but not too dreadful. There were dishes everywhere and the trash was overfull, but the counters were clean, and there were notes tacked up on the fridge with colorful magnets. After their parents had lawyered up, they'd been tight on money, and she and her brother had reacted in radically different ways. The summer Katie was sixteen—when, for the first time in her living memory, they hadn't returned to Eagle Lake—she took a full-time job at KB Toys in the mall. Everything around her was going to hell, but she could at least bring in a steady paycheck. It didn't really matter what the work was; what mattered was staying occupied. She was the youngest employee there, and she knew it made her father proud when she handed over her paycheck at the end of each week. It seemed that as David grew up, he'd had the opposite reaction: He learned that he could survive on almost nothing. He cultivated an appreciation for dollar pizza slices and musty vintage clothing. He was an expert at tracking down free events and never said no if you offered to buy him a drink or a meal. It came across as insouciant, though she suspected it was designed to camouflage the zeal with which he pursued acting. It was hard for her to imagine living that way, never sure what the next day would bring. But perhaps she envied David just a bit too. Her path was razor straight; it led right to the horizon, and then what? No turns, no hills, nothing that filled her heart with insane joy? David lived hand to mouth, but at least he felt things fully.

The freezer was empty, the ice tray furry. The whiskey tasted cheap, but the metallic zing signaled to her that she could relax: she was safe here. Katie took another deep slug and went back into the somber living room. "So, Davey. You talked with Dad recently?"

"Mm," he said. "Not really."

"When's the last time you visited him?" It was strange that David—the only son, the longed-for second child—had slipped into the contours of his new reality so much more easily than she had. After the divorce and the sale of the house, their mother had put some of their belongings in storage at the cabin before moving with David into a two-bedroom apartment near Clinton Hill. He'd commuted to PPAS, the performing arts school in Midtown. David had spent all those years alone with their mother while she was gone in college—she really couldn't expect him to feel the same way about Dad.

"What's up?" he asked. "He finally scheduled for release?"

"Three weeks."

David smiled. "Fuck me," he said. "Almost six years. Since I was just a kid. Be weird having him back."

"Have you heard from anyone? Like, anyone call you about the case?"

"From the parole office, you mean, or who?"

"Reporters," Katie said. She took a seat next to him on the couch. Her body felt insubstantial, as though she could float into the air like vapor, dissipating without leaving even an odor. "They're calling me. They want to talk to me about the case. It's really—I just don't know what to do. I thought it was all over."

"Damn." He leaned forward and studied his hands. "No, haven't heard a thing. But then I haven't been great about messages and stuff—and now, you know, no phone. What are you going to do?"

"Why does any of this matter anymore? He's served his time. You'd think they'd leave us alone."

He grunted. "Fat chance. But you don't have to talk to them. They'll give up eventually. Move on to another story, something more current."

"It just feels so . . . *invasive*. And Dad, he asked me to go to Eagle Lake. Get the cabin ready for him."

"No—no way, not me," David said. "I'm not going. That place is fucking haunted. I thought Grumpy finally sold it?"

"No, not the cabin," Katie said. "Look, Dad's getting out, and we've got to figure out how to put our family together again."

"There's no going back. You know, rewriting things," he said. "Whether we want to or not."

She wasn't sure she believed him. "Are you even happy he's getting out?"

"Of course I am." But there was something about David's tone that suggested he wasn't telling her what he really felt. "It's just, you know. Like I don't really even know the guy."

Should have visited him more often, she thought, but she didn't want to be mean spirited.

The heavy gloom of the apartment made it impossible to tell whether it was day or night, and they decided to take a walk around the block. Katie offered David a cigarette, and they both lit up, walking side by side in the cooling dusk. A light wind blew in from the Upper Bay, tinged with the smell of salt and fish. Surrounded by stunted brick buildings, the neighborhood felt far removed from Manhattan— so quiet, almost peaceful, yet in the silence, an unspoken conversation seemed to be running between the two of them: David telling her to not ask too much of him, to leave him be; Katie asking him to help her figure out what life would look like once their father was a free man again.

David held the butt between thumb and forefinger like a villain in a movie before grinding it out under a pair of canvas sneakers. "Come on; chuck that thing and follow me. We can talk a bit in here. It's nice." He headed up the stairs of an old church on the corner of the block. A sign outside read VISITATION BVM PARISH. The wooden front door was locked, and he headed to a side door, motioning for her to come.

Inside, low lights were on, and there was a chill in the air, as though the church were lagging behind by a few months and inside it was still December while outside it was already June. Katie's heels made staccato taps on the floor. When they were little, she and David had attended the Episcopal church in West Mills with Grumpy and Gram for a while, and she'd loved the weighty silence that seemed oppressive at first but became soothing the longer she sat and waited for something to happen. Usually she'd fall asleep, but Grumpy never woke her. Once Gram died, they stopped going. This church was different, starker, shaped like a ship in back but inverted like an upside-down keel. She slipped into one of the pews, and David took a seat next to her.

"They let me play the organ. No one can actually play that thing anymore; everyone's dead. It's an old Midmer-Losh. I come practice almost every day. I love it in here," he said. They sat in silence for a while. "Remember how Dad used to read to us at night? All those obscure English stories that Mum passed off on him. Way past the time when other parents were all, 'Go watch TV, and leave us alone.' I was obsessed with Babar. I think about that time a lot when I come here. It was nice, you know?"

"Yeah, those Uncle Arthur stories," Katie said, fiddling with the hem of her jacket.

"Enid Blyton. You loved that shit!"

"I was just pretending. It was Dad's voice I liked," she said. "You know I couldn't actually read till I was like eight, right?"

"Really? They didn't know?"

"Did a great job hiding it, I guess." When she was six, seven, even eight years old, making sense of the string of words on a page was a monstrous task. Her confusion was like a hideous scab she managed to hide from everyone, even her teachers. But before any of the grown-ups fully understood what was going on, Lulu figured it out. Though she told Katie that she didn't like books either—too long! too slow! too boring!—that very first summer, she would read to her aloud in the den at the cabin, helping her sound out the words. When they got frustrated, Lulu would goof around, using funny voices, stretching and scrunching her face to act out the story. Eventually Katie switched schools, got special tutoring. Learned that she was not in fact stupid, just dyslexic.

"You know what I think of, when you tell me things like reporters are hounding you, or when I think about Mum and the divorce?" David said. "I remember when Dad took me with him to go visit this woman at Eagle Lake—Constance, remember? Constance Nichols?"

"Yeah, sure. The one who used to wear kimonos to the beach."

"Right. Well, she was sick or something. We went over there, Dad and I, and took her this pile of cupcakes. Orange cupcakes. And he was so nice; he felt so bad for her. Her face just lit up, and she ate one right away. It was a small thing to do, but it mattered." David ran a hand through his hair. "On the way back to the lake, he was all emotional. I remember his eyes welled up, like he was going to cry. And I was scared for a bit, thinking, like, something was wrong and maybe she was dying, but then he told me that her husband didn't take good care of her, he'd cheated on her, and how he was so dishonorable. That's what he said: 'You've got to treat people right. It's important to be honorable.'"

"Yes," she said, smiling. "It's a lot to live up to."

"Man, I think about that a lot," David continued. "'There's nothing more important than being an honorable man.' How ironic. Everything got so fucked up once he went to prison, didn't it?"

"Before then," she said, "when Lulu started spending summers with us."

"Did you ever talk to her again? After?"

"Hell no," Katie said, heat pressing against her neck. A small diamond earring winked at her from under David's dirty-blond hair. His profile was quite sharp, noble, even. There were times when he seemed to shrink in front of her eyes, become her chapped-lipped little brother again, as though trapped in her memories of him. And other times, like now, he seemed to swell, to assume a stature that had little to do with size and more to do with an aura of competence.

"What about that kid, Jack? You guys were crazy about him," David said.

"No, no—I never saw either of them again." It was surprising how, all these years later, their competition for Jack still felt in some way shameful. This was a boy she'd only known for a few weeks, and still the mention of his name shifted something inside her, set her on edge. Made her yearn for something unnamable.

"So, I don't know. Maybe it's time you looked them up?"

She let out a puff of air as if to say, *Are you kidding?* Inside her, always, was the emptiness of having lost her best friend, but she had become accustomed to that. And even Jack had betrayed her, ultimately—even Jack had erased her from his life after that summer.

"If you ask me, I think you miss her. You wonder about her; you just won't admit it." David stood up and ran his hands down the front of his jacket, smoothing his clothing in an endearingly fussy way. "Wait here, okay? I want to show you something. Be right back."

A minute later, the sound of the organ emerged—deep, blowsy, reverberating through her—and she was filled with awe. Her little brother had lived almost a whole decade without her around, and there were all sorts of secrets she hadn't even guessed at, like the fact that he could play the organ. The music was thunderous yet also languid, replete; it gave her a sense of the possibility and surprise of her world. But then, almost as quickly, the character of the sound changed, and among the resonant chords were some real stinkers. When her brother came back, Katie covered her mouth with her hand. He shot her a withering look.

"Don't wake the neighbors," she said, grinning.

"All right, all right," he said. "So I'm not that great. *Yet.*"

It felt so good to laugh with him. They walked back to his apartment and embraced in the empty streets, under a light that droned above them like a giant insect. As she turned away from him, she felt a slow and steady silencing of the inner voice that nagged at her, telling her to never turn back. There was so much about the past that was good. As she headed back toward Manhattan in a cab, weaving through Carol Gardens and Cobble Hill, over the Brooklyn Bridge now sparkling in the deep blue darkness, she mulled over what David had said in the church: *I think you miss her.*

God—I do miss her, Katie thought as she looked into the black water streaming below her and then up into an urban sky punctured with faint stars. Was it possible to know her father was an honorable man and still miss Lulu?

8

The lake is calm. The moonlight shimmies over the water, turning it into acres of gray silk. Katie and Lulu slip down onto the spider-riddled bottom of a canoe and lie in the middle of the lake, bored and not bored, staring up at the sky. Tonight it is crisscrossed with highways of sparkling space debris, and they count the shooting stars aloud, one after another—five, ten, thirty flashes. The very next day they are both going home.

"You know, I'm gonna miss you, Katie Gregory," Lulu says. When summer is over, Lulu returns to her world, and Katie returns to hers. They talk now and then on the phone, but it's nothing like when they are together, breathing the same air, egging each other on. "It's the pits, living upstate," Lulu adds, grabbing the bottle of Campari from Katie and sitting up so she can take another swig. A dribble of pink liquid creeps down her chin.

On long afternoons just the previous summer, they were still hanging around the grown-ups, hoping to be taken out for a sail on a Sunfish, or playing with the toddlers in the grass. But this summer the girls have no interest in grown-ups or toddlers. Weeks earlier on the very first night Lulu arrived to stay, they stole an old bottle of Southern Comfort gathering dust at the back of the linen cupboard that doubled as a bar. They drank almost half of it and ate ice cream to mask the disgusting taste. It wasn't the first time they'd had alcohol, but it was the first time they purposefully drank it in order to get drunk. When Katie threw up in the middle of the night after her parents had tumbled into bed, she and Lulu snorted with laughter, terrified of getting caught but incapable of suppressing the joyous frenzy of discovery. They became more and more daring. At night they smoked Katie's mother's stolen Pall Malls under a canopy of hemlocks as the adults drank and chatted on the deck not ten feet away. Once they sneaked out of the cabin in the early morning hours and headed back to the clubhouse, stealing a bottle of wine from behind the bar and then driving the Ford Falcon around the dirt roads with the lights off as dawn began edging its way over the trees.

And then, of course, they both discovered Jack Benson. And later what Katie remembers most about lying there in the canoe that night is how guilty she felt.

Jack has been gone for almost a week: tennis camp. The ache inside Katie is unbearable. The feel of his skin on hers, the warmth and slickness of his tongue in her mouth. She thinks: *We've barely even gotten started, and now summer is over.* She thinks: *Why don't I just say something to Lulu, just spit it out?* If their bond is so fragile that Lulu would turn against her for this, then what does that mean? But Katie stays quiet not so much because their friendship seems precarious but because of the wild look in Lulu's eyes as she spins her tales, dreaming up a future for herself. A look of sudden vulnerability that surprises Katie with its fierceness and then just as quickly disappears. Katie just can't bring herself to hurt her friend's feelings.

The last time she saw Jack, he and Katie were again alone, the morning after the first kisses in the shed. They were on the dusty gravel behind the clubhouse saying goodbye, tripping over each other in their eagerness to talk. He was telling her about his father, the unrelenting pressure to please him; the way he only asked his son questions so he could supply the answers himself, after a millisecond's impatient pause. She'd talked about David, how she worried that he was too quiet. That her brother sometimes hid in his closet and talked or sang to himself. That her mom was always so withdrawn, and she thought maybe it was her fault somehow. She told Jack how she loved numbers, how each number seemed to her to have a color. Without warning and in full view of anyone who might be walking by, he bent his jutting shoulders forward and brushed her lips with his, a whisper of a kiss.

Then he pulled her close and kissed her again. His body felt good against hers, the promise of something unknown in the light press of his hip bones against her stomach. In that moment, Lulu did not exist.

Afterward, when Jack is gone, Katie still does not say anything to Lulu about what's been happening. She doesn't mention it the next day or the next. Six days and she hasn't said a word. Yet Lulu talks about Jack every day that he is not there, fretting about when he will return, *if* he will return. Each time she talks about Jack and Katie doesn't say anything about the kisses, the door to the truth closes further until it is all but locked. Not telling her friend is no different from lying.

The Campari is almost finished, and Lulu takes a last sip, letting the final drops fall into her mouth one by one. She smacks her lips together. "I'm supposed to start thinking about, like, vocational shit," she says. "No one even asks if I want to go to college. Like, literally no one goes to college from Blackbrooke High."

"You're going to move. You'll join a band," Katie says, trying to imagine what it's like to live in this area year round, in a town where there is nothing to do. She's only once been to Lulu's apartment, and it was a disaster. Paper-thin walls and a kitchenette with stained plastic counters. Neighbors smoking and drinking on the outside walkway, leaning heavily on the railing that overlooked Mission Street. The stories Lulu told late at night in the safety of the woods seemed exciting, novel, but the reality turned out to be something quite different. "You don't need college to be a singer, right? Blackbrooke, it's just, I don't know. A blip. You'll be out of here in no time. You'll be on some stage in some cool place, and I'll be your roadie."

Lulu throws her torso to the right and then the left, wildly jerking the canoe in the water. "I order you to take me back to West Mills with you!" she hisses into the hot darkness. "Stick me in your suitcase, and I promise I won't be any trouble."

"Stop—you'll tip us over," Katie says, laughing, gripping the sides of the canoe.

"Ugh. And what's up with our little princeling? I wonder if he'll even turn up agai—"

"Don't call him that, Lu." A little lurch in Katie's chest.

"But it's perfect—the prince and the pauper, right? What could be more fitting?"

Katie hates when Lulu talks like this. Her sharpness and hard-edged laughter make her seem so mature, such a wiseass. Katie wishes she could joke around about Jack too—or, better yet, tell her friend about the lost hour in the changing shed, the sudden kisses in the parking lot. That things have moved forward and that Lulu's being left behind. But she's tongue tied and oddly lonely, as though Lulu isn't even there anymore.

The water stretches out inky and unknowable until the girls paddle closer to shore, when it catches the lights, bursting into flame. The string of bulbs that connects the corner of the old building to the railing around the deck casts a yellow glow over the grown-ups sitting outside smoking and drinking.

Heat presses down. Lulu pulls out a lipstick from the pocket of her shorts and deftly swipes it across her lips. "How do you *do* that?" Katie asks as they clamber out. She's tried putting lipstick on, peering at herself in the bathroom mirror, but she looked like a specialty act in a circus show.

Rolling her bottom and top lips together in slow motion, Lulu spreads the color around evenly and then puckers her lips. "Let's go kick some ass," she says, and although Katie doesn't know exactly what her friend means, she likes the sound of it.

The rickety building that faces the lake is an old icehouse converted into a place for kids to play Ping-Pong and eat sloppy hot dogs, with a bar area on the side for the grown-ups. Cupping her hands around her eyes, Katie peers in through the clubhouse window, searching the crowd for Jack, who was supposed to be back yesterday but never turned up. The square dance caller stands on a raised platform and drawls into his microphone. A tan cowboy hat covers his eyebrows. Charlie and John Gregory stand at the edge of the crowd, disheveled, skin gleaming. The women wear checkered dresses and big aprons, their hair puffed up, gallons of makeup smeared around their eyes. Katie's mother doesn't like these theme nights as much as her father, but she plays along. She can get away with being reserved because she's foreign. "Your mom's mysterious," Lulu once said. "People adore mystery."

John looks ridiculous but somehow handsome, too, wearing an ascot and a pair of green polyester golf pants. He is a man who moves through the world chest first with a grin on his face. The tiny gaps between his teeth make him seem to be in constant good humor even when he isn't. When he smiles, his face takes on the quality of a child, mischievous and knowing. It makes you laugh in complicity; you just can't help it.

Little kids race around, chasing each other—and suddenly there he is, Jack, standing by the makeshift stage, leaning his long body against one of the old speakers. His face deeply tanned, the waves of his too-long hair almost white under the lights. He is all angles and pent-up energy. Long limbed, bony. There is a hole on the breast of his Lacoste T-shirt where he must have snipped out the crocodile logo in a fit of self-consciousness. The fact that he is here, that they have the night ahead of them after all—this almost eclipses the worry that takes root again about how on earth she will tell Lulu that Jack has decided between them, and that he has chosen Katie.

9

Each day after going to see her brother, Katie came to consciousness in the predawn hours, four or five o'clock in the morning. She'd drift in and out of sleep for another hour or two, waking finally in the steely morning light with a feeling in her heart so heavy, stonelike, she was dumbfounded. She dreamed of epic struggles around the smallest, most mundane things. Her father helping her with an untied shoe elicited a torrent of yearning; kissing Jack was a tragedy that made her dream self weep inconsolably. But she also dreamed of murder, the delirious, terrifying thrill of plunging a blade into a young girl's rib cage. She would live whole lifetimes in a flash.

Her father was calling her more often, with laundry lists of things he wanted her to do. She tried to make sure to plug the phone in only when they prearranged a time to talk. When he called on Thursday, he had to stop twice in the middle of asking her to tell him the ins and outs of social media, his voice breaking a little. "Honey, sometimes I feel like I'll never catch up," he said.

"It's easy, Dad," she said. "You haven't been gone for that long, in the big picture. You'll pick this stuff up in no time."

"The whole world has been moving ahead, and I've been in here."

She sucked on her lip, not wanting to give away how moved she was by his fear. "You've always taught me to be brave, to just keep going, right? That's what you'll do. There'll be some adjustment, sure, but knowing you, it'll take you, like, a whole day."

He laughed on the other end. "Give me two days, okay, sweets?"

Above all, she wanted him to feel strong, to launch into his new life with hope and energy. Of course she didn't say anything about the renewed interest in his case or the nightmares she was having. At work, the hours dragged by till she could make some excuse to head home. Zev caught a ride with a friend back up to Vassar, and she was alone. She forced herself to run every day when she got home, so weary and spent she wanted to cry. She began biting her nails again. Saturday morning she lay in bed, having slept only a few hours, looking absently out the window onto the apartment building opposite hers. She had been dreaming about drowning, and upon waking, she'd remembered something she hadn't thought about in years.

It had been a bitter, colorless February day, with winds that could shred skin. Her grandparents were at Eagle Lake for the day to attend the Winter Carnival, and her father had packed her in the car along with her very pregnant mother. Katie was five years old. "We've got to get out of this shit hole!" he'd said. At that point they were living in a tiny apartment near the West Mills train station. It would be another year or so before Gram died and Grumpy moved out of the West Mills house, allowing his daughter's growing family to claim it as their own.

One of the teenagers had strung the rope back up on the maple so the kids could swing over the lake. People were drinking mulled wine and clapping their hands together trying to keep warm. The lake was entirely frozen and covered in a thin layer of snow. Katie grabbed the rope and swung out over the ice, once, twice. Her legs were weightless in the cold air. And then—she never quite knew why—she simply let go. She opened her fingers, released the rope, and fell straight down onto the ice.

Her feet plunged into the water, her flailing arms broke the ice, and a channel sprang up instantly, linking the hole to the water that rushed under the ice toward the dam. As soon as her head dunked under, her small body became as heavy as a sack of concrete. Her father didn't hesitate: he shucked off his coat—his woolen hat still on his head—and jumped in.

The lake was not deep at the shoreline, and he could stand, though she didn't know that. He grabbed her so hard that bruises blossomed on her pale arms, and she clung to him so fiercely that his head went under for a second till he found his feet and stood up. He pushed her away from his body, and she shrieked; she could not believe that he was saving her only to push her away again. But he was trying to lift her up to dry land, and to do that, he had to disentangle himself from her grasping arms. She clung to him even harder, and they tussled, and she screamed, "Daddy! Daddy!" Afterward he had joked about it, but she had never learned to find it funny.

In many ways, he'd been doing this all her life—proving his paternal devotion. Sometimes it was an almost literal act (giving her the last peanut crackers at the end of a long car ride, when she was losing her mind with hunger), and sometimes it was through the plain but powerful magic of his trust in her. He'd stand on the sidelines as she passed the lacrosse ball to a teammate, his belief in her abilities making the ball sail to its desired destination. Tasked with calling local vendors for a career project, she stuttered into the receiver, but her father's earnest smile made the words come out with greater intention. She couldn't explain it, but with her mother she had always felt less than. With her father, she was not merely good enough—she was great. Just the way she was.

Katie rose from her bed, fuzzy headed. She grabbed her jeans and a light cotton sweater from the chair, slipped her feet into a pair of Converse sneakers. The day loomed ahead of her, empty. Standing in her kitchen, unable to eat or read the paper, she tried to think of every excuse she could to avoid heading up to Eagle Lake. Thinking about the lake and the teeming woods made her sick to her stomach with fear: she knew that she'd no longer be able to access those pure feelings of ease and happiness that she used to get from being in the woods. That last summer with Lulu, those moments with Jack—they had been so perfect, until Katie had ruined it. She clamped her jaw together until her teeth began to ring.

But there was so little she had been able to do for her father over the years; she could at least overcome her childish reluctance to go to the cabin. She needed to step up and prove that she was the girl he thought she was.

Zev's ancient Datsun was parked just two blocks away, and he'd left the keys with her. So what if David wasn't going to come with her? She'd better get over it: she had promised her father, and anyway, she couldn't just mope around, avoiding the inevitable. Who knew—maybe going back was just what she needed. She had wanted to be more resolute, to face things head-on. Here was her opportunity.

Under the looming pines, the cabin was cast in speckled shade. Katie stopped short on the driveway and stared, her breath pressing like a thumb on her windpipe. The place was shabbier and smaller than she remembered. Curtains were pulled shut over the front windows, and a plastic flowerpot on the stoop held a scramble of dead plants. The door was locked. Katie picked her way to the back patio over the clumpy grass and rocks. She had a dizzying sense of a clock's hands speeding backward, unstoppable.

Peering through the windows into the den, she saw the two old sofas, perpendicular to one another, pushed up against the walls, their stained plaid looking so familiar. She just couldn't believe nothing had changed, especially in the den, of all places. This was where she used to play with her little brother and clutch his sticky fingers as he learned to walk, tripping over the shag carpet in his eagerness. Later, it was where she lounged with Lulu on long, indolent summer nights with a stolen beer or two, frogs singing outside in the deep backwoods. It was through these windows that she'd caught a glimpse of the rosy flush of dawn on that last day of summer in 2007, the three of them—Lulu, Katie, and her father—sprawled on those very couches, sleeping the agitated sleep of people who were not where they were supposed to be.

The back slider was locked, too, but the window near the kitchen was unlatched, and she hoisted herself over the sill and climbed in. The air inside was close and cool, smelling of something earthy. She groped along the walls and flipped on the light switches, then headed toward the front window and ripped the curtains aside. Diffuse light filtered in. One by one, she opened curtains and blinds and yanked windows up. Dust covered every surface, and there was clutter everywhere. Magazines, a towel on a chair. She sneezed. When Katie was a child, her mother had kept the cabin spotless, but all around her now, familiar objects were thrown into unfamiliar disarray.

So it seemed the electricity worked. It was almost a decade since the house had last been used, and she wondered whether Grumpy was the one who still paid the bills. No water came from the faucet in the kitchen, and the downstairs toilet was dry. She'd have to get the superintendent to turn the water on if her father was really going to move in. It seemed a crazy idea for him to come back here. The local papers had been full of the story when the trial ramped up; surely everyone would know his name, would remember the scandal. Not to mention the people who spent their summers at the lake, all those old friends—there was no way they'd be happy to see John Gregory. A wave of compassion washed over her. He must be really desperate to be willing to come back.

The living room was unchanged, and she sat briefly on the large corduroy couch as memories crowded her head. Learning to dive. Fires in the pit behind the boathouse. The old red bikini. Taking out the canoe. Her father throwing a deflated football with David. She saw these as snapshots, shuffled like a deck of cards. Her mother had loved taking photos and for the longest time kept carefully annotated photo albums: when Katie lost her first tooth, when she attended her first day of kindergarten—all of it, every little milestone. She'd been a patient photographer, never asking for poses and smiles but catching people in action, unaware. Where were all those albums now? she wondered. Katie would clean this place up—it was the very least she could do—but not now. Though . . . maybe she could find those old pictures. Maybe when they'd moved from the house in West Mills, the albums had ended up here, along with the other detritus from their former lives. Those pictures might tell her something about her parents that she'd forgotten: that they'd been happy, once.

Tucked into the corner of the living room was a narrow stairway with a railing made of irregular pine branches that led to a second floor. In the master bedroom, the heavy oak bed frame with the carved headboard was gone, and in its place was a ratty-looking mattress lying on the carpet. She thought of her mother's trim, compact body stretched out there, her reading light casting an amber glow on her cheek. She'd never been quite like other mothers—and not just because of her accent and her mannerisms. Katie's parents had married because they'd found themselves unexpectedly pregnant, and then, in a cruel twist, they hadn't been able to conceive again. Charlie suffered three miscarriages, one of which Katie witnessed: her mother sobbing on the toilet, a fat trail of blood soaking into the plush white bath mat.

When Charlie finally got pregnant with David, Katie had been five. The firm, convex mound protruding from under her mother's breasts was a baby—a brother, *for her*, coming soon, after they had waited so long—but each night when that strange belly nudged up against her, hard yet soft, it seemed as though a living thing had taken her mother over and turned her into someone else. The sense of unease made Katie clingy, and her mother couldn't tolerate it. She'd give her a quick good-night kiss, flick off the overhead light, and disappear. Even now, Katie didn't understand why it had been like this, whether she'd done something wrong or somehow disappointed her mother. Over the years, Katie had yearned to bridge the gap that had widened between them, but they rarely saw each other anymore, not even at Christmas (her mother went to the Bahamas with Michel). It seemed Charlie had simply decided to let the distance grow, and Katie had followed her lead.

On the top shelf of the closet, there was a row of six or seven shoeboxes and a few plastic milk crates that held random relics. A few faded Polaroids of Grumpy and Gram at cocktail parties. A pedometer. A small silver bell. A schedule from one of the theme nights at the clubhouse. No photo albums. It was true: the secret of her father's conviction and her family's disintegration had crowded out everything good from the past.

Across the hall, her brother's old room was crammed with excess furniture, the walls still covered in posters of musicals and old playbills. Lulu and Katie had spent so much time in that room, summer after summer, reenacting shows with David as their little helper, taking turns at playing Sandy in *Grease* or Tracy and Penny from *Hairspray*. Lulu had a beautiful voice. Once they'd spent days stitching together costumes and making wigs, singing "You Can't Stop the Beat" and shrieking so loudly that John came up, red faced with laughter, and told them to pipe down or they'd set off the Cauleys' dogs.

She went downstairs and stood outside the den. It was just an ordinary room, she told herself. Nothing to be afraid of. She cracked open the door and peered in. It was a small, misshapen room, pine paneled, dominated by a row of large windows facing the woods. Stepping inside, Katie held her breath before letting it out in a burst. Ridiculous to be so timid! And yet Lulu Henderson's presence was there amid the unchanged dimness. The whites of her eyes seemed to flash at Katie like a feral cat's. She remembered her musky smell, a combination of soap and skin. She heard the way Lulu spoke, her voice strong and melodious, flattening out when she didn't get her way. Lulu was imbedded in this place; it made no difference that she'd always remained an outsider at Eagle Lake, a visitor, despite the hours she'd spent in the lake's shallows or drinking Dr Pepper in the clubhouse. But Katie had never thought of her as someone who didn't really belong here. For her, Lulu had been a fixture, a given, as permanent as the lake or the pines. *Lulu belonged to Katie; Katie belonged to Lulu.*

Yet each year by late August, that feeling faded in spite of her ardor. They would drive out of the stone gates and drop Lulu off in front of her apartment complex, and she would not invite them in, and they would not ask to come in. She'd thought she knew so much about her friend's life, when in reality, she'd known so little.

For example, Katie hadn't known that Lulu played hooky a lot, that she was often in trouble for unauthorized absences. That she already played in a folk band or that she saw a court-ordered psychotherapist every week. Katie certainly didn't know that, just a few months after they said goodbye to each other for the last time, Lulu would tell a teacher at her school some outrageous story about crazy things happening to her in the den—in this very room—as Katie slept on the couch nearby.

That she'd say things had happened that were unthinkable, impossible—that Katie's father touched her late that night. More than that, *more.*

From the den, Katie could see out the window to the perimeter of the woods where the patio petered out. The forest was a mysterious, tangled place, full of mixed oak, fir, and red spruce. She caught sight of the old shed, where her father used to store their bikes over the winter. A compact wooden structure, it had a tiled roof that was almost entirely obscured by a layer of luminous green moss. Her mother kept brooms and buckets there, cleaning supplies. Katie hadn't been thinking ahead; she should have stopped in Blackbrooke and bought supplies so she could start in on getting the place tidied up. She picked her way over the loosened stone, shivering in the spring breeze.

The padlock on the door hung open on its rusted hook. Katie kicked aside some matted leaves and inched the door open. Inside, her father had nailed metal grips along the walls and painted the outlines of his tools on the rough boards so he'd know where everything went. They were empty now, faded ghosts. She switched on the overhead. No bikes, just a push mower and a broken bookcase. In the back corner stood a plastic trash can and a bunch of cardboard moving boxes from when they'd sold the West Mills house, including a midsized wooden box that she recognized as David's old treasure chest. Stenciled on the lid in fading black was the image of a pirate wearing an eye patch and a hat.

She crouched down beside the box, ran her finger over the dusty lid, and then lifted it open. A tiny black spider with long, articulated legs scuttered away. The box wasn't filled with children's toys anymore, nor did it hold photos; instead there were a bunch of spiral-bound notebooks and a manila folder full of loose papers. There were bills and old bank statements and some scraps of drawing paper. With a start she realized the folder held paperwork from the trial. Letters from lawyers, a huge envelope marked "bills." There was a thin pack of letters in there, too, held together with elastic bands. Just as she was about to shove the letters and the paperwork back into the box, a name caught her eye, and her head flooded with static.

Jack Benson.

She puzzled over his name, written on the left-hand corner of an envelope that was addressed to her. The date on the stamp read May 2010, shortly before her father's trial. The letter seemed a relic from another era, one that dated from long before her time; she couldn't remember when she'd last received a bona fide, handwritten letter— maybe from Grumpy, who didn't use a computer. The envelope was thick, creamy, good paper stock. Jack had written her name in ballpoint pen, chicken scratch for letters. Larger *K* and *G*. She turned it over and over, handling it gently as though it might disintegrate. It had been opened.

Jack had tried to reach her . . . he had written her a letter! She'd had no idea. They hadn't been on Facebook back then, but she'd definitely had email . . . and then she remembered that her mother had made her change her email account. When had that happened?

It was in the spring of 2008, when the lawyer first started coming around to the house. Her mother had forbidden her to use the computer, and Katie had grown to like the isolation, the sense of protecting herself from a world that gave not one shit about what she was feeling.

To calm herself, she laid one hand on her stomach. Her body seemed to ache all over, her muscles pulsing and sore. Yesterday she'd had to stop twice in the middle of her run to catch her breath.

All this time she had thought Jack had turned his back on her. The letter was radioactive in her fingers.

10

Sometimes it's the voices that break through—the varying timbres. Her father's, always laughing, teasing, cajoling. Her mother's British cadence, clipped and precise.

And Lulu's—full, deep, yet feminine. Breathy and rooted at the same time; a contradiction. So lovely in song, making the hairs on Katie's arms shiver. There's something powerful about it, even in regular conversation.

"You know, Katie, I love this place. I do," Lulu says as Katie comes back toward her. She's sitting in the darkness beneath the maple that leans out over the water. "But please? If I ever turn into one of those old cronies in there, wearing dress-up clothes when I'm forty fucking years old and getting drunk on vodka and soda, just shoot me, okay?" She makes a gun with thumb and forefinger and points it at her forehead.

"Jack's back," Katie says, toeing the grass at the water's edge. "He's inside."

"Oh!" Lulu cries, jumping up. "We'd better go in—he might think I've already gone home."

"Why do you assume that he's . . ." Katie starts and falters instantly. This is ridiculous; she should just come out with it. But there is something unspoken between them, a fact they both accepted long ago: Lulu is the pretty one, with her burnished skin and wide-set eyes. The contagious energy. The brown belly boys can't drag their eyes away from. That strong voice, daring you to challenge her.

Dad. His green polyester pants glow in the dark. In the heat, he smells of musk and sweat. "Hot as Hades in there," he says, emerging from the clubhouse, where the country music pulses. But it's hot outside too.

"Anyone want to swim?" Mum's eyeliner is smudged. Her purple linen dress has fallen off one shoulder, revealing a lacy bra strap, and her big brown hair is a tangled nest. A beaded necklace swings between her breasts, and she carries a glass of rosé.

"No!" Katie says. They are talking about skinny-dipping, which is humiliating and awkward and far, far worse whenever grown-ups get involved. "Mum, no, really, *please*. It's too crowded."

Lulu laughs so loudly that Katie is irritated. Sometimes it seems like Lulu understands her mother better than she does.

"Oh, lighten up, will you," Dad says to his daughter. He is laughing too.

Katie looks away. Over the lake, steam rises in a thick, levitating curtain. Thin clouds are blotting out strips of the star-studded sky, and the heat of the evening has an edge to it, as though it might suddenly drop. When Katie licks her lips, salt floods her mouth. The heat presses into her, but it's not unpleasant.

"Hey," comes another voice. "You're all out here."

Katie spins around: Jack, walking toward them.

"Hiya," says Lulu, jutting out one soft hip: both *Don't mess with me* and *Come hither*. Katie studies her, wondering how she does it. She is so womanly, her skin, those curls, her lips bright red and luscious, almost black now in the darkness. She checks to see Jack's reaction, but she can't really tell what he's thinking.

"Come out here to flirt with the girls, eh?" Katie's father asks the boy. John concentrates on taking a sip of his beer. His hand is unsteady.

"Of course, sir," Jack says.

"Of course, sir," Dad repeats. When he tilts his head back to laugh, the creases in the tan lines on his neck yawn open. "You in the marines or something? Quit with the 'sir' business. Makes me feel old."

Charlie finishes her wine. She runs a finger under each eye and pushes her damp hair out of her face. "Come on, John. Leave the kids to their fun. Let's go get some water."

But he hesitates. What is he waiting for? *Is* he waiting? Eventually he turns, and Charlie follows. In the silence left behind, Katie takes a shallow breath. Jack's front is cast in darkness, his messy hair haloed.

And then, suddenly—a blinding burst of light, bleached of warmth. The spotlights on the diving board have been turned on. They light up the air, wildly exaggerating every tiny rupture in the water's surface: snakes, snapping turtles, spiders skating on tremulous legs.

Lulu shields her eyes. "Dammit," she says. "Can't we have any privacy around here? Why does Tommy do that?"

"Will you go ask him to cut it out?" Katie says to Lulu, blinking rapidly. "He'll listen to you."

"Why me? You go," Lulu says, glancing sideways at Jack, who has been so quiet. (So very quiet it makes Katie wonder if he has maybe changed his mind about her.) Then Lulu bunches her hair in one hand and rubs her lips together, seeming to reconsider. "Never mind. I'll go. Back in a few. Wait here." She storms away.

"So. Yeah." Jack says this as though the two of them have been having an ongoing, entirely silent conversation already.

It is time for Katie to say something clever or, at the very least, something that doesn't make her sound like an idiot. She opens her mouth and closes it again.

"You know," he continues, "my dad wanted me to go straight back to New York, after tennis camp? Get ready for school and stuff. It's all about college prep now. That's all I ever hear anymore: college, college, college." He sighs. He has a plastic bottle tucked under his left arm, and he holds it out toward her. "Want some?"

They sit down facing the water. She takes a swig and screws up her face; it is lukewarm vodka. "You missed a boring week. Tons of rain."

"I wanted to stay." He pauses, considering something. "I gotta head back tomorrow. My parents already left."

"Yeah, I'm going too." The vodka burns in her chest like gasoline. She doesn't really like the taste of alcohol, but she is getting used to it. "I wish we didn't have to," she adds, and that admission knocks something loose inside her. When Jack takes the bottle back from her, their fingertips touch. He is cautious, but behind that reserve something is brewing. He is staring at her, his face bright now in the klieg lights. He lays his hand on top of hers on the broad arm of her chair. His fingers are long and tapered. He traces her bones with his thumb. They sit in silence, and she turns her hand over. With his index finger, he traces the life line in the hollow of her palm. Back and forth, back and forth. It tickles, but she doesn't move at all. Frozen in the heat.

She thought boys would be rough, fast, but Jack isn't, and though he does no more than touch her hand, there is a roar in her ears like when you're in an airplane, taking off.

"Double dare," Lulu is saying to someone as she approaches Katie and Jack. Katie can hear from her voice that she's excited. "Bet you won't do it!"

Katie snatches her hand from Jack's. When she lets go, the night air whooshes over the skin of her palm. Her heart begins pounding. The lights are still shining full blast, and some boys begin emerging from the clubhouse, punching each other in the arms. Lulu is carrying a couple of red plastic cups. She has high color, and her eyes are bright.

"Tommy says he has to keep the lights on. Safety when people leave the club, yada yada," she says, putting the cups down on the arm of the chair, where seconds earlier Katie's fingers had been intertwined with Jack's. "Dance is almost over. So, you know, whatever."

"What's this?" Jack asks. "Nectar of the gods?"

"Don't you know it." Lulu grins at him. "I sweet-talked Tommy into pouring us a couple of beers."

The party is about to wind down; people who've been drinking and talking on the deck are heading back inside as the square dance caller announces the last dance. "Now grab a little lady and go, gents, go!" he roars, and the music starts up again. A fiddle sawing away. Thumping bass. Hoots from the crowd. The music is very loud, and she feels it in her bones. Jack, standing, reaches out for her elbow, taking her by surprise. He raises his eyebrows at her, an invitation to dance; she stands and slips her hands in both of his. She doesn't resist—she can't. It's all in good fun, after all.

They lean away from each other and then thrust toward each other in an exaggerated way as though it's a joke, though it isn't. They swing their arms around their heads wildly. Neither of them knows any of the steps, but they make it up as they go along, exaggerating their movements and snorting with laughter. The song goes on forever, and finally she trips over his feet, and they topple over onto the grass. But instead of stopping, they roll along the ground, laughing and laughing, and his body is so powerful and long against hers that she feels as though the hours they've spent joking around as friends all summer have been a prelude to this exact moment when they are sandwiched in each other's arms. They roll to a stop, and he kisses her again, and this time it is another real kiss, less gentle than before. They are invisible to everyone.

But they aren't invisible. Lulu stands, openmouthed, not two feet away. Her face is naked, shocked; she takes a clumsy step back. "You bitch," she says. "You fucking bitch."

11

Dear Katie,
  *I found an email for you in the old directory from
Eagle Lake. Is it still Katiemeaowmix@aol.com? I've
tried writing to you there but it bounces back. I know
it's been a while. I also tried calling but the phone rings
and rings. Maybe you moved?*
  *It's hard to know what to say, but I really need to say
something. I still can't believe what's happened. Where
are you? I want you to know that I think about you all
the time.*
  Are you angry at me?

It was too much; she stopped reading and sat back on her haunches.
Her curiosity had gotten the better of her, and she'd dragged the box
into the kitchen. Lovely, earnest Jack. She didn't understand why he'd
thought she was angry at him. He'd tried to reach out to her, and she
hadn't known that. Would things have been different if she'd known?
Would she have gone to see him, after the conviction?

  *I can't forget when you left. I didn't even realize that
you were saying goodbye! You looked so pretty in the rain
and then I tried to find you again and I couldn't. I just*

*feel so bad about the trial. Now I can't reach you. I don't
know if you've had enough of me or if you don't know I've
been trying to get in touch.*

The other letter had also been torn open. Who had intercepted
them—her mother? Her father? Why would they have kept them? A
small bud of fury lodged in her chest: *How dare they.* She wondered how
she would have reacted if she'd received the letters, if she would have
felt less alone. In her gut she knew that things would have, somehow,
turned out differently. Or was that just the flimsy yearning of her teen-
age self?

The second letter was dated five weeks later. It was written in ballpoint pen on lined paper torn from a notebook.

> *My parents and the lawyers said I'm not allowed to
> contact you but I'm worried so I'm writing again. I need
> to tell you that I'm very sorry. I'm sorry about what I
> have to do and if I had a choice I wouldn't do it. But
> I have to. I thought it was important to tell you that. I
> can understand if you're angry. But I'm not the bad guy.
> I think if we could see each other again, I could explain
> things to you.*
>
> *My mom said I had to just tell the truth and I'm
> trying to focus on that and on knowing that the truth is
> always good, but it doesn't always seem like that.*

He signed the letters with a flourish that betrayed his youth. What
was it that he had done, and why were lawyers involved? She had
always assumed that until the verdict was made public, he wouldn't
have known anything.

The old pirate box was full of junk, but now that she'd started
looking through it, she didn't want to stop. A sense of resolve had

built up inside her, and though it was uncomfortable, it also promised a kind of freedom—the freedom to stop running and to start facing the questions she still had. There were reams of handwritten notes on trial strategy, dry stuff that was hard for her to understand. A few photocopied articles about past cases that her father's lawyer must have used to bolster his defense, the legalese impenetrable; she didn't recognize the cases they referred to. There were a few business cards and a series of bills for tens of thousands of dollars; she suspected the trial had bankrupted the family, but she didn't actually want to know the details. Had her mother kept all this because of the divorce and the settlement?

Then she stumbled on two photos of Lulu, both taken around the same time and from a distance. In them, Lulu wore her dark hair short and was looking down at the sidewalk as she walked. In one picture, she was with her mother, Piper, and they appeared to be having an argument. Judging from the background, it was springtime, maybe outside their apartment in Blackbrooke. Katie guessed these might have been taken in the months leading up to the trial.

Running her fingers through everything, she alighted upon a thick, cream-colored business card with raised black script on it that read *Hugo Montefiore, 12c Elgin Crescent, Chelsea W12 9EU*, with a London telephone number scribbled on the back. Odd, she thought, holding it close. The number 8 was made up of two circles, one on top of the other, just like her mother used to write them. Katie tucked it into her back pocket, figuring she would ask her grandfather if he knew what it was about. Over the years, they'd spent a lot of time together at the lake, of course, but she wasn't aware of him playing any special role during the lead-up to the trial or afterward.

There were other letters in the box too. Letters with her father's spiky writing on the envelopes. The back of each of them bore a faint stamp:

THIS CORRESPONDENCE IS FORWARDED FROM A NEW
YORK CORRECTIONAL INSTITUTION. THE CONTENTS
MAY OR MAY NOT HAVE BEEN EVALUATED, AND THE
DEPARTMENT OF CORRECTION IS NOT RESPONSIBLE
FOR THE SUBSTANCE OR CONTENT OF THE ENCLOSED
MATERIALS. IF YOU HAVE RECEIVED UNWANTED CORRE-
SPONDENCE FROM THIS INMATE, CALL 1-866-956-8745
TO STOP FUTURE CORRESPONDENCE.

Love letters from prison, dozens of them, all addressed to her mother. Katie's hands trembled as she slipped the papers from their envelopes. The first one was dated a week after they took him away.

> *You looked back at me when you were leaving today,*
> *and I couldn't read the expression on your face. What did*
> *you expect from me, to be superhuman like your father?*
> *One thing I am not is anything like your father.*

And then another letter, just one day later:

> *I miss the kids so much it's killing me. Give them*
> *both big hugs from me.*

A few months later, in December, he wrote:

> *We need to talk about your father. I know you don't*
> *want to, Charlie, but we need to. I could see it written*
> *all over your face yesterday. It's going to kill us if we can't*
> *talk about what he's doing to us.*

Katie wondered what her dad could possibly have meant by that. How had Grumpy been involved? A disorienting sense of all that she couldn't possibly know or understand overcame her again. It sounded as though her grandfather had done something to her parents, to his own daughter. It didn't make sense.

John wrote about his bunkmate, the books he was reading. He asked for crossword puzzles. Again and again, he wrote that everything would be all right. Katie's head throbbed with an incipient headache. Her father had been so wrong about it all working out, but how could he have known? She felt caught in some way she didn't fully understand, but it was a familiar feeling, like being in a very small room with one very small window. That window was high up, the walls were close in, and she could touch each wall with her hands. If only she could clamber up to the window, she could free herself from this feeling of claustrophobia.

She rose and unlocked the cabin's back door to get a breath of fresh air. She was being so stupid, so dramatic—she was neither trapped in some tiny room nor helpless. The need to talk with someone was overpowering, but David didn't seem ready, and Charlie had already declared her unwillingness to be an emotional touchstone. Katie checked her phone and saw that it was evening in London. She dialed her grandfather's number in the assisted-living facility. As the roar of an overseas connection came over the line, she felt instant relief.

When she was little, her grandfather's dispassionate focus on her, his many cozy rituals, had made her feel cherished. Each night when she stayed over at his house, as she often did in the years before David was born, Grumpy would tuck her into bed and recite "For Want of a Nail." He loved the singsong cadence that emphasized the poem's circular mystery. Once she was older and had learned the words by heart, they'd each trade off saying the lines one at a time. Then as they got close to the end—"for want of a message the battle was lost, for want of a battle the kingdom was lost"—they'd both take a deep breath and shout the final line: "and all for the want of a horseshoe nail!" He'd peck her cheek afterward in a cheerfully complicit way that suggested she understood its meaning, but in reality she had no idea what the poem was about. It wasn't until years later that she even heard about the "butterfly effect," the idea that failing to anticipate or do something tiny—forgetting some seemingly insignificant thing, like a horseshoe nail, for example—could lead to ever-increasing disasters. But she didn't need to understand the poem to love the chanting, the way it made her feel part of something bigger than herself, something grown-up and mysterious.

"Grumpy! Is it too late to call?" she said when she got through to his room. Cradling the phone awkwardly between chin and shoulder, she managed to strike a match and light a cigarette. "They put you to bed right when the sun sets over there, don't they?"

"Right after tea, dear," he said. "They seem to think we need a solid sixteen hours."

She took a deep drag.

"You smoking again?" Grumpy asked.

"No—well, not much. Not really."

"I thought runners don't smoke." He chuckled faintly. "You are so like your mother. So stubborn."

"Don't say that. I'm nothing like her."

"It's a compliment, dear. Your mother's a tough little thing, if ever there was one."

"And anyway, Mum quit smoking," Katie said. She wasn't hungry, but she felt the need to consume things, to fill herself up in some way. Pacing the flagstones, she picked a fleck of tobacco from her bottom lip. "Grumps, you'll never guess where I am." Then, in a falsely bright voice: "I'm at the cabin."

The sound of him clearing his throat came over the line, and she held the phone away from her ear.

"It's, um, well, it's in pretty good order here," she continued. "Have you been back?"

"What are you doing up there? Your mum send you?"

"No, actually, not Mum." A little nauseated, Katie ground the cigarette out against the stones and noticed that the light in the bleached-out sky above the fir trees was already beginning to fade. It had gotten late. "I'm cleaning it up a bit. Dad's, um, you know he's getting out soon, right? In a few weeks, actually."

"No, sunshine, I was not aware of that." Another guttural throat clearing. "And for the life of me, I can't see what that has to do with Eagle Lake."

"Mum said he could stay here. Just for a bit, until he gets back on track." She rooted around in her back pocket for the business card she'd found.

"Back on track, eh?" Grumpy repeated.

She decided to ignore whatever it was that he was implying. "So anyway. I found a bunch of stuff from years ago. There's a card here, a business card. From some guy, in London, Hugo Montague or something? No, Montefiore. I'm wondering if you know anything about it."

"Not sure, dear. I'm afraid I don't remember things sometimes." Grumpy sounded uneasy, and she thought of how her family had always insisted on marching ahead, never looking back, impatient with too much navel-gazing. Was it a British thing, or had her father played his role in it too?

"It's just, with Dad getting out, you know . . ." She tried again. "It's all beginning to kind of come back."

"I lost my stomach for it," her grandfather said. "As soon as your friend, that child, took the stand. For me it was all over right then and there."

"You mean Lulu?" Katie asked.

"No, no—Lulu, I missed her testimony," he explained. "And your mother didn't hear it either. Charlie wasn't allowed in—something about being called as a witness."

"I don't understand. Which friend are you talking about?"

"The one who saw them, the two of them. That boy you spent the summer with."

Her back stiffened. "You mean Jack? He, what—he saw my father with Lulu?"

"Yes, that's right, Jack. Handsome bloke. So tall. Was he already over six feet then? Awfully nervous, poor fellow. But, dear, I don't see how any of this is in the least bit helpful. Your father was convicted. Guilty or not is rather beside the point now, isn't it?"

Everything around her seemed unsteady and fragile in light of this news—the incredible news that Jack had been involved in this whole mess in a tangible way. Now the letters she'd just read made more sense to her; he had testified at the trial! His testimony may well have affected the outcome, and somehow she had never known this. She tried to swallow over the hard lump in her throat. It couldn't be true that he had seen anything—she remembered that night. There had been nothing to see, nothing.

"It's not beside the point to me," she said to her grandfather.

"Don't be so romantic. These things are never black and white. You must know that," he said, his voice scratchy, and then he coughed so loudly and in such a prolonged way she had to hold the phone away from her ear again.

"You all right, Grumpy?" she asked, standing very still. "You don't sound very good."

"I've seen better days, sunshine," he said.

12

The phone in her apartment remained unplugged, and as she left to meet up with Zev for an early drink, she decided not to plug it back in, even though it was Sunday. She sat sipping a cocktail and talking about work-related disaster stories, noting out of the corner of her eye that the hands of the clock above the bar were steadily inching forward. Dread rose inside her until it reached her throat, but still she sat there, forcing herself to wait it out. To let the minutes tick by. To make him wait. Right up until six—which was when she would need to jump on the subway in order to make it back in time to get her father's call—she thought she might change her mind and head back, as she always did. But as the longer hand inched toward the twelve and she did not get up to leave, Zev became more and more garrulous, as though somehow realizing he was on borrowed time. He was telling her about his first year teaching at Vassar, when he was twenty-six. He'd been a waiter in New York for three years and had a bad breakup with a girl he'd met in London at design school. "The world's worst waiter," he said, twisting his beer glass in his fingers, leaving damp circles on the wooden table. "Twice I spilled an actual meal on someone. But—I don't know why—I always got great tips."

"It's the eyes," Katie said.

"Well, they did not help me with the teaching. Those kids were so bored, looking at me with these blank stares, waiting for something. As though I could light the fire for them. So I did it, literally. Burned the homework and made them work with the paper, the wood, soot, yes?" He grinned at her. "They were very confused, but it worked. Shook them up."

They laughed, and when he ordered another drink, she did not say no. She was drinking something called the Shitkicker—one of those artisan gin cocktails that took ten minutes to prepare—and it was delicious. The clock ticked, time shifted and flickered uncertainly, and just like that she missed her weekly call.

She didn't want to make small talk with her father. He shouldn't have asked her to go back to the cabin. But was that really it? She plucked the tarragon leaf from the rim of her glass and thought about the letters from Jack and all that paperwork, and she tried to remember if her father had ever clearly told her what had happened that night. Had he given her any sort of logical explanation? He must have, but she couldn't remember. His voice had become mixed up with everyone else's over the years—the lawyers, the judge, her mother and grandfather. Her brother. Everyone with an opinion, everyone taking sides. Now she felt a sudden, sharp confusion that stalled her.

Zev secured her a fresh drink; it was ice cold and should have tasted good, but there was a hint of something musty or maybe slightly off in it. He had started talking about his huge family, cousins and aunts and a million uncles on his mother's side. There was one uncle in particular, his mother's oldest brother, whom Zev had loved as a little boy. He was called Menashe: a huge man with a head of black hair that he could shift forward and backward on his scalp like a wig, using some magic alchemy that made kids go crazy with joy. Zev smiled, but his eyes were sad. "We adored him. Then one day I just never saw him again."

Feeling suddenly dizzy and sick, Katie clamped her jaws together and took a small breath through her nose. "What happened?"

Zev twisted his mouth into a grimace. "Ah, there was a huge political scandal. He was the minister of housing in the seventies. Turns out he was embezzling money from the Labor Party and using it for gambling. But all I remember is that hair. How we all laughed so much we would choke on our own spit."

She took another sip of her drink, but something was very wrong with her. She jumped up, wild eyed. "Be right back," she said. "Sorry."

Shouldering her way through the early evening crowd, she made it to the bathroom and managed to yank her scarf away from her face and lift up the yellowing toilet seat before throwing up.

Zev rode with her on the subway back to her apartment and walked her to her door. "Are you going to be all right?" he asked. "Do you want me to stay?"

"No, I'm okay. I don't think so," she said. "Thanks, though." He released her elbow and kissed her on the cheek. Katie's stomach turned again. "I'm so sorry. I didn't realize I was sick—I should have just stayed at home."

"Call me, okay? Let me know how you are." He began to walk away but then turned back to her. "We should talk, Katie, okay? Find some time to talk about, well, my studio and so on. Maybe after I'm back from Spain."

"Yes, right, I forgot about your trip," she said, forcing a smile. He was heading to Barcelona for a week to attend some symposium. "Of course."

Once upstairs, Katie pulled back her hair from her face and brushed her teeth. After almost twenty years of being part of the art scene in and around New York, Zev had a huge network of friends and connections to stay with when he came to the city. Months earlier, when they first started sleeping together, he would often leave very late at night, and she didn't ask him where he was going. He wove in and out of her life without creating a sense of obligation in her; she'd loved that about him from the very beginning.

Now things were changing. First he'd turned up at her apartment that night without any notice. She knew it was supposed to be a nice surprise—and it was; they'd both been swept up in it—but it also meant he'd crossed a kind of boundary. Now he wanted to move in. The fact that she hadn't told her father they were a couple (let alone told Zev anything about her father) must be proof of some sort of resistance or fear. She couldn't quite shake the idea that Zev was the wrong man for her in the long run. That their easy intimacy was not enough to build a life on.

After sitting at her small kitchen table for a while, her hands wrapped around a mug of mint tea, she booted up her computer. When she had come to the city and begun working full time, she would come home at night to her first apartment (a tiny studio sublet), wired from the excitement of her day, and she'd lie on her bed and think of Jack. He was in the city somewhere, she'd felt certain of it, and she had liked the idea that she wasn't really alone, that there was someone not that far away who knew her the way she had been during the first half of her life, the part that had unspooled without a snag. Over the years in college she had kept a distance from her family, but she had new friends; she had her studies. In her first six months in the city, her school friends hadn't graduated yet, and she had seen almost no one outside work. It had been comforting to imagine Jack, his hair still thick and very blond, his long, lean body filled out. She'd wonder idly if he still played tennis, where he'd gone to college.

But she had not been tempted to look him up back then. She'd become accustomed to the sense of herself as separate from all others, and there was something comforting about that. It was best to keep the past just out of reach, hovering a little more than arm's length away. While she knew it was there, could sense it, she carefully kept those memories out of her grasp, and she sometimes seemed to forget the past entirely. But that was an illusion. Her memories of Jack, of Lulu—of life *before*—were not actually gone and forgotten; they lived on inside her, shadows of a bleached-out stain.

Really, she wanted to type *Lulu Henderson* into Google, but she could not bring herself to do it. To warm up, she started with *Herb Schwartz*, her father's lawyer. Up came a series of entries, a few from lawyerly sites, but she was not actually interested in what had happened to Herb. Yesterday, she'd left David's old pirate box in the kitchen at the cabin, knowing she would have to go back there soon, but she kept thinking about Jack's letters to her—the fact that he had tried to contact her. It changed the way she thought about him. She'd never understood why he hadn't found some way to reach out after the trial. It hurt to think he hadn't bothered to show her any sympathy. To know, now, that Jack had cared about her—had, in fact, tried to contact her—softened her memories of him. She remembered how he'd observed her while they had all horsed around at the lake, too shy to butt in. That he'd watched out for her when they had all drunk too much. It was all coming back.

She massaged the stiff muscles in her neck, trying to relax. Mixed in with her tenderness toward Jack was a bubbling anger that she couldn't quite place. Her fingertips were cold against the skin of her neck, and she dug them in as deeply as she could tolerate. Maybe she was infuriated with her father because of Jack's letters, because he hadn't let her see them or hadn't stood up to Charlie. Either way, her parents had denied her something that was hers, that was *private*—something that would have been meaningful to her in ways they must have suspected. And Jack had written that he'd seen something; it was unnerving. Had her parents been afraid of what he might have seen? What *had* he seen?

Anger was more galvanizing than fear, so she typed in *Jack Benson*. Up came a Wikipedia entry for a poet from the sixties and an obituary for a journalist from Florida. She clicked on the images tab, and a series of pictures showed an old man named Jackson Benson with thinning orange hair; a boy with a soccer ball; a teen with a green mohawk. And then there he was among the imposters—Jack, with his disarming smile. Snapshots of Jack lounging on a settee, playing bass in a crowded bar, wearing a mask at some Mardi Gras festival. One picture showed him without a shirt on, unabashed in front of the camera. There was a large tattoo on his upper arm, a hummingbird in motion. Not the typical tattoo with crisp black lines, filled in, cartoonlike, but a bird flying, fluid and colorful. Blurred like a watercolor. *Oh*, she thought, *that's new*. Instantly, she understood just how much must have happened in the ten years since they had last seen each other. There was so much about him that she couldn't possibly know.

She tried finding him on Facebook, but no one matched Jack's description. She clicked through to the Exeter Academy website and tried to find an alumni page but wasn't allowed in without a username and password. LinkedIn offered her ten different Jack Bensons, and a quick scan revealed they were from Illinois and Mississippi, Virginia and Washington State. He could have moved, of course; he could be living anywhere in the world. One Jack Benson was a technology audit and risk strategist, another a high school teacher. The accompanying thumbnail sketches were tiny, and at first glance she didn't see anyone she recognized.

Slow down, she thought. *There's no rush*. She took a deep breath before scanning the images again. One looked as though it could possibly be him, and she clicked on it.

It was Jack. His hair was far darker, slicked back, and his forehead was wider than she remembered. Green eyes, a direct gaze. A small smile playing on his lips and two-day stubble. Next to his name it said

"Realtor." Jack had become a real estate agent? That seemed highly unlikely. Scrolling down, she checked his credentials and saw that, yes, this Jack Benson had attended Exeter Academy and then UVA.

A blue button offered: "Send a message."

Her memories of him were suddenly so close, right within her grasp, and she wanted to reach out and grab them. But it was like jumping off a ledge into a tide pool when she wasn't exactly sure how deep the water was.

The letters. She needed to know about what he had seen. What he had testified about in court. She clicked on the blue button and typed into the space: jack it's katie gregory.

That was all. Quickly, before she changed her mind, she hit send.

13

Katie cannot smell fern without thinking instantly—like the burst of those old-fashioned camera flashes—of the dirt path that leads from the cabin through the woods to the lake. Ferns speckled with black dots like peppercorns, frilly and luminous in the summer light.

The colors of that night, the night she's tried so hard not to think about, are black shot through with red. The red of Lulu's lips. The red of the plastic cups they were drinking from. The deep, pulsing red of her own heart, hidden inside her but bursting with each stolen kiss.

The clubhouse is packed and steamy now, and the square dance is drawing to an end. Jack stands close to her as they scan the crowd. Mr. Herman is at the mic. He and Katie's mother dated for a couple of summers when they were around Katie's age; now they barely acknowledge each other. An off-center cowlick makes him look like an overgrown child. John and Charlie Gregory move their heads toward each other, and Charlie goes over to the bar area, waving to get Tommy's attention.

"Laaaadies and gentlemen," Mr. Herman cries out. "Step right up for the prizes! Prizes galore! Come on, people."

The room hushes except for the banging of the screen doors on their loosened hinges. Where has Lulu disappeared to, with her righteous indignation? After she cursed at Katie, she ran off, and Katie hasn't been able to track her down. She is nowhere to be seen in the crowded room. There is David, by the counter, almost ten years old and gawky, drinking a milkshake. Behind the counter Tommy and his girlfriend, Alexi, are running around, every move a balletic dance of fast food service.

Mr. Herman doles out prizes for best twirl, do-si-do, curtsy turn, pass-through, and pull-by. And there she is now, Lulu—just as he is finishing up, she enters through the back door. Her hair pulled off her face into a tower of curls. She has reapplied the red lipstick.

Jack squeezes Katie's hand, and a surge of adrenaline shoots through her. When she looks across the room again, Lulu is staring in their direction. She doesn't need to say anything for Katie to understand what she is thinking. Her eyes are flinty and unblinking. Rosy cheeks and those bright lips.

Lulu says something to Katie's father, and he leans his body in toward her, trying to catch her words. The skin on his forehead gleams like chrome. He stares at her lips, moving silently, a slash of red on her face. Then he reaches out and wipes his thumb over the corner of her mouth. Once, twice, pulling her lips apart; there is a flash of white teeth.

No one else is paying any attention, but Katie can't move her eyes away. Surrounded by cheering and laughing, by the rising voices of people fueled by too many sweet drinks and too much beer, Lulu and her father appear to be in a room all by themselves. Lulu takes a step back, and the noises swell again. Katie's father accepts a beer from Charlie and drains it in one long series of gulps, his Adam's apple jerking up and down. When he is done, he wipes a sleeve over his mouth. He has the look of a man caught in a desert.

Though Lulu has turned away, it feels as if she's looking squarely at Katie, daring her in some way—but daring her to do what, she does not know. And then she is gone again.

How long does Katie keep searching for Lulu that night—was it long enough? The heat presses down like one blanket too many. Out on the diving board, a body radiates a vaguely steely light as it rises and falls through the air. There is a short shriek, and the person jumps in the water with a splash. It's not Lulu. There are people on the float and by the docks, but Katie can't tell if she is among them or not. Someone has put on "Who's That Lady" by the Isley Brothers. "Look, yeah, but don't touch," an off-key male voice sings from the bar area.

"A swim might be kinda fun?" Jack asks Katie uncertainly.

She shuts her eyes, and sparkles streak over her inner lids. Getting cold and wet seems like the last thing on earth they should be doing right then.

Jack presses close to her. "Listen, come on," he says so quietly she has to strain to make out his words. "Let's get out of here, okay?" His fingers curl around hers, and he pulls her over toward the bike rack.

And Lulu—should Katie just forget her? Maybe Brad is with her now; maybe they are back inside, dancing together. He is too old for her, but it would be exciting to have a college kid pay attention to you. Maybe she is behind them on the deck, trying to persuade someone to give her more free booze. Or she might be in the boathouse, bumming a cigarette.

"Grab a bike," Jack says, rattling them loose from the rack. "We'll bring them back later."

Some of the bikes are neatly filed side by side, wheels freshly pumped with air, children's stickers adorning the handlebars; others are disintegrating, leaning against the spokes of the rack, pedals dislodged, seats askew. She hesitates before yanking one out. The pull she feels toward Jack is thrilling, elemental, and she can't let it go even though she knows she should. She sits down on the bike, and the rims kiss the hard-packed earth as the air hisses out of slits in the rubber. Casting the bike to one side, she grabs another and bounces up and down lightly on the seat. Jack and Katie share a glance and grin at each other.

It is then that she makes her decision: *good to go*. She could choose to stay at the lake so that whenever Lulu decides to stop being angry, Katie will be there. But she feels so free in the humid night air, flushed with excitement and infused with a lingering, mellow energy. She decides to take what she wants and pushes Lulu from her mind. Is that when everything really starts to go wrong?

The woods echo with the thump of their wheels bouncing off sudden dips in the earth. Riding through the night air is exhilarating. Everything seems at once dreamy and intense, as though there is more of everything, an abundance awaiting her: more love, more textures, more heat, more sensation.

The Dolans' house sits at the top of an incline on the far side of the lake. In the light from the garage, Jack's body on the whippet-thin bike casts long shadows that melt into her as she draws close. He reaches up above the door and fishes a key from the ledge. The house is one of the oldest in the area, immortalized in a black-and-white 1880s photograph hanging in the clubhouse. As with most of the houses in the club, Katie has seen it hundreds of times from the outside but has never been inside. Once they enter, they are thieves, uninvited guests, intruders—what Jack and Katie are doing alone in this closed-up house is forbidden, nerve racking. The outside light clicks off, and the darkness is so dense that for a second she can see nothing at all: no furniture, no windows, no Jack. It takes her a while to trace the windows with her eyes, the night sky outside a slightly different shade of black.

"What happens if we get caught?" she whispers.

"They're gone already. Back to Connecticut. I'm the only one who knows where the key is." He takes her hand again, and this time his skin is cooler, more papery, and she grasps it a little tighter, brings her body close until her hip touches his. They stand together until their breathing slows and their eyes adjust. Then he tugs on her hand slightly, and she follows him up the curving wooden stairs.

He stops on the landing at the top of the stairs, and she bumps into him. The trees outside the window are silhouetted against faraway stars. Their upper bodies touch, Katie's breasts tucked under his rib cage and her head reaching the crook of his neck. She could lay her head on his chest easily, and they would fit together perfectly, her cheekbone in the hollow above his collarbone, but instead she holds her head up and looks, as he does, out the window. There is something tense and beautiful in this holding apart and touching at the same time.

Katie breaks the spell first by looking up at him. His face is angled and earnest, and she sees that he will always have a boyish quality to him. The slight curve of his shoulders seems to come from some invisible weight he carries, and she thinks, *I don't know him at all; he's full of secrets.*

The curtains in the guest room are drawn over a single window, and a narrow bed in the corner is made up with a white terry-cloth bedspread. Jack goes over to the bed, and, crossing his arms and hooking his forefingers under the hem, he lifts his shirt right over his head and drops it on the floor. Katie does the same. Her fear has evaporated, and she feels only the thrill of what is to come. Jack kicks off his sneakers, unzips his jeans, and draws one leg out and then the other, stomping softly until the pants release his luminous feet. She unbuttons the waistband on her shorts and shimmies them over her hips. He stands in his underwear and she in her bra and panties. She unhooks her bra and plucks it from her breasts.

They are barely breathing. They slip out of their underpants and lie on the bed facing each other. Katie reaches out to touch him, and his muscles tighten under her fingers. She looks down at his chest and the bone-sculpted whiteness of his hips. Her breath catches. It is like the releasing of a coil: she swells with desire as though her body is doubling in size.

Jack's chest is impossibly smooth. When her fingers trail lower over his belly button and touch the soft hairs flat against his stomach, he shudders. The entire world opens up to her. Their fingers find the warmth between each other's legs, and the lean muscles in their thighs come alive.

They are alone together in this infinite moment. She can't get enough of him, of his warm skin. She squeezes her eyes shut and touches him everywhere.

When the phone rings, they freeze, their bodies—softened, primed—becoming as rigid as wooden slats. The phone trills again and again.

It must be downstairs in the kitchen, because even though the ringing is shrill, it sounds far away, as though removed by the expanse of a dulling ocean. It exists in another universe, and it takes six, eight, ten rings for it to penetrate their reality, for them to realize that their time is over and they have to get up and leave. That sound draws them away from their bodies and puts them back into their heads: They are naked on a stranger's bed. They are not supposed to be there, and they are definitely not supposed to be doing *this*. Someone is on to them, and whatever they have started is over before it has even begun. (She will, from then on, forever despise the ringing of phones, startling each time, her heart quickening painfully.)

The ride back to the clubhouse is their long, silent goodbye to each other. With every invisible bump in the road, Katie's body jangles its way back to earth. Even though she has never wanted anything as badly as she wants to be with Jack in the Dolans' bed, doing anything and everything, she isn't yet in despair. She thinks to herself, *The night's not over yet. It's not over!*

14

Jack screeches to a halt. Close behind him, Katie does the same. Her breath comes hard and fast from the pace they kept up getting back. It is almost one o'clock in the morning. Someone has moved the Falcon from the back of the lot, and it is parked near the bike rack, wet towels hanging over the bucket seat. The top is down, as it almost always is, the back seat operating as a sort of roving supply truck. There are two paddles in the front seat, a pair of pink flip-flops, and a single leather dock shoe. A cardboard box with tools in it. A packet of Charlie's Pall Malls.

"Hey," David says from the other side of the Falcon. This startles Katie so badly that she drops her bike, and its rusty metal kickstand cuts her shin. Blood trickles along the inside of her ankle. Most of the younger children have probably been hauled off to bed, but her brother is standing there, holding a flashlight.

"Wanna see what I found? Look under here!" he says, shining the beam of his light toward the car.

"Shouldn't you be home by now, Davey?" Katie catches the blood with two fingers and wipes it off, then licks her fingers clean.

"It's a baby rabbit!"

She and Jack kneel down and peer under the back wheels of the car, where David is now prone, his head partially under the rear bumper.

There is a tiny shivering heap on the gravel that could be almost anything, except that the shivering means it's alive.

"He's scared, poor little thing," she says.

"I want to keep it," David says. "But it wants to be left alone."

"Once we're gone, it'll make a run for the woods," Jack says.

Katie gets up and dusts off her knees. "Where are Mum and Dad?"

David clicks the light on and off, on and off. "Dunno," he says, "but don't worry; it's okay. I'm going back now." He pulls his bike from the rack, attaches his flashlight to the handlebars, and rides off into the darkness with a wave.

The lights in the bar are blazing, and a throng crowds around the counter, keeping Tommy and Alexi busy. Katie's flustered about the call, wondering whether it was a mistake to let it spook them. Was it her father calling, or her mother, wondering where she was? But they don't care who she is with or what she's up to. They have barely said a word about Jack all summer. How would anyone have known to try calling them at the Dolans', anyway? Was it just random—a total accident that catapulted them out of their moment? If they had let the phone ring into the night, would everything or anything be different?

A few boys are playing pool inside. One of the dads is sitting by the counter playing a chaotic game of Go Fish with Tommy, his belly pressed against the scuffed wood. Kendrick and Brad come crashing in, their laughter puncturing the other noises. Brad is shouting and gesticulating wildly. He goes over to the counter and slides open the gate so he can get behind it. His T-shirt is darkened with sweat or maybe lake water. As he bends over the industrial-size blender, his expression is intensely concentrated, as though he is trying to thread a needle.

Brownish hair with a hint of orange sticks up from his forehead. A swelling red mark runs along one cheekbone.

"Dude," Jack says. "Raccoon come at you in the forest or what?"

Brad ignores him. Katie wonders whether one of the boys told Lulu where they might be and whether she was the one who tried to call them. She bites her nails and looks around at the laughing people, searching for her friend's face. When the blender starts, nothing can be heard above the grinding.

She nudges Jack. "Let's go back outside," she says. The noise is intrusive. Time keeps stretching out, thinning, and it feels as though an infinity has passed since they were listening to the square dance caller, watching as the prizes were handed out. When she thinks back to the Jack who'd been in the guest room with her, that memory is already fading.

"Huh?" Jack asks, screwing up his face. "Can't hear you."

"Okay. Lulu—I'm gonna go find her. All right? I'll be back," Katie yells.

Outside, a rusted tin can full of cigarette butts lies tipped over on the flagstones, leaving a trail of stained filters. A few people are on the Big Float, trying to rock it from side to side on its enormous oil barrels. The Adirondack chairs beneath the maple are empty. She looks through the picture window into the bar; her mother is at one of the low tables talking with Mr. Davidson, gesturing with her hands. Dad is at a table drawing something on a paper napkin.

No sounds come from the changing sheds, and she heads toward the boathouse. The air seems to hum as though the currents are rubbing each other like a bow on a string. Above her the sky appears purple, swelling, and the stars have mostly disappeared. From the woods the faint sound of rumbling emerges, but when she turns her head, it disappears.

Even with no lights on, Katie sees Lulu before Lulu sees her. A curtain of fog hangs over the lake, pulsing dimly in the intermittent moonlight, and it envelops Lulu almost completely, so Katie can only see a white block that she recognizes as a T-shirt. Her back toward Katie, Lulu is sitting on the dock that extends from the boathouse into the water.

Among the old canoes and kayaks, the strings from the sails suspended from the ceiling rafters hang down like lichen. Until Katie steps onto the wooden platform, Lulu doesn't realize anyone is behind her. She whips around. "Who is it?"

"It's me," Katie says. "Where've you been? I've been looking for you."

"Go away."

"Did you just try to call me?"

"Leave me alone," Lulu says in a voice so soft it makes the hair on Katie's arms stand up.

"What's wrong?" she asks, though she knows Lulu must be angry at her for the kiss, for disappearing. Her flip-flops are obscenely loud on the dock. Katie squints at her friend: she isn't wearing the same clothes as before. Instead of the old pink T-shirt with the blue bubble letters on it, she has on a huge white one and a pair of boxer shorts. "Lulu? Everything okay? What have you been up to? I'm really sorry about earlier."

Katie is afraid Lulu will ask where the hell *she's* been, and in telling her about the Dolans'—as she thinks she must—she'll ruin everything. But Lulu doesn't answer her.

"Did you go swimming?" Katie tries again. The sky seems to press down on them. There is that strange rumble again, making itself felt on her skin.

Briefly Lulu raises her head, and a trace of lipstick is still smeared on her mouth. She sees Katie noticing and draws the back of her hand over her lips.

"We just went on a ride. A bike ride. It was no big deal," Katie says.

Lulu's T-shirt is cold under Katie's fingers, damp around her shoulders. Her bones feel solid, but Lulu is shivering as she pulls away from her friend. "Christ, I really, really wanna go home," Lulu says.

The slight chill of the early morning, tinged with a promise of fall, is mixed with an undercurrent of heat or electricity, something oppressive, and Katie shivers too. The sky seems to contract, sucking energy into itself, and then in an instant it is bloated, pressing down on them, and it lights up like the flash of a thousand bulbs, and there is the deafening sound of total silence as they are bathed in frozen light, and then the crack of thunder, a splitting open of the sky like a white wound.

And then chaos over by the clubhouse. A scream followed by another scream, shouting, splashes, the sound of someone falling onto wood, cursing, and high above the other sounds, a child crying. The swimmers head to shore like panicked rats. With the next lightning bolt comes the rain. So soft at first, just the faintest touch of raindrops on skin, and then a deluge. The noise of it drowns everything out. They are instantly soaked.

Katie grabs Lulu and steers her toward the clubhouse, running, clutching her arm. Their feet slip on the wet flagstones. White flanks and breasts flash as swimmers snatch up their clothes and run under the awning to shelter from the driving rain. Not everyone is out of the water yet, and as another crack of lightning shoots across the sky, one man stands next to the water and screams, "Get the hell out! There's lightning!"

They run around to the back of the clubhouse. A few people are struggling with the Falcon in the parking lot, trying to get the roof up. "I'll be right back," Katie says, motioning for Lulu to wait there under the overhang.

Jack is so surprised when Katie says goodbye that his body barely yields to her quick embrace. She can't explain that she needs to take care of Lulu now, that, in a way, she's already betrayed her. He looks down at her soaking clothes and laughs, at first, until he realizes what she is telling him. She tries to let him know she is sorry without actually saying so. Their limbs jangle against one another as they teeter forward into each other's arms. He is confused, holding back, as though she's changed the rules of the night on him without notice.

Katie runs upstairs and grabs some random dry clothes for them and brings them down to the den after checking that David is tucked in his bed. Turning her back to Katie, Lulu slips off the boxer shorts and T-shirt and puts on a thin cotton dress. She wraps her hair in a towel Katie has brought from the bathroom.

The front door slams. "Girls?" Charlie's voice rings out. "David?" The thunder has abated, but every now and then a crack as loud as a gunshot makes them jump.

"In here," Katie calls.

"Christ almighty," comes John's voice.

Charlie pokes her head into the room. "Thank heavens you weren't in the water," she says. "David here? Do you know?"

"He's in bed. I checked."

Her mother yawns. "That Patterson girl refused to get out of the lake. Her father dove back in to get her. What idiots. They could both be dead."

In the den, a long brown plaid couch is pressed up against one wall, with a comfortable two-seater at right angles to it against the back wall. End tables made of rattan are covered in spent Coke cans and an empty bag of Doritos. Lulu sits down on the bigger couch and rubs her eyes. The rain pelting the roof sounds like the drone of a motor. Katie turns on the TV to drown it out. Sitting next to Lulu, she pulls a fleece blanket over their bare legs. Lulu's body begins to relax into the cushions.

"I'm going to bed," Charlie says. "Up bright and early tomorrow, girls. Back to the real world."

If they stay awake long enough, Katie thinks, maybe Lulu will soften up again. Maybe they can fix things before they have to say goodbye in the morning. They stare blankly at the bald man on the screen, who juices carrot after carrot and then adds eggplant and parsley. Katie yawns enormously. The soft skin of Lulu's thigh presses against hers.

John comes in. "What's this crap you're watching?" he asks. He's changed out of the green polyester pants into a pair of sweats. He looks wide awake, invigorated, even. He stares at the girls for an extra beat.

"Your car okay?" Lulu asks him.

"Sure, honey," he says, his voice thick. "A little water won't do the old girl any harm."

"I'd think it would be bad," Lulu says. "Getting water on the leather and stuff."

"Ah, that car's been through a lot worse." They look at each other without saying anything, and then he walks over to the DVD player and starts rooting around in a pile of old discs collected in a basket. Picking one, he unclips the plastic housing and slips it into the machine. Static, followed by jazzy music, and then the title *Body Heat* scrolls across the screen.

"Oh, my mom loves this movie," Lulu says, sitting up, alert.

On screen William Hurt smokes a cigarette and gazes out over a hazy skyline. Katie's eyes are so heavy. If the phone hadn't rung earlier, she would have stayed with Jack at the Dolans' all night long. Eventually she and Jack would have fallen asleep, his skinny limbs entangled in hers. She would have woken up in the early morning, stiff and cold, with his skin still touching hers, his eyes ever so slightly open in sleep, his hair a mass of lake-dried curls. She would have started kissing him again, and he would have kissed her back, and neither of them would have cared about morning breath or needing to go to the bathroom or the fact that they had not gone home and were going to be in serious trouble.

"Hey, Lu, move over a bit, will you?" she says, yawning again.

"Sorry, Princess," Lulu mutters. Absorbed by the movie, she adjusts herself a bit to make room. "You're too heavy," she whines when Katie lays her legs on Lulu's lap.

"Who's the princess now?" Katie asks, feeling as though a warm blanket is descending over her head. Her yawn threatens to pull apart the muscles in her face.

"Mr. Gregory, tell your gargantuan daughter to make some room for me on this couch, will you please?" Lulu says.

"Mr. Gregory? What's that about?" John asks. "I think you're old enough to call me John. Don't you already call Katie's mom 'Charlie'?"

"Yeah, but that's different." Lulu doesn't sound sleepy, nor does she sound angry or sad, like she did back when they were at the boathouse. "*John*," she adds.

"There's plenty of room over here, if you want."

Lulu moves to the other couch, and Katie pulls the throw over herself. Lulu is acting so weird: hot and cold. Let her go sit with Dad if she wants to; Katie doesn't care. The movie is clearly supposed to be sultry, but it seems awkward and dated to her. She closes her eyes and sinks into her dream like a swimmer sinking into wet sand. It covers her completely and weighs her down until she is cocooned. In her sleep, her throat is parched, and as the room turns a lighter and lighter shade of gray, she wakes up a few times to take a sip of her Coke. The sound of the movie seems endless until there is silence. Even the rain stops.

Outside the windows, the edges of the night sky burn with the palest mauve and then, later, a fierce orange. At one point, she thinks she sees someone at the window; she is sure it is a face, darkened in shadow, faintly rosy from the dawn light. There is rustling and sighing, and the screen is fuzzy, and before long she falls back into the quicksand of awakened desire.

That is what happens. At least, that's the way she remembers it.

PART TWO

15

Next time, Katie was sure to be better prepared for going back up to the cabin. She scheduled a couple of days off work; the superintendent turned the water on and confirmed that the heat was still functioning. Verizon reconnected the cable, and the internet was up again. Her father was thrilled. She felt awful about avoiding his call on Sunday, so she plugged her home phone back in and hoped he'd call her spontaneously.

"I guess our routines are changing, huh," he said when they spoke a few days later, "and that's all good, right? A whole new paradigm."

They agreed he'd start calling her on her cell, which would allow them to be in touch when she went to Eagle Lake. She told him about some websites she'd found that were geared toward helping released prisoners get acclimated to freedom. "So apparently, if you want a successful reentry, you have to be sure and go talk with your pastor," she said. As far as she knew, her father had never attended church, not even when they all used to go with Grumpy and Gram. "Oh, and humility. You need that. I read on one blog that it's the number one thing you have to have."

"Oh dear," John said, chuckling. "That doesn't bode well for me, then, does it?"

Before Zev left for Spain, he and Katie grabbed lunch at a small Thai place around the corner from the Hamlin Group. He was excited; the deal for his paintings had already gone through, and two of them had been shipped off to San Francisco. He was giving a talk and teaching some workshops at the Museu d'Art Contemporani de Barcelona on the intersection between politics and art, and he'd stayed up all night writing. With the US election coming up in November, everyone wanted to talk about the insanity of the nomination process, but Zev was less interested in the mechanics of politics and more interested in its cultural implications. A few recent paintings of his that made veiled references to celebrity influence were generating serious buzz.

As they talked, he sketched on his napkin with a pen, light lines she couldn't decipher from upside down. They were so wrapped up in their conversation that it didn't occur to her until it was time to get back to work that they hadn't touched on the topic of moving in together.

"Hey, one thing," she said after they'd paid the bill, rising. She only had a few minutes, but she at least had to tell him that she was also headed out of town. "Um, I'm leaving for a few days. Going up to my grandfather's cabin."

"Oh, your family has a cabin? That's great," Zev said, pocketing his change and standing up. He wore a white T-shirt and a navy blazer with black jeans. His face was drawn from lack of sleep but animated. "Somewhere in the country?"

Already this conversation was veering off into territory so banal she didn't know how to bring it back. "Near Poughkeepsie, the Hudson River Valley area?" she said. She badly wanted to be more open, but she couldn't think of how to start. It was part of a much longer conversation. As she looked at him, readying herself for the coming two weeks, she wondered what he thought about love. Did he believe in it? Was he the kind of guy who, once he said "I love you," would say it all the time, or was he someone who thought the whole idea was outdated? He must have been in love before, but what about now—did he call what they had "love"? It was a first for her, this feeling, this strange combination of intensity and fear. She had always assumed that real love was about feeling no fear.

"That's good. You'll get some rest," he said. "You can use my car, if you like; it's still in that lot not far from you. I left you a set of keys, right?" He didn't realize she'd already driven up to the cabin in his car once before, just the previous week.

Of course he suspected nothing; he was so kind. "I'll miss you," she said.

He reached out and touched her chin lightly with his calloused fingertips. "I'm excited about the trip, but I'm more interested in what happens when I get back."

She nodded, rattled. She hated this dance of deception she was perpetuating: *I'm heading out of town for the weekend*. As though this were a spa break or a girls' getaway weekend. It was astonishing how you could be telling the truth and lying at the very same time.

Blackbrooke's main drag was a wide, stately avenue built for horse-drawn carriages in the early 1800s by two brothers who had been counting on the arrival of major roads and the railroad. A jumble of highways passed close to town, shaving off the southwest corner into a forlorn wasteland of gas stations, Qwik Stops, and discount liquor stores. But the men had been wrong about the railroad; engineers had picked Port Leicester instead, twenty-five miles to the north, and that slight miss had spelled a slow and certain death for the grand old town.

Katie stopped at the A&P on Main Street to buy some food and cleaning supplies. It was impossible to avoid sleeping at the cabin—theoretically, Motel 6 was an option, but she was afraid to stay there, with the Trans Ams in the parking lot, the broken windows, and the black-rimmed aboveground pool. She'd left work early and made it to Blackbrooke in record time so she could get settled in before nightfall. There was a lot to do. Tomorrow was Friday, and she'd convinced David to come by for a few hours before driving over to Bethel Woods to see the Goo Goo Dolls. She was going to need help trying to get the Falcon going again.

Before heading to the lake, Katie took a detour past the Blackbrooke courthouse, pulling the Datsun over to the side of the road and idling. People were milling around the wide granite steps. Girls in tiny shorts, hands clutching naked elbows. Lawyers in rumpled suits, distracted looking, cutting their way through the loiterers, papers tucked under their armpits. Stolid granite walls rose toward the sky, flanked by Greek-temple porticos and topped with a golden dome that winked as the clouds flitted past. It made sense, she thought, to try to find the trial transcripts, which were part of the public record. She got out of the car and stood on the pavement opposite, taking in the courthouse's incongruous vastness. Every federal crime in the county was tried here, in this dying town. She herself had climbed these steps to give her testimony, nudged on by her father and his lawyer.

It was four thirty in the afternoon, and the courthouse was still open. Katie resolved to move, but she couldn't quite do it. The muscles all along the length of her body were rigid with fear. The option to turn around and get back into the car was there; it was a viable choice. But if she wanted to be a person who was not afraid of the truth, then she had to grab opportunity, stop being passive. She no longer wanted to let things happen to her. Shifting her weight forward, creating a slip of momentum, she put one foot in front of the other, climbing the stairs before yanking at the heavy glass-paneled door.

The woman at the front desk barely glanced up at Katie as she put her bag through the x-ray machine. To the left was the clerk's office, behind oak doors with scratched glass panels. A piece of A4 paper was tacked onto each pane with yellowing Scotch tape: No CELL PHONES OR CAMERAS IN THE COURTHOUSE. No one had worried much about cell phones during her dad's trial. Back then, she had kept her eyes on the floor until they'd reached the courtroom itself. The day had been stiflingly hot, the air-conditioning broken. She tried to shove those thoughts aside. Her damp cotton shirt stuck to her ribs, chilly against her hot skin. She took one deep breath to steady herself.

A warren of mismatched desks and file cabinets filled the clerk's office. "Hi," Katie said, putting her bag down on the floor between her legs, her hands trembling. The office was a throwback, no gleaming laptops, frosted cubicles, or halogen desk lamps. The strip of fluorescents overhead buzzed.

When no one looked up, she cleared her throat. "Hello? Um, I'd like to see a court transcript, if I may."

Three sets of eyes rose simultaneously, only mildly curious. "Transcripts?" a lady at the back said. "We don't keep complete transcripts here."

"Oh, all right," Katie said. For a second she was deeply relieved, but then a kind of stubbornness seeped into her bones, and she stayed rooted. It was her right to see those transcripts, to know what had happened in court. They couldn't deny her this right. All three women remained rooted behind their desks. "But so, okay, where are they kept, then? The transcripts?"

The woman closest to her checked her watch, then turned her eyes back to her computer. A thin, middle-aged woman in a fitted green T-shirt regarded her through thick glasses. "You need the case number, all right?" Her voice had the ring of finality to it. She was definitely giving Katie the runaround. "Without the case number, we can't help you."

"What type of case was it?" the woman at the back called out.

Katie swallowed. "Statutory rape."

The two women exchanged glances. The one who told her they didn't keep transcripts leaned into her chair and flipped a pencil back and forth between two fingers. "You want to see the transcripts of a rape trial? Is it over?"

"Yes, it was a while ago. In 2009, uh, sorry, summer of 2010."

"Was there a conviction? Did it go to appeal?"

"He was convicted and then appealed. It went to the New York Supreme Court."

"You a journalist or a lawyer?" the woman in green asked.

Katie's shirt clung to her shoulders, and she tried to resist fiddling with it. "The defendant, I'm his daughter. And, he's, um. He's getting out of prison," she said. "I have a right to know what happened. Those court documents, they're in the public record. And I'm his *daughter*."

There was a long silence, and the woman in green sighed. "Get hold of the case number, and we'll see what we can do."

It was almost dusk by the time Katie arrived at the cabin and unloaded everything. Stripping the sheets in the bunk room, she stuffed them in the washing machine and ran the old vacuum cleaner over the matted carpet. It would have to do for now.

She went for a long run around the lake, earbuds in, music blasting. The drumbeat of her heart was constricting her throat, and she wheezed as she ran. It took almost two miles before her breath became regular again. The sun was cooling, and she wondered whether the old fireplace still worked. Her playlist ended, but she wanted to keep moving, so she started it again from the beginning and went around the lake two more times. Her body thrummed with a shredded, lingering sort of energy.

By the time she arrived back at the cabin, she felt truly resolute, almost calm, for the first time since the reporters began calling her. She was going to do this. No one was going to give her answers unless she asked for them—and she wanted answers. She began to make a to-do list in her mind. The first thing on her list was to find the case number. And the second was to call Jack Benson.

Jack's email had read, in its entirety:

> Katie Gregory! Good to hear from you! Call me any
> time on 2129956732.

She sat in the living room, the air smoky from her attempt at making a fire, drinking a bottle of wine she'd picked up at the discount liquor store. The first glass had gone down quickly, and even though she felt queasy, she filled her second glass to the brim. So they were neighbors—this news was both unsettling and a thrill. She'd been right, after all; they had probably been circling each other from a distance for the past few years. Finishing that second glass of wine did not make her feel more courageous, so she picked up her phone and dialed anyway.

"Benson," he said.

"Jack!" Katie said, then hesitated, trying to get control of her voice. "Hi. It's Katie. Katie Gregory?"

"Whoa," he said. She could hear that he had not expected it to be her. "Christ, you surprised me. How've you been?"

"Um, okay," she answered, realizing instantly that this call was a terrible mistake. To ask *How have you been?* when the last time they spoke was before her father was sent to prison was like asking a man who was about to be strung up on a tree what he'd miss in life. It was mortifying, utterly inadequate. "And you? How are you?"

"I'm fine. I'm good. Busy, you know." A pause. "Damn, Katie. Wow. This is *hard*."

"I . . . well, yeah. I'm at the cabin again, at Eagle Lake."

"Oh shit," he said.

"My dad's getting, um, released soon. I'm cleaning up, going through things. And I . . . I was . . ." She stopped, uncertain how to phrase her question about the letter, about his testimony. The beginnings of a headache crept along the bone above her eyes, pressing down on the delicate nerves.

"Katie, look, I never felt great about how we said goodbye. And I never got to tell you how bad I felt, you know? About the whole fucking shitshow."

There was something comforting about his cursing, as though he were still a teenager and not a man. It took her back to when she too had been careless and unconstrained, when words would pop out of her mouth instead of stewing inside her. She got up and walked to the window. Now that she was actually talking to Jack, her obsession with what had happened between the three of them that night seemed misplaced. How had they influenced what had happened? But she couldn't shake the feeling that Lulu had done something, said something, decided to take back control by wreaking havoc.

"So where're you, Katie?" Jack asked.

"I said—I'm at the cabin," Katie answered. "At Eagle Lake."

There was a noise on the other end of the line, like a door slamming. "No, I meant where do you live?"

"Manhattan."

"No kidding . . ." There was static, a brief lapse in the phone connection. "So do I."

"Look. I found all this stuff," she tried again, but they were cut off by more static.

There was a distant honking sound and the screech of brakes. He was in his car, driving. "Katie, I—can I call you right back? I'm headed to a showing. The traffic's insane. Is that okay? This is your cell, right? I'll be like ten minutes."

"Sure, yeah," she said. "Call me."

But her phone did not ring again that night. She waited an hour before trying him again. Voice mail clicked on instantly. Furious, she checked his number and punched each digit in again, more carefully this time. No answer.

16

She was in bed the next morning when her phone buzzed on the covers beside her; the movement woke her, but only slightly, like the touch of a mosquito on a warm shoulder—only enough for her to emerge momentarily and then be dragged under again.

The sheets were saturated with the smell of what some chemist in a lab somewhere considered to be the essence of wildflowers. Deep, deep in the static-filled gray of sleep, she opened her eyes every now and then to question where she was, to breathe in and register the strange competing smells, before being pulled again into an uneasy yet irresistible sleep. It took her a long time to open her eyes and realize that she was in the bunk room at Eagle Lake again. The residue of the late-night sleeping pill she had taken after trying Jack again and again coursed through her body, and she struggled to understand that the day had begun without her. Making an immense effort, she uncovered her bare legs, and the cold air hit her like the slap of a rattled parent. The next time the phone buzzed, her eyes opened wide, and she stared at the slats on the bottom of the top bunk. The mattress above her was stained with years of children's accidents.

She'd missed a call from Zev, but when she tried to call him back a few minutes later, it went straight to voice mail, as though his phone had run out of juice. Briefly, she thought about calling her old friend Radha, who knew a few bits and pieces of what had happened. It was strange that no one, not even her father, knew what she was up to. Katie badly wanted to escape her own mind, put into words what she had set in motion by coming here. But she also knew that she wouldn't be able to explain this to Radha or anyone else without risking their pity—or even worse, much worse, the greed of their prurient curiosity. She did not think she could tolerate that, so she waited to see if Jack would call her back.

The sight of the yogurt and bread she had bought yesterday repelled her, but she downed two cups of black coffee—she'd forgotten to buy milk. Thankfully, David would be there soon. Goose bumps spread over her legs and arms as she opened the front door and stood on the lintel, looking out and yawning widely. Across the gravel driveway and beyond the stand of pines was an undulating meadow, unkempt and woodsy, and then the Big House, grand in size but modest in design. Three stories, shingled, with dark-green window frames and a red roof. From here she could see the back porch—the new owners had done something with the stone patio—and into the kitchen. That was where her grandmother had slaved over her apple crumbles and shepherd's pie. Grumpy had complained about all the maintenance on the house even though they had all known he loved it. John used to spend hours perched on ladders helping his father-in-law clear out a gutter or crouched down by some worn tread, paintbrush in hand. There had always been something that needed fixing.

David arrived an hour late—no surprise there. All his life he'd run behind, always late for the school bus, eyes crusty with sleep, teeth unbrushed. Today he looked again like he'd just rolled out of bed, hair flattened, one blue sock and one argyle. Katie jumped right into his car with him (a tiny Jeep, borrowed from a friend, with a cloth roof and no sides), and they drove over to the other side of the lake, to the Nicholses' house.

"How do you feel?" Katie asked as they drove along the dip by the club, where the road descended toward a small bridge over the dam. Through the trees, the clubhouse with its green siding was just visible.

"A bit tired, but otherwise pretty decent," he said.

She sighed. "No, Davey, I mean about being here."

"Pretty weird. Yeah. But I did come back once with Mum. You'd gone off to college already. She brought me up here one day, kind of like to say goodbye. But I hated it—I mean, it was so bad. It's always been the two of them here together, you know? And he was gone. I cried all the way back home."

"Ugh, sounds awful," she said. "I never came back even once."

"And Mum cried too. I think that was the worst part. She kept talking about how people should live with 'integrity.' Like we hadn't already known that. I think that might be the first time I ever saw her cry. It was totally fucking unnerving."

When Katie was little, she'd been fascinated by the way her mother grimaced, pulling her lips down over her teeth so she could get the eyelash curler in the right place on her eyelids. How she'd put on John's worn-out shirts from the office, tying them at the waist, making them look sexy with a pair of jeans and some sandals. Katie had imitated her voice, how her mouth cupped her tongue, her lips narrow and often pursed. But her mother had so often seemed impatient with her. She'd sigh as she squirted out some extra face lotion when her daughter asked, or she'd snap at her to go play when Katie stared too hard at how she was filling in her eyebrows or sticking Gram's diamond studs in her ears. Katie always had the sense that her mother expected something more from her, that Katie had failed a test without even knowing she was taking one. But she never figured out what it was her mother really wanted from her, and eventually she gave up trying to find out.

Constance Nichols was sitting on the front porch of her house, wearing an oversize straw hat and a red kimono and reading a book. Her skin was very pale, almost bluish, her neck long and elegant. She seemed out of place in the woods. Katie remembered her from before: she always sat in the shade, and even when she swam, her arms and legs were covered. She looked up warily and walked across the porch as they rolled in.

"David? Is that David Gregory?" Constance asked as David and Katie climbed out of the Jeep.

"Mrs. Nichols," said David, leaning in to kiss her cheek. "Good to see you again. You remember Katie, my sister? How are you? Is Joshua around?"

"Joshua?" Katie asked.

"Our younger son," Constance said. "Brad's brother. He works at the gardening supply store now, down in Blackbrooke. You know the place?"

"Yeah, I think so," David said. He ran his hands over his hair, but it sprang up between his fingers. "Nice."

Constance folded her bony hands in front of her. "We're very happy about it."

"So Katie says you have the Falcon. That's crazy—I had no idea."

"Oh. Well, yes. Your mother decided she would rather just, you know. Keep it, for when . . . for later." Her eyelids fluttered. She looked stricken, as though to even mention John Gregory's name would break some unspoken rule.

"That's so kind of you," Katie said. "Thank you. Uh, my father, he asked us to see if we could try to get the car going."

"Ah," Constance said. "He's being released, is he?"

Katie's cheeks went hot. "Yes, that's right."

"Well, dear, it hasn't been driven in forever, but who knows. I'll wrestle up that key." When she returned and handed it over, she held Katie's eye. "What good kids you are. How loyal. Your father is a lucky man."

The garage was little more than a lean-to behind the main house, a gray clapboard structure with broken doors.

"Did you know he was my first kiss, that kid Joshua?" David hissed at his sister. He helped her heave open one of the doors and then dusted his hands off on his jeans. "Perfectly nice guy, just a little wacko."

"How old were you, like, five?"

"Yeah, I know." David laughed. "We all have to start sometime, don't we?"

In front of them, a blue tarp stretched out over the car, lumpy and covered in debris from the rafters. There was a fluttering in the corners, a frantic flapping, and something darted above their heads before escaping through the open doors. David yanked the tarp off the back end of the car, sending particles of dust flying into the air. With two hands he hauled the cover up over his head and folded it back on itself, releasing the powerful smell of damp corners, cracked leather. Nesting animals with their hard-won scraps. Rotting pine needles and something chemical.

Both of them stood still for a while, surveying the scene. The car was still as bright as nail polish. The chrome bumper was rusted but intact, both tailpipes shooting out like exclamation points above the packed-dirt floor. The candy-red taillights like jewels set into a silver mount, the dash of the Falcon insignia connecting them, the word "FALCON" spaced out, rusty with the passing of years.

John had polished this car every weekend during the warm-weather months. During the winter he had parked it in the heated garage at West Mills. In the summers, the roof had always been down, kids clambering with wet feet over the back seat. Now the roof was up, but the windows had been left lowered. Katie looked toward the Nicholses' house, dappled in the shade like a hen's egg. Constance was standing on the listing front porch, sun hat in hand, watching them. "She's sorta creepy," she said under her breath. "Staring at us like that."

"She's okay," David said. "She was really good to Mum after the trial. They were kind of friends."

Katie sidled into the darkness of the garage and tried the passenger door, but it wouldn't budge. The roof's sagging fabric was clogged with pine needles and mouse droppings. Together they hauled it back like a huge black tongue, something diseased or contaminated. For what seemed like a long time, they both stood looking at the leather seats, graying from years of disuse. Coldness emanated from the interior, combined with the faint smell of mold.

Cautiously, Katie leaned forward and slid into the passenger seat. David clambered into the back and began rooting around under the seats. He held up a sneaker and a T-shirt. "There's tons of shit back here. There's even some empties. Schlitz, for Christ's sake. We've got to clean this out."

"First we gotta get it rolling," Katie said. "Dad'll be so happy."

"And that's the most important thing, right? That he's happy."

She stopped in midmotion. "You being sarcastic?"

"No, no. I get it. It's just . . ." He shook his head, frustrated. "I don't know. Sometimes I feel like everything revolves around him. If he's here, if he's not, whatever, it's always about him."

"Davey . . ."

"I know. Sorry. I'm just saying what I think."

The ignition wouldn't turn at all. David went into the house and came back with some olive oil, a handheld brush, and a few plastic bags. They tried again; now the key turned, but there was no sound from the engine. He peered under the hood and swept away some debris.

"This thing's a mess," he said. "We probably need to get it towed."

Katie looked up a garage in Blackbrooke that she remembered her father using when the car kept stalling one summer. They would tow it into town and see if they could get it running. "This is going to cost us a fortune," she said when she hung up.

"Let's at least get the junk out," he said.

Katie noticed something David was holding. "What's that?"

"It was stuffed under the front seat."

Curious, she took the rag from him. Shaking it out, she held it up in front of her. The material was thin, and even in the stippled light of the woods, it was almost transparent, a faint rosy pink from years of being wet and drying and then getting wet and dry again. Holes by the neck and short capped sleeves. This T-shirt was familiar to her: It had been left countless times, soaking wet, on the floor in the laundry room. It had been hung on the line to dry. It had been worn by Katie, and once even by David, who had only taken it off when John had remarked on pink being a strange color for a boy to wear. It was crinkled and dirty. The blue print on the front was so faded as to be almost illegible, but she knew what it said.

It said *Hawaii* in bubble letters. Lulu had been wearing it that night, the last night of summer.

17

Holding that flimsy material in her hands, Katie could almost *smell* Lulu, feel the texture of her skin, see her impish frown. How had her father gotten hold of that T-shirt? Maybe he had gone swimming with Lulu while Jack and Katie were at the Dolans' house, but what—if anything— did that mean? Maybe her father had played a trick on Lulu—snatched her clothes away while she was in the water. It could have been entirely harmless. But Lulu had been upset when Katie found her at the dock. None of this was adding up.

"This is Lulu's," she said to her brother.

"Oh," David said. "We should just throw it away, right?"

"I mean, Lulu was wearing it *that night*. You know? During the square dance?"

He cocked his head to one side. "Shit, that's weird, right? Why would it be in the car?"

"That's what I'm wondering."

"Look, all this rooting around? It's not going to end well."

"What do you mean? Why not—do you know something?"

"Nothing more than you do. I promise," he said. "Really. But . . . but I don't know. I have a bad feeling. I just do."

"Well," she said, cramming the T-shirt into the trash bag, "I guess at this point what we feel isn't really all that relevant, is it? He's our father, and we love him, and he needs our help." Even as she said it, she knew it wasn't really that simple. Yes, she loved him. Yes, he needed help. But she also knew that to move forward, she was going to have to keep going backward. Stars specked the black beneath her lids as she rubbed at her eyes. It felt as though she hadn't slept in days. She couldn't explain it to David, or she didn't want to—at least not yet, not until she knew more. He had his own path to take, and she didn't feel like justifying herself to him.

Armed with the case number, which she found among the papers in the pirate box, Katie went back to the clerk's office at the courthouse later that day, after David left for his concert. The woman with the glasses told her to come back in an hour, and when Katie returned, they had located the folders relating to her father's case, which did in fact seem to include the transcript and some of the ensuing legal paperwork regarding the appeal. They pointed her toward a dingy room next to the office in which two metal desks sat back-to-back, covered in papers. There was a broken chair leaning against the wall, and the blinds over the windows were slanted at an angle. An enormous copier lurked in the corner. Periodically, harried clerks rushed by and glanced in, but otherwise she was left undisturbed.

The transcript was like a screenplay for a movie, except there were no italics saying, "*The defendant leans back and rubs his eyes, his shoulders stooped.*" Or "*The accuser begins to sob uncontrollably, her hair falling in her face.*" Instead, there were breaks in continuity. Questions stopped, and there was a blank half page, and when it resumed, it seemed something had happened—something wordless that the court stenographer did not put down on paper. And those details were what crowded Katie's imagination. She saw her mother in her ugly blue suit, a blank expression on her face; she saw how she must have turned toward Katie's father every now and then, making an effort to appear firm, unflustered. John sitting there, believing that this would all work itself out, that it *had to* work out because this girl Lulu Henderson was clearly troubled and jealous, and most important of all, she was lying.

Pages and pages of testimony; Katie flipped ahead. She would read everything her father had said and every word of Lulu's testimony, but first she had to see if Grumpy had remembered things correctly or not.

Then she found it.

> Q. Good afternoon. Could you please state your name for the court?
>
> A. Yeah. It's, my name is Jack.
>
> Q. Jack . . . ?
>
> A. Jack Benson.
>
> Q. Can you tell us how you came to be at Eagle Lake Park that summer? Just some background so we understand.
>
> A. My parents rented a house.
>
> Q. To clarify, this was from July through to August of 2007, yes? Your parents rented a house at Eagle Lake Park, and you were there during those months?
>
> A. That's right.
>
> Q. Okay, go on.

A. So they rented a place, and I spent a few weeks there, like, maybe four, five weeks total?

Q. Thank you. You knew the Gregory family well. Would you agree with that assessment?

A. I knew the kids well. I mean, I still know them.

Q. Katherine and David, right? You would say you were friends.

A. Yes, that's right. David's still just a kid, I mean—

Q. The girl, Katherine, she's your age.

A. Yes. And yeah, we were friends.

Q. And what about the victim—

THE COURT. Counselor, please.

PROSECUTOR. Sorry, Your Honor, my mistake.

Q. The alleged victim, what about the alleged victim? You were friends with her, too, Lulu Henderson.

A. Yeah, sure. We all hung out together.

Q. And before we get to the night in question, just tell the court about your relationship with the defendant. You interacted with him on a number of occasions, is that right?

A. Yes.

Q. Can you characterize your relationship?

A. I'm—sorry . . . I'm not really sure.

Q. You don't understand the question?

A. I didn't have a relationship with Mr. Gregory. I mean, I barely knew him except from seeing him around the clubhouse, you know?

Q. We don't know. We need your clarification. The clubhouse? What is that?

DEFENSE. Relevance? Your Honor? Is any of this relevant?

THE COURT. I'll allow it. But get to the point, counselor. It's getting late.

PROSECUTOR. I'm establishing the setting. What happened prior to the rape. Excuse me, the alleged rape.

Q. Okay, son. Tell us what you mean by "the clubhouse."

A. It's a place where we met at night. During the day, too, actually. To play Ping-Pong, you know? Drink shakes and just hang out.

Q. And the defendant?

A. Oh, Mr. Gregory, yeah. He was there a lot, too, mostly weekends. There's a bar area where the adults can have drinks. He was very active.

Q. Can you qualify what you mean by "very active"?

A. He was always there.

Q. Yes. Go on.

A. Uh, he was sort of a drinker, I guess.

Q. So this place, this clubhouse, drinks were served there? Beer and such? And Mr. Gregory was an enthusiastic participant, is that a correct characterization?

A. Yes, ma'am.

Q. Would you say he was often drunk?

DEFENSE. Your Honor! The kid was fifteen years old; how would he know?

A. Sixteen. I was sixteen.

She put the paper down on the desk. Really? The prosecutor didn't know what she was talking about. Just because people drank at the clubhouse didn't mean they were drunks.

THE COURT. Don't interrupt, son. Ms. Sofigny will address you directly when she asks you a question. Okay, this is about establishing mood; I get it. Let's move on. The facts are what we're trying to get at here, counselor.

PROSECUTOR. Yes, Your Honor.

Q. Would you say that Mr. Gregory often appeared to have had a lot of alcohol when you encountered him at the clubhouse at night?

A. Yes, I guess. But so did everyone.

Q. Can you speak up, please?

A. Yes, he was often drunk.

Q. Let's go back to the night in question, the night of August 31, 2007. Tell us what happened that night.

A. We were hanging out; people were swimming. There was a party, a square dance. And a big storm.

Q. You were with the alleged victim at one point, isn't that right?

A. Yes, but, I mean. I was with everyone, on and off.

Q. Okay, so it was a party night, and everyone seemed to be having a good time. Did you encounter Mr. Gregory during this period?

A. Yes, I did.

Q. And what did he say to you?

A. He—well, he wanted to go swimming. Skinny-dipping, in the lake.

Q. Uh, hold on. You are saying Mr. Gregory, the defendant, he wanted to swim naked with . . . with the children?

A. Everybody does it. You're making it sound, like, I don't know.

Q. Did this happen? Did Mr. Gregory, a man of forty-five, swim naked with all of you? With underage girls, with Ms. Henderson—

A. No, no, I mean, I don't know. But it was normal. And I left for a bit, so I don't know if he even went swimming in the end. I'm not saying he did that. Maybe he didn't; I don't know.

Katie stopped reading, heart pounding in her ears. The questions were so leading. That's not what had happened; it was Katie's mother who had been so overheated, who had come out of the clubhouse sweating and wanting to cool off, not her father. Wasn't Charlie the one who had suggested going swimming? And Jack was right—the prosecutor was making it sound perverted, when skinny-dipping at night was normal.

Q. Okay, let's move on to later that night. The party broke up. It was what time? Around one a.m.?

A. Yeah. There was lightning. A big storm. So everyone went home.

Q. But you didn't go home, isn't that right?

A. No, I mean yes. But then I went out again, later. I wanted to see Katie one more time.

Q. Where did you go?

A. To her house.

Q. What happened then?

A. I thought they'd all gone to bed. But there was light coming from the den.

Q. And what did you do?

A. I thought maybe they were watching TV.

Q. Okay, so what did you do?

A. I didn't mean to be, like, spying or anything.

Q. That's okay. That doesn't matter. Just tell us what happened.

A. They were in the den. Mr. Gregory, Katie, and Lulu. I looked through the back window.

A face at the window in the murky early-morning light—so Katie *had* remembered that correctly. She was afraid to read on. But she had come here to get facts, to better understand what had actually happened, and that meant she had to keep going, no matter how hard it was. She clamped her teeth together and continued reading.

Q. And what did you see?

A. The couch, there was a couch against the opposite wall. Everything was blue—the light, from the TV, it made everything blue. But I couldn't see very well.

Q. Just tell the court what you believe you saw.

A. I saw Katie asleep on the couch.

Q. There were two couches? Who was on the longer couch?

A. Lulu. She was on that one. Well, she was sitting, and he was on the floor.

Q. He, meaning the defendant. What was he doing?

A. I couldn't really tell. He was—there was a blanket over his back.

Q. Just tell the court what you thought you saw when you looked through the window.

A. I saw a man. It was Mr. Gregory. He was kneeling in front of Lulu. I think she had her eyes closed. I couldn't really see much. He was, like, kind of bending down in front of her.

Q. Did it look as though Mr. Gregory was committing a sexual act?

A. It could have been. She was facing him. There was a blanket. And that's all. That's all I saw.

Q. Thank you.

A pulse at her throat, blood rushing through her veins. Pain in her bones, everywhere. Was this "evidence"? She couldn't be sure what she was reading, what it really meant. She had thought she'd find a definitive answer, a word or an explanation that would illuminate the truth. Instead, she was flooded with dread and confusion. What had her father been *doing*?

Cross-Examination

Q. Were you drinking the night of August 31? What had you had to drink that evening?

A. Some beer. The older kids, they had vodka.

Q. You drank beer and vodka that night? Even though you were not of age.

A. Yes.

Q. Had other kids been drinking too? Underage teenagers?

A. Yes.

Q. Lulu Henderson, for example. She was drinking alcohol?

A. I'm not sure. I can't be certain.

Q. And Katherine Gregory? She was drinking?

A. Yes. A little.

Q. Okay. In terms of your own behavior. Can you tell the court how much? Approximately how much alcohol or marijuana had you consumed that night?

A. Not very much. I mean, I was totally clear headed. It was late too. Everything had worn off.

Q. So you were drinking beer and vodka all night, and it was late, and you decided to go visit Katie Gregory one last time?

A. Um. Yeah.

Q. Can you tell us why? Why did you want to go to her house in the middle of the night?

A. I just wanted to see her again. And I thought Mr. Gregory—I don't know. I thought he might, I guess, be angry about things? I was worried about Katie.

Q. Why would Mr. Gregory be angry?

A. Because we had been gone for, like, a while, Katie and me. We weren't supposed to be alone together, you know? I think he saw us earlier, kissing.

Q. You'd broken the rules, you'd been drinking, and then you went to see if everything was all right, and you say you saw Mr. Gregory through the window with Lulu Henderson, but it was dark, and you couldn't really see what was happening.

A. No.

Q. No, you couldn't see? Or no, you didn't look through the window?

A. I couldn't really see what was happening.

Q. It would be correct to say, then, that you are testifying that you did not see Mr. Gregory and the plaintiff engaged in sexual activity?

A. Um, I don't know. Can you repeat the question?

Q. Are you saying that you did not witness any sexual activity between the defendant and the plaintiff?

A. What I'm saying is, when I looked, I saw them—I thought it was weird—

Q. We've established that you saw them. But were they engaged in sexual activity?

A. Honestly, I don't know. I couldn't see what they were doing—

Q. No further—

A. —but it was weird—

Q. Thank you, no further questions.

Katie put a hand on her chest, feeling the urgent beat of her heart under her fingers. A tangle of unanswered questions remained. The lawyers didn't seem to have proven anything with this line of questioning. Jack had testified, but he hadn't known exactly what he had seen when he'd looked through that window in the den, and it was established that he was unreliable because he'd been drinking. The prosecutor had overreached.

But at the same time there was no denying the fact that Jack had seen something that made him acutely uncomfortable, that hinted at transgression.

A terrible thought occurred to her. Was it possible that Jack chose not to remember exactly what he saw? That he lied or obfuscated on the stand to protect her father—and therefore, by extension, to protect her too? Was that why he had tried to write to her about his trouble with telling "the truth"? *Christ.*

Just then, a woman poked her head around the doorframe, causing Katie to start. "We're closing up here," she said.

Katie checked her watch. "But it's . . . it's . . ." and she realized it was already a few minutes past five o'clock in the evening. "Damn. You're not open tomorrow, right?"

"Weekend, hon. We don't work weekends."

She stood, shaky, stretching her legs one after another. Her entire body was numb except for her damn chest, where a battle was raging. The rest of the transcript would have to wait. She thought about Jack's letters to her, his attempt to make peace when he thought she knew he was a witness. How could her parents have denied her those two letters? All these years, Katie had thought she was alone in her particular brand of pain and confusion, when in reality it hadn't been like that—Jack had felt it too. He had had questions.

The bad news was this: He had seen things, things that didn't seem right. And she was leaving the courthouse with more questions than answers.

When Katie got back to the cabin, the sun had dropped behind the wall of black pines, and a chill set in. Being alone in the country was a discomfiting experience, and she wished David had been willing to stay over. She had her laptop and another bottle of wine, but when she tried to sit still, the sounds from the woods seemed to amplify around her, and the cold seeped into her fingertips and her toes. If only Jack would call her back, but her phone was silent.

Breaking out the cleaning supplies, she started in on the kitchen. The radio was tuned to a jazz station, and after a while she switched to Oldies 90.3. Tidying up wasn't so bad, really. It took her three passes with a mop to get the old linoleum floor to shine again. The kitchen table was scratched up and dusty, but once she'd scrubbed it and applied some Old English, it shone in the lamplight, warm and friendly. She picked some ferns to display on the counter in a small vase. Sometimes she sang out loud, and sometimes she worked in silence, the songs bringing up waves of memories as she worked. When Shania Twain came on, Katie stopped in her tracks, one arm raised above the refrigerator, where she was clearing away years of mouse droppings. *Shit*, she thought. *Shania Twain is not a goddamn oldie!*

18

John Gregory is a horrible singer. He stands in the West Mills kitchen, "You're Still the One," by Shania Twain, playing on the radio. Each time it reaches the chorus, he stops what he's doing and waves whichever utensil he's holding high in the air, arching his back and singing in high falsetto, "Looks like we made it; look how far we've come, baby!" David and Katie burst into giggles.

It is her parents' wedding anniversary, January 14, 2008. Outside it has been snowing lightly for hours, and summer seems so long ago. Charlie's Union Jack apron is strapped across John's torso, and he is on his second or third rum and tonic. They are making a surprise dinner for Charlie of beef tenderloin wrapped in phyllo pastry, with sides of carrots and a big salad. John has thrown Charlie off the scent by claiming he has a town basketball game to coach and sending her to a spa. The vent above the oven rattles, and the kitchen windows are steaming up with moisture.

He plans on glazing carrots in apricot jam and cinnamon, which will take at least twenty minutes. Katie grabs the peeler from David. "Go help Dad," she orders. "I'll do this."

"Let him finish," her father says. His cheeks are pink from the steam. "Boys should know how to cook, too, these days."

"You want to surprise Mum, right?" Katie looks at the clock over the door. "If so, we'd better get a move on."

"Nervous Nelly," he says, and then to David: "Get me three bottles of wine from the basement. The merlot, okay? In the crates to the left of the boiler."

When Katie has finished peeling, John shows her how to chop the carrots into julienne strips and create a glaze. It smells rich and sweet, like dessert. Shania Twain is still playing on repeat. Again and again. The dining room at the back of the house overlooks the yard, a large rounded doorway leading into the kitchen on one end and the vestibule on the other. The oak table is set with the white china from Gram and the silver with the vine pattern on the handles. When a car pulls into the driveway, John waves them over frantically.

"Holy Mother of God, Jesus Christ our *Lord*, that woman is punctual," he hisses, flipping the radio off. Katie dims the lights. They hold their breath as a key turns in the front door.

"John?" Charlie calls out from the front hall. "Hello? What's that smell?"

Katie clamps a hand over her mouth, suppressing a laugh.

Candles cast fingers of wavering orange light over the table settings. David's body is rigid with excitement.

"Hello?" Mum stands in the arch of the doorway. She wears a sweatshirt, and her hair is greasy and tied in a low ponytail. In her arms she holds a pizza carton and a big bottle of Sprite. Katie waits for a look of delight to cross her mother's face; why is she always such a downer? "Oh my goodness," Charlie exclaims. A beat later, she breaks into a smile. "What on earth . . . ?"

During dinner, John lets the children have wine, and Charlie doesn't complain. When he brings out the ice cream cake, he places it in front of his wife and sticks a huge spoon in it. Written on the cake in pink cursive is *Charlie & John Forever*. "All yours, honey," he says. "You sure deserve it."

The planes of Mum's face are long and angular, and when she is happy, the angles soften perceptibly. In the candlelight she looks almost like a young girl, and Katie wonders if she will look like her when she is grown. She wants to jump up and hug her, but she's not sure how Charlie would react. Sometimes her mother will stroke her hair, say how pretty Katie is, but she looks sad when she does it. Other times she seems opaque and unknowable, as though her daughter isn't of interest to her.

"I'm going to get fat on you—just you watch out," Charlie says, digging a spoon into the cake with gusto.

"Fat, thin, whatever," John says, grinning. He spreads his arms wide. "Don't matter to me either way, woman, 'cause you're still the one . . ."

Charlie rolls her eyes, licking vanilla ice cream from the corners of her mouth with quick darts of her tongue.

The grown-ups have almost finished a third bottle of wine, and John sends David to fetch another one.

"Go easy," Charlie says. "It's only Tuesday."

"And what a lovely Tuesday it is." John motions to his son to keep going.

On his way back to the dining room, David calls out, "Wow! Still snowing. Think we'll have a snow day tomorrow?"

"It's, like, two whole flakes," Katie says under her breath. In the last few months everything David says has been getting on her nerves. "It's all gonna melt."

"Hey, cool." David comes into the room, two new bottles cradled in his skinny arms. "There's a police car out there. Maybe the neighbors got murdered or something."

"Ugh, please," Katie says. "That's so morbid."

John shoots his wife a glance and stands up, laying his cloth napkin next to his plate. "I'll see what's going on. Finish up, okay?"

The tenderloin has been massacred and sits in a pool of cooling blood. Katie is sleepy from the red wine. Mum is talking about the gutters, of all things, worrying about whether they'll withstand a heavy snowfall. "It's not a good sign that it's already so cold," she says. "Anyone know what *Farmers' Almanac* predicted?"

"Charlotte, come here, will you?" John's voice rings out from the front hall. "Charlie?"

David and Katie look over at their mother.

"Coming," she says. "Start clearing up, you two."

Katie puts down her cutlery and scoops up the plates, running them under the faucet and slotting everything into the dishwasher. Her body is in a sudden dichotomy: though she is slipping knives and forks into their plastic baskets, every fiber of her being is attuned to what is going on in the hall at the front of the house.

People standing on wooden floors, footsteps, a shifting of weight that makes the floorboards creak. Multiple voices, one low and steady. At one point her mother cries out. Undergirding it all is the even tone of her father's voice, like a steady drum rhythm in an experimental modern tune.

Katie goes over to the doorway that leads to the vestibule.

A policeman, in uniform. The swell of his stomach rests on a wide black leather belt from which hangs a nightstick, a pistol in a holster, and a large flashlight. His hands are clasped together in front of his groin as though protecting himself from an oncoming soccer ball, and from his fingers hang a pair of silver handcuffs. Charlie is talking with the other policeman, who stands by the door. Young, with short-cropped brown hair and a baby face. His posture defensive and uncertain.

The older policeman reaches out with one of his soft white hands, grasps John's elbow.

Something is at Katie's side: David. He puts one arm around her waist and leans into her. He squeezes her hip hard with his hand, and she frowns at him as though to say, *I have no idea!*

John nods at the older policeman, and this must lead to some agreement, because the man nods back curtly. The two officers follow John onto the front porch. "I'll call you as soon as I can," he says over his shoulder to his wife. "No need to worry."

The door slams shut.

"Mum? Where are they taking Daddy?" David calls out, propelling himself toward the door, his voice high pitched.

Katie grabs him, fights the urge to press him tightly to her chest. He isn't a baby anymore, but his face betrays an innocence he hasn't yet outgrown. Why is her father leaving, during dinner, with two policemen? Why is her mother not going with them? David starts to cry.

"Get back into the kitchen, and clear the table," Charlie says in an uninflected voice. "Everything's fine. Dad will be back in an hour." There is a familiar finality in her voice. Her guarded manner warns the children not to ask questions, and they remain silent all that night and many more to come. The questions are powerful—they want to be heard, and they do not stop insisting on it—but the kids tamp them down with force, one after another, like swallowing bitter pills that lodge uncomfortably somewhere in the windpipe, not that far from the heart.

Reasons. Explanations. Logic. What fits where in her mind, or in reality? Katie lies in bed. This is when she begins learning to deflect, to shift to another idea, another image, to head somewhere that feels safe. She tells herself that this probably has to do with some jock from one of the teams her father coaches, some hoodlum who got in trouble. There is always drama going on with those kids. It is no big deal.

But she can't go to sleep until she hears a car in the driveway, close to two o'clock in the morning. It is the police cruiser, inching its way up the incline. It stops in front of the house, and John Gregory steps out. He heads toward his front door, holding his arms stiffly by his sides. He left without a jacket, and it is still snowing. Katie can see the bald spot on his head but cannot read the expression on his face. The cruiser door slams shut, and her father enters the house without looking back. Katie can do nothing other than crawl back into bed.

When she wakes up the next morning and sits at the breakfast table, everything is so normal that she can't bring herself to ask a single question—it will tip the balance, bring them bad luck. Her father says offhandedly that it was all a mix-up, and then he gets up to pour himself another cup of coffee to take along on his commute into the city. His navy suit is a little wrinkled at the elbows and the thighs, but he's got good color. He smiles at his family, tucks the paper under his arm, and grabs his briefcase.

It's easy to accept his explanation. Asking gives life to fear—it's better to be silent.

19

It was well after midnight before Katie exhausted herself cleaning the kitchen. She slept only fitfully, dreaming wildly. Nonsensical dreams that ended with her lying in her father's arms on a prison cot. This image flooded her with a sense of warmth as she woke to the new day, as though she'd opened an oven to check on the bread. Even though the testimony she'd read the day before was shocking, today she was less rattled—after all, it had also been inconclusive. In the end, Jack hadn't seen much of anything, at least nothing that proved her father's guilt. He could have simply been mistaken about it seeming "weird." He'd been upset—hadn't Katie also been confused that night, uncertain about people's motivations, about what was actually going on?

In the cabin, the joy and mayhem of golden summers had leached away, leaving an emptiness she couldn't fill on her own no matter how hard she tried by putting on music or buzzing around cleaning. The place had always been full of people and signs of life—her brother and his friends, damp towels draped over the rattan, Charlie in a caftan, smoking a cigarette and leafing through the *New Yorker*. Lulu jumping from the bunk, the thud of her feet a minor earthquake, or singing in the bathroom, her voice with its lilting, weightless tone, so different from her speaking voice. And her father always deep into some project.

Hovering at the periphery of all this, just out of sight, was the specter of Lulu. Katie had never allowed herself to be curious about what had happened to her. Was she in LA singing in a lounge, dressed in cheesy red velvet? In Nashville, tucked into some recording studio, having swapped her dirty sneakers for cowboy boots? It would be so easy to find out; it was all just a click away—but the thought of opening that door and letting in that reality made her shrink into herself.

Her phone pinged with a text and an attachment from Zev. He was giving his talk the next day, and he'd been sending her various quotes he was considering using. In quick succession he'd sent her a Nietzsche quote, "We have art in order not to die of the truth," followed by "All of that art-for-art's-sake stuff is BS," from Toni Morrison, and the contrast made her laugh. Now he sent what looked like a pastel drawing. She tapped the image to make it bigger.

It was a rough sketch of a woman in strong colors, a slash of bright yellow for hair, dark-brown eyes that seemed to pop from the page. It was a picture of her, she realized with a start; that was what he'd been drawing on his napkin when they'd been at lunch together. It was fascinating to see how he saw her, this woman with the guarded expression, a strong, sensual mouth, flyaway hair.

You're supposed to be working, she texted back, leaning up in bed on one elbow.

It's helping me concentrate ☺, he wrote.

Katie headed into Blackbrooke to pick up more paper towels and a new broom. It was almost midday on Saturday, and the streets were empty, as though everyone were still sleeping off some epic hangover. It wasn't hard to see ghostly images of herself and Lulu wandering the deserted streets looking for fun and trouble. Here was where they bought a bottle of Jack Daniels one day with one of the older boys. That alley was where she'd had her first puff of a cigarette. The two of them had spent so much time at the lake and so little in town that she could probably list every single instance they'd set foot in Blackbrooke together. But of course, this was where Lulu had lived—this place had been her home. She'd haunted these streets all her life, and for all Katie knew, she might still be there. At that thought a wave of nausea rolled over her. She climbed back into the Datsun, slinging her purchases onto the back seat.

With both hands, she clutched the steering wheel. She needed to finish cleaning the cabin and setting it up for her father. Find out what Jack was up to, why he wasn't answering her texts or calls. Maybe she would take Monday off work so she could go back to the courthouse and finish reading the transcripts; she wanted to see what her father had said about that night.

When she peered into the future—into the moment of her father's release, into the still unknown happinesses and ordinary sadnesses that awaited her as she aged—her vision was obscured in some profound way. It was as though she were wearing blinkers, could only see part of the picture. And that was a sensation she didn't like, that sensation of partial blindness. Because it was voluntary, and who in their right mind would willingly remain blinded?

No matter how hard it was, she had to keep digging. She was going to have to go to the source. She started the car and headed toward the street where she thought Lulu Henderson had once lived.

A black girl with braids ending in a cascade of plastic baubles drew on the road with chalk, jumping at the sight of Katie's car. At the corner of Dempsy and Hart Streets, a man wearing a Steelers hat was walking with a pronounced limp, holding a crocheted bag in one hand. An old couple sat on a porch, both wearing ragged slippers and drinking

Pabst. So this was where the people were, in the side streets. A sense of life lived in the shadows, away from the eyes of the drivers along Main Street, eyes that calculated and pitied and made assumptions. Katie inched along, driving like an old lady without her glasses. When she reached Mission Street, she pulled into an empty spot.

The old building where Lulu's place had been was just as Katie remembered it, down to the uneven yellow brickwork at hip height. It was a squat building with an open-air corridor running along the front on both levels. She'd only ever been there once, but she thought Lulu's apartment might have been the second to the left on the top floor. Katie played out a scenario in her mind: storming up there, rapping on the door. Her stomach was sour and tight, and she told herself to stay calm, to think clearly. The likelihood that Lulu would still be there was incredibly slim. On the second floor of the apartment building, a man emerged to throw a ball down to a kid on the street. A few minutes later, the door of Lulu's old apartment opened, and a woman came out, leaning over the railing and lighting a cigarette. Languid movements, either relaxed or bored. Puffs of smoke dissipating into the air. The woman had a round face, open. Her hair was brown and slicked back as though she'd just stepped out of the shower. Katie stared at her, astonished. For Chrissake, it couldn't be, and yet it was; it was Lulu's mother.

There was a time when Katie was about ten that she had insisted on staying the night at Lulu's. They'd been spending a few weeks together for the past two summers at Eagle Lake, but Katie had never seen where her friend lived. Like a lovestruck girl, she was infinitely curious about Lulu's life: the color of her bedspread, the size of her desk, what kind of backpack she used for school. It wasn't her family she wanted to know about (the lack of a father at home only registered vaguely, partly because, of all the stories she told, Lulu never talked about her father, or her mother's boyfriends). It was her environment Katie wanted to observe, touch, smell. What did a life like hers look like close up?

When John dropped the girls off that night, a dirty gray area rug was hanging over the railing outside Lulu's door. "You'll call me if you need me, okay, honey?" he'd said, his tone alerting Katie that something wasn't quite right. He started to climb out of the car.

"I'm good," Katie said in a rush. "I'm fine. You don't have to come with us."

Lulu was already on the other side of the street. "He wants to meet my mom," she said. "He thinks we're poor."

"Honey, that is not true," John said. But he got out of the car all the same and went with them to the door.

Inside the apartment, the curtains were drawn, and *The Price Is Right* was playing on the television. When Piper Henderson clicked the TV off, the silence afterward felt thin and precarious, as though in a second there'd be a bang on the wall or a car misfiring in the street. Katie and her father hovered on the doorstep. Just a second earlier his face had been drawn and serious, and now as his eyes sharpened, his mouth slackened. Before he even spoke a word, she knew he'd noticed too: Lulu's mother was beautiful. Katie had only seen her a few times before and always from a distance. Usually it was Charlie who picked Lulu up and dropped her off. Katie's own mother was lovely in a regal way, wiry and poised, a distant look on her face, her accent a barrier that didn't invite people in. In contrast, Mrs. Henderson's face was unformed and round like a young woman's.

Her movements were quick, as though she only decided to move or talk a split second before she did it. Even then Katie recognized this quality as unusual in a parent. Her expression was open and uncomplicated, her skin pale as skim milk and nothing like her daughter's. She had dark eyes that moved restlessly from Katie's father to Katie and back to her father again. When they shook hands, John's face broke into a toothy smile that made Katie cringe.

Later, when Mrs. Henderson leaned over to hand her some brownies as they sat watching movies in the living room, her breath—sweet with the smell of alcohol—grazed Katie's cheek like a light kiss that was familiar and comforting. The brownies were gooey in the middle, and she ate them ferociously, as though she hadn't eaten in days. Mrs. Henderson cracked another wine cooler and sat facing the girls in a large armchair, taking off her nail polish.

"Wanna do my nails?" she asked Lulu.

"Ugh," Lulu said, not moving her eyes from the television. "Do it yourself, Mom."

"I'll do it," Katie said. Her hair stuck to her face; the apartment had no air-conditioning, and she needed a shower, but their one bathroom had only a plastic shower stall tucked in the corner, and it was small and dirty.

"Lu," her mother said sharply, "I'm talking to you."

"Mom, I said I'm busy," Lulu whined. Her expression stayed blank, but her mother's face transformed instantaneously: something gathered behind her eyes and her lips.

"Don't talk to me like that when you've got your fancy friend here!"

Lulu and Katie straightened up. "I didn't mean it that way," Lulu said. "It's just—this show? I love this show."

Her mother lurched forward, and her hand shot out so fast there was no time to anticipate the slap. "Thankless little hussy." A vein crossing Mrs. Henderson's neck cast a pale-blue shadow, the faintest river of blood pulsing under her white skin.

The air trembled with unpredictability. This was not what Katie had expected, and she felt the urge to protect her friend in some way. She thought about the next day, when they'd both be heading back to

Eagle Lake; they only had to get through this one night, and they'd be back on Katie's turf. She had never before heard a parent talk that way to a child or strike one in the face, or anywhere else for that matter. Mrs. Henderson tipped her head back and drained her pink sunset cooler. She seemed cold, when just minutes earlier she'd been so warm.

Katie stood up, her legs uncertain under her, and went over to the side table, where there were a few sticky bottles of polish along with a file and some cotton wool. "Here," she said, her voice ringing out in the silence. "Let's try this color, okay?"

The girl and the woman sat side by side on the couch. Mrs. Henderson's nail beds were narrow, the skin on the backs of her hands soft, as though she never washed dishes or cleaned bathrooms. Lulu had once said her mother brought in extra money as a hand model. "Um, your hands," Katie said. "They're so pretty."

But Mrs. Henderson said nothing. The color in her cheeks faded back to normal, and her eyes seemed to fade too. The nail polish bled over the edges onto her skin, and the more Katie tried to wipe the excess off, the messier it became. When they'd arrived, Piper had promised them a macaroni casserole, but Lulu and Katie went to bed that night hungry. They didn't stay up to talk or play cards. It wasn't until the next morning when they climbed back into the Falcon—after John Gregory had kissed Mrs. Henderson on both cheeks, the sharp odor of his aftershave cutting through the smell of brewing coffee—that they could hold each other's gaze again.

Without saying anything, Lulu was telling her friend, *Don't ask.* The dull shuttering of her eyes underscored that Lulu badly needed Katie to play along. That she knew Katie saw her for who she really was, and that was okay, but only if no one said it aloud. Lulu needed her, and feeling needed was amazing.

Katie never asked to stay over there again. Later, when Lulu was at Eagle Lake, chatting mindlessly about whatever came into her mind,

Katie would think back to that night, to the slap and all that hadn't been articulated. If she was honest with herself, it might have been then that she stopped entirely believing everything Lulu said. She'd started to understand there was a chasm between how people saw their lives, how they wanted others to see them, and how they really were. A chasm that was too deep and dark to explore.

20

There was nothing else for her to do other than climb out of the car and head toward Piper Henderson. When Piper saw her approaching, she cocked her head and clattered down the stairs. Katie couldn't take her eyes off the woman; she was girlish, but there was something off about her. Velour leggings revealed long legs and bagged around her knees. A white sweatshirt bore the logo of Manchester Community College, the collar cut off. Her body was still slim, but her eyes had settled back into the folds of her face, which was puffy like the face of a child in the early morning. Pulling fiercely on her cigarette, Piper let the smoke stream out of her nostrils as she approached.

"You who I think you are?" she asked, not hostile but not friendly either.

The last time Katie had seen her was at the courthouse when Katie had taken the stand. The pouchy, sickly look of her skin was alarming. Katie smiled nervously. Her hands were clammy, and she rubbed them on her thighs. "Yes, Katherine Gregory. Um, Katie."

"Thought as much." Piper's voice was deep, a smoker's voice. She smelled of gin and cigarettes. Katie didn't remember her smoking when she'd stayed over that night. It occurred to her that she should never sneak another cigarette again, no matter how infrequently. "What the hell you doing here?" Piper asked.

"Uh, I'm back at the cabin for a few days," Katie said. Her mind was racing ahead to whether Piper might be able to help her in some way. "Cleaning it up. At Eagle Lake, you know?"

Piper did not feel the need to respond. She seemed like the kind of person who could wait for hours for you to be who she expected you to be. Her eyes were narrow and watery.

"But, um, I was wondering . . ." Katie continued. "How is Lulu? Have you been in touch with her recently? How is she doing?"

Piper crushed the cigarette under the toe of her slipper and pulled out a pack of Merits from the sleeve of her sweatshirt. "Yeah, well. She comes around sometimes, always wanting something from me. Like I have the answers. And she expects me to sit around and give them to her? After she went off like that, you know—after that whole mess she started with you all."

Katie felt a rush of relief: Piper was on her side. "Do you know how I can reach her?" she asked. They looked at each other as Piper dragged on her fresh cigarette. Her hands were still elegant, the fingernails long and chipped, painted blue.

"She's not in witness protection, if that's what you mean." Piper laughed, tight lipped, and Katie saw that she would still be pretty if she were happy. "Look her up. She's in Vermont now, or New Hampshire. Up north."

"You're not, uh—you guys aren't close?" Katie thought of her own mother, up north, sitting in some pretty house on a lake with a man named Michel.

Piper inspected the cuticle around her thumb. "My cousin got in deep with this guy, and that pig dumped her as soon as she got pregnant. Me and my husband, we couldn't have kids. So we thought we'd take her . . ." She trailed off and then shrugged. "I didn't think I'd be doing it alone."

"Oh, wow. I didn't know. I mean, Lulu was adopted?"

"Mm-hmm. And the thanks I got. What a lot of trouble she stirred up. You read that stuff about her? After the trial and all?"

Katie shook her head. Just moments earlier she had been feeling a sense of relief, but now she was sickened. Shouldn't a mother always be on her daughter's side, no matter what? There was something horrifying about Piper's betrayal of her child that stirred up Katie's pity, even if it seemed to support the idea of her father's innocence.

"Well, she's a pretty piece of work. Her saying my cousin wasn't looking after her right and all. That Jody's boyfriends did bad shit to her. That girl would say anything to get her own way."

And with that Piper was done. She walked away and did not look back.

As soon as Katie got back to the cabin, she brewed a pot of coffee and sat down at the kitchen table with her laptop. She wanted to find out right away what Piper had been talking about. First she typed in *John Gregory*. There were hundreds of entries for such a common name. A preemie and a British author. A skinny middle-aged man posing in the nude. She typed in *John F. Gregory.* Up came what looked like the title of a master's thesis, written four years earlier: *Dissociative Disorder Arguments in Rape Cases: Bogus Claims or Breakthrough?* Her father's name emerged in bold amid the two-line description.

Defendant Cannot Present Testimony
in Rape Trial
on Alleged Victim's Prior Abuse
By George C. Manta

A recent ruling by the Supreme Judicial Court stated that a rape defendant may not introduce expert testimony on "dissociation disorder." In addition, the defendant may not present evidence that the alleged victim was sexually abused as a young child and that, as a result of a possible "dissociation disorder," she might have fabricated her allegations of rape. The previous district judge had also ruled the expert testimony inadmissible.

Alleged rape

In August 2007, fourteen-year-old "Sarah" spent much of the summer with her best friend at a private lake community near the Catskills in New York State. Sarah, who was adopted at age four years and three months, had allegedly suffered sexual abuse by two of her biological mother's boyfriends as a young child, before being adopted.

At the end of the summer, defendant John F. Gregory, the father of Sarah's friend, allegedly had intercourse with Sarah. Four months later, during a discussion of issues pertaining to sexual abuse in her tenth-grade classroom, Sarah brought up the alleged incident. According to her, during class, "it popped into my head, what happened with Mr. Gregory at Eagle Lake." Shortly thereafter the defendant, John F. Gregory, a resident of West Mills, New York, was indicted in Superior Court in Deloitte County, in the town of Blackbrooke, on two counts of statutory rape.

At a jury trial before Judge Jemima P. Sonnenheim, Sarah's testimony revealed major gaps and inconsistencies in her memories of the night the alleged abuse occurred.

Defense counsel sought to present two theories about why Sarah's allegations against her friend's father were not believable. The first theory was that Sarah had been seeking attention and had acted as she did because she believed "this is what all men do." This belief was based on the fact that she claimed to have previously been raped by two men who were considered to be "close family friends" of her biological mother.

The second theory was that Sarah's memory was negatively impacted by a "dissociative memory" disorder, causing her to wrongly attribute early memories of abuse to the defendant. The defendant sought to introduce expert testimony by a psychologist to underpin this theory.

Judge Sonnenheim excluded testimony from both the expert and Sarah's biological mother, as well as evidence of Sarah's alleged abuse before her adoption. The judge found that the prejudicial effect of what she considered "entirely speculative" testimony outweighed its probative value.

John F. Gregory received a maximum sentence of six years and was denied a stay of his appeal.

"The error in prohibiting the testimony of his expert witness was prejudicial, and the defendant deserves a new trial," said defense counsel Herbert L. Schwartz of Schwartz, Danneberg, Weissman, Bein & Johnson in New York. "The state's case rested wholly on the alleged victim's credibility. Excluding evidence that could have affected the jury's evaluation of her credibility was extremely damaging to the defendant's case."

Schwartz explained that in sexual abuse cases, the state always poses the question "Why would the victim say this if it isn't true?"

Out on the stone patio, Katie paced back and forth in her socks. Back and forth, back and forth. The legalese in the article turned their story into something inanimate and distant, a cold-blooded argument. But for her, it was as real as a flesh wound. For a while after her father went to jail, she dreamed of bumping into those jurors in the course of her ordinary life. One night she'd dream of the heavyset woman in her pretty red dress, and the next it would be the older man who sat at the end of the second row, taking notes with a fountain pen. In her dreams she would punch these people in the face, her arm shooting out and smashing through skin, bone, cartilage. There was blood, tons of blood. And there was silence, during which she savored the fear in their eyes, their blood staining the webs between her fingers. When she woke up, that delicious satisfaction would disappear, and she'd be back in her bed, an ordinary girl with no special powers, a girl whose father was in prison and who could do nothing about it.

Now she remembered, too, other dreams she had suppressed, snippets that were just as powerful and that left her drained when she opened her eyes to the reality of another day. In those dreams, she did not rail against Lulu but cried for her, for their lost friendship. But when she woke, that pain was subsumed by the avalanche of her anger. She knew what to do with anger but not what she should do about her grief.

Reading now about Lulu's past reanimated that chaos. All along she had sensed something was wrong in Lulu's family, something that no one would confront—not Charlie or John or even Lulu herself. But Katie had felt it, hadn't she? An indistinct yet disconcerting sense of peril that lay like a scaffold beneath their friendship, giving it strange ballast. It seemed cruel that as close as they had been, they hadn't really told each other much of anything.

Now it seemed the jury also hadn't known about the claims that Lulu suffered trauma before her adoption. Had Piper been telling her earlier that Lulu had lied about the rapes when she was a little girl or that she'd been lying about Katie's father raping her? The jury had no reason to suspect Lulu's memory might be distorted. But *had* her memory been distorted? Was it possible that she wasn't really lying, just remembering the order of events incorrectly? Getting men and pain and fear mixed up?

Finally, she typed *Lulu Henderson* into the search field.

Lulu Henderson, Profile & History, Ancestry.com
Harriet Lulu Henderson, records
Lulu Fifi Dog Care, New Hampshire
Lulu Henderson, underwear, CafeMom

She clicked on the images tab. There was a gravestone, a puppy, comic books, a puppet wearing office clothes. And then there she was: Lulu's hair formed a black halo around a soft face. Her expression was wary, her eyes squinting slightly as though she were asking the photographer, *And who exactly are you?* She was carrying a stack of books and wearing an enormous black sweater that dwarfed her upper body. Under the thick wool the swell of her breasts was unmistakable, but her shoulders were pulled forward, and Katie was hit with the realization that this woman, this grown-up Lulu, was trying to hide herself. She did not look like the person Katie had thought she would become.

There wasn't much she could glean from Facebook because of the privacy settings, though there were some pictures of Lulu with a bunch of dogs and various dog paraphernalia, which was curious. All along she'd assumed that Lulu would have become a singer, but there was no sign of that from what little she could see. Back then, Lulu's energy had thrown a shadow over Katie's—she hadn't minded, because she'd instinctively known how much Lulu had needed her. Katie had watched and admired, wondering in an almost abstract way what she herself wanted for her future. Lulu's longings had been enough for the two of them.

She worried at the skin around her fingernails with her teeth. Her father's lawyer had forbidden Katie to contact Lulu, but she'd ignored him. After the verdict had come in, she'd created a new email account—eaglehaslanded@yahoo.com—and sent her a note. No holding back, a torrent of hateful language. She'd said everything in that email that she had dreamed of saying to Lulu's face. Days of careful crafting, not a word wasted. Each sentence a punch in the gut. It had been an incredible release, and she hadn't regretted it. Afterward, she'd disabled the email to be sure that she wouldn't get some sickening, self-righteous response.

She had never admitted to anyone, not even to herself, that her anger hadn't been as pure as she had wanted it to be. Now she thought of the article and the expert witness who hadn't taken the stand. She wondered about this issue of dissociative memory, whether it could be true. With those thoughts, a tug of pity pulled at her. Lulu may have lied, and she may have destroyed their lives, but she'd been just a kid. Katie should never have sent her that email.

After a little more sleuthing, she found a phone number. There it was, just like that, a bridge she could walk across. She jumped up from the table as though it were on fire. Was it betraying her father to call? In the bathroom, she stared at her face in the mirror and saw a girl who was still afraid to make a move. It wasn't the person in the picture Zev had sent her. That picture had been of a woman with a backbone. Someone who wasn't derailed by a messy life.

Screwing her eyes shut, she thought about the reporters who had been calling, claiming that Lulu had spoken to them. It wasn't fair that they knew more than Katie did. She had given Jack the upper hand by approaching tentatively, allowing him to back away from her, and she didn't want to do that again. The old rules about who you could and couldn't contact didn't count anymore. But she felt nauseated, so utterly drained that her body shook as though she were standing outside half-clothed. Opening her eyes, she grimaced into her reflection: she was going to call. Now. If she hesitated for another second, she would never do it.

The phone was slippery in her fingers as she dialed. A woman picked up, her voice loose and distracted.

"Hi, I'm looking for Lulu Henderson," Katie said, going back to the kitchen, heart hammering, and pouring herself a glass of water. "Is this the right number?"

"Yeah, this is Lulu. How can I help you?"

It seemed an absolute miracle that at this very minute, Lulu stood in some room in some house in New Hampshire, holding a phone to her ear, and that she was about to have a conversation with Katie. All these years she had calcified in Katie's memory as the girl from that last summer—billowing, frizzy hair, a light rash of pimples on her chin, full lips pulled into a mischievous smile. It was impossible to believe she existed now, an adult, a changed woman.

"It's Katie Gregory."

There was a pause, a sharp inhalation. "Well, fuck me. No kidding. To what do I owe this pleasure?"

Anger and confusion had been backed up inside Katie for so long that she'd forgotten that Lulu would be angry too. It was impossible now to launch in as she'd thought she would: *It's been so long, I wanted to say sorry for the email I sent you, I know you've had some really awful experiences, awful, I understand better now, I think. Nothing is as straightforward as I thought* . . . Instead there rose within her a hot tide of defensiveness, automatic, entirely out of her control.

"You talked to a bunch of reporters," Katie said. Her will met Lulu's aggression, and the two instantly were at war. "How you could perpetuate this, this horror show, after my father spent six years of his life in jail! I want to—"

"You've got some nerve. Why shouldn't I talk to whoever the hell I want to talk to? At least they take me seriously."

"You don't think we took you seriously? You kidding? Didn't you already get what you wanted, Lulu?"

"What I *wanted*? I didn't want any of this."

There was a pause, during which it felt as though the conversation could go in several very different directions, and then in the background, Katie heard an odd noise, a sort of snuffling or hiccup. She stilled her breathing to listen more closely and realized that it was the sound of a hand over the receiver, and behind that, the sound of a person crying.

"Hold on—we started out wrong. That isn't what I meant to say." Katie held her breath, waiting, shocked that Lulu carried her emotions so close to the surface. "Lulu? You still there?"

There were more muffled, choking sounds, and then the line went dead.

21

A constant dripping in the hallway. Buckets in the kitchen, in the basement. Her parents cursing the winter storms, the ice dams. The weather creeps its way inside the West Mills house, transforming itself into icy rivulets, gathering quietly, a secret army bent on invasion. New York State experiences record snowfall, and the house groans under the pressure: waterfalls pooling in the cracking windowsills, water dribbling through kitchen light fixtures, seeping through the bedroom walls. Bloated plaster and grim mouths.

By April, the skies clear, a sudden pulling back of the offensive; yellow crocuses pop on the lawn. But something isn't right. John brings the Falcon out of the garage to give it its first waxing in the weak sunshine. There is a forced quality to his joviality. When Katie is in bed, just before falling asleep, she can hear him fighting with her mother behind closed doors. There is talk of money, voices snapping and stinging.

Katie has things on her mind. She is working so hard, driven by a desire she's never felt before. She has started to notice the interconnectedness of all things, how history and science and philosophy and mathematics are all linked in a complex and infinite web in which she can lose herself for hours. She discovers that she is exceptionally good at algebra. The juniors in her advanced class are standoffish, a year above her, but she is cool under pressure, tests well. At times, while poring over a textbook or writing an essay, she feels a sense of excitement overtake her, and she can barely keep still. The energy is all directed back inside her, like blood rushing to her brain, feeding her curiosity. It is this discovery—the deep energy of engagement—that teaches her how to shut off those things she does not want to know about.

She is a master of focus. A deep diver, but only in certain waters.

John sits behind his desk in his study, wearing his reading glasses. A polo shirt is tucked into a pair of ironed khakis. He stands up as Katie enters. Next to her father is a man she has seen a few times to whom she hasn't yet been introduced. He has a wild head of curly gray hair and wears glasses with light wire frames. His face is broad and textured, as though he suffered from acne as a child. The pants of his blue suit are unfashionably wide.

The man throws a magnetic smile in her direction, and she is instantly on edge. "Hello," he says, extending his hand. "Pleased to meet you. I'm Herb Schwartz."

"Nice to meet you too . . . I'm, uh, Katie."

He motions her over to an armchair. "So, Katie, great. There's nothing to be worried about, but we do need to talk."

"Sorry, but you're who exactly?" she asks, looking over at her father.

Her father gives her a half smile. "Herb is a lawyer. See, we've got a bit of a problem. Has your mother told you anything?"

"Okay, folks," Herb says, raising a hand to stop them. "Let me deal with this. Why don't you let Katie and me talk for a bit, and we'll get the facts straightened out."

"I think I should be here," John says, his voice lacking conviction. And he is too fidgety, strangely subservient.

"Where's Mum?" Katie asks. She feels like a little girl again in the presence of these two awkward men. "Can Mum be here too?"

Her father and Herb exchange quick glances. John says, "You two have a little chat on your own. I'll be in the kitchen if you need me."

In the study that day, Herb explains what is happening: During health class five months earlier, in December of the previous year, Lulu Henderson and a group of students were talking about date rape in college after her teacher initiated a conversation about the meaning of *consent*. Lulu said, casually, that she'd had sex with her friend's father, "And I'm not even in college yet."

Herb's fingers make air quotes.

"Is she all right?" Katie blurts, horrified, imagining her friend bleeding in some alleyway, crying. Just like that her heart is stripped bare.

"All right . . . ?" Herb asks, his hands hovering in midair, before recognizing the misunderstanding and pointing to her. "Katherine—your father, it is *your father* she's talking about."

And with those words, with that awkward gesture, Katie's life changes irrevocably.

Herb's hands are pudgy, the skin like suede, and he uses them often as he speaks, circling through the air, touching his chest to show his sincerity. What Lulu is accusing Katie's father of amounts to a felony indictment. Herb looks at Katie over the top of his glasses. It is considered statutory rape, he clarifies, his face freezing briefly, as though it takes great effort to say these words aloud. It is then that Katie really begins to comprehend: Here is a grown man who can barely bring himself to say the word *rape* in front of her. This is serious.

"That's not possible," she says, straightening up in the chair. She tries to think back to when she and Lulu last spoke on the phone, maybe after Christmas? Or was it Valentine's Day? She can't recall anything specific they talked about. Yes, now, now she remembers. It was short. Awkward. They spoke over one another.

Nothing makes sense.

"What's not possible?" the lawyer asks. "That your friend is accusing your father or that this alleged crime took place?"

"You mean, when the police came," Katie says, feeling as dumb as a cow, "they were arresting Dad?"

"That's the procedure. He's been out on bail, and we think there's going to be a trial. Probably not for a while if we can help it," Herb said. "Listen to me—this girl, she's saying this incident happened while you were present. She claims the three of you were watching television at the cabin, on the last night of summer. She said there was a storm and you were all together, very early in the morning. Do you remember that?"

"She says it happened in the den—the . . . whatever? Something between her and Dad?"

"Yes. Do you remember that night?"

Katie nods, slowly. A piercing anger makes her ears ring. *I am so fucking dumb*, she thinks. *How can Lulu be so cruel, so selfish? Why would she say something so incredibly, unbelievably stupid?*

Because it's obvious: no one with half a brain is ever going to believe that Katie's father would have sex with a girl, let alone *while his daughter was in the same room*. People will laugh at Lulu. Everyone is going to think she is a batshit-crazy liar.

As Herb Schwartz talks, a constant thought runs through her brain, like a frigid undercurrent: All along there is the fact that Katie disappeared with Jack that night. That she had chosen him over Lulu. That Lulu knew it.

She must really hate my guts, Katie thinks.

But there is not much time for reaction; Herb is in action mode. He wants answers. He's looking to lay out the facts for her. Katie remembers little of what he tells her, other than the basics. There was a counselor who took Lulu to be examined by a doctor and to give a statement to the New York Child Protective Services Abuse Investigation team. There was, of course, no evidence of abuse, and it is clear to everyone involved that the story is full of holes, Herb says.

"So, Katie. Here's the problem." Herb knits his thick brows together. This part she will remember clearly. "Once Protective Services becomes involved and a claim is filed, it sets in motion a chain of events that can't be stopped, not even by a full retraction of the accusation. Your friend was a minor, and she stated that an adult molested her. She said, in fact—just to be precise," he continues, "that she had been, uh, penetrated."

"What, I mean, how do you mean? At knifepoint? And I slept through it all—seriously?" Katie lets out a snort. "*Rape?*"

"To be clear she did not, at least not originally, use that word. *Rape.* And no, there was no violence involved."

"I don't get it." Katie is stunned. It's as though the world is spinning in the wrong direction. "What exactly is she saying?"

"In New York State, a girl under the age of seventeen is considered incapable of giving consent. The Deloitte County prosecutor has decided to press charges, and there's going to be a trial. Eventually. It will be held in Blackbrooke, where the alleged incident took place."

Herb stands with the fingers of one hand resting on the edge of the desk. "And because you were in the room when she says the offense took place, you are going to have to take the stand in your father's defense. Do you understand what I'm telling you, Katie?"

She nods again, biting her lip. This can't be for real. "I think so."

Now he smiles. "And that's good, very good for us, actually. About you being in the room. We're very lucky she admitted it. We've basically got this thing tied up. Now, why don't you tell me what you remember? Try to be as exact as possible."

And that is when the idea is born. That she has some control. That she can think back, play the night over and over again, piece together the details and make sense of this. The movie, the storm, the sleepy end-of-night warmth in the den, while outside—

"You watched the entire film with the two of them?" Herb says. "From beginning to end? And then you went upstairs to bed, with Lulu? You were awake?"

"Of course I was." She tries to remember the end of the movie, what happened. A pinkening sky, a face in the window? An itchy blanket. Her mother looking for David. What had William Hurt's fate been? She vaguely remembers being embarrassed by the story; it was kind of cheesy. Did Lulu like it—hadn't she said it was one of her mother's favorites? Katie had been sleepy, yes, but she probably hadn't totally fallen asleep. She would have definitely known if something weird had happened between Lulu and her father.

"I was awake the whole time, and nothing happened," she says quietly. "Nothing."

Would I have known? The question sits like fragile china way up at the very back of a shelf in a corner of her brain; Katie looks it over, examines it, and then puts it carefully and completely out of sight. It is not possible. It is absolutely not possible that she would not have known.

Herb tells her that she may never contact Lulu again, under any circumstances.

"But what about . . ." She is thinking of the summer. It's as though her mind hasn't quite caught up with reality. What will happen now?

"If you contact her, it'll be disastrous, Katie—and your father will not be able to recover from it. Am I being clear? There can be no calling, no emails, or anything whatsoever. You will do the case irrevocable harm."

So—there will be no more Eagle Lake, at least not with Lulu. It's over. She feels the backup of salty tears in her throat, finally seeing the divide between *before* and *after*. Until then, she has never thought of the future in that way. She and Lulu had such ordinary dreams, as girls do. They assumed that one day they would live together, get an apartment—maybe somewhere far away like California or Texas. They could go anywhere. They'd share clothes and give each other makeup and boyfriend advice, spend weekends drinking with impunity on some rooftop deck overlooking the city lights. They'd argue about paying for utilities and buy each other gifts when they were feeling down. She thought the future was something that unspooled like a ball of yarn in front of you, bouncing along, unimpeded.

Now she glimpses the path ahead of her and understands that whatever happens, her future is going to be one that does not contain Lulu. It hardly seems possible: she will never see her or talk to her again. Katie blinks rapidly, eyes stinging, as though she is drowning.

22

Whenever the phone rings, Katie jumps. It is never, ever for her. Her father hangs on it like a teenager, pacing, skin coated with sweat, snapping the cord impatiently. Her parents live on the phone. They talk and talk and talk, and Katie shuts it all out. Once, when they are both out of the house, Katie dials Lulu's phone number.

The phone trills in the distance until Katie remembers about caller ID and slams the handset back on the cradle. She knows she's not supposed to contact her, but she also knows that no one understands what's happening to her: she hates Lulu, but she also doesn't. It's impossible to just switch feelings off. She wants desperately to know what Lulu is thinking, to understand her, but what Katie wants doesn't matter.

School happens around her and to her—SATs, college applications. In many ways, from the outside everything is almost exactly as it was before. Except for the once languid, childish months at the lake during summertime; those are over. For the first time in Katie's living memory, the Gregorys spend the summer in West Mills. Only once do they fight about this.

"Why?" Katie yells at her parents as the two of them sit eating a cobbled-together dinner at the kitchen counter. "Why can't we go back? I don't understand!"

There are fumbled explanations; her mother flushes, her green eyes cloudy. But there is no real answer, other than the answer they all know deep down inside but cannot bring themselves to say. Eagle Lake is Chernobyl; it is fear and confusion and poison. It is Lulu and her fucked-up family and her lies.

Life cants at a strange angle but still moves forward. Nothing will stop time but death, and even then that's not certain. The West Mills house goes on the market, but it doesn't sell. Grumpy delays a planned move back to London. Sometimes he and Katie drive into the city to catch a show or to stop at the cliffside picnic spots on the Palisades Parkway to kill time (he does not come for dinner to the house anymore). They eat cheese-and-pickle sandwiches on Wonder Bread folded into wax paper that he grabs from her and crunches in his enormous fist until it shrinks into a damp ball. He tells her about England when he was a little boy. They find safe topics. She tries to dwell on happy, ordinary memories like these rather than wonder why Grumpy wants to leave them to return to England. This leaving, running away, seems like an act of cowardice to her. Gram died years ago; why does Grumpy want to leave *now*, when their world is imploding? Does he even know what's going on? He is so stoic, his back so straight inside his corduroy blazer, his neck crisscrossed with wrinkles. But they can't talk about what's happening.

Her mother takes a job at a local flower shop and is no longer at home when the kids come back from school. She works weekends, special occasions. One morning Katie comes downstairs for breakfast to find her asleep, curled up on the armchair in the living room like a little girl, a book splayed on her lap, feet in thick socks. Her mouth hangs open and her face is relaxed. She's been there all night. Katie gently touches her shoulder. "Mum," she whispers, afraid to wake her but also needing to understand what's happening.

Charlie startles. Under her eyes are thick smudges of mascara. She runs a hand over her hair, totally disoriented.

"It's time for breakfast," Katie says. "David's not up yet."

"Sorry, I . . . I fell asleep," Charlie says, rising. Her book falls to the floor.

"Mummy, are you all right? What's going to happen to Dad? Are we in trouble?"

A hundred thoughts appear to flit across her mother's face, yet Katie can't read any of them. She's tried to ask before, and all she gets is a panicky glance that quickly turns distant, blocking her. Now her mother seems to be wrestling with making up her mind about what to say.

Anger rises inside Katie. "Dad won't talk—he's all, 'Everything's fine and dandy.' And you, you're . . ."

"I'm fine, darling. We'll all be just fine, I promise." She lays a chilly hand on Katie's forearm. "We're all doing the best we can. I think it's wise to concentrate on your schoolwork and think about your own future, and Daddy and I will sort everything out in good time."

"How am I supposed to do that? How should—"

"Listen," her mother snaps. "You're not helping matters. Just get on with things, all right? Think about the things you can control. Focus on that. Now I have to go get David up, or everyone's going to be late."

Katie wants to bark something at her in response, but she notices that her mother's eyes have filled with tears, and she can't bring herself to make things worse.

Two years pass after "that summer"—the axis upon which Katie's world has been turning, the invisible yet foundational structure for all that is to come in her life. She sets the alarm for five fifteen every morning and runs through West Mills before the sun comes up. Here and there, lights flash on, and she spots a bathrobed mom at a sink, the kitchen window aflame in the steely morning, or a man bent toward a bathroom mirror, shaving. Children sleep as parents rouse themselves to face the world, and Katie runs and runs. At home and school she is lethargic, always yawning, but on her runs she is tireless, pneumatic. She gets leaner, faster. Her fear fuels her—and as time counts down (finally, finally) to the day when she will testify, she is furious at everyone. At David, now a teenager, for his red-rimmed eyes and shredded lips. At Charlie for her fortressed silence. At her father for suffering in a way she can't do anything about and for expecting too much from them all. She often dreams of her friend, of screaming at her until the veins in her neck burst, and she wakes up even angrier. Her anger lurks, voracious and annihilating, behind the door she has slammed shut, and she cannot risk letting it out.

But she needs someone. Someone who will understand; she knows she needs this, or she might go mad. Yet there is no one.

Once the trial starts, her parents drive the one and a half hours back and forth from West Mills to Blackbrooke each day, leaving the house early in the morning and returning late, eyes crazed with red tracks, blank expressions denying trouble. John tells bad jokes as Charlie lays the table and serves up lasagna or her disgusting spinach pie. His good cheer is pervasive, the exhaustion so subtle that it's not that hard to be lulled into a sense of security.

But that changes when Katie takes the stand.

In the front row, Grumpy sits, stooped, and seeing him like that makes her falter. He looks so old, his back weighed down by whatever it is he's thinking. The judge sits on a raised mahogany throne, or so it seems, surrounded by intricate woodwork scrolls and stacks of leather-bound books, wearing an impressive black robe. Judge Sonnenheim's narrow, lined face is impassive, but her eyes are kind as they track Katie's movement toward the witness stand.

At a table next to Herb and her father, facing the judge, sits a youngish woman in a pale-gray suit with severe blonde hair tied back in a ponytail: the district attorney. A man with a swarthy complexion and ludicrously thick eyelashes sits next to her, taking endless notes.

"Come on up here," the judge says to Katie, gesturing with a sweep of her bat-winged arm toward the podium. "Right here. That's it."

As Katie takes the oath, Herbert Schwartz chews his lip. She promises to tell the whole truth and nothing but the truth while Herb works on his bottom lip as though he hasn't eaten in days.

"Who are you going to look at?" Herb asks her over and over again during their practice sessions in her father's study.

"Only at you," she answers. "No one else."

"Or you can look at the DA. You can look at either of us, all right? Only at the people who are addressing you directly." While he does not raise his voice, he enunciates each word as though he is talking in caps. *Do not look at the jury.*

"Why?"

"I'm not saying they're not on your side. You just don't want to confuse matters. So it's better just to focus on whoever is talking to you."

"Okay," she says.

"Who else are you not going to look at?"

"I won't look at my father."

"Do not look at your father. Right. Who else? The plaintiff. You're not going to look at the plaintiff . . . or at her table or at anyone sitting next to her. Don't even take a glance."

"It's stupid to call her the plaintiff," Katie says.

In the courtroom, the windowpanes create a latticework of shadows that ripple along the wooden benches in a kind of underwater dance. Katie only moves her eyes fractionally to the left, and there she is, Lulu. It can't be more than a few seconds that she allows her eyes to rest on her, but it seems to last forever. No detail escapes her. Lulu looks radically different than she looked when they said goodbye on the pavement outside her apartment building years earlier. The wild, curly hair is shorn off and appears to be wet. Her face is round and naked, her complexion surprisingly sallow. She wears a blue shirtdress made with thick, shiny material. The rounded Peter Pan collar is laughably juvenile.

Her gaze is unwavering and flat. Here, in real life, she is not telegraphing Katie that she misses her, that she wishes they had a chance to talk, or that she is sorry and has made a terrible mistake. She is not asking for Katie's forgiveness, laughing about what a silly misunderstanding all this is, or blaming herself for being a drama queen.

What does it mean, that bare, untextured look? It's unbearable. Katie's heart is trapped in her mouth like a thumping animal.

Both Herb and the DA ask Katie almost identical questions. They show her picture upon picture, trying to untie the critical knot in the story: how this alleged violation could have happened with the defendant's daughter in the same room. They show her a map of the cabin's footprint. A sketch of where the den was in relation to the kitchen, the main entrance, the stairwell. Questions about the door, whether it was obscured in any way, if she remembers anyone peering into the den. There are disquisitions on the couches and how they were positioned, where she was lying, and whether she ever once turned around and looked behind her.

But everyone is focusing on all the wrong stuff. No one knows what Katie did to set it all in motion. No one knows about her stolen time with Jack at the Dolans', except whoever called them, and she never says anything to anyone about finding Lulu on the dock, how she had seemed so unlike herself, as though something had happened while

Katie and Jack were gone. The confession of her fumbling intimacy with Jack sits on the tip of her tongue, but she tells herself that no one cares, that it isn't what they want to know about, that it is what happened afterward that is important.

What does she remember about watching TV? At what point did she fall asleep? Can she recall the last scene from the movie? Did she ever turn around to see Lulu and her father behind her? Does she remember talking to her father? How many blankets were in the room? Did she fall asleep?

And she tells them what they expect to hear, what she told Herb: that she was awake the whole time. She says nothing about the vodka earlier that night or the sleepiness that overcame her in the early morning. She looks down at her bleeding cuticles, the dry, ragged skin of her fingertips, and she says what she believes to be true: nothing escaped her. It turns out that no one believes her anyway, and that lack of belief in her festers, infects her through and through—because, in her heart, she wants to be an honest person, and she thought she was. But she is not fully honest with anyone, not even with herself. It turns out she cannot give voice to uncertainty; this is not allowed. She does not need to be told this to know it is true.

So she becomes quiet; she continues her journey inward, a journey she will be on for years, alone, unable to share with anyone, not her family, not her friends, not her lover.

23

Earlier, Katie had driven to Sears and bought two slip-on sofa covers for the den, a set of plush white towels and sheets, and a base for the bed in the master bedroom. The bed frame was very heavy, and she stood for a while at the foot of the steps leading to the second floor, wondering how to get the box up there. She'd just have to drag it behind her. The washing machine rumbled steadily, drying the new sheets; the best she could find, four-hundred-thread-count sateen.

Her father called her again as she was prying open the cardboard and laying out the metal frame on the carpet of the bedroom. "I'm getting your room ready," she said. "It's going to be so nice."

"You sound tired, hon. Don't push yourself too hard."

"You're one to talk. You're the slave driver!" She laughed, glad for the break. Her skin was sticky and her muscles shaking. "I couldn't get David to help me, go figure. Too busy with concerts and the like."

"Ah, honey," her father said. "Compassion beats complaints, okay?"

"Yeah, but no one likes a skiver," she said. "No, really, I guess it's okay. At first it was weird, up here alone, but I'm getting used to it."

"Hard for me to even imagine the space. A bed I can actually stretch out in. The smell of trees and grass."

"You're not, like . . ." She hesitated. "You're not worried about coming back? Like, people being weird with you?"

He dismissed her with a grunt. "No, not at all. You get what you project, and I'm all about positivity. Moving on and moving up. I think it'll be just fine. You don't need to worry about me."

"I know. But I do."

"You're the best, sweetheart. Don't know what I'd do without you."

After the call, she sat on the floor thinking for a while, unmoving. A thick, moted ray of sunlight came in from the open window; the June air outside was far warmer than the air inside the cabin. She stuck her bare foot into the ray of light and let the sun warm her toes. Time for a break. Time to get outside.

The clubhouse was closed, of course; it would be a few weeks before the volunteer committee swept it out, wiping down the floors with Pine-Sol and clearing the mousetraps. It seemed desolate without the cries of children playing in the sand or music coming from the bar. Cupping her hands around her eyes, Katie peered in just as she had the night of the square dance. The shelves, still laden with paperbacks. Speakers in the corner. A pile of chairs stacked high. The old piano, missing some keys. Incredible—a place where nothing ever changed.

Surprisingly, the lake water was not unbearably cold. In the summers her mother used to swim every day unless there was a lightning storm. Charlie often wore a crocheted orange bikini she dug up from the bottom of a musty drawer. Against her skin, the color made her freckles stand out. It always looked as though it might just slip off her, resting so lightly on her delicate bones. When she emerged, it stayed wet for hours, and she would lounge in the sunshine, leaning back on one elbow and dragging on her Pall Mall, waiting and waiting for the threads to dry.

Katie left her clothes in a pile by the maple that leaned over the water's edge like an elderly man peering into a well. Once she started swimming, she couldn't seem to stop. The blackness was like a weight over her body, and even though it pressed on her, it could not contain her, and with the movement of her arms she propelled herself through it, on and on. The first gulp of air was painful; her hair streamed free behind her, her scalp numb.

The buoy was gone, but she swam far out to the other side, heading for the imaginary turning point, ignoring the pain that began in her chest and reached down to her knees. She thought of the boy Brad and how he would swim to the buoy and back without ever seeming to stop for breath. Under her feet she felt something every now and then and didn't know what it was—fish, turtles, snakes?—and she kicked violently, her breath only half-formed. It was both freedom and constriction, joy and pain.

Lifting her head for a gulp of air, she saw that she was about halfway back, the clubhouse crouching on the shore, low and green, the maple tiny and misshapen and—something moving in front of it. An animal or a person? A few strokes more, another gulping breath: yes, it was a man pacing on the flagstones.

He was very tall, his body a familiar *S* curve, light hair ruffled. *My God*—it was Jack Benson.

He was as familiar to her as was the shape of her own face, the curve of her brows, the topography of her hands; she would have recognized him in a crowded room or far away at the end of an empty train platform. The pace of her swimming slowed as numbers crowded her head. Almost ten years since she had last seen him. Two unread letters from him. He was the first boy who had seen her completely naked. She was almost twenty-five years old, which made him twenty-six, or perhaps twenty-seven; she wasn't sure. It was less than forty-eight hours ago that she had read the testimony he'd given at her father's trial. How many times had she called him since Friday—how many times had he not answered her call?

Jack stopped pacing as she drew closer. She dropped her feet and touched the gooey soil at the bottom of the lake.

"Hey there," he called out. He wore an army jacket, faded to a pale green with epaulets that might look foolish on a smaller man, the kind of jacket bought at a department store, not a thrift shop. Blunt-cut light-blond hair, longer at the crown. He could be a Swede or a Dane, an elegant Nordic type with defined features. He pushed the hair off his forehead in a self-conscious gesture she recognized immediately, and in an instant, that simple gesture stripped away the last decade.

"Jesus Christ," Katie said.

"Sorry to surprise you. I thought we should talk?" He bent forward slightly in an effort to camouflage his height; he had done that when he was a kid too.

"Something wrong with just calling me back?"

"Yeah, but, you know." His eyes took her in, shifted to the lake, the ground, back to her face, her mouth. She remembered his nervous energy, the way he always looked as though he were about to propel himself forward. His face had thickened, but his eyes were the same, slightly hooded, with hazel irises surrounded by a dark ring. "Calling just seemed—I don't know, Katie; that call was so bad. So uncomfortable . . ."

She gave him a rueful smile. "And this is better?"

The tension seeped from his features, and he smiled back. "You said you were up here. Figured I'd check if you were still here and come see the old place again. Thought it'd be better to talk face-to-face." He stuck his hands into the pockets of his jeans. "And, uh. I guess I wanted to see you again too."

Katie's head and shoulders were peeking out from the water, but the rest of her body remained submerged. There was some water in her ear, and it was so cold it hurt the inside of her head. "Throw me that towel, would you?" she asked, pointing toward the wooden deck, empty of its usual tables and umbrellas. A scruffy towel lay where she'd dropped it.

"Uh," he said, squinting and looking around himself, first in one direction and then in the other, "it's going to get wet, isn't it?"

She could see that having him throw her the towel was ludicrous. Her heart clattered as though she were fifteen again, shy and fierce at the same time. Of course it was ludicrous to have him throw her the towel while she was in the water. While his back was turned, she approached the low wall that ran along this part of the lake and put both hands flat onto the concrete, making an awkward little jump to haul herself out. Through the wet cotton bra her nipples stood out, sharp as stone chips. She grabbed the towel. Her jeans stuck to the damp skin of her thighs. Jack kept his back turned to her as she dressed. He flexed his shoulders, and the material on his jacket shone where he stretched. It struck her that she had never seen Zev fidgety like this, that his energy was static compared to Jack's.

"I just want to say I'm really sorry," Jack said. "You know? About everything."

"Don't know why you should be sorry."

"There wasn't even any evidence," Jack said. "It's crazy that you can be convicted without evidence. I didn't think that would ever happen."

"Yeah, well," Katie said. "That's justice for you." She felt totally unprepared for this conversation, a little resentful, even. The knowledge of what he'd said in court throbbed in her head, but there was no way to go from "How are you?" to "What were you *thinking*?" How could she ask him what he thought he'd seen? Did he realize that he was probably partially to blame for her father's conviction?

There was no way to broach the subject, not right now. Damp and chilled, she struggled to get her clothes back on.

"Haven't been back here since then," Jack said.

She straightened up and ran her hands over her wet hair, aware that she probably looked pale and thin. "Neither have I." They walked toward their two cars, parked in the dusty lot behind the clubhouse.

His was a small black Mercedes. She glanced at him quickly. A Realtor. It just seemed so incongruous.

"The lake—it's still so beautiful; it almost hurts," Jack said. "That summer wasn't all bad, was it?"

They were in the open, yet it was as though they'd been thrown into a tiny room together. Goose bumps appeared on her damp skin, and she hugged her arms around herself. This was so not what she'd been expecting.

24

Back at the cabin, Katie headed upstairs to warm up under the shower while Jack took a seat in the living room. Under the needles of hot water, her skin was aflame. Her fingers seemed almost to belong to someone else, so alert was her skin to the brush of fingertips slick with soap. It was like covering her body with rubbing alcohol. After she threw on a pair of jeans and a big sweatshirt, she stared at herself in the mirror. Her eyes were bright, clear from her cold swim, her face bleached of color except a vivid pink on her cheeks.

She wondered how much she'd changed or stayed the same over the years. When she knew Jack, her hair had been longer, and then for a few years she had shorn it off completely; now it was shoulder length and wavy. Still blonde, but lacking the glamorous tousle so popular now; it was just sort of plain. She was aware of not being a great beauty, though men often catcalled her in the streets, almost always to tell her to *smile*, or *cheer up*! As always, and without intending to, she clung to her deep sense of interiority—it was this, she thought, that made people feel excluded. But not everyone. Those who loved her, understood her like her father did—they could bridge the gap between who she seemed and who she really was. She might appear to be cold or distant, but who could know what was going on in her head? Running a finger over her upper lip, she thought about Jack sitting downstairs in the flesh, wondered whether he felt he knew her the way she felt she knew him.

Their story had taken on a different shape in her mind since she'd discovered that he'd tried to write to her. They had barely even known each other, but it hadn't felt that way. To her, he was a boy she loved. There was no question of whether it was real love or not—she probably loved him more *because* she hardly knew him, because the promise of him had been allowed to bloom and live on in her imagination. They'd fallen for each other before all kids had cell phones, before social media existed, and afterward it had been so very easy to lose sight of one another, as though they'd lived on different continents. In the fall, when the memory of his hands on her body and the heat of his tongue in her mouth was still vivid, she carried the knowledge of their intimacy with her like a secret at parties filled with panting, uncertain teenagers. Among them afterward, she'd been infused with a kind of pride; she felt powerful and beautiful in a way no one could even guess at.

Of course, after she found out about her father's arrest, her life was recast. At those weekend parties, she became desperate to make some kind of concrete connection. She needed to feel real, alive. She would start off eager, ready to be daring, to prove that she could do whatever she wanted, whenever she wanted, to hell with it all—but as soon as a boy started breathing too hard, or she felt the dull thrust of his hard-on against her thigh, she'd back away.

She went into the kitchen and poured two glasses of wine, wishing she had a bottle of tequila or some ice-cold vodka or something strong that would smudge the sharp edges of her apprehension. Jack sat with his back to her, and she stood quietly at the lintel, a glass in each hand, knowing that this was one of those before-and-after moments. Life was lurching forward in a direction she hadn't anticipated. Her numbers were not adding up, and her trajectory was changing.

She held out a glass to Jack, but he shook his head. "On the wagon, two years already," he said. He smiled, but it looked pained, as though he'd practiced in front of a mirror and decided that it might do the trick but wasn't entirely sure.

"Oh. Right," she said, putting his glass on the old side table and taking an inadvertently enormous gulp from hers. She coughed. "Sorry to hear that. Want something else?"

"Ah, it's okay," he said. "Long story."

She was curious but didn't want to ask. "So my dad gets out soon"—she studied him to gauge his reaction—"from Wallkill. He got six years."

"They didn't let him out for good behavior? You're shitting me."

She shrugged, her neck stiff. "There's no such thing as good behavior," she said. Maybe she could get to the bottom of what he thought he saw. But something held her back: fear, perhaps, or propriety. "And I guess, I don't know. I guess he got in some trouble, helping out some of the other guys in there he wasn't supposed to fraternize with. You know my dad, always trying to teach someone something."

"Christ," Jack said, knitting his silky brows. "When's the last time you saw him?"

"I go up there once a month, something like that. He counts on me." A pause hung between them until it became bloated and burst. "It feels really weird that you're here, Jack. How come you never called me back? On Friday?"

"I—you gave me the scare of my life, Katie. I mean, I hadn't heard from you in like ten years. When you never answered my letters, I figured you—"

"I never got them," she broke in. "I mean, not until just now. I found them last week. I've been clearing the place out because Dad's coming."

"You never got them?" he asked, straightening up.

"Nope." Her collarbones flared with heat, sweat prickling at the base of her neck. "I mean, I didn't even know you testified at the trial, Jack. Did you realize that? That I had no idea?"

"Look, I didn't know anything. I was, like, totally in the dark about everything! I knew he was convicted. I knew what I read in the papers."

"Yeah, the fucking newspapers," Katie said, taking another sip of her wine. "That's been fun." As they talked, they began to assess each other more openly. His cheeks were covered in stubble, light and soft, concentrated around the chin. If it weren't for his expression, the serious look in his eyes, he could have passed as much younger. "What happened to your parents?" she asked. She'd only met his father once; she remembered him as a huge man with shins as big as dolphins. His mother was a beauty, friendly in a noncommittal sort of way. Always checking her reflection in the clubhouse windows.

"Nothing, really," Jack said. "Don't see them all that much." They began catching each other up, and she started to relax—he told her he had gone to UVA on a tennis scholarship and then lost his spot on the team after a hazing incident at his fraternity. For two years after graduating, Jack moved into his parents' Upper West Side apartment. His "forgotten years," he called them, during which his parents ignored him so effectively that he got away with snorting cocaine in the marble-tiled bathroom, leaving white dust and empty baggies on the countertops that the housekeeper cleaned up without complaint or comment.

"Ugh," Katie said. "Sounds bad."

"What about you, after the conviction?" he asked. "Didn't you freak? How does someone even deal with that?"

Briefly, she thought about Zev and how she dealt with the whole thing by never talking about it, but then she tucked that thought away. After draining her wine, she held it up, the pinkish stain on the glass viscous in the dying light from the window. "This stuff helped, though it was mostly tequila back then," she said, choosing to wrap it all up in a neat package, when it had been anything but neat. She had logged so many miles, sometimes in the middle of the night, running and running. Yes, there had been booze and boys—pitiful, fumbling attempts at intimacy and rage-filled, drunken fucks that had left her reeling. But there had been so much else: time within herself, unpredictable, dissipating and then clumping like chalk in water. "Forgotten years," she said. "Yeah. I know what you mean."

"To think of how much time I wasted." Jack pulled his mouth into an exaggerated frown. "And you never get any of it back."

She was disappointed with herself for not being able to open up, as she knew she should, but she felt so weary. "Hey, can you help me for a second?" she asked him, standing, stretching, her thigh muscles igniting with fatigue. "Set up this thing upstairs?"

The narrow staircase to the second floor was awash in cooling shadows that swallowed her as she ascended. Jack almost bumped into her at the top of the stairs, and she jumped, as skittish as a deer. She remembered the Dolans' house, the absence of moonlight on the woods.

"In here," she said, going into the master bedroom, the only room left that she hadn't yet finished. "No one's been here in a long-ass time. What a sorry, sad little place. But not when I'm done with it," she said, pushing her sleeves up to her elbows.

"What's that?" he asked, pointing to her arm. "Noticed it earlier, at the lake."

A few inches above her a wrist, a tattoo of a sprig of blueberries surrounded by leaves circled her forearm. The blueberries were larger than life, saturated in light and shade, dark powder blue, ciel and Egyptian blue, the leaves a bright pop of green.

"We used to go blueberry picking together," she said, "me and my dad." Under the intensity of his gaze, Katie began to falter. She discovered that she couldn't tell the story, so she didn't.

Jack folded his body into three long sections, bending at the waist and knees. They knelt to dismantle and then reassemble the pieces of the bed frame one by one. They danced around each other, careful not to touch, his smell—Old Spice, soap?—filling the air. Lying on his back, he inched his head under the rails and tightened the metal screws laboriously, his legs thrust out, endless dark-blue jeans. They slowly resumed their conversation, small talk about work, and Katie ribbed him about being a Realtor.

He would have none of it. "Pays the bills," he said, "and I have a decent apartment on the East Side." She felt a kind of guilty pleasure staring at him, watching his eyes light up and become subdued, noticing the creases by his eyebrows, the shadow under his cheekbones, the shift of muscle over bone. His boyishness, a reminder of how things were, moved her.

"So, um, Jack," she said as they sat, finally, on the floor on either side of the enormous frame. Over the last hour she'd managed to relax a bit, but now that she had stopped moving, she felt jumpy and uncomfortable again. She had to ask—she had to finally hear him say, in his own words, what he'd glimpsed through the window. Had he been telling the truth when he'd claimed he didn't really know what he'd seen? Was he protecting her? "I didn't know you came back to the cabin that night. After the storm."

"The lawyers, those guys scared the living daylights out of me," he said, his eyes with their strange ring of darkness considering her carefully. "I was so immature—people thought because I was tall, I was, like, a man already. But I was just a kid. They said, you know, I wasn't supposed to tell you anything. Call or write or anything."

"They told me the exact same thing," she said. "But I, uh. I really need to know what you think you saw."

"I told them everything I saw, on the stand. I wasn't holding anything back."

"So you still don't know if you saw . . . if they were . . . ?" Her breath caught in her throat. It seemed that so much was riding on this moment, on his answer. She so badly wanted him to have seen nothing.

He shook his head. "Sorry. I wanted to be the one who could fix everything, make it all go away. But I couldn't."

"I tried that too." For a long moment, they looked at each other, unblinking. "Told them I'd been awake all night long, that I hadn't slept a wink," she admitted. "And the thing is, it wasn't really true. I don't think so at least."

"Wow."

"Yeah. I know." She had to move. She jumped up and leaned over, and together they hauled the mattress onto the frame and pushed the whole contraption back against the wall. "I'll get the bedding," she said.

As they stretched the cotton sheets onto the bed, neatly tucking in the corners, he kept talking. He told her he'd wanted to say goodbye again, that he'd freaked out after she left the clubhouse, thinking he'd miss seeing her the next morning for sure. Once the top sheet was smoothed down, she dragged the comforter over, and they spread it out, neatly folding the top down to reveal the two plumped pillows.

"Okay," she said. "Done. Thanks."

They each drank two enormous glasses of water in the kitchen, their gulps loud and vulnerable against the steady whir of the electric clock on the wall. All this time, and that clock had never stopped running. It marked the passage of every second, every minute. It was past six o'clock, when she usually spoke with her father, but they'd agreed not to talk tonight. It hardly seemed possible he'd be getting out next week. There was so much more she wanted to know, but she could sense that Jack was pulling away, that he would tell her in a minute that he had to get back to the city, that he had a dinner or some kind of appointment, an engagement he couldn't break. And she was tired to the bone, reeling from the day.

She put her glass in the sink. There was one more question she wanted to ask, but her hand was shaking. "Do you think she was lying, Jack? You think Lulu actually made the whole thing up?"

When he didn't answer right away, she turned to look at him and was surprised to see his face suspended in a kind of painful hesitation. His expression was open, as though he was about to say something.

There was an entire story playing out behind his eyes, those intelligent, soft eyes; he was always waiting to see other people's reactions, gauging his impact and adjusting himself accordingly, like a chameleon. "I'm sorry," he said finally. "I really don't know what I think."

That wasn't the answer she'd been hoping for. As they said goodbye, promising to meet up again in the city, he tried to hug her, but she was stiff and unyielding. When he turned around on the front stoop one last time, his eyes did not stop communicating with her, even though something was holding him back and he was not speaking his mind.

25

John Gregory is stoic, the faint smile on his face like a placeholder for better things to come. He sits at his lawyer's table in the Deloitte County courtroom, the top of his head glistening under the harsh overheads. Local TV news cameras aim at him, perched on tripods. The cameramen swivel on their hips, bored. Their eyes land on the Gregory family as it enters, calculating which shots are worth getting. The air in the courtroom is stale, the hum of air-conditioning resoundingly absent. Katie has dressed so carefully, praying that it will make some kind of difference: if the judge remembers how nice they all are—this man's family that loves him, stands by him—maybe she'll give him a light sentence, let him stay at home while awaiting his appeal. In the oppressive heat, her mother's borrowed silk shirt clings like a damp spider's web to the rise of Katie's breasts; she plucks at the material with thumb and forefinger and surveys the courtroom.

Amid the apple faces, shiny and upturned, there are four or five seats across the room that remain conspicuously empty. As before, Herb has warned Katie not to look for Lulu, but as soon as she enters, she begins scanning the room for her. It isn't a conscious decision; she just does it. Eyes strafing the rows, searching—she sees nothing but the emptiness of those seats. The vacuum caused by Lulu's absence leaves Katie disoriented.

It's only now that she realizes that she thought there would be some kind of final reckoning between them. Last time they exchanged glances, it was Lulu who dominated, telegraphing her separateness. She seemed *done*, done with Katie, done with the Gregorys, whereas Katie had been expecting some brief connection, a thread that bound them. Now that she sees the empty chairs, she understands that there will be no reckoning. She will not have a chance to see Lulu, to convey with a glance and a squaring of the shoulders that she will not allow this to destroy her. That whatever Lulu has done and for whatever reason, Katie and her family will forge ahead.

And yet Lulu is not here, and nothing passes between them.

"Katie," her mother says under her breath, spitting out the *t*. "Stop fidgeting, will you?"

Charlie's dress bunches up in folds around her narrow hips. Her body is small, thinner than ever before. She's tied her brown hair back at the nape of her neck. Her skin is as pale as skim milk. Tortoiseshell reading glasses perch on her nose, which is strange because she usually never wears them in public and certainly not when she isn't reading.

Twice Grumpy has laid an enormous, wrinkled hand on Katie's thigh in an attempt to still her quivering. It takes everything in her to resist pulling away from him, lifting that concrete hand off her leg. Her love for her grandfather is rooted in the idea of his invincibility, and seeing him cowed throws her.

David sits on the bench swinging his feet above the scuffed wood floor. In his blue blazer and red tie, he could be attending a confirmation or a wedding. He is thirteen, his face an angry terrain of pimples. The tender flesh around his lips is brutally swollen and cracked. It shines with Vaseline.

Judge Sonnenheim enters, and quiet falls over the room. She is far prettier than Katie remembers from when the trial ended a few weeks earlier. Her lips are brownish red, her hair soft and styled away from her face. Every eye in the room tracks her movement. She calls the room to order and begins talking. People are standing up and sitting down again. Her mouth with its painted lips opens and closes. Katie's forehead is burning up. The sun on her back brands her through her shirt. Sweat gathers at her waistband, under her armpits.

Herb has sent the judge dozens of letters from supporters. They tell of how John Gregory runs a Saturday chess club for public school kids. That his jokes turn run-of-the-mill backyard barbecues into parties. That he babysits for neighborhood children, cooks for his family, washes their laundry, teases his wife mercilessly because he adores her. All this is true; all this is her father.

But as soon as the judge starts talking, Katie understands that none of this makes any difference at all. This judge doesn't care about her family one bit. Not about her little brother or her, her mother or Grumpy—and least of all about her father. The reason the judge is wearing lipstick today is because of the television cameras. This is not about dinners and laundry; this is about making a statement.

"I recognize that the defendant is considered an upstanding member of his community," the judge is saying. "But one must consider the lasting damage he has done—the psychological trauma. I have a letter here, a statement from the victim . . ."

This is really happening, and it is not going to go as her father or Herb promised.

" . . . one must consider the age difference. The victim was only fourteen years old, three years younger than the age of consent in the state of New York. There is an age gap of over thirty years. The defendant groomed this child over a period of time, seducing her into . . ."

But the words are not adding up. For one, Lulu wasn't fourteen years old, was she? Katie tries to remember: her birthday is sometime in September. Is it possible—is it actually possible that all along Lulu let her believe they were the same age, when really she is a whole year younger? But this isn't so surprising, really, considering how much Lulu talked and how little she ever really revealed.

" . . . the request for a stay of the sentence, pending appeal, is denied. Given the severity of the crime, I sentence John G. Gregory to six years in state prison, with five years' probation."

The DA, with her wrenched-back hair, jumps to her feet. Her eyes dance as people pat her on the back. Everyone at her table stands. Everyone everywhere stands. People are moving, talking, crying. Security guards in white shirts and black pants surround her father. Tears run down Grumpy's cheeks. The crowd begins jostling around them. Charlie's glasses slip down her nose, and she does not push them back up. She nudges forward through the crowd with one shoulder and heads over to her husband.

Raising both her hands, she holds onto the sides of John's face. They look at each other. They kiss on the lips. The red lights on the cameras pulse.

Herb whispers into her father's ear. John empties his pockets out, depositing his wallet and keys and some coins into his lawyer's cupped hands. Through the murmurs, the breathing, the shuffling of heels on the floor comes the unambiguous, elemental thrum of the air conditioner finally turning on.

Her father places his hands behind his back, and one of the guards reaches over and clicks a pair of handcuffs onto his wrists and leads him away.

She will never again see him in the kitchen of their home, preparing breakfast. He will not lean over her for a quick peck on the cheek or smooth her ponytail with his fingers or tell her to put away her shoes. There will be no vacations together, no movie nights or family dinners, ever again. The future lies ahead of her, the years when she will become a woman, and this man will be absent from it all. The hole this will leave is as gigantic as a crater, the shocking emptiness of which rings in her ears as though she has been struck across the face.

26

The last days of high school. A cluster of parents lingering by the secretary's office clamp their mouths shut—snap! snap! snap! snap!—as Katie walks through the front doors. She stares at them, daring them to say something, and they cast their eyes downward. *Good! Fuck you too*, she thinks. The boys just return her cold looks, and while a few snicker or make crude gestures, they aren't as embarrassed by their contempt for her as the girls are.

Girls avoid her, their eyes filled with pious false pity. She senses a curiosity so intense it borders on erotic. Their faces flush as they lean in toward each other at lunch, talking breathlessly. "Was she, like, pretty?" Katie can just imagine them asking. "Are her parents getting divorced?" "Do you guys think it ever happened before?" "Did she hear them *doing it*?" "Wonder if she'll go to jail, to, like, you know—visit him?" They've read the articles, seen the local news. This is by far the most exciting thing that has ever happened to them.

The family's life is suddenly smaller, trapping them in a tightening mesh. There are all these new rules, this pretense they are supposed to keep up. The new certainty they live with is that they can't count on anyone or anything except themselves. Katie's father believes that together, they can be strong against the screwed-up world—but the truth is that they are all on their own, and it is lonely, like being the only human being left alive on a ravaged earth.

She's in a suspended state of being until the day she visits her father in prison, some weeks later. There are only a few other visitors. In the waiting room, the chairs are the same type of molded plastic used in school lunchrooms and are bolted to the floor. A thin girl sits hunched over, playing with the cuffs of her sweatshirt. At first glance she doesn't seem much older than Katie, but there are streaks of gray in her dirty-blonde hair.

Waiting to see her father is like taking a test for which Katie doesn't know the rules. It is a medium security prison north of Blackbrooke, in Deloitte County. From the outside, the concrete building seems to go on forever, surrounded by barbed wire fences and spotlights as big as the ones used to light football stadiums. There is overcrowding, her mother explains, and that's why Daddy is here; as soon as things are sorted out, he'll be moved to a minimum security prison. But that will never happen.

At home, Charlie is mostly expressionless and quiet, reading obsessively, but in the prison waiting room her skin assumes some color again, and her movements become brisk and efficient. She pushes ahead with a sense of purpose, whereas Katie feels more and more lethargic, incapable of agency. The lockers require tokens, which Charlie produces from the bottom of her handbag. She folds up her long cashmere sweater and places it in the locker and tells David and Katie to do the same with their jackets. David is operating at half speed, which Katie finds infuriating.

At the yellowing pass-through window in the front of the room, Charlie gives her name and hands over her driver's license to a female guard. Her mother's face is gaunt, the freckles almost entirely gone. Sometimes, when David or Katie ask her something, she appears not to hear them at all. Maybe she is taking pills or is depressed. But in the middle of the night when Katie crawls into her bed, Charlie doesn't kick her out. In her own bed, Katie feels as though darkness is pressing in on her like a thousand heavy palms, and when that happens, she can't understand which way is up and which way is down. In her parents' bed, her body is heavy against the sheets, weighed down and substantial again. In the mornings, when she opens her eyes, she buries her head in her dad's pillow and breathes in his scent. In just a few weeks she'll be in college—gone. She's too old to be in her parents' bed.

The idea of leaving home is also the only thing that is keeping her from losing her mind. Over the summer, she changes her name on all her paperwork; she's becoming someone new, someone with no history. As much as shucking off her father's name gives her a hollowed-out feeling in her gut, she has to do it—if she can't talk about these things at home, she certainly can't talk about them anywhere else. And one day it will all be over, he will be free again, and they'll be able to forget this ever happened. It's just a matter of getting from here to there.

A middle-aged woman puts coins into the slot in a locker, turns the key, and then opens it. One by one, she slips gold rings off her fingers. Four . . . six . . . seven. Then a bracelet.

"This is okay, right?" she asks her husband, pointing to her necklace.

He scans her neck: a gold cross on a thin chain hangs on the tired skin above her breasts. "Yeah," he grunts. He is wearing a smaller cross on a thicker chain.

Katie wonders who they are visiting. The woman's face is heavily made up, pale-blue shadow and purple eyeliner. Her crisp linen shirt is tucked into black slacks. She pulls a rhinestone-studded belt from the loops of her pants. Her movements are assured. There is no trace of conflict or embarrassment in her expression, yet her face falls when she catches Katie's eye. A guard comes to the back door and calls out: "Honey Rivera! David Price! Marsha Atkinson! Charlotte Gregory! David Gregory!" he says. "Katherine Gregory!" The six of them stand obediently.

A female guard lifts Katie's hair off her shoulders with one hand and runs her fingers along the ridge of her back. "Shake it out, would you?"

she demands. "Take those off," she adds, pointing to the little earrings in the extra holes Katie punctured into her ear with a blunt needle during a long night when she and Lulu were bored.

The older lady yanks off her cowboy boots and puts them through the scanner. "It's Trish today," she whispers to Katie as they pass along to the next barrier. "She's real picky. Sometimes they let you through without a problem; sometimes they don't." She shrugs and smiles, high wattage but pained.

Katie wants to ask her who she is visiting. A son? A nephew? A father? What was he accused of? Does she know whether he is really guilty or not?

Katie has so many questions for her father. When he is outside his cell, does he have his arms pulled back behind him, his wrists cuffed together? Do the shower stalls have doors or curtains? Is he afraid of the other men? Are any of the guards nice? If it's hard for Katie to sleep, what is it like in here—can he fall asleep at night? Is he allowed to take his pills? Is he afraid when it's time to shower? Does it make him feel better or worse to know that guards are watching him when he is naked? And where does he get shampoo? Does he want her to send him his Selsun Blue extra strong dandruff shampoo? Does he miss his rum and tonics? What does he do all day?

Her blood seems laced with caffeine as they walk in a pack across the jail yard. Something about being surrounded by barbed wire and gates and fences and buckled concrete makes her want to run very fast. She looks up at the rows of gray windows overlooking the yard. Are they allowed to smoke? What if they don't want to come outside? Are there ever prisoners who just want to stay in their cells all day?

The thick glass in the cubicles is milky and scratched. The ubiquitous phones, attached to the wall. The bars clang shut to lock each inmate into a booth, where they sit on a stool bolted to the floor and pick up the phone. The hands that reach up to touch the glass, leaving oily fingerprints. The guards pacing up and down, beating on the bars every now and then to make sure they are locked.

Prisoners come in one by one. *Where is Dad?* she frets. He isn't coming. David takes a seat next to his mother, and Katie remains standing. Clammy palms, questions swirling. Everyone else is murmuring into their handsets, leaning toward the partitions as though this will help them make their point.

And then there he is. His face is curiously blank, but when he sees the children, it lights up. His hair is longer than usual. As he sits down, the guard slams the bars shut and locks them behind him. There are only two phones on their side of the glass. David turns away, not ready to talk yet. His chapped lips are cracked and scabbed, and he licks them. Just looking at those broken lips, swollen and pink around the edges, is painful. She wishes he were a little kid again so she could wrap him in her arms, but she can't protect him anymore.

John grins at his wife. "Charlie Gregory," he says, "you are so fine. I swear you are looking younger by the minute."

"Stop trying to flatter me," she says.

"I'm not trying," he says. "I'm just doing."

So much small talk. This and that, none of it important. Washing machines and letters, car maintenance and a broken doorbell.

"What's the matter, Katie? Cat got your tongue?" John asks his daughter. He's telling a story about helping an inmate write a letter. His eyes are sharp, but his face is relaxed, as though he's waiting for them to get some joke that he is enjoying. "These guys are harmless."

"It's *prison*, Dad," she says under her breath.

"What's that?" he asks. "Speak up, will you?"

"Nothing." And then, giving in to the need for small talk, "So who's Gus, then?"

"Nice-enough guy but can't string two words together. I helped him with a letter to the appeal board. Basic stuff—I mean, no English degree necessary." John laughs. He asks how the summer is going, and Katie tells him everything is fine, great; that is what he wants to hear, after all. She doesn't tell him about the girl who's been in her class since second grade who burst into tears when she bumped into her at CVS and then looked so relieved when Katie didn't ask her what was the matter. There's no mention of stomach cramps or sleepless night. Or the dreams, the ruinous dreams.

"Come on, Katie," John insists. "Talk, will you? I want to hear what's going on out there."

"I beat Grumpy at chess," David says, but John doesn't appear to hear him.

All Katie can really think about are the endless questions she has that she knows she's not supposed to ask. Does everyone have to use the same toothpaste, or does he have his own tube? Is he allowed cream in his coffee in the mornings? What does he do if he's hungry in the middle of the night?

"Charlie, listen," her father says. "Can you leave us be for a minute?"

Her mother's eyes narrow; she wants the kids to entertain John, make him laugh, and help them all pretend this isn't really happening.

"I can't just get up and leave, John," she says. "You know how it works."

"Take a little walk, then, would you?"

She hesitates but then stands up and strides out of the booth toward the guard. Their heads come together, and she murmurs something, and he shakes his head.

"Katie Gregory, you wipe that sorry look off your face, do you hear me?" John hisses over the phone. "I want you to sleep in your own bed, okay? You stop getting into your mother's bed like a baby. You're eighteen years old, for Chrissake."

The blood drains from her face. David kicks lightly against the floor with his sneaker. "Dad," he says, his voice an octave too high. "Come on."

"I'm counting on you kids to keep things going at home, like, you know, normal. You've got to trust that everything's going to work out all right. The appeal looks good, really, really good. It's just a matter of time, and if I can suck it up in here, then you guys can too. No wallowing, okay? No crying, no complaining."

"I wasn't complaining," Katie says.

"Yeah," David says, his liquid eyes so innocent, "she wasn't!"

"Promise me you'll pull yourself together, Katie. Be brave," her father says. "Promise."

It is that word—*promise*—that strikes her to the core. It is her constant ballast in the years to come, a flashing beacon that leads her way. Now she knows what to do. Her brain is plugged back in, her circuits firing: she can promise her father to be brave; she can try her very best, always, not to be just another disappointment.

27

Very late at night after Jack left, Katie called Zev in Spain. She had been lying in bed in the dark, unable to sleep. An early riser, he picked up immediately, his image emerging on her screen like a man underwater. Half his face was covered in foam, and the other half was clean shaven. "Wasn't expecting it to be you," he said, wiping a towel over his mouth. "Isn't it the middle of the night?"

"Yeah, but I know you've got your talk today. I wanted to wish you luck," she said. She was so desperate to talk to someone. "And I'm lonely. Wishing you were here."

"Well, me too. What are you wearing?" he said, grinning.

She smirked back at him. "You don't have time." She turned on her side and propped the phone up on her pillow. "Are you nervous?"

"Not really. And it seems the less I care what people think, the more they want to hear what I say, so it'll probably be a smash hit."

"Thanks for the picture. Nobody's ever drawn me before. I'm flattered."

"So you should be. I'm a very famous artist." He sat down on something, maybe the edge of the bathtub, and took a sip from a small ceramic cup. "How is the countryside? Seen any bears?"

"It's okay," she said. "To be honest, it's a bit strange. It's—uh, I grew up here, and I haven't been back in a long time. A really long time. Last time I was up here, things were, um, kind of complicated."

"Complicated . . ."

She smiled. "Yes, and I'll tell you all about it when you're back. In the meantime, shave that hairy face of yours, and go slay them." After they hung up, she felt a little better, but only a little. After all, now there was even more that she wasn't telling him. And no matter what she did to distract herself, she could not stop thinking about when she was going to see Jack again.

The next morning, she put her bag into the Datsun and gave the house one last walk-through. The rooms were tidy, years of neglect dusted away. New curtains, throw blankets, hangers in the closet, soap at the sink. A few nonperishables in the cupboards.

She drove back to the courthouse in Blackbrooke. Since Jack's testimony was inconclusive and she hadn't gotten a straight answer from him, maybe she'd learn something from Lulu's testimony and her father's. The same ladies who had been there on Friday let her in with no fuss. It took them a few minutes to get her the transcripts, and then they left her alone. Thumbing through the document, Katie went straight to Lulu's testimony.

Direct Examination

Q. Good morning. Can you state your name for the court, please?

A. Loretta Henderson. People call me Lulu.

Q. That's with two *t*'s, is that correct? L-o-r-e-t-t-a?

A. Yes, that's correct.

A barrage of questions followed about her schoolwork. (She was a B student.) Was she in band? (Yes.) How many instruments did she play? (One, badly.) How many siblings did she have? (None.) There were dashes all over the transcript, which must have meant pauses in the testimony (what was *happening* during those silences?). As Katie read, a middle-aged man with disheveled hair hovered by the door as though to ask her what she was up to, but he disappeared as soon as she looked up.

> A. Then, um, he—then all of a sudden, he started to put, or he started—we started kissing, and he started to put his finger in my—
>
> Q. Let's slow down. You were kissing? He leaned toward you on the couch, and you began kissing?
>
> A. Yes, that's correct.
>
> Q. He initiated this? John Gregory did?
>
> A. Yes.
>
> Q. And you didn't stop him?
>
> A. No.
>
> —
>
> —
>
> —
>
> —

—

Q. Okay. That's fine. You just have to tell us what happened, bit by bit, so we understand, okay?

A. Um. Okay. Could I have a drink of water, please?

Q. So you were saying he kissed you.

A. That's right.

Q. What happened then? Did he talk to you?

A. I don't know.

Q. You don't know, or you don't remember?

A. I don't remember.

Q. Okay, continue.

A. One time, he was saying, "Do you like this?" So he asked me if I liked it. And I think he said, "This is how it's done, gentle."

Q. What did he mean by that? What was he referring to?

A. I . . . I don't know.

Q. Okay. And then what happened?

A. After we started kissing, and then, it—he put his
fingers in my vagina.

At that word, a flush prickled up Katie's neck. She could not find
her breath, her rhythm; she began counting to herself. Breathe in;
breathe out. Slow down and count. It would be okay, she thought. She
just had to read the words, and she could make up her mind about what
they meant later.

Q. Were you wearing anything? Did you have clothes
on?

A. Yes, I was wearing a dress. My clothes had gotten
wet, earlier, in the rain.

Q. So you changed into different clothes?

A. Yes, and we got a blanket. Um, he got—there was a
blanket, and, um, he covered me with it.

Q. So you were covered, partially, with a blanket. And
then what happened? He touched you under your
clothes?

—

—

—

Q. Would you like to have a minute?

212

THE COURT. Are you okay? Take a deep breath.

THE WITNESS. Yeah.

THE COURT. You can take a break if you like, but we have to get through this.

The WITNESS. Yeah. I am good.

Katie stood up and shucked off her sweater. Her body was on fire and her throat parched. She stumbled around the corridors, avoiding eye contact with anyone, until she found an old-fashioned drinking fountain at the end of a narrow hallway on the ground floor. The water was lukewarm and tasted of metal. She gulped it down and splashed it over her face.

Q. You were wearing a dress, you said. What kind of dress?

A. Like a big T-shirt thing, kind of loose.

Q. So it was flimsy, a light kind of dress? Like you might sleep in?

A. Yes.

Q. And were you wearing underwear?

A. No.

Q. Do you usually wear underwear under your clothes?

A. Yes.

Q. So can you explain—just tell us why you weren't wearing underwear, that night, when he put his fingers in your vagina.

A. Earlier, we'd gone swimming. In the lake. Um, and then, like, later, when I got out of the water, I was all wet, you know? I didn't put my underwear back on.

Q. This was not something you planned, or is it something you do often?

A. No, it was because I'd been all wet. But I did—I mean, um, when I was in the TV room—I had clothes on then.

Q. Okay. But he could slip his fingers under your dress. Did you tell him to stop?

A. No.

Q. Was he hurting you?

A. You mean, um—because of his fingers?

Q. Yes, because he was touching you.

A. No, it didn't hurt.

—

—

—

—

—

—

THE COURT. Are you all right?

THE WITNESS. Yeah.

THE COURT. Yes, you're okay, or yes, you need a break?

The WITNESS. Yes, I, I need a break.

Direct Examination Day 2

Q. I want to go back to the part when you were talking about John Gregory touching you.

A. Okay.

Q. Did he speak to you, say anything to you during this time?

A. I think he was afraid Katie would wake up. We were real quiet. Except, um. He asked me did I like it this way.

Q. How did you respond?

A. I don't know. I'm sorry. Um, I don't remember.

Q. You don't have to be sorry.

Katie stopped reading and sucked at the blood in her mouth from where she'd bitten her lip, a bruised crack that radiated pain. The women were talking next door, and she listened for a moment, unable to distinguish their words but comforted by the gentle rhythms of their speech, the meaninglessness of everyday communication. Life was normal, people chatted, people ate; they walked to work and drove cars and wasted time on Facebook. People loved each other and fought and picked their teeth and gave birth.

And what she was reading, that was what people did too.

A. And then, at the end, um, he told me to sit on top of him—and—um—

Q. Did you do that? Sit on top of him?

A. Yes.

Q. And then what happened?

A. And then, um, he pulled his pants down, and he took out his penis, and I sat on top of it, and—

Q. What happened?

A. His penis went in my vagina.

This was so much worse than she'd expected.

It was stupid, but she had not been prepared for everything to be spelled out like this. A clear-cut mechanical narrative, so appalling in this context. So unforgettable.

Q. Did you say anything?

——

Q. Sorry, is that "no"? Can you clarify for the court?

A. No, I didn't say anything.

Q. And the defendant? Did he say anything?

A. No. He was quiet.

Q. And you didn't scream or cry or say "stop."

A. No. But it—

Q. You can tell the court.

A. But it hurt. I didn't say anything, but it was hurting me.

Q. Can you tell us why you didn't say anything? Why you didn't tell him to stop hurting you?

——

——

—

—

—

—

THE COURT. Do you need a break? It's okay if you need a break.

THE WITNESS. No, I'm okay.

THE COURT. You're sure?

THE WITNESS. Can I please have a glass of water?

Q. Did you see your parents the next day?

A. I saw my mother. My father, he doesn't live with us.

Q. Okay, you saw your mother the next day. Did you tell her what happened to you?

A. No.

Q. Why? Why did you not say anything to your mother about John Gregory hurting you?

A. Because he is my best friend's father.

Lulu had used the present tense here, and what did that mean? "Best friend"—those simple words added sparking embers to the sense of panic overtaking her. Of course they had not been best friends anymore at that point. But they used to be; they used to love each other, and that reality had been wiped out, along with the life Katie had taken completely for granted.

There were hundreds of pages of testimony, and Katie began frantically flipping through the pages, looking for something specific. She snagged her lip again with her teeth, then stopped herself before drawing blood.

She saw her own name on page 114, day six, when she took the witness stand.

There was Piper's name, Lulu's mother, when she took the stand.

There was some guy from her father's office, and the new West Mills town soccer coach, speaking on her father's behalf. In the old pirate box at the cabin, Katie had uncovered a sheet with a list of names on it, and many of those same people were listed in the transcript, called up as character witnesses. On and on with the names, questions, reworded questions, breaks in the narrative, more names, objections, sidebars. Rape crisis counselors. Doctors.

The image of Lulu on the stand—stuttering and crying as she talked about Katie's father's fingers—threatened to blot everything else out, and she shoved it away, yet Lulu hovered alongside her, whispering, and Katie couldn't tell what she was saying, though she desperately wanted to understand.

There was one person mentioned on almost every page, at least obliquely, whom she could not find under either Direct Examination or Cross-Examination. One name was missing: the name *John Gregory*.

Where was his testimony? How could this document be missing what must surely be among the most important components of the trial—her father's side of the story? As she flipped back and forth, something dawned on her, and every drop of moisture evaporated from her mouth.

The reason it was not there was because he had never taken the stand in his own defense. He had never told his own side of the story, either in court or to his family.

Cross-Examination

Q. Hi, Loretta. My name is Herbert Schwartz.

A. Hello. I, um, can you—I mean, call me Lulu, please?

Q. You don't need to be nervous. I'm not going to try to trip you up, okay? And I will certainly call you Lulu if you like.

A. Okay. Thank you.

Q. So, according to your testimony, you were in the den of the cabin, here on the diagram. Your Honor, I move to admit this evidence as Exhibit #4.

—

—

Q. Is this a fair depiction, in this diagram, of the layout of the house?

A. Yes, I think so.

Q. Well, let's see. You've spent many summers at the cabin with the Gregory family, is that right?

A. Yes.

Q. Since you were about six years old?

A. I'd just turned seven when I first started staying with them.

Q. You were seven years old. So that is over ten years ago, right? You had been spending every summer with them for about, what, seven years in a row?

A. Yes.

Q. So it would be fair to say they are like family to you? Mrs. Gregory, Charlie, is like a mother, and Mr. Gregory, John, is a bit like a father. Perhaps a surrogate family?

A. I suppose so.

Q. They took care of you since you were little, fed you, comforted you if you were upset?

A. Yes. But I, I have a mother, too, a real mom.

Q. I understand. Your mother, your adoptive mother, she's here today, right?

A. No, she's not here. I mean, not today.

Q. Okay, I'm sorry. I thought she was here. So, in addition to your mother, your adoptive mother, not that long after you were adopted into her family, you also started staying with the Gregorys for weeks at a time?

A. Yes.

Q. Back to my question, then. This diagram, it is an accurate representation of where the den is in relation to the rest of the house? The den is right next to the kitchen? It is not in a basement, down a long hallway, or tucked far away, is that correct?

A. Yes, it's next to the kitchen.

Q. So anyone in the kitchen or the hallway, or even coming out of the living room, could look into the den? It would be right in view of anyone who was in the house?

A. It was the middle of the night. It was, like, dark. Everyone was asleep.

Q. Is the den in view of many of the most heavily trafficked places in the house or not?

A. Yes, it is.

Q. Okay, thank you. I'd like to play a tape now, from the resource center. Your Honor, could we play the tape, please? Lulu, you're nervous?

A. Yes, I, I . . . sort of.

Q. You don't have to be nervous.

A. Okay.

Q. Just listen to the tape, and you'll be okay. Just answer my questions.

A. Okay.

This is where they would have brought in the expert witness, Katie thought—they would have wanted to follow up Lulu's devastating direct examination with a cross that questioned her ability to recall events properly. They would have put someone on the stand who testified that if she had been raped as a young child—before she was adopted—Lulu might simply be wrong about what she was remembering. She wasn't lying, exactly; it was just that her memories were jumbled up.

Katie's forehead was covered in a filmy layer of sweat, her hands cold and clammy but her body too hot. A lurch and a tug in her stomach, the need to get air. She hated this. She wanted it to be over.

Q. So you say on the tape that it just "popped into your mind" that the defendant had touched you, had had sex with you? During class one day, it "popped into my mind," you said. Correct?

—

—

Q. Where were you when the assault popped into your mind? Why did you not remember it earlier, say, the day afterward when you were with your own family, your adoptive mother, again?

—

—

Q. You do not need to be upset. Just answer my questions.

—

—

THE COURT. Let's take a break.

—

—

Q. Could you please speak up?

—

—

Q. Your Honor, I think we may need to take another break.

—

Q. Lulu, Lulu? We will resume tomorrow. There's no need to be so upset.

PART THREE

28

Katie drove back to the city, her thoughts so scrambled that she missed her exit and became lost in the confusion of highways by Secaucus, thinking at one point she might have to pull over to blow her nose and look at a map to reorient herself. Every muscle in her body ached as though she were getting the flu. Her stomach clenched in on itself like a fist. The day was heavy with bluish clouds low on the horizon, and the air was shockingly warm, the temperature almost seventy degrees, as though the earth were battling with itself about how spring should unfold.

When she arrived back at her apartment, she flung the windows open and gulped down a few glasses of water. Jack had texted her earlier that morning, and she'd resisted responding right away. But she looked down at his words now—Can I see you again?—and could not bring her mind to focus on anything else. He wanted to see her, and she wanted to see him. She ignored thoughts of Zev, so far away at just the wrong moment. After all, she and Jack were old friends. Would it be so wrong to meet up with him again so soon? How could she possibly wait longer when it had been so many years since she'd last seen him, and he was the only one who really understood what she and her family had gone through?

Yes, let's, she texted back, and she jumped in the shower. By the time she got out, he'd responded with a time and place. The relief and anticipation that flushed through her pushed all other feelings aside, and for the first time that day, she felt almost normal again.

They met up at an Italian place called Luigi's in the Village after work the next day. The restaurant was worn out, flattened velvet drapery and ripped banquettes, stuffing bursting out like swollen gums. A cliché of family dining from another era. This was the kind of place her father would have loved: $12.99 all-you-can-eat buffet between 3:00 and 6:00 p.m. Half-price beers and double well drinks. A couple stood at the bar, the woman wearing an orange polyester dress, the man with a head of bottle-black hair. Jack was already seated in the back corner. He looked very tired, his chin unshaven, sharp creases fanning out from the outer corner of his mouth. A black T-shirt, fitted.

"I ordered you a martini," he said without preamble, nodding toward the frosty glass sitting in a small puddle next to a basket of bread. "Figured you could maybe use some fortification after your weekend."

Katie slid onto the bench. She'd applied lipstick and brushed her hair before leaving the office, and it fell loosely around her face, clean and wavy, smelling faintly of coconut. She tilted her head toward the empty martini glass and the half-full beer in front of Jack. "Am I late? You've been here awhile?"

"Nah." He hesitated as though considering whether to address the obvious. "I'm sorta on the wagon with one foot, you know? Sometimes I get off and then jump right back on again."

A sensation uncomfortably close to pity pulsed in her chest. "Isn't that just called 'drinking'?"

He studied his hands; his fingers were elegant and articulated like those of a musician. "Some people can do it. It depends."

Katie took a sip of her drink. This was no artisanal cocktail made with carefully sourced elderberries or garnished with a sprig of caraway thyme from Majorca. Pure vodka, three fat, briny olives. Jack unsettled her, and yet it was not a bad feeling. They were both known to each other yet utterly unknown. For long minutes at a stretch, they sat without talking at all, and it was just fine. The conversation worked its way around to whom they were dating. Jack had met a girl on vacation in Greece, and they were hanging out, but it wasn't really going anywhere. She was a student, originally from Alabama, training to be a physical therapist. When Katie told him about Zev, his gaze became pointed, his entire body listening. "So it's serious?" he asked.

"I don't know yet," she said, which was the truth but not the whole truth. With every half admission, there was a sense of taking a curve too fast in a car, of getting a little winded.

"I think I should tell you. I'm, uh—Lulu got in touch with me a couple of years ago. I wanted to tell you at the lake, but it somehow, well. Didn't feel right, or I was nervous or something."

Her head was wooly, and she wasn't entirely sure she'd understood. "Lulu," she said, like a moron. The hunk of bread she was chewing was like putty in her mouth.

"Yeah. I got a message from her. It was maybe two years ago? This friend request on Facebook, and I had absolutely no idea who it was. I mean, she looks nothing like how I remember her." He considered his words. "It was like this glam shot, one of those things they take at the mall. She had on tons of makeup. Her hair was different. She was heavier. She had this look on her face, like, I don't know. Twinkly." He raised his brows as though he knew how absurd this sounded. "I definitely don't remember her as twinkly. And her name was different, too, not Lulu. Loretta, I think."

"And you friended her."

"Sure. Look, I was trying to get into real estate. I have loads of so-called friends I don't know. I didn't think twice about it, and then she sent me this private message, and we started having a conversation. Nothing too important. Just catching up." Jack motioned to the waitress to bring them each another drink. "We switched to email, and then she started really telling me a lot. You know how email can be. It was wild—she just really opened up. She told me about her life when she was a kid, her relationship with her mom—her real mother, before she was adopted. Did you know that—that she was adopted?"

The waitress came over with another martini for Katie and a beer for him. He took a long pull from his glass and then sighed. "Guess I'm really off the wagon now, huh?"

"I read her testimony," Katie said, "and I can't get it out of my head. Did you—did she talk about that? What did she tell you?"

"Well, I mean, she told me tons of stuff. Not much about the trial, though. It was sort of like—I guess she wanted to let me know more about herself. Like, who she was, not so much what had happened. But it was kind of strange 'cause we'd never been like that, talking and sharing things. But the way she—you know how people behave when they've been alone for a long time? Isolated, or away somewhere foreign? Like they just can't stop talking. That's what it was like."

"Is she with anyone?" It was hard to tell if the pit Katie felt growing in her stomach was a bitter coil of pleasure at thinking her old friend might have had to pay in some way for lying or if it was a prickle of empathy. "What'd she end up doing?"

"She was moving. There was some guy—I can't really remember. She'd tried singing for a while, but I guess that didn't work out. I kind of just stopped responding. To be honest, she sort of freaked me out." He tipped his head back to finish his beer. "I felt like she wanted something from me that I couldn't give her. She asked a lot about you."

Jack's eyes were resting on Katie as though appraising every inch of her face for some secret sign, something that would tell him what to say next. "She was disappointed I didn't have anything to tell her. She seemed to think we kept in touch, like, actually dated."

Katie took a small sip of her second drink, and the salty bitterness of the olive juice tasted like food to her on her empty stomach. "And all summer long I thought you liked *her*. Christ, it took us a long time to get anywhere, didn't it? And then it all went nowhere."

He smiled. "I liked you from the minute I saw you the first day, running by the tennis court, and then, oops . . . go figure, your shoelaces come untied . . ."

"Oh shit. That's so embarrassing."

"Yeah. You guys weren't exactly subtle." He held her gaze. "Don't take this the wrong way, but do you think about the summer—I mean, not about your father or about Lulu, but about the two of us?"

Heat rose up her neck and seeped into her face. "We were just kids. It was—"

"Your dad, that business eclipsed everything, but that doesn't mean there weren't other things that happened, things that meant something. It's just, sometimes I think back to what was sort of the simple life, right?" he said. "And there's a moment—we keep coming back to it, again and again, for whatever reason. It's not even necessarily a big thing. It's just this sort of hinge or something, on which everything seems to turn."

"Not sure I understand," she said, buying herself some time. But she did know what he meant; that summer had been full of seemingly innocuous moments that turned out to be indelible, that came back to her in all their strangeness and meant something while also meaning nothing.

"For me—when you said goodbye at the clubhouse, I remember you were soaking wet. I couldn't really hear what you were saying. You looked so pretty, so incredibly serious. If I'd just stopped for a minute and asked you what was going on . . ."

She looked down. "You remember when we stood at the window at the Dolans', looking out? We'd just gotten there, and it was pitch dark. We couldn't see a thing. It was like I was blind, but then, slowly . . . slowly things sort of began to take shape. You know, like a picture developing?"

Her heart began beating madly. "We hadn't even done anything yet. We were just sort of hugging."

"Yes, I remember that," Jack said.

"Right then," she said, "for me, it felt like everything was possible. It was all going to happen, and there was so much of it. All good. And then, yeah. It all went fucking haywire."

They couldn't hold each other's eyes anymore. She wondered about the years he hadn't told her much about—the lost years of drugs and drinking and unhappiness. It wasn't clear if all that was really over yet.

"I'll be back," she said, sliding over the bench. "Ladies' room." When she stood up, the martinis hit her with full force. She tripped a little, lurching toward the bathroom. The cold water on her face was a huge relief. Four, five deep breaths, and she felt better. Her cheeks were deeply flushed. She would ask him more about Lulu. What she was doing now, whether she seemed happy. A sudden sob clutched her throat. It had been so long since she'd had a friend like Lulu, since she'd felt that kind of complete connection. No one in college or in the city had come close to being an adequate substitute. There had been plenty of nice girls, girls to go out with, to get drunk with, to share stories with. But not the stories that really mattered.

29

Emerging from the ladies' room, Katie squinted to adjust her eyes. Someone bumped into her in the dark hallway. It was Jack.

"Katie, can I, can I just . . ." he said, as though he were short of breath. He cupped his hands over her shoulders. The tips of his fingers pressing on her bones were like warm stones on her skin, pinpoints of sensation; the pressure was a shock. And then he leaned forward and put his mouth on hers and kissed her, barely, as though asking for permission. He tasted like beer, like summertime; he smelled of warmth and sun. The tension in her body seemed to focus all in one place, at the base of her neck, and her skin began to prickle, rain on water, needles on skin. She couldn't think. She kissed him back. The release was instant, a swooping sensation that was irresistible and sickening.

He leaned against her with his full weight then, pressing her to the wall. Soon she was lost in the feeling of weightlessness. It seemed to have its own momentum, a kind of inevitability. The skin of his face was rough against her lips.

Her phone rang, and she ignored it. A patron walked past them, briskly edging his way down the hall, but they didn't pause. It was like being submerged in warm water. She was light, yet her limbs were oddly heavy too. A terrible urgency gripped her. They couldn't hold each other closely enough. Jack slipped his hands under her shirt, and her skin burst into flame. His hip bones dug into her. The phone rang again.

She pulled away a little and caught her breath.

"No, no," he murmured. "Don't."

She met him again in a kiss and pressed her fingers into his back. But the feeling of elation didn't last; the urgency wasn't what they'd thought—it wasn't erotic; it was desperate. In that instant she saw that the dreams she'd had of this man were misplaced. Those memories of the time they'd shared as kids had assumed a significance, a kind of bloated purity, that was all out of proportion with reality; they had been sweet moments she could hang on to, promises of how life could have been. But it wasn't real. Jack was not the solution. Jack was part of the problem. This was not going to work.

"Hold on—hold on a second," she cried, recoiling when her phone buzzed with a message. She was heavy lidded with desire. She ran her tongue over her lips. "We have to stop. I'm sorry. I don't know what I'm doing. I'm a mess right now."

"Shit," he said. "Katie—"

"I have to deal with my life. Sorry, I'm sorry. I can't."

"Fuck," he said.

Wiping a hand over her mouth, she squeezed her eyes shut. Her lips were raw and swollen. "It's always going to be the wrong time for us."

"Don't . . ." he said, and he drew his breath in sharply. "Don't think about everyone else, for once. Think about what you want!"

"It's just wrong. I'm trying to figure things out." She stepped away, pressing her back against the wall. The black of his pupils was enormous. "We were just teenagers, Jack. Now we're grown-ups." But even as she said this, the low-slung excitement was still there in her stomach—the thrill of behaving badly, of breaking the rules. Of sinking recklessly, wanting something that she predicted wouldn't end well for her. She pulled the strap of her bag up to her shoulder and began to head back toward their table.

"I didn't tell the whole truth," Jack called out to her. He was still in the darkened hallway, leaning against the wall. "On the stand."

"How do you mean?" Katie swiveled to face him. The hair on her arms prickled. "You didn't see them, through the window?"

"No, no, that was true: I did see them, your dad and her." He scrubbed at his thick blond hair, pushing it back again and again. The bright blue of his hummingbird tattoo peered out from the edges of his T-shirt sleeve, like an iridescent petal catching the light. "But something else happened. Something pretty bad. Earlier that night."

"I've got to get out of here," Katie said, feeling faint.

"I knew I should tell someone, but I couldn't. I wasn't sure, you know—was it really relevant?"

"Just say it, Jack," she said. "Just spit it out."

"It was Brad. Remember Brad? He—uh, he cornered Lulu. Remember, we hung out with him at the changing sheds for a while a few days earlier. He was a swimmer, a college kid."

"Yeah, I remember Brad," she said, fiddling with the buckle of her bag. The vents hummed with cool air at her ankles. "What about him?"

"He told me when I got back to the clubhouse. They'd screwed; he was bragging about it. But she'd said she didn't want to, and he just—you know, it was kind of one of those things."

Katie's insides took a slide over this unexpected precipice. "She didn't want to? When was this?"

"Earlier, when we went off to the Dolans'. Remember that call? That was her. I think Tommy must have figured out where we'd gone and told her."

It seemed so obvious now, Brad asking Katie about Lulu. Lulu sitting on the dock, refusing to meet her eyes. Her lipstick smeared. And she had thought Lulu was furious with her about Jack. It struck her now that Katie had been seeing everything from her own narrow perspective—it was awful to think that she might have been completely off base about Lulu being angry at her. "I don't understand why you didn't tell the investigators. You didn't say anything during the trial!"

"Don't you think I was torn up about that? If it was relevant or not? Of course I was. It was a super confusing time," he said. "The lawyers, they gave me instructions. Just answer the questions. Don't ad-lib. Blah blah blah. Christ, I was barely seventeen. I was scared to death."

Katie saw Lulu in the dark, crying, her breath coming fast, her eyes wild; she was thinking, *Where is Katie? Where is she?* Later, by the lake, Lulu had told her, "I want to go home." Things were clicking into place in her mind. Brad was the monster; he had messed with her friend's mind. And Katie was to blame, too, for being so selfish. "This changes things," she said. "You should have told the lawyers."

The whites of Jack's eyes glinted at her. Whatever electricity had flowed between them was gone. "How does it change anything?" he asked. "Don't girls always say no at first?"

"Whoa," she said. "That's not very evolved, Jack. You don't really think that way, do you?"

"Look, I just don't get how it impacts what happened with your dad."

"She was mad at me, you know? Maybe that's why she went with him, with Brad, in the first place. And then she said it was Dad, blamed him. She was just really messed up." Closing her eyes, Katie felt the sting of tears. Until recently, she had never thought of her friend as vulnerable, and now she saw just how wrong she'd been.

All of a sudden, things were happening too fast. A minute ago her insides had been fluid; she'd been in a dream, and Jack was in that dream too. And yet he had never spoken up about this—to her, to the lawyers, to anyone. Maybe it could have made a difference at the trial—who knew? It spoke to Lulu's state of mind. It threw into question the kinds of choices she might have made. How could Jack have taken the risk and kept quiet about it? Her sorrow for Lulu quickly transformed itself into fury at this man who had dismissed the importance of an appalling incident even though he knew it to be true. How could it not be pivotal?

"He went to jail for *rape*, Jack. Almost six years of his life. My father can never coach kids again. He has to find something to do, someplace that will hire felons. My mother had to get a shitty job. Our family fucking imploded!" Her voice rose as she spoke, and one by one people sitting near the corridor started craning in their seats to see what was going on. "And all along you knew that boy had done something terrible to her, and you didn't say a word. I . . . I'm sorry, but I find that kind of sickening."

Jack seemed to shrink as she swelled with anger. She was glad now that she'd tested the durability of her desire and discovered it to be shallow and sad. She was looking for something that was already right in front of her: a solid mass, something concrete, not ephemeral. A person whose quiet forward motion created a place for her—not to hide in but to be safe enough so she could become herself again.

She grabbed her suit jacket from the booth and stumbled out of the restaurant into the early summer evening, the air so humid it strafed her skin like soaked muslin, cloying.

Jack. Foolish, immature Jack. How she had loved him that summer. Her dream of Jack had hardly even begun before it was over.

30

A few days later, on the way up the stairs to her apartment, she stopped on a riser to catch her breath. She didn't feel right, and she realized that she hadn't felt right for weeks. That time in the bar a couple of weeks ago with Zev—she never just threw up like that. Her dizziness, the swooning feeling that often overwhelmed her when she woke up. The constant soreness in her bones, the sour stomach . . . Even when she had been with Jack, she hadn't felt like herself. She'd attributed it to nerves, to the stress of what was going on, but was it that? Her body just didn't feel normal.

She began a calculation that ultimately could only end one of two ways, with a positive or a negative. She and Zev had been together since October, and now it was June; that was about eight months. Sometimes, when he stayed over, they would make love two or even three times. Often, in the middle of the night, they reached out in half sleep and slid their hot, searching hands over each other, still mired in the cocoon of their earlier lovemaking. Silently, ferociously, they would fuck in the darkness, keeping their eyes closed. She had never experienced that sensation with anyone before, that kind of out-of-body experience.

Those times, those pitch-black moments in which they lost themselves feverishly, they did not use a condom. She tried to remember how long ago they had had one of those episodes. Then she tried to remember when she'd last had her period. And with that calculation she knew that it was a possibility that she was pregnant with Zev's child.

Doubling over, she sucked air in sharply and huffed it out again. A child. Once in college, she'd had a scare, and it had proven to be nothing but stress and a bit of anemia. She'd gone on the pill and then off again and had planned to get an IUD. But she hadn't done it—she'd allowed herself to become lazy. Eight months with Zev, only using condoms—what were they thinking?

But it was also possible she was wrong. Her periods had never been all that regular, and she didn't bother to keep careful track of them. This was a time of high stress, and perhaps her body was reacting in strange ways. She had been running—and that long swim!—and hadn't been eating very much. What with her father's release and Zev's overture about moving in together, she was under a lot of pressure.

And then there was Jack—the fact that she couldn't deny that she had been so drawn to him that she'd almost launched into an affair, if you could even call it that. It made a mockery of her careful planning and her calibrated reactions. Since Tuesday she'd been ignoring all his efforts to reach her, but the truth was that part of her still missed what might have been if reality hadn't conspired to get in their way when they were kids. Would she have seen him the following summer? Would they have had the chance to become a real couple?

She put her key in the lock. As soon as she changed out of her work clothes, she was going to call Zev. She longed to hear his raspy, singsong voice, to begin the hard work of opening herself up to him. It was what he deserved, and it was what she wanted. Over the last few days she'd started examining some of the feelings he elicited in her. For instance, why did she often feel a guilty thrill after sex, as though she were doing something she wasn't really supposed to? Why had she not told her father that they were a couple? She'd thought it was because she wanted something that belonged only to her, but she was beginning to suspect it was more than that. Maybe she worried that her father wouldn't think it was a good match, that he'd want more for his daughter. But what did *she* think? It seemed to her now that her feelings for Zev were tangled up with the past in a way that had been holding her back.

Her landline rang when she entered the apartment, and she remembered with sickening clarity the intrusiveness of the reporters, the media's ghoulish fascination with the relatives of criminals, their unhinged loyalties. She dropped her bag to the floor, snatched the phone off the hook, said, "Fuck you!" and then slammed it down again. Once again she had forgotten to unplug it. The phone rang again, and she stared at it. "What the hell do you want from me?" she hissed into the receiver. "Why can't you all leave me alone?"

"Katie? What's going on?"

It was her mother. Relief raced through her like a flush of alcohol, until she realized that something had to be wrong if her mother was calling her. "Mum?" she said, falling back onto the old velvet couch. "Sorry! I thought you were someone else."

"I'll say. Everything all right?"

"I don't know. Depends on what you mean by all right."

Her mother sighed. It was always like this, a tense, clipped exchange in which every sentence hid behind it another one that flayed at her. They couldn't seem to talk normally anymore, without hidden accusations blistering under the surface. "Who did you think it was?" Charlie asked. "Have they been calling you too? Those reporters?"

"I'm not going to talk with them."

"Quite right," Charlie said. "I'm sorry, it must be awful"—she paused—"with your father getting out so soon, on top of it all."

"Mum, I'm not sure I want to get into this."

"No need to be short, Katie. We're all just doing the best we can with the hand we've been dealt," her mother said. "And this isn't a social call. I'm in London for a few days. Grumpy isn't doing well. It took me a while to get it out of him, and finally I called Henrietta. You remember her—the head nurse?"

Katie's grandfather lived in a nursing home in Ravenscourt, London. Once every year or so, when the airfare was low, he flew Katie and David over there to visit him. "Is he okay? Did she tell you what's wrong?"

"Age is not for the weak of heart, that's for sure."

"Is he sick?"

"That's what I'm trying to tell you. He has pneumonia. Started with a cough some months ago, which he ignored, of course. Now it's settled in, and it's getting worse. He's ninety-six years old, you know. All right in the head, hardly a surprise. But the body, it's fragile. It eventually just gives up the ghost."

This time the upwelling of tears was less like a wave and more like a punch in the throat. It took a while for Katie to be able to swallow properly as her mother went on and on about the nurses, what they were and weren't doing. How cruel it was to age and lose your independence. "I have to see him," Katie said, strangled. "I don't want him to die."

"Of course, darling. That's why I was calling. You must come visit very soon."

The softness of her mother's tone, the quiet hesitation before she said *darling*, unleashed something inside Katie. How she missed the mother she wished she'd had. Why had it always been so very hard between the two of them? Was it because she was English and had so fully bought into the stiff-upper-lip approach to life? She tried to think back to when it had started. Maybe when Katie had found her crying on the toilet, bloody panties at her ankles, yet another baby unrealized. Children weren't supposed to know a parent could be so helpless and vulnerable. Maybe her mother had been trying to protect herself in some way. Or maybe that hadn't been it at all.

"Pumpkin?" Charlie said. "You there?"

Katie couldn't remember the last time her mother had called her *pumpkin*; it was as though Katie were deep inside a cave and ahead of her she glimpsed the wavering glow of open air. "Mum, I'm really having a hard time," she said. And when her mother murmured some-thing, Katie burst out: "I think—I don't know—I think it's possible I could be pregnant."

Her mother let out a startled cry.

"This wouldn't be good news, Mum."

"You're not considering . . . ?" Charlie asked.

"I haven't even bought a test yet," Katie said. She would never have expected this—her mother, so sentimental. "Ugh. I shouldn't have said anything. It might be a false alarm, anyway."

"Who is the fellow? Is it serious?"

Katie told her about Zev, and her mother's *mmmm*s and *ahhhh*s in the background encouraged her to keep talking. Their relationship still felt so new, so full of possibility, both good and bad. She wasn't sure how to feel about him—this was different from anything she'd experienced before, undefined, vertiginous.

"That's called love, dear," her mother said.

But how could Katie know for sure? And the prospect of a child, especially now, was not something she'd ever considered. She didn't know how she felt about becoming a mother. And it was such bad timing, with Dad about to—

"You're getting ahead of yourself," her mother interrupted. "Go to the pharmacy and buy a test. All right? And, Katie. Don't let your father consume you. You know how he can be. Protect yourself."

"It's not like that—"

"I'm just saying. Take care of yourself. Because the man can take care of himself. Trust me on this."

As the bodega owners started packing away their sidewalk wares and locking up their grills that night, Katie walked down the blinking streets in the Meatpacking District. It had been warm again all day, and the night air brought out crowds, women in stretched-out tube tops and short skirts, teetering over the cobbles, men in ironic T-shirts without jackets. At the corner of Gansevoort and Hudson, a gaggle of teenage girls—too young to get into the clubs—shivered in cutoff jeans, faces lit blue as they huddled over their cell phones, giggling.

A strange tension infused Katie's body, and in the night air it seemed that her muscles were taut and twangy, as though the descent into darkness were filling her with an energy that couldn't find a way out. She had been too tired to go running, but she had badly needed some company, and Zev hadn't picked up the phone earlier. When Ursula texted her that she and a few others were going dancing, Katie jumped at the chance to get out. She rarely went to clubs, but she did love to dance. It occurred to her that she should go dancing more often. Zev had taken her once to a salsa bar up in Spanish Harlem, and they'd danced together, arms clasped around each other and feet clacking and stomping beneath them, the drumbeat sending shivers through her. He had led her with his great flat palms pressed against her skin. Lulu used to love dancing, and whenever there were theme nights at Eagle Lake, the two of them would throw themselves around like missiles. But they'd outgrown that quickly, suffering from self-consciousness, preferring to watch from the sidelines and cast judgment on others.

Each step she took toward the club, her body loosened in anticipation. A group of men were gathered around a lamppost, dressed in black like crows glistening under the light, smoking. Cigarettes crunched between thumb and forefinger, eyes darting. One of them, wearing overdesigned glasses, called out to her as she passed, but it was half-hearted. They were not young anymore and not yet old—like her, really, stuck between being hopeful and careless and the alluring tug of orderliness that was their future. Some would insist on living out the dregs of their youthful freedom; some would throw themselves into domesticity, by choice or necessity. But now they hovered, quivering with eagerness that was as fragile as it was obvious. Katie took it all in as she strode past in her heels and summer dress: the jockeying, the foot shuffling, the smell of inexpertly applied lotions. Her birthday was in just a few months—she was halfway through her twenties already!—and she shared the same feeling of precariousness that she sensed in these young men.

At the club, she thought guiltily about the Duane Reade bag lying on her countertop with the unopened pregnancy test inside it. Her friend Ursula was chatting up the bartender, the bangles on her forearm sliding up and down as she laughed and played with the cardboard coasters. Danielle and Radha went onto the dance floor and joined the crowd that pulsed like gems in sunshine. Radha and Ursula had been at Vassar with Katie, serious girls with jobs in fund-raising, mission driven in both work and play. Radha's black hair had streaks of cobalt blue in it that shifted like ropes as she moved.

Thirsty but unwilling to break in on Ursula's exchange at the bar, Katie leaned with one elbow on the sticky wood and surveyed the crowd. She had ordered a beer but already finished it and was reluctant to drink any more. Things were just getting started on the dance floor. The DJ spun a curious mixture of old-style disco and electronic music, which had people gyrating with jerky hesitancy.

She felt a jumpy tension in her limbs, the need to move. She'd hoped the noise and sweat and energy would take her away from herself. It had crossed her mind to confide her pregnancy fears to Radha, but saying those words aloud again—*I'm worried I might be pregnant*— would give even more heft to that possible reality. On the floor, Radha was motioning her over with big circular gestures. Someone tapped her on the back; it was a young man with a pale shaved head and a bushy black beard, carefully tended, as soft looking as mink. He raised a beer and his eyebrows at the same time, making her crack a smile. What would it be like to run her fingers over his smooth head, the egglike roundness of it? She marveled at the way humans tried to connect with one another, everywhere, all the time. In each person she encountered, she detected a whiff of sad-eyed need, the perpetual desire to be noticed and understood.

But she wasn't interested in meeting men. Scrunching her face, she shook her head and mimed, *Not for me.*

Radha waved again, and Katie joined her to be sure the bearded boy didn't think she might change her mind about the drink. At first she was stiff, but when the music changed to something slower, a deeper, more drawn-out beat overlaid with staccato drums and a repetitive chorus, her body started to respond. She imagined herself moving, serpentine, along the jungle floor like a snake. The tightness inside her resisted release, making her fingers twitch, distracting her so that she caught herself looking toward the bar again and again—as though she were in fact interested in the guy—until finally the tension surged over the wall of her discomfort and released her.

31

Trudging to work, she tried to distract herself by counting the hours and minutes until her father's release, until Zev returned from Barcelona. Until her hastily planned trip to London to see her grandfather with David the following week. The incessant loops her mind was making were exhausting but effective; she managed to go for minutes at a time without telling herself, *Take the goddamn pregnancy test.* But she wasn't sure she could do it on her own. Last night she had talked with Zev for a while, but it seemed wrong to bring it up over the phone. He was in the thick of his presentations, and it wouldn't be fair to distract him, but also, she wanted to see his face, to know for sure what he was thinking. Besides, she needed to know if she was pregnant or not before it made sense to broach the topic of parenthood with him.

When she imagined taking the test, she couldn't picture Radha there with her, or any of the other women she knew, for that matter. And while she loved her brother, he was not the person she would choose for this particular mission.

Of course, it was Lulu she wanted by her side. Even though she knew, especially after what had happened with Jack, that the idea of her friendship with Lulu was simply that—an idea, long ago extinguished— it was still what she yearned for. So often it had been Lulu who'd comforted her, persuaded her things would be okay. When Katie gouged her leg on a nail and the wound was thick with grit, Lulu kept a cool head even though the grown-ups were all gone. When Katie drank too much whiskey after they'd sneaked out one night, Lulu had given her a piggyback through the darkened woods, not even stopping once. She had a herculean strength, it seemed, the ability to withstand almost anything with a wry smile or a dismissive shrug. Never hysterical, never flippant. Katie thought she'd put all that longing for what she could no longer have behind her, but no. It was hard to accept that this hurdle—finding out if she had a child growing inside her—was one she'd have to figure out on her own.

From the outside, her life looked pretty ordinary, but the revelations of the past few weeks had shifted her self-perception. She wanted agency over herself, the freedom to make her own mistakes and to be her own person—the irony was that this was the life she *thought* she'd already been living. Now she was realizing that she had been in thrall to the past, allowing it to define her every move. Keeping new friends at arm's length, minimizing her relationship with Zev, awaiting her father's release like a child eager for the comfort of being tucked in at night. She even felt differently about her mother, who had revealed a tender side on that call that she'd previously kept hidden—or that, perhaps, Katie hadn't been able to see.

Upon waking each day she slipped a finger between her legs and searched her bedsheets for a drop of blood. Every time she got up from her cubicle to go to the ladies' room at HCG, she prayed to see a splash of red on her underpants. Knowing whether she was actually pregnant was complicated by Zev being away all this time: as long as he was physically absent, she could trick herself into staying in this false limbo. Last night after they'd spoken, she had almost cried with relief at having heard his mellifluous voice again. But at the very same time, she dreaded his return and all that it would mean for them.

If she were actually pregnant, how would he react? She really had no idea. What did he even think about children? The only clue she had to go on was watching how he reacted as they walked around the city together—watching out for a child amid the crowd jostling to board a subway carriage, grinning at a baby peeking out from a blanket-stuffed stroller as they waited in line at the supermarket. But it wasn't clear what any of that might mean in terms of how he felt about becoming a father himself. And what did *she* think? Could she consider becoming a mother at such a young age—could she do it?

John Gregory had taught his daughter to drive in the back streets of West Mills, where the spiky fruit of the sycamores would batter the car bonnet like hail, startling her. But mostly she had learned on the dirt-packed roads of Eagle Lake, starting when her feet could barely reach the pedals. At dusk you had to keep your eyes peeled for deer, invisible but for their wild eyes and the flash of a white tail. They'd lunge out at her as she drove by, sometimes four, five of them on one short ride. She quickly learned to keep her cool. By the time she was ten years old, she knew how to navigate the clutch. Sitting next to her in the Falcon, John had been patient, slow to startle, always ready with a word of encouragement. He'd place his hand over the birdlike bones of hers as she yanked the gearshift around, the car bucking in protest underneath her.

A few days after meeting up with Jack came the day of her father's release. The Falcon was in decent running order again, after an $853 tune-up at Ricky's in Blackbrooke (Katie used money from her savings account). David had offered to fetch it, and she let him. He'd parked it in a vacant lot behind a friend's restaurant down in Red Hook, then drove into Manhattan to pick her up in the morning. She thought then, in the car, of telling him that she might possibly be pregnant, but it seemed wrong to complicate the day in that way.

Wallkill prison was a long drive up 95 from the city, and she'd usually gone up there alone, always by Greyhound bus. This time they drove the Falcon with the top down, David at the wheel, keeping it steady at sixty miles per hour. The silence between them existed in a neutral sort of place, as though they both hadn't quite decided how they should be acting toward one another. It was a good day, good things were happening, but a sense of something unsettled, off kilter, made it seem precarious.

They pulled up the wide, buckled driveway, past the giant plastic marker reading **WALLKILL CORRECTIONAL FACILITY**, and swung around toward the main entrance—and there he was, just like that. Standing with his hands stuffed into the pockets of an unfamiliar black anorak, wearing a pair of aviator glasses. The sun bounced off his forehead, the glass in his lenses blasted into shining discs. He was pale, unsmiling. As they pulled up, he remained stiff, his face unmoving. For a second Katie thought maybe it wasn't him after all. She and David left the car idling and climbed out, neither of them making a sound—and that's when John raised his fists to the air, lifted his head to the sky, and shouted, "Waaaahooooo!"

He hugged them each so hard their breath caught tight in their chests. Katie could not control the grin that took over her face. It was happening—her father was free, finally free!

"Scared ya," he said. "Suckers!"

"Dad." David pulled away, smiling. "I see prison hasn't sobered you up."

"Hell no," John answered. "Let me look at you, son. It's been a while . . ."

"I know, but—"

"Nah, just joshing you. It doesn't matter. Man," John said, slinging a small sack into the back of the Falcon, "will you look at this baby. Let me have her for a minute, will you?"

He jumped into the driver's seat, and as David and Katie stood side by side watching, he raced down the driveway, tooted the horn a few times, revved the engine, and then did a spectacularly brazen U-turn in the intersection—one hand on the wheel, the other raised high—and returned to them. Watching him move through the free air, unimpeded,

Katie was ecstatic one second, jumpy the next. She looked at David to see if he was as unsettled as she, but his face gave nothing away.

"Rides like a dream," her father said. "Thanks, kids. This makes my heart sing. Climb in."

The car rumbled, a deep, throaty murmur, as it cruised along the back roads. The sky and trees whizzed over their heads like a too-fast movie reel. "Where are we going?" Katie asked.

"Where do you want to go?" her father said.

David pulled his baseball hat lower over his forehead against the wind. "Your call, Dad!"

The car barreled toward the Hudson River. When the trees swallowed them in their stippled embrace, John slowed down. He tapped on the car door with his left hand, his right hand loosely clasped around the steering wheel. The Falcon nosed out of the shadows onto the open road again, and the vista unfolded in front of them for miles in every direction. In the distance a few tiny round dots hovered in the sky, but they didn't seem to be moving. They were pink and green, some striped with blue.

"Hey, no kidding," John said. "Hot-air balloons!"

They looked like M&M'S, gaudy and bright, and there were at least ten of them, floating effortlessly, creating no noise, and leaving no wake. As the Falcon approached, the balloons loomed along the road to their right, dancing ever so slightly. Katie grinned to herself. The muscles in her shoulders began to loosen up; the world was complicated, yes, but also full of beauty, and now they could all move forward and embrace it.

"Always wanted to go up in one of those things," John said. "But your mother was too damn scared."

"No surprise there," said Katie.

"Ach," her father said, dismissing her with a wave of his hand. "Not a word you say will change the fact that I think she's damn near perfect."

It was sad, his enduring dedication to her mother. How much sweeter his release would have been if Charlie had pulled up today in the Falcon with his children.

They left the balloons behind them. "Get ready," John said when they reached the crest of the hill. "You guys ready?"

No time to fret over what came next. John floored it. Katie's stomach turned over as they swooped down the hill. The speedometer topped eighty miles per hour, and the car shuddered with effort.

"Hot damn!" John Gregory shouted. "Fly like a bird!"

They stopped at a diner outside Walden, even though it was a cliché because every newly released prisoner headed straight there to get his hands on some home-style cooking. John ordered a beer as they sat down and then another as they perused the menu. They chatted about the upcoming election and the deaths of Pat Summitt, the basketball coach, and Muhammad Ali. He folded his glasses carefully and slipped them into the breast pocket of his plaid shirt. It was such a comfort to see him in this setting, a normal man doing normal things; Katie pushed aside the unnerving questions that scuttled into her thoughts from time to time. The past was the past, no? He was happy, and she was too. They all were—by God, they deserved it.

The food came quickly, brought by a waitress in pigtails with thin coral lips who must have been approaching sixty. Two specials (lasagna and meatloaf), a stack of pancakes, a side of curly paprika fries, and a piece of apple pie—far too much for the three of them. The men dug in, as though in competition with one another for which one could eat the most, lips glistening with juices and syrup. Katie tried to keep up, but she couldn't eat much, shreds of mozzarella sticking to her palate like cardboard. A delirious mood set in, as though they'd rolled back time and were little again. David burped, holding his hand in front of his mouth like a teenager. Katie pulled out her cell phone to show her father the latest model, giving him a tutorial on how the apps worked. He pressed the keys with the thick pads of his fingers, clumsily, leaving behind a thin, oily residue.

"Hold on a minute," John said, digging into his sack and pulling out an envelope. He studied the piece of paper and typed into Katie's iMessage. "This right, hon?"

"Who're you texting?" David asked, using his hand to wipe his mouth. Katie passed him a napkin.

"Wouldn't you like to know?" John laughed and handed the phone back to Katie. "Let me know when you get an answer." He scooped out a big spoonful of pie and rolled his eyes in bliss as it went down. His face was slim, the skin sagging at the jawbones. There was stubble near his lips that hadn't been shaved off completely. He stretched out his back and sighed. "We'll have to get me one of those phones, okay, hunbun?"

The trip back to Manhattan was quiet, each of them wrapped up in the noisy embrace of the wind. A sense of calm had settled over Katie as they rose from the leatherette seats to begin the journey into the city, to her little place, her home. She turned to David to smile at him and was pleased that he smiled back. John drove all the way, one arm dangling over the door. At Katie's apartment, he traced his fingers along the ridge of the old couch and along the top of the wooden coffee table as though eager to feel with his own fingers the varied texture of her life.

"Love this place," he said. "So proud of what you're doing."

"Thanks, Dad, but you're giving me way too much credit, really. My life's not that exciting."

"Yeah, but look at all this."

David sat down and took off his baseball cap, his hair flattened underneath. His eyes were big as he followed his father's frenetic movements around the apartment. "That all you've got, Dad?" he asked, nodding toward the one small sack.

"Yep. Except for the things your mother kept for me. She's got some stuff in storage."

"Want me to do some shopping with you? Those pants are from the last century."

John smiled. "I think I might prefer to go shopping with this fashionista here," he said. "Though you didn't exactly dress up for the occasion, did you?"

Katie looked down at her clothes: worn cutoffs and a deep V-necked T-shirt. All the many times she'd visited him in prison, she'd been forced to wear slacks (no jeans) and cover herself up (no cleavage) in order to be allowed in, and today it had been liberating to grab whatever she wanted to wear. He was right—she should have made a bit of an effort. "We'll have dinner out somewhere later," she said. "Maybe I'll put on a pretty dress, okay?"

John headed toward the kitchen area and started looking around. When he leaned over the counter and reached toward a cabinet above the fridge, his plaid shirt rose up and showed a stretch of white belly, almost concave, hip bones sharp above the loose band of his pants. He had always been somewhat stout, wearing his muscles from years of teenage football like an extra layer of padding. Now he was lean, thin, even. Right there on the counter, next to him, was her bag from the drugstore. She was still dithering, hoping against all hope she wouldn't need to use it. But the truth was that physically she felt dreadful. The little she'd been able to eat at the diner earlier sat heavily in her stomach. She shoved aside thoughts of what that might mean.

Katie's phone buzzed in her back pocket. It was a text from a number she didn't recognize; the first message read, It's John and I've got wheels, and the incoming one said, Come on over.

"Sweetheart," he said, "don't you keep any beer in this place?"

"Shit, sorry, forgot to get any. I've got tequila?" Katie said, getting up to grab the bottle from the credenza.

"I'll take a glass too," her brother said.

"You got a text, Dad." She handed her father her phone. As he read, the creases in his forehead smoothed out; his jaw relaxed. He took the glass she handed him and drank it down slowly.

"I press here?" he asked, pointing to the space bar with his thumb.

Katie nodded. It was the strangest thing, having her father move around in space next to her. For so many years she had seen him in only one fixed place: the visiting room at Wallkill, sitting on the same stool. Only in her memories had he walked, stood, sat, eaten. Only in scenes from long ago had he interacted with the world of people and objects. Now, in her apartment—where she had lived so many hours invisible to him, where she had made love to men and cried out in Zev's embrace—he moved just the way she remembered: with a kind of automatic fatherly authority. She was the child; he was the adult. It was familiar, but it wasn't like she had imagined it would be.

John gave Katie back her phone, and she summoned all her will-power not to look at the text he'd just sent. "Got some music? Jazz, maybe?" he asked.

She found some Ella Fitzgerald on the radio. The music seemed to change the composition of the air between them, filling it with a kind of honeyed softness that was lighter than the silences. For hours they talked and laughed, stretched out their limbs and punched each other in the arms, and listened to each other's stories. Finally, after dusk had passed and the sky hung dark above the streetlights, David headed to the bathroom, and Katie went to her room to change into a dress before heading out for dinner. When she returned, her father was hunched over, his face sunk into his hands.

"Daddy?" she said. "What's the matter? Are you okay?"

He raised his face to her, and his eyes were small and bloodshot, his cheeks glistening. "Those balloons, Katie." His voice broke. "I can't stop thinking about just how—how *beautiful* they were. Just so crazy, goddamn *beautiful*."

32

After a big breakfast of scrambled eggs and bacon the next morning, John Gregory said he had to go. He promised to call as soon as he got his own cell phone.

"Aren't you staying with me?" Katie said. "I took the morning off."

"Of course I am," he said, rising. "But I've got to get out there a bit, see what's going on. Ride the wind a bit. You know? Just let the freedom sink in."

"Okay, but all alone?" Katie asked. Her father out there wandering the streets on his own didn't seem like much fun.

"Well, who said anything about being alone?" Her father smiled, hitched his bag to his shoulder, and threw the Falcon keys up in the air, catching them in one hand.

She felt a quick stab of jealousy. Of course he had people in his life she didn't know about, relationships that were as unknown to her as her relationships were to him. He had his freedom now; who were they to make assumptions or have expectations? He was a grown-up, for God's sake, and she was not his mother.

"And soon I'll be settling into the cabin," he added. "You'll come see me there, spend weekends, right?"

She asked if he had enough money, and he waved her away. "Your mother and I came to an arrangement. Don't worry about me."

She was aware of feeling disappointed, like a child who asked about the constellations and discovered that grown-ups didn't actually know much of anything; it just seemed as if they had all the answers. John scribbled a number down on a scrap of paper and kissed her on both cheeks, his stubble reminding her of endless nights in her cool sheets, his warm breath on the top of her head as he read to her.

When her father left, she strapped on her trainers and went for a run. Halfway through, her phone started buzzing: yet another text from Jack. To her surprise, her insides turned over, and she wondered why she even cared anymore, why she wasn't more angry at him. The confusion she'd felt after their kiss in the hallway had not entirely disappeared. Beneath her spiky anger was an undertow of tenderness, as though in the end she would forgive him anything. It was mysterious to her why she felt this way after so much time had passed. Though she sensed that there was something unsteady or untrustworthy about him, at the very same time she held an entirely different version of him in her mind: a boy's self with a pure-hearted essence. A boy who had shared a timeless moment with her. Those two selves were as real to her as the pavement beneath her feet.

She slowed to a walk and made her way back to her apartment. After showering and dressing for work, she looked up Jack's number in her contacts and blocked it, then blocked him. A small pang, a goodbye of sorts, pinched at her, and she let it pass. Then she got out her laptop and stared at the screen. Perhaps, with great care and delicacy, she could type out for Zev the story of what had happened. Perhaps black words on a clean white screen would be easier, or at the very least safer, than words from her mouth into the air. Could she explain herself?

Dearest Zev, she started.

She imagined Zev at a podium, his shirtsleeves rolled up, face shadowed by his angular features under slanted lights. She deleted the two words she'd written.

Hi Handsome! Can't wait till you get back.

Uncertainty buzzed in her ears.

We do have a lot to talk about

No, this was a bad idea. She would have to find the right way to tell him, face-to-face. Then she thought, *At least I can write that I love him.* But it seemed wrong to send those fragile words on that kind of journey—to an SMTP server where they would wait in an outgoing mail queue, clunky and manifestly inhuman. Instead, she would whisper them into his neck, the heat of her words giving life to possibility. They would stumble toward each other as best they could when he was back.

I'm really missing you and can't wait till you get back, she wrote instead, and she pressed send and headed out to the office.

What was different when she woke up the next morning, after going to bed far too early and sleeping badly? Nothing and everything. Spinning her feet from bed to floor, she rose, stretched her neck a bit, and headed straight to the kitchen area to get the pregnancy test. It was a basic version: pee here; watch the plus or minus sign emerge. She sat and peed, urged on by the sudden desire for certainty.

Her head was still lost among the night shadows; she stared at the pale-pink tiles, the missing grout. While waiting, she made herself coffee and picked her outfit for work. There was no rush—it was done, the damp plastic indicator lay on the windowsill in her bathroom, and all she had to do was look. Rushing would make no difference. The coffee was strong and gave her a sour kick. Her head began to clear. She checked her email again, but there was still nothing from Zev, even though it was daytime in Spain and he must have finished his speeches already. What a relief that she hadn't written him an overblown email in a moment of weakness telling him she loved him. In a few days he'd be back, and they would talk this all through sensibly. There was an email from her mother telling her that Grumpy had briefly been in the ICU again but was improving. Katie and David had tickets to London for the following weekend: an eleven-hour flight including two layovers, but she was happy she'd get to see him again.

In the bathroom, the plastic wand waited for her. The seconds before getting the answer were crystalline, perfectly empty. It was strange to know that reality had already happened, that it was a *fact*—she was or was not with child—but before she entered the bathroom, this reality did not yet exist for her.

She crossed the threshold, picked up the test, saw the sign. Now she knew: she was pregnant.

At work, the ringing of the phones and the susurrant voices formed a soundtrack to the whirling sandstorm in her mind. At this point, she would have paid to be given some real work to do rather than sit there twiddling her thumbs. There was some accounting she was helping a colleague with and a little research to do for Jonas, but other than that she was trapped in her cubicle with only her thoughts. As she pondered the reality that she was indeed carrying the tiny seed of a baby in her body—a child over whom she had the godlike power of life—she kept circling back again and again to her own mother.

Charlie had once told them she'd wanted babies since she understood that she could just cook one up in her belly like one of her own mother's rhubarb pies (this was before she understood the role men played in the culinary process of baby making). Talking with her kids about her childhood in England, she seemed charged with an almost melancholic energy, as though those days had been magical and real life hadn't lived up to the dreams she'd concocted for herself. It struck

Katie as odd, then, that Charlie seemed to get so little joy from being an actual mother herself. So odd that she'd begun to think motherhood had been disappointing in some way Charlie hadn't anticipated. It scared her.

Perhaps it was in fact the miscarriages, the steady loss. With each one, Charlie withdrew further. When Charlie finally gave birth to David, Katie had become so accustomed to her mother's frostiness, how she seemed to close herself off, that she wasn't sure if she should even show her happiness at having a baby brother.

It was two in the afternoon already, and there were no messages yet from her father. The phone at the cabin rang and rang into the emptiness, and there was no answering machine. She had no earthly idea where he could be. It occurred to her that he might have decided to drive up to Montreal and find her mother, but that was too crazy to be true.

Thank God Zev would be back soon. That night they'd had cocktails, when he'd tried to talk with her about moving in together, seemed as far away as the speck of a freighter on a watery horizon. She had been pregnant then, and she'd run away from him. How much of that was avoidance, and how much was simply because she'd felt sick? If he hadn't gone to Spain, would things have been different? She could have asked him to go to Eagle Lake with her; they would have had time to talk. Now she feared it might be too late: she'd withheld too much from him for too long. The lack of emails from him had her spinning.

That cold swim in the lake seemed so distant. The courthouse, those transcripts. Could it really have been only a few days ago that she had kissed Jack? Since Zev had been gone, she'd lived an entire life—and he had missed it all.

33

The other freshmen see only the person Katie chooses to present to them. It's been a few hours since her mother dropped her off on campus, and her roommate hasn't arrived yet. In the mirror of the communal bathroom, Katie is met with a surprise: the person staring back at her feels no relief. Violent furrows tug at her mouth. It's been a couple of months since her father went to prison. Over 254 more weeks to go! The house will be gone soon, sold. Charlie and David are moving into a small sublet in the city. Her life is a pocked moonscape. A rush of anger comes over her. She grabs the scissors from her toiletry bag, the razor she uses on her legs.

It takes almost an hour, but when she's done, she likes the face she encounters in the mirror. The shock and newness in the eyes. They declare: *Here I am! Look at me!* Two girls come in while she is in the process of shaving her scalp, but they don't pay much attention to her; they smile. It is all in good fun. Fun, fun—that's what college is about, isn't it?

The skin on her head is alarmingly white and raw. Katie wears a cap at first but soon becomes accustomed to the garishness of flesh stretched over her skull. This strips away the complications of being a girl; it puts people a little on edge. Asks them how they want to respond to her. Her eyes look enormous, and she starts wearing black eyeliner and lots of mascara. She's never worn much makeup before, and now she piles it on. The only thing that bothers her is her father's expression of shock when she visits him. But every time she brushes her teeth and glances at the mirror or catches someone's startled expression, it is confirmation that the timid girl she once was is being choked off like an unwelcome vine.

Winter, second semester. Too many neon lights hurting her eyes, too many books lining the endless shelves in the library. Katie runs track, running and running until she is so tired she can sleep. It probably isn't a good idea to go to the party, but she wants to relax, just like everyone else. She and her roommate, Marissa, get a ride to a rental house shared by three boys on the football team. House music blasts from the speakers, and a boy in a black baseball cap and skintight jeans starts handing out Ecstasy. It doesn't take long for her to decide to take one; after all, she is here to have fun. She pops a tablet in her mouth and swallows it dry.

The beer tastes like liquid heaven. Her body sings along with the music; she has never before been so in sync with the rhythms, so primed to move. With her arms raised above her head, she closes her eyes and sways, and every now and then someone bumps into her, and they let their bodies melt into each other for a while before moving apart again.

When she opens her eyes, the crowd has become dense. The air is tangy—marijuana and beer and sweat. Nudging through with her shoulders, she makes her way to the door. The sweat dries on her instantly as she steps outside. Reaching into the pocket of her cargo pants, she pulls out a pack of cigarettes and taps one out. She's taken up smoking regularly. It's her new thing. She can always blame the cigarettes if she fails to win a race or beat her own speed at track. Cigarettes as an insurance policy against feeling failure too keenly.

A bunch of kids mill around on the pavement, smoking, and there is a couple leaning against the aluminum siding, making out. The houses crowd into each other like misaligned teeth. The air around her pulses with noise. She will always remember the feeling of the music in her body, thrumming. One towering streetlight a few blocks down gives the impression of a yellow moon strung up on a sky-high clothesline. The cold feels great. Across the street, an old man walking his dog stares in her direction. She looks down and searches her pockets for matches. When she looks up again, the old man is standing in front of her.

"Hello," he says. "Here you go." He holds out a lighter. She leans forward into the flame and pulls back sharply when the heat hits her face. She sucks in and watches with astonishment as the paper catches fire and the tobacco starts to glow and then blacken. The fire seems to travel through the skin of her face, down her neck, and into her back. Her body is melting and liquid, yet she is not hot, nor is she cold. The man lights a cigarette for himself. One arm, thick and hairy at the wrist, has a leash looped around it. The hand itself is covered in paint, with blunt, creamy nails.

"I'm trying to quit and failing miserably," he says.

He has a strange accent. She looks into his face dreamily. Close up she sees that he isn't really old at all, in his thirties, perhaps. In the mixture of darkness and artificial light coming from the house, his skin looks creased, like a shirt left in the dryer too long, and tanned, even though it is wintertime.

"You shouldn't be smoking," he says after a while. "Bad habit."

She is busy studying his dog, a fluffy brown bundle who has curled up next to his foot. The intimacy between the man and the dog is palpable.

"This little one," the man says, tipping his head, "he's tired. And lazy." His eyes, hidden behind a squint, are trained on her. "I should take him home, but I'm trying not to smoke in the studio." He gestures toward a large building a few houses down that looks like a warehouse.

Katie throws her cigarette into the gutter, careful to clear the dog, whose sides are lifting and sinking like miniature bellows.

"May I ask," the man says, the cloud of smoke swirling in the air between them, "do you speak?" When he smiles, his eyes disappear entirely, and his teeth gleam as though illuminated from inside. They are pulsing at her. She wants to lick them.

"Yes," she says, as he turns to go, "I do."

Inside, the floorboards vibrate with music, and the reverberations travel through the soles of her feet, through her pelvis, and to her neck bones. Trudging up the stairs, she looks for her roommate in the bedrooms. One of the boys who lives in the house, Damian, is leaning against the wall in the hallway talking to an Asian girl. Their eyes meet as Katie passes. She knows who he is; she's been watching him from afar since orientation. Sometimes in the mornings he gets bagels—always plain—at Francesco's near Blodgett Hall, where she's taking an econ class. There's a cubicle in the library where he often sits, wearing big black headphones. His eyes, overhung with thick, pale eyebrows, are wary, as though he too keeps himself hidden just on the other side of his expression.

He shoots her that quizzical look she is now so familiar with: *Something wrong with you, or are you bald on purpose?* She brushes past, her body infused with sudden desire that tingles in her neck and between her thighs. In the bathroom, she puts her arm onto the wall to steady herself. The wallpaper is a garish pink and turquoise, a floral pattern only a grandmother or absentee landlord would choose. Toothbrushes with splayed bristles crowd the sink.

The bathroom door opens behind her. "Oh—" a boy says. But instead of stepping away and shutting the door, he steps forward. It is the boy she likes, Damian. Katie jumps up and makes to yank up her panties, but he is next to her in a flash, grabbing her wrist. "I saw you looking at me out there," he says.

"So what?" she answers. In that second she thinks of Lulu and what she would do—then she turns away from that thought. Who does Katie want to be right then? Blood pounds in her ears from excitement or fear. They stare at each other for longer than seems possible. Close up, the boy's eyes are small, his face chapped looking.

"Fuck," he says, his breath stinking of beer and smoke, "you're some kind of freak, aren't you?"

"You are too," she says. "You just won't admit it."

He takes her hand and puts it on his crotch. He flips her around so she is leaning over the toilet, bracing against the wall with the palm of her hand. Her throat is tight; she didn't expect things to go so fast, but his hand is between her legs, and she is wet, and her disgust melts away, and she stops wondering how he knew that she would let him do this to her, even though she doesn't really want to, not this way.

A hand on her head. The air smells of something faintly tart. Her chin lifts, propped up by two stubby fingers. "You all right?" a voice asks.

She opens her eyes a bit and through the cracks sees that she is outside on the street. The sky has turned from black to blue and is brightening. Something wet is on her hand. It lies beside her on the pavement, and she turns, very slowly, to look down, and there is a small brown dog licking her knuckles.

"You need to go home." It is the old man who isn't old, crouched back on his heels. He wears painter's pants and scuffed suede trainers. "I came back. The music is still so loud. I'm usually up late, but even so." She wants him to cradle her face in both his huge, warm hands. With the pad of his thumb, he wipes her cheeks. "Where is home? I will take you."

"Cushing," she whispers.

"I knew it," he says, but he doesn't tell her what it is that he knows. Instead, he holds on to her elbow and guides her upright. "Come with me."

Her head begins spinning, and she turns away from him and retches against the fence. There is no one else on the street. The house behind her continues to pulse with music, and she tries to swallow the noises and the pain.

The little dog is off his leash, and when they get to the other side of the street, the man calls, "Mira!" and the dog scampers across the road to his side. He unlocks an ancient Kia, puts his hand on Katie's head again, and guides her into the front seat like a police officer guides a perp into a cruiser. The car smells of turpentine and ropes and is filled with boxes and bags and canvases. After sinking into the front seat, Katie leans her head back, and a shudder courses through her.

"You don't need to be afraid," he says, putting the key in the ignition.

"I'm not afraid." Her head throbs with every syllable.

"Well, good, but you should be more cautious. You can't just trust everyone"—he interrupts himself by hesitating—"in general, I mean to say." He pulls into the street. In the fog of her stupendous hangover, she thinks to herself that under different circumstances she would consider him handsome.

"What's your name?" he asks. His hands on the steering wheel are scrubbed clean. That is where the fresh smell is coming from.

"I'm Katie." She tries to smile. "Do you know where to go?"

"Yes, I know where to go," he answers. The interior light of the car is still on, and when he looks at her, his eyes are washed out, a weak blue. "I'm Zev. I teach at Vassar. Studio art, sculpture. I've seen you around campus before."

"So you're a stalker, then."

He laughs. "Yes, and you are just a little girl, though you don't seem to think so."

"Am I in trouble? You a provost or something?"

When he doesn't answer, she thinks he might be a weirdo after all, someone who wants to teach her a lesson. But he is intent on the road, his mouth curled upward slightly. At Collegeview Terrace he pulls up to the dorm, and he doesn't get out of the car to take her into her room as she thinks he might. But the way he looks at her when she pokes her head back in to say thank you—his gaze is so penetrating that it makes her think that maybe this is the beginning of something, but she doesn't know what.

34

The sound of running water, a sharp smell. Katie kicked the door of her apartment closed behind her, lugging three plastic shopping bags. Could it be her father already? He had finally called to tell her he was coming over that night, and she'd gone food shopping after work. But he didn't have a key.

"Hello?" she called out. Then she smelled it more distinctly: oil paint.

A large canvas was propped up against the far wall, about three feet by five. It had three figures on it, a woman and two men, one looming and stretched out, something soft, feathers perhaps, stuck in the black paint of his bones. The other man had no face but papier-mâché hands attached to the canvas that reached out, painted a luminous white. The female figure was somewhere between a girl and a woman and had been rendered in amazing detail with vibrant yellows and reds. Zev called this technique sfumato; he'd apply lighter colors over a dark glaze so the paint pulsed with life. The female appeared to hover over the other figures, to emerge from the darkness of the picture, delicate, ephemeral. Tiny gold buttons on her jacket glinted, and she wore jewels in her ears. In her hands she held something that seemed to be the focus of the painting, but it was smudged, as though purposefully unclear or unfinished. The girl's hair was blonde, almost incandescent. Like Katie's.

Zev emerged from the bathroom. His silvery hair was slicked back, darkened by water, his skin a glowing brown hue as though he'd just come from picking grapes in Greece under a punishing sun or visiting family in Tel Aviv. Katie's towel was slung around his hips, threads trailing along his damp shins. In his hand he held a razor.

She dropped the bags and grinned at him like an idiot. "What the hell? You're back already!"

"Hey, there. My last panel was canceled—I took an earlier flight back." He indicated the door with the razor. "It's okay? That I let myself in?"

"Oh, yeah. Sure," she said. So he'd been traveling; *that's* why he hadn't answered her email. She pointed to the painting. "Wow, Zev. It's incredible. It's supposed to be me?"

He smiled. "I've been working on it for the past few weeks. A friend was storing it for me."

"It wasn't in your show?"

"It's for you."

"Thank you, Zev. I mean, it's . . . I don't even know what to say." When they embraced, his skin was damp against her face, and it felt so good. She fought back a sudden surge of tears: *He doesn't know*, she thought. *He doesn't know anything. What am I going to say?*

"You okay?" He held her at arm's length.

"I'm so glad you're here," she said. "I need to tell you something."

"Is it about the test? I'm sorry—I saw it in the trash can."

They eyed each other, trying to assess what the other one was thinking. She could not still the percussive pounding in her chest. His voice was neutral, his face composed. He'd been smiling at her, and now he was serious. Did that mean he was hiding anger or fear—that he hated the idea of having a child? Or was he waiting to see what she said? She needed to know at least on some level what his gut reaction was before she could begin the work of knowing what she wanted.

"You are shocked," he said. "I didn't mean to snoop; it was right there, lying on the top."

"I—I just took it. Yesterday morning." She hoisted the bags onto the kitchen counter and kicked off her shoes. She had bought steaks for her father.

Zev lingered on the other side of the island. "I'm so sorry; we were careless, and . . . and that I put you in this position."

"I'm a big girl too," she said, unable to tell from his tone if he was saying this was a disaster from which they had to recover or an opportunity. Was he saying it was up to her to choose? The uncertainty and fear made her sharper than she intended to be. "I know how babies are made."

"A surprise like this. It's disorienting, no? But that doesn't mean it's bad."

Certainly, she couldn't regret those heady moments when they'd lost themselves in the timeless dark. Katie couldn't imagine flicking on a light, reaching for a condom. She wanted the dream of losing herself to be possible; she wanted to be safe while also being free. But that didn't mean she was ready to be a mother. Freedom and motherhood were not synonymous.

"What are you thinking?" he asked. His sad eyes made Katie want to run a finger over his brows, smooth out the worry lines. "I have so much I want to say . . . but I don't know."

"I just—I mean, I don't feel ready. I can't make a decision just like that," she said. "I'm not ready."

"Of course, I know. I'm sure." He paused. "It's not the same for me; I know that. But Katie, a child? A child is a beautiful gift."

She looked away. He wanted the baby.

"I can't tell you what to do. I would never tell you what to do," he said. "But we can choose to see this as a gift. A chance to build something together. Something very, very important."

It wasn't just a child he wanted; he wanted to have a child *with her*. He trusted that she could be the mother she would need to be for the sake of their baby. This was incredible; this was beautiful and good— and yet a sickly, creeping anxiety overtook her. It was one thing to admit her tentative hopes for them as a couple, maybe even as a *family*, and another to finally come clean about her past. How could she know that he wouldn't be disgusted with her for keeping so much from him?

"Come here," he said, pulling her by the hand toward the couch. He put one arm over her shoulder, and she nestled in, the scent of her own soap and shampoo on him. "It's not a disaster. This doesn't have to be a bad thing."

She began to cry, trying to swallow the noise, hide the tightening of her muscles.

He pulled back to get a look at her. "It will be all right, Katie," he said, his eyes an unstable gray. "I promise you. We will work it out."

"There's something else I really need to tell you," she said.

Zev made her some Manzanilla tea he'd brought back from Spain while she changed into leggings and splashed her face with cold water. He threw on a T-shirt and jeans and took a seat on the armchair. He'd pulled away from her, not just his body but his spirit, his whole being screaming of separation, as though their sense of communion had been a brief delusion. Perhaps he thought she would tell him she had been sleeping with someone else, that the baby was not his. After all, they hadn't agreed to be exclusive; they had been careful, both of them, to keep their options open.

"It's not about being pregnant," she said. "It's, um. It's about my father. Something I haven't told you."

"Okay . . ." he said.

"Something awful happened, at that place I went—my grandfather's place at Eagle Lake. When I was a teenager."

"To you, Katie?" Zev's careful, neutral expression collapsed. He leaned forward, elbows on his knees. "What happened?"

"No, no—not me. To my father, and, well, my friend was part of it. She was my best friend."

She started with meeting a girl named Lulu at a Walmart. The endless carefree summers at her grandfather's house. The cabin, the rope. They met a boy; they were so young—the memories tumbled out. An insidious jealousy, a sense of competition began growing between them—then, months later, the accusation of rape, out of nowhere.

That ugly word: *rape*. When you spoke it aloud, it changed the very air you breathed. Zev remained silent as she was talking, but his face told the story of what his heart felt.

She explained that her father had just been released from jail, and she had been getting calls from reporters that stirred up something murky inside her. That his freedom was not like she'd expected. She was—and she hesitated here, picking her words carefully—she was confused.

"You think it was wrong?" Zev asked. He looked as though gravity had tugged at his face and body and he could not resist the terrible downward pull. "You think he did not deserve to go to jail?"

"I was so sure, totally sure it was all a lie." She stared at his face, and the intensity of his concentration gave her courage. "But I could never figure out why. I mean, why would she lie?" She told him about the transcripts, about finding the paperwork from the trial at the cabin and how all this had set her off on a journey. The explanation came out of her in an astonishing rush of energy and fear. She choked on her words and just kept going.

When she mentioned the article she had read about dissociative disorder, his eyes sharpened. "And this girl, Lulu. You have spoken with her?" Zev asked.

"I called her last week. But she wouldn't talk; she, um . . . she hung up on me," Katie said. The tea was cooling, and she took a sip, but the mug clanged against her teeth, and she set it down. "It was awful. Awful. I felt so bad for her, and I was trying to tell her I understood things better now, but it all came out wrong."

There were footsteps on the stairs leading to her apartment, a rap on her door. She hadn't even noticed night falling. Windows looked out onto the building opposite, where lights were being switched on, like fireflies awakening. While they'd been talking, she'd forgotten her father was coming, and now he was at the door, iridescent shadows under his eyes and even more stubble on his chin, his clothes unchanged.

"Daddy!" she said. A flash of impatience was almost instantly supplanted by concern: Had he slept at all? "Are you okay?"

"Hello, beautiful lady," he said, bustling past her and putting down a large blue nylon bag, which still had a cardboard price tag attached to it. "Your father has been one busy man, and he's here to get some nosh. My lord, it's good to be back among the living."

Turning toward her, he caught sight of Zev in the living area, standing with his hands deep in the pockets of his jeans.

"Aha," John said. "You've got company."

"Dad, this is Zev. My, uh, boyfriend," Katie said, letting out a tentative laugh. "Zev, this is John Gregory, my father."

"I see. Your boyfriend," John said, reaching out to grab Zev's hand and smiling broadly. "Delighted."

It had been six years since John had eaten seafood, so they decided to get sushi instead of eating the steak Katie bought. The three of them headed off to a hole-in-the-wall restaurant two blocks from her apartment. They sat in the back at a small table near the kitchen. Zev was oriented toward her father, as though pulled in by the net of his energy. John talked unabashedly about his years in prison, telling one ludicrous story after another, and after a while Zev relaxed and began to laugh along with him. Katie could see this was her father's intention: normalizing that which usually made people feel uncomfortable. He didn't want to be treated like a leper. He wanted people to admire his fortitude, his good humor, and his strength. See that he'd turned this experience into something positive, something that made people at dinner in a restaurant laugh into their glasses of sake.

Her father shoveled the food in, chewing hastily, as though someone might snatch the next *unagi* roll away from him. Zev replenished their sake, and Katie abstained. She watched the two men feel each other out, Zev tentatively as was his way, allowing John to be the funny man. Once they'd had sufficient sake, Zev became ebullient, too, relaxing back into his chair, swirling the cup in his blunt fingers. They began to compete as to who had the most disgusting story to tell about the foods they were willing to eat. This developed into stories of traveling, and Zev talked about his "starving artist" period, when he'd lived in a squat in Brixton. The antinuke rallies in Trafalgar Square that he and his girlfriend treated like a day out, taking along a picnic of sausage rolls and cans of pale ale. John said he and Charlie had spent two months in London once, when they were first dating. He told them about the bedsit in Hammersmith where they'd had to feed the meter to keep the electricity on.

"So, my friend," John said, untucking the napkin he'd hung in his shirt collar and wiping his chin and mouth with it. His face was haggard, but his eyes were lit up. "You're forty...what? Forty-one? A Peter Pan type, I guess?"

"Youth is a crown of roses; old age, a crown of willows, as my mother used to say," Zev answered. He had not caught the slight shift in John's tone, the sharpening of his focus, but Katie noticed it right away, and she sat up taller. "They say students keep you young, but I suspect it's the exact opposite. Teaching takes years off your life." Zev was smiling, still having fun.

"Teachers allowed to date their students these days?" John asked.

"Dad, I wasn't one of his students, not ever," Katie said. "We met here in New York. I'd already been working a couple of years."

"Didn't you first meet at college?" He reached out to touch her forearm. "I just feel really in the dark, hon."

He probably thought he was looking out for her, but she hadn't asked him to do that. She had grown up since they'd last lived together like regular people; she'd become a woman who didn't need to ask permission to make her own decisions.

Zev looked from her father to Katie and back again, his brows snagged over his heavy nose. "Are you suggesting we've done something improper?"

John poured himself more sake. "When I was in jail, I met a man with the name of Emmet. He was a sculptor, covered in tattoos. On his neck, right up to here"—he ran his finger under one ear, along his chin, to the other ear—"skulls and playing cards and girls riding missiles. He was near seventy years old. Boy, he loved those tattoos. Oiled them with some kind of coconut potion he had to bargain for from the commissary. *He* didn't think much of getting older either."

"So, Dad, okay . . ." Katie said, seeing the gap widen between her father's perception and reality. He was embarrassingly off base. "Zev's a professor, not a teacher. There's one of his paintings in the apartment, did you notice? He's very talented, really good. After his opening, his show at the Gaslight, there was tons of . . . of . . ." She petered out when she felt pressure on her leg; it was Zev, putting his hand on her thigh, asking her to please stop.

"That painting with the hands?" John asked. "The big one—that's one of yours?"

"He just gave it to me today," Katie said. "Isn't it incredible?"

"Yes, it is. Very interesting. She's in a position of power, the girl, or she's overshadowed by the others, the dark types?"

"I think that's probably the point, right? It's ambiguous."

They sat looking at the food before agreeing to box it up and head back. When John asked for the bill, the waitress said it had already been paid, and Zev waved his hand, as though it meant nothing. He must have given them his credit card when he'd gone to the men's room earlier.

"You planning on staying over tonight, Dad?" Katie asked as they approached her place. A drifting sense of disorientation had overtaken her in the restaurant, a tilting of expectations, and she didn't know anymore what she wanted from him. Earlier, watching the hot-air balloons, she had slipped back into the delicate fold of girlhood, of being his child. Now, there was a surge inside her pulling her away; she was no longer the same person she'd been back then.

"Well, provided the Israeli's not staying too and we have to wrestle for space, ha ha," John said.

"Please don't call him that," Katie said. "And Zev sleeps in my bed, obviously."

"Aw, so sensitive," John said. "I'm just joking, sweetheart." He shook Zev's hand and looked him in the eye. "Thanks for dinner. And for taking good care of my girl."

"You're very welcome," Zev said.

John took the keys from Katie and headed up the stairs.

"I should go," Zev said quietly. "Right? You need some time together."

"Sorry. It's been so long. He just wants what's best for me."

"You are both finding each other, still. I understand." A shadow passed over Zev's face. "Wait—is it tomorrow that you go to London? Already?"

She nodded. "Just a few days," she said. They held on to each other for a while, kissing briefly, but it seemed as though neither of them could wait to pull away.

"Okay." Zev started to walk down Hester and then turned around. "Katie?"

"Yeah?" she said.

He pulled his leather jacket around him more tightly. "Nothing," he said. His smile was grim, and she couldn't blame him. The night had certainly not unfolded as he'd expected. "I wish you didn't have to go right now. But yeah. I hope it goes well. Maybe I'll get to meet your grandfather one day."

Why did she feel as though she couldn't take a full breath? The idea of losing herself to someone was no longer what frightened her most, she thought as she climbed the steps toward her apartment. It was the question of whether she could be vulnerable in that way while at the same time being a good mother. Her own mother had stumbled badly, and Katie still didn't quite know where her father had taken the wrong step. It seemed that parenthood turned you into both a hero and a patsy, torn by competing impulses. And the question was if she wasn't up to it, if she really wasn't ready for motherhood—not *now*—could Zev still love her?

She rested a hand lightly on the flat of her stomach. It was time to ask her father some questions too. The door was ajar and the radio set on low to Jazz 88. Fresh, mismatched sheets were stretched out over the old couch, and her father lay there fully clothed with his shoes off.

"That was nice," Katie said, hanging up her denim jacket. "I'm so glad you got to meet Zev."

When he didn't respond, she went over to the couch. He was fast asleep; his mouth hung open slightly, and his face, even in repose, was as fierce and tender as it had always been. But with his eyes closed he was stripped of something; she couldn't be sure what it was. She reached down to touch his shoulder. "Dad?" she said.

He rolled his head to the side and brought his arms up over his chest. The skin on his neck sagged, and she was hit with the realization that as his child she would never know him fully. Gently, she raised his dead legs to the couch and pulled the sheet and blanket up over him.

There was no need to rush things. Tomorrow she would fly to the UK and take care of her grandfather. After that, she would turn to everything else—her father, her lover, herself. In what order exactly, she didn't know, but did it matter? Probably not.

35

On the plane, David was full of chatter about his understudy work at the Broadmore; it was good to see him opening up when for so many years he had been like a moth confused by the interplay of light and dark, easily crushed. The joy of discovering something he was good at was visible in his quickened cadence, the serious pull of his mouth. They settled in, talking a bit about their father, about how he seemed, his look and demeanor, but not all that much. They had no habit of sharing concerns or fears, no vocabulary for doubt. It was what they had learned among the silences and turmoil of their teen-age years. After throwing up twice in the minuscule, water-splattered airplane toilet, Katie decided to tell David about being pregnant. His eyes widened, and in the rush of his surprise he sounded like a child, and then—just like a child—he lost interest as quickly as if he were turning a page in a book. It was a relief to have that news turn out to be, somehow, so very ordinary. After a few hours in the air, he crashed hard, sleeping with his head twisted awkwardly, undisturbed by the flight attendant bringing food or the heavyset man struggling to sidle his way toward the aisle.

The road into London from Heathrow wove above the streets on an elevated highway from which the billboards and office buildings seemed to be close enough to touch. Once the black cab reached the outer suburbs, morning traffic thickened into a writhing snake. The road narrowed down to the A4 and became the London Road, shooting through identical brick row houses with tiny front lawns, remarkably clean of litter, overhung with the pall of exhaust.

The cab headed straight for their hotel on Marylebone Road. There was a tidy familiarity to England that Katie found comforting. Weaving through central London, she was struck once again by its orderliness, the way everything had its place. Patterns everywhere you looked: in the multicolored bricks scalloped along the rooftops; in the fluted iron railings bordering front lawns; in the rows of trees, all pruned just so, leaves supple and ever rustling. There was far more sky visible than in New York, and when the sun came out, it was so vast and shocking that the streets glinted with surprise. One ray of sunshine, and Londoners shed their coats and jackets with joyful exuberance, as if they'd suddenly found themselves transported to a beach in Majorca—a whole country for which a simple change of weather led to a transformation of personality.

They showered and drank some coffee but wasted no time walking over to the nursing home. Grumpy was sitting in a chair by the window. He wore clunky glasses that made his eyes look twice their normal size and held knitting needles in his fleshy fingers. The window was cracked open, and a stream of air whistled in, ruffling the blanket laid over knees as giant and misshapen as boulders.

"Sunshine! Boyo!" he said, his face brightening. "What a fabulous treat!"

"Am I seeing correctly, Grumps? You, *knitting*?" Katie asked, peeling off her jean jacket. "Are we in some kind of alternate universe?"

Harry Amplethwaite held up a long, thin scarf that snaked over his armrest and onto the floor. "Nothing like fashion accessories to spiff up a dull wardrobe. As your grandmother always said, idle hands are the devil's work. And if I'm working, it means blood's still pumping through my veins."

"Yo, Grumpy," David said, and they did a complicated fist bump and then hugged, slapping each other on the back. They loved playing up the kid slang for fun. "You look rad."

"Yes, well. Could do with a bit of a spit and polish," Grumpy answered.

"You always look dashing," Katie said. Though his face was animated, it sagged at the edges like melting wax, his heavy eyebrows drooping in the middle as though pressed down by two invisible thumbs. His hair was gloriously thick and near black, neatly parted to one side. "How are you feeling? Any better?"

"Rotten," he said. "But then I'm well into my tenth decade, so who's complaining?"

They sat around his little table, and he filled them in on the various simmering feuds going on in the nursing home. For a mathematician and an engineer, he was an excellent storyteller. David turned on the electric kettle, and they drank some Tetley's, using Gram's wafer-thin china cups with the gold edges and watching the birds peck at the privet hedges outside.

As they talked, Katie managed to inhabit multiple places at once: she was in the room with her grandfather, absorbing the smell of wool and the faint tang of privet, while also being in her apartment with Zev and then her father. She was still trying to make sense of it. All along she had made the assumption that Zev was too different from the man she had imagined for herself for the two of them to actually stay together. Across that gallery that night she'd caught sight of him again, she remembered thinking, *So what if it's just for fun?* The pull she felt didn't have to have a reason other than being a physical imperative. But that had changed. The abandon wasn't just a fleeting revelation—it permanently loosened something inside her. And having her father react to him in that awkward, prickly way made her understand that she would have to claim Zev, assert her right to love whomever she chose.

Securing a van and a wheelchair from the nursing home, David and Katie took Grumpy to the British Museum. In all the years they had visited their mother's family in England, they'd never missed a trip to the museum, hours-long strolls through echoing halls, legs buzzing with fatigue. They always headed straight for the Assyrian rooms, with their winged-lion sculptures and carved stone panels. Grumpy had flown a Vickers Wellington bomber when he was twenty-one years old and a member of the RAF during the war. They'd engaged in battle at Habbaniya, eventually ending up on the outskirts of Baghdad (where he'd been mildly injured by an even younger soldier who was a member of his own regiment). He loved to regale his grandchildren with stories about his haplessness.

They made their way slowly through the Nimrud rooms until they landed in Room 9, Nineveh, with its human-headed winged bulls. After a short but alarming coughing fit, Grumpy motioned for them to stop, and Katie and David took a seat on a bench while he rested. They had begun talking about the chain of command in the British military when David said, "You know Dad got out of prison, right? Did Katie tell you already?"

"Whoa," Katie said, "talk about a non sequitur."

A flush mottled the skin of her grandfather's neck and crept up toward his jawline. "Well. The military operates in a hierarchical manner; its leaders demand respect and loyalty. And they deserve it. We gave our lives readily for those we admired. They were trusted. They were men of their word."

"What do you mean? Are you saying Dad isn't?" Katie asked, her eyes locked on his face. There was a fluttering of something unpleasant in her chest—doubt or the desire to defend?

Grumpy lifted his thick glasses up, balancing them near his perfect hairline, and rubbed at his eyes. His head swiveled decisively toward the display to their left, a fragment of an enormous stone slab with an image of a vessel on it and multiple oars. *We have to talk about your father,* John had written in letters from prison to her mother. "Did something happen between the two of you?" Katie continued.

Grumpy made a snorting noise. His big eyes were harder now. "Your father was what we call a runner. He ran away from his problems. Never one to admit his weaknesses. That man, I have never in my life met a man so capable of avoiding reality."

"Yeah, well, he sure didn't manage to run away from *all* his problems," David said, shifting his weight uneasily.

"Why do you think he was always finding yet another new and exciting career opportunity? That foolish business idea in the early years, then what? Commercial banking and—what was it in the end—day trading? Or the other way around—I don't remember. Could barely make a living for himself, let alone keep you all afloat."

Katie realized she had never really thought much about her father's profession, except to notice that the money—whatever money it was they'd had coming in, previously—had dried up after the conviction. She remembered the business card she'd unearthed, with her mother's handwriting on it and a London address. It had struck her as unusual because of the name, the obvious foreignness. "Grumpy, so, remember that thing I asked you about a while back, some guy called Montenegro? Do you know who that is? I found an old card when I was tidying up at the cabin."

Her grandfather stiffened visibly, and when he tried to adjust his glasses, his fingers were as ineffective as putty. "*Montefiore,*" he said. "If you must know, he was a private investigator. Hugo, the son of a friend from Cambridge, he arranged it for me. He'd lived in the States for a while, knew the system."

David, his black leather jacket like a carapace, zipped to his chin, stood up and cracked his knuckles. A young Japanese family made their way through the room, the little boy trailing a piece of string with paper tied to the end. They all watched until the family was out of sight. "To help you do what?" David asked.

"Get evidence to present to Charlie. So she could see what she was dealing with."

"You mean, evidence on, uh—against *Lulu*?" Katie asked.

"Goodness," Grumpy said, gesturing emphatically, as though she were too stupid for words. "About all the other things, dear. Now take me home, will you please. We've had quite enough excitement for one day."

She and David exchanged a glance. He seemed pale and bothered, sorry he'd brought up their father in the first place. But maybe he'd been stirring the pot on purpose; it wasn't clear. On the streets, the sun shone on the speckled sidewalks, but the chill of the museum stayed with her, as if she'd been standing too long in a windy corridor and hadn't noticed that her fingers had started to go numb.

36

In the next few days, they met with Grumpy's physician, Dr. Abad, a small, round Persian whose hairline cut across the apex of his skull in an almost straight line. In precise, accented English he relayed that Grumpy's blood pressure was still extremely low, but the infection was waning; he was a remarkably healthy man given his advanced years. Katie and David had tea with the home's head nurse, Henrietta, a Miami Dolphins fan, and gave her a turquoise jersey.

They spent an entire day helping Grumpy sort out his tattered photo albums from when he'd lived in Kenya as a young boy. Later, she tried to ask him about the evidence he'd mentioned when they were at the museum, but he held up his hand, trembling ever so slightly, and she retreated. That night, Katie opted out of seeing *Mamma Mia!* at the Novello Theatre with David and a friend of his who was studying at Richmond. Grumpy and Katie ate a lukewarm roast-beef dinner at the cafeteria in Ravenswood, and afterward, as she helped him maneuver his massive frame onto the bed, he pointed her to his dresser, where a battered manila folder lay.

"I was thinking," he said. "Silence isn't always empty, is it? It can drive a person quite mad. Give me that, would you?"

She brought the folder over to him on the bed and looked at him helplessly. He was frail and yet at the same time imposing, with his broad shoulders and implacable eyes. He opened the file and grabbed a tidy bundle of typed reports held together with a paper clip, a plastic bag containing photographs, and another one that appeared to contain receipts, fanning them out on the bed.

"What's all this, then?" she asked.

"About your father, dear. You asked, and, well, you've never asked before, have you? It bothered me for years, this whole damn thing." He coughed harshly into a soft cotton handkerchief. "Your mother, poor dear. It wasn't clear what she really wanted back then, but I think that die has long been cast."

Her grandfather kept talking as she picked up one item after another. The heading of one sheet read, *Surveillance Report, Insight Investigators*. The language was straightforward; there were dates and times and lists of phone numbers, interviews that had been typed up, and surveillance log sheets. There was a letter of termination from a RE/ MAX Realty in Pennsylvania and a copy of a police report dated July 19, 1991, and another from November 22, 2002.

Names and dates and facts were visible to her, but even stitched together in this way, they didn't assume a significance larger than themselves. As she shuffled some papers between her fingers, her head started clouding over. She wasn't sure what all this was supposed to mean. Grumpy sensed her growing alarm and began talking more quickly, picking up first one document and then another.

There was so much she hadn't known. She had not known that her father never actually graduated from Harvard (wasn't there a diploma that used to hang in the master bathroom in West Mills?). She had not known that Grumpy bailed him out of jail when he got his first DUI and that the year he took town cars to work was not because he'd been given a raise, as she and David had thought, but because his driver's license had been suspended. Her father had been laid off three times: Grumpy's investigator had unearthed complaints from coworkers at his places of business. He'd been fired from a job selling insurance, back when he first met Charlie.

"But nobody's perfect, Grumpy. Haven't you ever done something you're embarrassed about or made a mistake?" Katie asked. She felt almost panicked, as though she were being told to jump from a plane. It seemed very important to defend her father, to put this into context. This cataloging and piling on of his minor misdemeanors was mean spirited, petty, even. "This isn't really playing fair."

"My dear, you're entirely missing the point. What I'm saying is we reap what we sow. Everything we choose to do has consequences. And people do not change unless they want to change. They show us their colors; we just don't see them."

As they continued, her grandfather's fingers became steadier and his voice stronger. She had not known that when she was three years old and her mother had her second miscarriage, her father was having an affair with a young woman named Dana Huntington, whose father was the CEO of Ulster Bank. At this last piece of information Katie turned away from him abruptly and searched for a glass she could use to get herself some water from the sink in the corner. She could not swallow properly. The brown linoleum shifted under her feet, and she steadied herself with one hand on the edge of the porcelain.

Grumpy flapped an interview form in the air. He'd known about that one, he said. He discovered the affair by accident when he was in the bank executing a transfer. Grumpy called the woman's father, Barclay Huntington, and the next day she put an end to the affair. It turned out John had been invited to their estate in Westchester twice for family dinners. No one had known about the existence of a wife or a baby girl back in West Mills.

"I often wonder if things would've been different had I told Charlie about that one. But he insisted, your father. He'd made a dreadful mistake; he was repentant." Grumpy held her eyes with his yellowed, watery ones. She could barely register what he was telling her now. "He seemed sincere, and I believed him. I thought he'd strayed once and that would be it. I didn't want to ruin my daughter's marriage! It seemed cruel not to give him another chance."

Page after page, there were women's names, details, photos. The pictures and notes revealed an unassailable truth: This woman here, she was real; she was flesh and blood. She was a student, a mother, a businesswoman, a teacher, a socialite. She looked haughty or tender hearted. Perhaps she was clingy or perhaps standoffish. Her hair was long, short, brown, blonde.

Katie gripped her glass of water. She took tiny sips, but no amount of drinking could lubricate her throat or put her body back into its normal state. Where had all this happened? Where had he taken these women? Their faces crowded her mind, and in among those clamorous women was her father, throwing a smile at her in a messy kitchen after they'd made turkey meatballs. Watching her with an ecstatic look on his face as she twirled around in the dressing room at Macy's, trying on Easter dresses. Shouting, louder than any of the other dads, on the sidelines when she scooped up a ground ball on the lacrosse field in middle school. That man, that man she loved, had had an entire life she'd known nothing about. She wondered: Had he loved his family at all?

"But why did you . . . I mean, was it—did Mum know about it? And about the investigator, the affairs?" she asked. The enormity of what she was learning was beginning to overwhelm her, how it changed reality the way nuclear transmutation changed chemical elements. This all seemed utterly impossible, yet it was not impossible at all—if anything, it was *common*. In some ways, it was the ordinariness of this betrayal that was so shocking.

"Not at first. But it was my duty, Katherine. I was her father. I was supposed to look out for her."

She held Grumpy's hand, and they sat for a while in strangled silence, his breath loud and labored. Under her fingers her grandfather's skin felt as thin and dry as tissue paper. Her brain was racing, but it had nowhere to go; she was stuck in an infinite loop. Then she caught sight of a photo of someone she recognized: Constance Nichols, the woman who had garaged the Falcon at Eagle Lake. "Where did you get this one?"

"That?" said Grumpy. "Don't remember. The investigator was terribly thorough. I imagine he interviewed the woman. Look on the back; perhaps it says there."

"I already know who it is." Constance had chiseled features and a nose that was a little too long for her face. In the picture, her hair was swept up in a loose bun, and a pearl choker lay at the base of her neck, tight against her skin. She had been an actress when she was younger.

When Katie thought of her parents during their marriage, she saw them dancing the tango in the clubhouse; driving on the highway with the roof down; diving, one after another, into the water, lean and athletic. Tanned shins and sandy toes. Her dad with his drink, eyes crinkling. Where did Constance fit into this picture? She barely looked like she'd have the energy for emotion. Not that long ago, David had told her how kind their father had been to that woman: *It's wrong to break your word; you've got to treat people right. It's important to be honorable.* And meanwhile, he'd been having an affair with her?

As a child, she'd seen the way people's faces lit up when her father told a joke or complimented them. Now another piece of the puzzle was in place, and she saw what that might have meant for her parents' marriage. She sat very still. It felt as though if she were to move, she might break. "My God, Grumpy. So you told Mum about all this?"

"Yes, dear. I had to."

"And that's when she decided to leave?" Katie asked. Her heart ached for her mother as she thought back to the prison visit when her parents had told her they were getting divorced. Katie had slammed down the receiver and run away, but the guards wouldn't let her leave the visiting rooms. Thinking her mother was capable of that kind of disloyalty and selfishness had cut off something inside Katie, making it impossible for her to love in the same way anymore. What if Charlie had told Katie then about what she had known?

"I'm sorry, sunshine. I know this must be absolutely dreadful. Perhaps it was selfish of me to want to get it off my chest," Grumpy said, "but it never felt right that you children didn't know. Especially you, dear. You were so curious once." His face was drained of color, his elastic mouth sagging. He closed his eyes and laid his arms by his side as though he were depleted, ready for sleep or death.

37

Running through the streets of Hammersmith later that night, Katie turned over memories of her father in her mind. She tried to drown them out in a tide of music, cranking the volume up so high that her headphones vibrated, but she saw him again and again: unassailable, unrelenting, sentimental. Teaching her to swim the crawl. Dancing on disco night at the clubhouse wearing a silver spandex shirt. Gathering Katie in his arms at the hospital when David was born, tears of happiness falling into her hair. Her feet pounded on the pavement as the memories consumed her.

Then Grumpy's words from earlier hit her in the stomach, and she felt sick all over again. *He was a runner, your father.*

The other images came, and they were revolting. Her father's face pulled into a grimace of ecstasy. Having sex with women in cars and in sheds and probably in his own marital bed. In his office. In hotels. She began to imagine him with Lulu, and she ran harder, trying to exorcise the image from her head.

He had lied to her mother, to her, to David—he had lied to himself. He was a man with no integrity. It all connected somehow, surely. But did it mean her father was guilty of rape? Did it mean that he could do the unthinkable, take advantage of a *child*? Underneath her feet, the ground was yawning open, ready to swallow her whole. All along she had believed that he was a man of honor. That his love and dedication to his family were larger and stronger than anything else in the world. That belief had defined her life, guided her in so many of her decisions. Where she went to college (she had briefly toyed with the idea of UCLA, but he thought Los Angeles was full of airheads). What she studied (he believed in practical majors, like accounting or economics). Her eventual job (the offer of an internship at a fashion magazine had made him laugh out loud during one visit, as though being interested in something so flighty was ludicrous). It had led her to be wary of friends like Janice or even Radha if he so much as hinted they weren't good enough for her—and to hold back a part of herself from Zev, which could so easily have ended in disaster. It seemed almost farcical now. All along she had been chasing shadows.

It was almost ten o'clock, and she didn't know what to do with herself, so she kept running. She could run all the way to Kensington Gardens, jumping the fence and racing in the moonlight through Hyde Park to Soho, accompanying the lumbering night buses along Piccadilly, on into the city, on and on, next to the silent black muscle of the Thames. The private garden squares hidden away between terraced houses crouched like black beasts around every corner; behind their locked gates were tennis courts and fountains and sheds that held gardening tools. During the day they were filled with nannies jostling their strollers and toddlers tripping on the gravel, but at night it was different. The silence was like a quiet death.

In that suspended darkness, the image of Lulu came to her—not as she was as a child, but as she must be now, a woman. That voice on the end of the phone line, faltering. Hurt because she had been doubted, was *still* being doubted all these years later. When they were younger, Lulu's private world had been like a railroad track you failed to notice running alongside the train you were on: always there but invisible until another train came barreling along in the opposite direction. She'd existed in a whirl of self-contained energy, this child who had created around her a sense of possibility, of adventure and immediacy. Katie had only been able to see her in one way, had *needed* Lulu to be that way so that Katie could figure out who she herself wanted to be. She had thought of Lulu as invulnerable, a person who barged ahead no matter what, who did not care about the fallout—and in opposition to that, Katie believed herself to be meticulous, observant, empathetic.

But she had also been cautious and uncertain. She had lacked a voice, and now she asked herself if she even liked who she had become. A woman apparently unable to deal with having a child. A woman struggling to commit to a man who was patient and fascinating and creative, with whom she felt a deep, instinctive connection—because *why* exactly? Because she'd accepted without question that she wanted someone like her father, or the person she'd thought him to be, and she'd assumed he wouldn't think Zev was right for her. Katie had proven herself an unreliable judge of character . . . it was all a mess.

But she had been happy, hadn't she? Her job paid the bills, and she had friends in the city she could drink and dance with, a lover she could hook up with. Her future had looked promising, and she had worked hard for it. Now that seemed a sign that she had gotten things upside down. What she thought was security was actually a chain wrapped around her ankles, keeping her in place. She'd been on hold, waiting, waiting—but for what? For a father who turned out not to have been real.

All those nights she'd lain awake before the trial, full of questions, and she had never insisted on getting answers. Grumpy had said so himself, that she had been curious once. Why hadn't she confronted her father, asked him outright what had happened? It seemed inconceivable to her that she'd so readily given in to her family's culture of silence. First during the trial and then during the divorce. Her brain had been waterlogged with neglected questions. She'd had every right to be afraid, to be full of doubt—she'd had the right to voice those questions and to have them answered. But having a right was not the same as exercising it.

She slowed her pace, remembering a pillow, a vast bed, her mother staring up at the ceiling. It was the middle of the night, they were both awake, and sleep was finally weighing down Katie's eyelids. They'd been to see her father that day in Wallkill. It was the day he told her to buck up, to sleep in her own bed, to be brave, and there she was again, lying where he used to lie next to her mother. She imagined she could smell him, that slightly soapy scent mixed with the vanilla smell of her mother's hair. Charlie had turned to her daughter and whispered, "Did Daddy ever touch you, Katie? You can tell me," and she was so sleepy, she was finally there at the brink, and she whispered, "No, no . . . ," and when she woke up, Charlie was gone, the words swallowed up by the night. She never thought of it again.

All along, she realized, it had been her father who was the outsider, not Lulu. It was her father who had lived a life he had not earned. It had been given to him, and he didn't even know it for the gift it was. He had always wanted more, too much; he'd never known when to stop, even when it meant hurting the people he loved. The people he was responsible for. Did it mean he was guilty, after all? That Lulu had, in fact, only ever been telling the truth?

It was possible, she realized, to know someone intimately and yet not know them at all.

The paving stones were uneven under her sneakers; the overhanging bushes scratched her bare arms. There was a sudden noise, a cry from the gardens, and she stumbled. Her vision telescoped, and her breath became uncomfortably short. She was hit by a wave of nausea.

When she opened her eyes, an elderly man was peering at her, and she was lying on the ground. She wrestled herself into a seated position; both knees were scraped, and her head was pounding.

"What you doing running around so late, lovie?" the man asked. His breath smelled of liquor, and his face was covered in white stubble that looked like scattered ash.

"I don't know," she said, trembling. "I must have tripped."

"You all in one piece?" He pointed at her knees, where blood was beginning to sprout. "Nasty-looking tumble."

On her feet again, Katie took a step away from him and was closer to the curb than she realized. He reached out and grabbed her arm as she lurched backward. "I've got to get back," she said. "I don't know where I am anymore."

"Bloody hell, and I'm the one who's been drinking." The man didn't let go until she was standing fully upright, both feet planted on the ground. "Go 'round the corner, love. You're at Camden Hill Square, but if you get back onto Holland Park Ave., you can catch yourself a cab to wherever. All right?"

Back at the hotel her muscles quivered with exhaustion, and her feet were tender, her mind racing like a phantom twin running never-ending marathons. David still wasn't back. She dialed Zev, not sure what she would say but needing to hear his voice, that silky tone. It went straight to voice mail; she had already messed everything up! Staring at the phone for a while, she tried to decide what to do. She hoped it wasn't too late, that he would give her a chance to explain her wavering, that it didn't mean she didn't love him—in fact it meant the very opposite. That she wanted to be the best version of herself she could possibly be—for him, for their baby—and she hadn't been sure she was capable of that.

Now it seemed to her that she was a simple person, not nearly as complex or opaque as she had feared. She knew what she believed in, the life she wanted. And she needed to understand the solid, unassailable truth of what her father did or didn't do, in words that came from his own mouth. Because it seemed likely that she had been very wrong about him, that she had trusted the wrong person. That summer day when she was seven, picking blueberries with her father, she had glimpsed her own singularity, her unbreachable otherness, for the very first time. Now it was this exact self-sufficiency that she had to learn to trust.

When did the damn play end—where the hell was her brother? For hours she lay awake, her body vibrating in the darkness, humming with newfound knowledge she didn't know what to do with. Finally, rooting around in David's toiletries bag, she found a bottle of Tylenol PM and took one. As she fell into sleep, she thought of her mother, recasting old scenes when Katie had interpreted her silences as disapproval or disinterest, when in fact they had likely been a symptom of her hidden sorrow. It seemed clear to Katie that her mother must have had suspicions about her husband's fidelity long before the trial. She hadn't known how to protect herself, so she'd retreated. And her daughter's slow but decisive turning away from her must have seemed like yet another unearned betrayal.

Shortly after six in the morning, she flicked her eyes open, and it was as though she hadn't slept at all. David was in the bed next to hers, deeply asleep. She went downstairs to the coffee shop in the lobby and dialed her mother's number in Canada.

"Mum," she said. "I know all about Dad. I wanted to say . . ." She gulped in a breath that failed to feed her lungs sufficiently.

"Katie? Do you know what time it is? Are you still in London?"

"Mum, listen, I want to say that I'm so very sorry. I'm so, so sorry."

"Darling, slow down. I don't know what you're talking about. What are you sorry about?"

"I talked to Grumpy, and he told me about the investigator. I know that he, that Dad cheated on you. That he lied. I know that things weren't the way they seemed." Katie closed her eyes. "I know why you left him—he cheated on you. He's a liar."

"Oh, Katie! No. I didn't want that," her mother said. "What was he thinking, telling you? I didn't want you to know that stuff, ever. I thought, you see"—she hesitated, made a strangled sound—"I thought you and David might be the only people left who really loved him anymore. I just couldn't take that away from you."

38

Katie carried the knowledge of her father's betrayals with her like a sack of rocks. Every time she moved, even when it was simply to take a breath, her insides ached. She began to worry about the seed planted in her womb; it seemed possible that even this early, when the embryo had just attached to her uterus—its nervous system forming, its heart—it could absorb what was going on in her own body and mind. Could you inherit your mother's pain in this way, through osmosis—could it become part of you?

You were supposed to be able to recognize bad people. When she was little and her mother told her not to talk to strangers, she'd had an image in her mind of what this meant: a stranger was a man with a scruffy beard wearing a greasy raincoat. It was like that with monsters too: they looked and acted like monsters. Even once she was older, Katie was invested in believing that she could distinguish good people from bad. Surely that was what human instinct and intuition were for.

It wasn't until she and David were back on the plane heading home that she told her brother about what she'd learned. It felt like a cop-out, stuffed in their seats surrounded by strangers, movies playing silently on tiny overhead screens, but her need to release the information was overpowering; she could not wait. Each second she held it inside her brought her closer to a tearing of her soul she didn't think she would recover from. No more secrets. David listened quietly, as she knew he would, wrecked. His face went rigid, and he looked down into his lap, her words violently readjusting his world. He didn't ask her a single question, in just the same way she had learned to suppress her curiosity until it became scar tissue, ugly but easy enough to overlook.

The skin around his pinched lips whitened, and tears fell; she forced herself to face him, to acknowledge his pain, accept it. She was hurting David by telling him, but it was her father who had caused the pain in the first place. It wasn't right that these truths remained unspoken.

"But he was so *adamant*—he made such a point," David said, flicking his eyes at her. "Talking about . . . what honor means! And yet, I don't know. There was always something. Something . . . *off*."

"I'm not sure Dad knows what honesty actually is," she said. She was beginning to see that truth could be multidimensional and that it was possible for those various dimensions to clash without canceling one another out.

She called Zev as soon as she landed at Kennedy, and once again the call went straight to voice mail. He was clearly avoiding her. But later that night, he texted that he was up at Vassar, where a few of the arts honors students were getting ready to ship their year-end projects to a gallery in Detroit for an exhibition. He was helping them select their best work. He didn't want to talk over the phone and hoped that was all right with her. We have some big things to sort out, he said. In person, and alone, I think. His words were so unadorned. Did that mean he felt as cold toward her as he sounded? Was he angry that she hadn't insisted he stay over that last night, when her father was with her? She was dying to tell him about what she'd learned in London, how it changed the way she understood her past, how she needed the courage to confront her father, but instead, *this*. These words, devoid of emotion.

Her phone also coughed out alerts about incoming texts from her father, one after another, released upon touchdown. He must have gotten himself a phone while she was away before heading up to Eagle Lake. That first night she was back, he texted her four times while at Walmart, telling her about the changes he was planning on making to the cabin. He had found a great new wine store on Route 28. The new sheets on the bed were amazing. Could she bring him some kimchi from one of those Korean places in the city. And on and on. His favorite emojis were the pink heart with the yellow sparks and the smiley face with the quizzical expression and tongue stuck out, and he sent them to her randomly. He didn't understand texting etiquette and didn't seem to expect a reply. Each text was an affront, part of a game he thought she was still playing.

She did not respond. The morning after she returned home, she could not get out of bed and spent the day vomiting into a bowl. She called into work sick and slept. She didn't care. It seemed to her that life could not simply go on the way it had before.

All these years she'd absorbed the lessons her father had taught her, only to discover they were flimsy and false. She slept, chased by dream snippets that made no sense. Her sheets were soaked with the tang of misery. When morning came, she looked at herself in the mirror and saw someone unrecognizable. She asked herself what this woman wanted, and the answer was so simple: she wanted to live her life with integrity. No one could do that for her.

She kept thinking of Lulu as she had been that last summer, brazen and lovely—and deeply and continuously disappointed by life. Surely things would have been different if Katie had had even an inkling of what her friend had gone through? She rested a hand on her roiling stomach and thought of mothers and daughters, of Piper and her ugly dismissiveness, of her own mother and her corrosive secrets. She wondered what Lulu felt about children, being one and having one. Katie knew she needed to do something, take a step toward living the life she wanted. She would go see Lulu. But first, she had to talk to her father face-to-face.

She texted Zev that she was coming up to Poughkeepsie later that day to see him, after going up to Eagle Lake to see her dad. Then she got online and looked up the Greyhound bus schedule to Blackbrooke.

John Gregory was in shirtsleeves hauling trash when Katie's taxi pulled up to the cabin. The barrels were already full, and he was crushing cardboard under his boots and stuffing it into the sides of the one container that had space. It was late June now, and the ferns of Eagle Lake had lost some of their pungent smell. The trees above them swayed, silver-backed leaves trembling. Pine needles spun in the steady rain. The purr of the cab doing a U-turn and heading back to Blackbrooke was accompanied by the crunch of John's boots on gravel.

"Baby girl, what a treat," he said, wiping his hands on his jeans. His hair was damp, cut very short. "I thought you were still in London!"

The sharp odor of his sweat rose off him. Her logical self kept repeating: *Just because he committed adultery does not mean he is a rapist.* But she wasn't actually his baby girl anymore, and she resisted the urge to put her nose into the folds of his shirt and tell him how the logic of her world was being turned upside down. She wanted him to tell her something that would make it all right again. She needed to hear him say that his endless cheating did not mean he was a monster, capable of harming a child.

The cabin was clean and warm. Above the stone fireplace hung a new flat-screen television. On the side table stood a framed photograph of John and Charlie holding pink cocktails. John's arm was draped around her shoulder, his hand dangling above her left breast, gesturing as though he would grab it. His face split wide in a grin, Charlie rolling her eyes.

"So how was the old geezer?" John asked. "Did you have rain?"

"Dad, you haven't been honest with me," she said. She remembered the baby in her stomach, the life she was responsible for. Her skin was clammy with fear, but she couldn't let herself falter. "I spoke to Grumpy; I know you weren't faithful to Mum."

"What on earth are you talking about? He was always one to mess around in other people's business," he said. His face registered nothing, no surprise or fear. Disappearing into the kitchen, he kept talking. "He's an engineer, you know, a busybody. Thinks if he gets involved, he can solve the problem, be the savior." When he came back in, he had a drink in each hand and passed one to her. "You know, he's the one who causes trouble, not the other way 'round. Doesn't mean to, but you know how it is."

"He showed me the investigator's reports, Dad. I saw them with my own eyes." Her throat was as dry as chalk. She sniffed at the drink and took a sip; it was water. She was relieved. Lying in bed yesterday, she had realized that in many of her memories of her father, he had had a drink in his hands. It had never occurred to her before that this could have something to do with why people made excuses for his behavior. Because she was sure people must have known about the affairs. Her hand shook so much she spilled some water down her chin.

"Your grandfather, he never quite came around to me, even in the early days. There was another guy Charlie'd liked; they'd been dating awhile. He was from where they grew up, became a hedge fund guy or something. Harry, he's someone who doesn't like surprises. Not one bit. He didn't like it when she picked me instead."

"You're saying you never had any affairs?"

"Your mother, she was the—"

"Is it true you'd been fired from your job before you were arrested? Who paid for the lawyers?" she interrupted, flustered by his evasions.

"My job? No," he said. "He's been confusing you, honey. I worked for Citigroup for years—I brought in tons of clients. They loved me at that place."

"But you lost that job, right? They let you go?"

"And *we* paid for the lawyer." John took a swig of his drink. He pursed his lips and studied his daughter. "Took out an extra mortgage on the house, as a matter of fact."

"So we owned it, the West Mills house?"

"Well, Harry gave it to Charlie. It was ours."

"We bought it from him?" she asked.

"I'm really not sure what you're getting at," John said, his voice tight. "Your grandfather was generous. He helped us when we needed help."

"And still, you think he made this stuff up, about you and Constance Nichols, for example?"

A flicker of something—discomfort? alarm?—crossed John's face. "Constance was your mother's friend," he said. "She was good fun. Her kids, though. Wild, totally wild. I was always glad you steered clear of them."

"Am I hearing what you're saying, Dad? You're saying you never cheated?"

"I adored your mother. And I adore her still. I'd have her back in a heartbeat." John tipped his head to one side. "You know, I thought you were smart enough to make up your own mind about things. You always seemed to have a good head on your shoulders. I worried about Davey, but I never worried about you. I don't know what's been going on while I've been gone, but you're acting like a spoiled teenager."

"We're not talking about me right now. We're talking about *you*."

"Well, I don't think an interrogation is necessary or fair. Haven't I already been blamed enough? Let's get things back on track. I don't know where you're headed with this, and I don't like it. I'm getting something to eat." He went back into the kitchen and rustled around in there for a while. She leaned against the doorjamb and watched him. He was calm, taking out a frying pan and some bread. Unpeeling plastic from a slice of American cheese. "Want a grilled cheese sandwich?"

"No. No, I don't." She filled her glass with water from the faucet. The afternoon was slipping away. "Why didn't you testify during the trial?" she asked, leaning back against the edge of the countertop.

"Herb advised me not to. It's always like that in these kinds of cases. It doesn't work to defend yourself. Such a scam, but people are people. They base their decisions on things like how contrite they think you look."

The tick tick tick of the flame of gas being ignited. The clock hanging above the stove reading 4:27. It was warm in the room, stuffy and sweet smelling. Sweat popped up on Katie's forehead.

"Someone like me takes the stand, and whatever I say is incriminating. You know, if I'm friendly and honest, then they think I'm too casual, not taking it all seriously enough. Heartless. If I fight back, tell it like it is, the jury thinks I'm too aggressive. You're a rapist in their eyes either way. So you've got to shut up and sit back and let the lawyers do the talking for you."

"And Lulu. And Jack."

He turned around, spatula in one hand.

"Yeah. I read the transcripts," she said. "I know he testified."

"Now why would you go and do that to yourself? Your mother and I went to a lot of trouble to spare you. Why're you causing yourself all this heartache? It's time to start fresh! I'm out, and everything is looking good, honey. Everything is *good*."

The smell of warming toast and melting cheese was overly rich. "Can you stop that, Dad? Can you stop with the cooking?" She went back into the living room and sat down on the couch. Her breath seemed stuck in her throat. She wasn't getting anywhere.

He came in behind her, crumbs on the corners of his mouth. Brunch used to be his big thing. On Sundays in the summer, he'd make his family an obscene amount of food: chocolate pancakes, omelets, fruit shakes. Her favorite had always been late in the season, when he sprinkled fat blueberries on top of the pancakes, and they'd swell and burst during cooking, purple juice streaming everywhere. "Honey, you seem really stressed out. Everything okay at work? Want to come up here for a week or two? The season starts soon; it'll be fun for us."

The beach in sunshine. Jumping off the diving board. Summer nights in the boathouse, clutching sweating cups in slippery hands. Everyone here knew what had happened, and one of the great disappointments her mother had been unable to hide was that no one at Eagle Lake had stood up for John. And now he was here again, behaving as though nothing had happened; it was astonishing. Katie thought of Lulu, sitting on the dock crying. She remembered the T-shirt David had found in the Falcon: *Hawaii*. Something had happened that night. It was not true that Lulu had fabricated the whole thing.

"Look, Dad. Since you didn't testify, why don't you tell me what happened? Just, like, tell me everything, okay?"

Waving a hand at her dismissively, he took another bite of his sandwich. He wasn't meeting her eyes. "Nah, let's not go down that road. Let's talk about something else, this awesome television, for example. Hell, prices have gone down since I've been gone."

He took a tiny step forward as though he'd lost his balance and closed his eyes for a second too long. Katie wondered whether his glass was really filled with water.

"What happened after the dance, Dad? Why was Lulu's T-shirt in your car? Can you tell me that?"

"Ack, Lulu's shirt," he said. He turned his head toward the front window, where they both heard a buzzing noise, a kind of muted rattling. The sound was rain, pecking at the gravel. "I thought you said you read the transcript. It's all in her testimony."

Katie leaned forward. He was most forthcoming, she realized, when she framed the question as a way for him to tell his side of the story. It was possible he could still say something that would help her understand, something that would prove to her he was not a bad man. She wanted to give him that chance. "Why don't you just tell me? What happened, Daddy?"

39

Charlie was at the piano playing some Joplin tune and called over to John to get her cigarettes, which she'd left in the Falcon. The square dance was over and most people had left. He could tell a storm was brewing; the air was so sticky, yet there was a kind of electricity running through it. When he got to the parking lot behind the club, he discovered that the car wasn't where he thought he'd left it. He spotted it at the far end of the lot, top down, under the basketball hoop in the pitch black. As he approached, someone jumped up from the back seat, vaulting over the door and running into the woods. He stopped and stood still for a second, listening. There was the rustle of the woods, but something else too.

It was too dark to really see much. A gray shape materialized in the back seat—a dog or something, not a human. It became paler as he neared, until it was the white of bare skin: it was a person on hands and knees, and the sound was the sound of crying.

John took three long gulps from his drink and wiped his hand across his mouth. "Lulu," he said.

She was almost naked. When she saw him, she screamed, an involuntary animal cry. "She was looking for her T-shirt. She'd been in there with that kid, that Brad guy. They'd been fooling around, and she'd taken off her T-shirt, and she couldn't find it. She was flipping out, just beside herself."

He told her don't worry, he told her to wait, and he ran to the lost and found near the sheds and grabbed an old T-shirt from in there, something dry and not too musty. When Lulu emerged from the car, she was crying so hard she was hiccuping, her whole body jerking back and forth, she was so upset. He put his arms on her shoulders, just her shoulders—nowhere else—and he didn't know she would do it, but she leaned into him heavily, and he couldn't push her away, so he hugged her, like he would hug Katie or some other child. He patted her on the back, and she hugged him hard and then calmed down a bit.

That was all that happened. He was trying to help her—she seemed so upset. He didn't know what had happened between those two, but that kid Brad was an asshole. He had upset her somehow, and John was glad that he could make Lulu feel a bit better. He was like a father to her—he was protective, you know. He just wanted to help. She was a mess.

In the cabin with Katie, John sighed. He finished his drink and went to the bathroom, stumbling on the area rug in the hall. While he was gone, Katie picked up his glass and sniffed the dregs. Vodka. How many times had he been drunk and she'd never even noticed? Her father approached life as though it had been designed with his entertainment in mind, while it was the opposite for other adults, who were compelled to accommodate him. Her mother, for example. Maybe Charlie had never had the chance to really be herself, always on alert for what her husband was up to. To Katie and her friends, John was the fun one, and her mother was the cold fish, distant and wary. The irony of this struck Katie as painful now that she was facing motherhood herself.

She stood by the window, looking out over the driveway toward the Big House. Daylight had been tamped down, and the trees were drained of color. The rain was coming down now in smeary gray sheets. The bobbing of a car's headlights flickered among the pines in the distance.

"I want you to stop drinking," she said when her father came back into the living room.

He turned down his mouth, the dark of his eyes like Teflon. "Now don't you go getting all prissy on me," he said.

A flash of light stroked her shoulder, and a car with its headlights on pulled into the other side of the driveway, facing the Falcon. The rain was really coming down now, striking the roof and windows loudly. Out of the car came Zev, a hoodie pulled over his head. He glanced up and saw her at the window and hesitated for just a second, then ran toward the front door. In the time it took him to get from the driveway into the cabin, he was soaked, his sweatshirt blackened with rain. He wiped a hand across his nose. When they embraced, it was as though she were falling into him. The smell of lemons hung around him like a perfume.

He pulled away to search her face. "I couldn't wait anymore," he said, his eyes kind. "I figured I could give you a ride back to the city. You okay? You look kind of pale."

"I'm . . . we're having . . ." Katie started, but when she turned to include her father, he wasn't there anymore. "I'm so glad you came. This is so awful. I think he's really drunk."

"I was worried about you. What's going on?"

"Zev, my man. Welcome to our little piece of paradise," John said, back now, his voice too loud. He was red faced, as though he'd become overheated. "What brings you here? Come to snatch away my baby girl?"

"I have a car," Zev said, his expression pointed. He seemed like a man who would stand his ground, a tree that barely creaks in the wind. "You might say I'm the designated driver."

"Very funny," John said. He had another glass in his hand. "The man has a car. I'm impressed."

"Dad, keep going, okay? What happened after that?" she asked. "After you found Lulu in the Falcon?"

"It started to pour, and everyone went home," John said. With great care and precision he placed his drink on the table. He glanced at Zev from under his brows, and even though he hesitated, there was something in his expression that suggested he was proud of himself. That he liked having an audience.

"And then what? I want to know everything."

The Falcon got rained on, but it was no big deal, and John and Charlie drove the Nicholses home, and then they went back to the cabin, he said. Charlie was worried about the kids swimming in the lake during the lightning storm; she was angry. She got like that when she'd had a few—always worried about everyone else. Wanted to be sure people were safe, whatever. He wasn't ready to go to bed, and the television was on, and he didn't think they'd mind, the girls, if he came and sat with them a bit, just to have a nightcap.

"It was the last night of summer, you see," he said to Zev, as if only a man would understand.

And they watched this old flick he'd seen years before—he forgot now which one—set down in New Orleans, he thought, or somewhere warm. The story was kind of funny, but Lulu started to cry again. He was helping her; she was still upset about Brad, and then she twisted it around, made it seem wrong.

"Helping her how?" Zev asked.

John continued looking right at him, and Katie seemed to disappear entirely—she wasn't sure either man even knew she was in the room anymore. Part of her wanted to stop this terrible momentum, but there was another part of her that dove right into the undertow.

"What would you know about the—the power of, uh . . . of empathy, huh?" John asked Zev. "Artists. You're all about yourse—"

"Let's keep it civil, okay?" Zev's voice was low but so firm that he could just as easily have been shouting.

"Like you know anything about women. No one understands them. Everyone thinks they know what women want, but no. No way." John leaned forward, pursing his lips, and tipped the entire glass into his mouth.

Lulu was crying; she'd been treated without respect, he explained. You see, women didn't even know what they wanted half the time, and when they did, they didn't know how to ask for it. Lulu hadn't known that she couldn't let boys touch her like that boy had touched her. That her own pleasure was important.

Katie recoiled. The immensity of it, the warped logic, hit her.

"So what did you do?" Zev continued. "How did you help her?"

Irritation clamped down on John's face, and he stood up. "I'm talking to my daughter," he said. "No one invited you here. In fact, why don't you just leave?"

"You're talking to *me*," Zev said, a sharp resolve in his eyes. "And I'll go when your daughter asks me to. Katie, you want me to go?"

"No, don't. Please stay," she whispered. "And then, what then, Dad?"

John was swaying, still staring at Zev. His skin shone with a sickly sheen.

"I can tell you this," he said, trying to talk slowly and clearly. "I can tell you I sure as hell didn't do anything I deserved to go to jail for."

Zev and Katie's eyes locked, confirming what they'd both heard. Tears clouded Katie's vision so that she saw her father as though he were no longer whole, body parts bobbing in a murky lake. She remembered then that first day of summer as she had watched him make his way through the water while Lulu had raced after him. She imagined gathering her old friend up in her arms, pressing her close: *This was wrong, so wrong. You deserved better. I'm so sorry, Lulu.*

"Oh my God," she said. "Let's go, Zev."

But her father grabbed her wrist, his fingers sticky against the naked skin, squeezing too hard, and she cried out. Zev pushed himself between them, making John stumble backward into the couch and fall on the carpet. "Just, just who . . . who do you think you *are*?" he panted, lifting his head, struggling to get up.

Katie yanked open the front door. The sound of the pouring rain was like flies inside her ears. She could barely breathe. She and Zev ran toward the Datsun. As Zev yanked the car into reverse, her father stumbled from the house and came toward them, still in his shirtsleeves. "Wait," she said, putting a hand on Zev's, and he pressed on the brakes. She opened her door, the whoosh of cool rain covering her cheeks. "Daddy, what are you doing?" she shouted.

Her father climbed into his car. When the engine roared to life, Katie tumbled from the Datsun and ran over to him, knocking sharply on the pane. He rolled the window down a fraction. "Of all people! I never, ever thought you'd be a turncoat," he shouted, his eyes blind like glass. "My little Katie!"

Water streamed into the neck of her shirt, down her spine. Underneath her feet the gravel began to shift and swim in the river of rain. "What are you doing? You can't be driving!"

"Stop telling me what to do," her father yelled, jamming the car into gear. He jerked forward, but the Datsun was in the way.

Katie ran behind the car, put her hands on the trunk, and screamed, "Wait! Just wait a second!" Banging the trunk with her hands, desperate. Hitting it again and again. "Stop!"

The car trembled beneath her palms as her father yanked it into reverse, and she pushed into it as though through the force of her will she could stop him from moving, and Zev was running toward them and her foot slipped on the tumbling gravel and she flew backward, knocking her head. Her legs shot forward. The car emitted a dreadful, high-pitched shriek and jerked backward, and she screamed as loud as she could, but he didn't see her—he couldn't see her—and the Falcon didn't stop.

40

It was warm and wet and there was an ice pick or a knife in her leg and people were everywhere. People touching her. Hands on her body, clothes ripping. A voice she knew, hands she didn't. Things were happening very fast, but she didn't understand. How could you bully a body like this and yet be so gentle at the same time? How could it be warm, like being in a bathtub, like being a baby, and yet pain was sparking through her body, a star shower of pain, a whole constellation blowing up?

And she tried, tried so hard to remember: Did he leave? Did he keep driving?

She thought he did. She tried to sit up, to tell someone, but all those people, they were not listening to her.

A man with graying hair was crying. He kept saying, "She's pregnant!"

The blinking lights were bothering her, but she couldn't turn away from them. Her shoulder was in some kind of contraption, her head as heavy as a block of granite. Like Morse code, the lights blinked and blinked some secret message she could not decipher. She was supposed to be at work; she had to get up and get dressed! She was never late—they would fire her, they would find someone else, and then what would she do? A hand pressed on her other shoulder, very lightly, a delicate touch that shot her entire body through with pain. "Stay still; you're not going anywhere. Calm down, honey."

When her body relaxed, it felt as though someone were lying right next to her, a body stretched out along the edges of her own, defining her and holding her in place. It couldn't be real (or there would be pain), but it was comforting: the softness of thin cotton, dark, silky hair on warm skin. Deep inside herself a sense of calm spread like syrup, soaking into the recesses, smoothing out the rough corners.

Time became a waterslide and then a stagnant pool. It was feathers in the wind and an airless room. A hare and a toad. Inside her, the life she had had and the life she now lived became steam that scalded her lungs, but it was also cool water that gave her goose bumps. She tasted blueberries and felt the sun on her feet and remembered laughter—so nice! She wanted to stay there, in the laughter, but they wouldn't let her. People she didn't know were moving her, pushing her around. Why couldn't she just stay in that moment in time and be surrounded by that life-sustaining, joyful laughter that made the whole world slip away, that turned time to dust? That made you happy just to be alive?

David was there when Katie woke up. He was sitting in the corner, in a chair by a large window, leafing through a paperback. The reading light struck him at an angle, dividing his face into knife edges. "Davey," she whispered. He jumped up and tapped furiously into his cell phone.

"Katie, Katie!" he said, leaning over her. His cheeks were sunken, bearded. He looked ten years older. "Promise me you'll never do that crazy-ass shit ever again."

"What did I do?" she said, but he only shook his head.

Her mother came rushing in, a gauzy scarf unraveling from her neck. She took Katie's head gently in her hands and brought her face close. Pale ginger freckles softened the wrinkles that crisscrossed her skin. "Sweetheart, we were so worried," she said. "How do you feel? Are you okay?"

"I'm okay," Katie said. "I think."

"Honey, do you know . . ." Her mother looked at David, and he shrugged.

Katie screwed her eyes shut. The baby! She had been pregnant. Now she was in a hospital, and everyone's face was racked with pain. "Is Zev here?" she whispered. "I want Zev."

"He's coming," David said. "He's just showering. He's been here four days straight."

She opened her eyes and gazed, stunned, around the hospital room. "Where am I?"

"Mount Sinai," Charlie said. "We're in New York."

"Mum," she said, hot tears spilling onto her cheeks. "What happened?"

"You were in an accident," David said. "Your leg was . . . you got run over."

"Oh God . . ."

"Honey, I'm so sorry about everything. I want to tell you—David and I've been talking. I thought I was doing the right thing! Protecting you. It's how I was brought up, to keep quiet, you see? To keep moving. And . . . and I thought—I just really couldn't see how talking about it would help."

Katie's head hurt. "I don't understand."

"He wasn't a bad man, not really," her mother said.

A shot of alarm buzzed through Katie's clouded brain. "What are you saying?"

"Did anyone tell you about your father, darling?" Charlie asked.

"No," Katie said. "What?" One leg was in a cast from her ankle to above her knee. Her right hand was purple and red, the skin of her palm shredded, covered in a glistening ointment. Her head was pounding from the drugs.

"Do you remember being at the cabin?" her mother asked.

The cabin . . . the car. Her father getting into the Falcon. "Where is Dad?" Katie asked, struggling to sit up, her heart galloping.

The New York State troopers chased John Gregory from Blackbrooke up toward 209 North and then onto the highway. Their lights were flashing, but he didn't appear to notice them. He wove in and out of the traffic in a way that would not have raised suspicion had they not been notified about the accident. Around mile marker 47 at exit 19, the Ford Falcon was in the middle lane, and just as he was about to pass the exit, he swerved violently to the right and took the off-ramp, bumping over the grass. The troopers were going too fast to take the turn and were forced to take the next exit instead. It was still raining heavily. They called in that they had lost him; another unit was on its way.

The second cruiser came up from the south and took the exit. It drove carefully because of the poor conditions. The sumac at the side of the highway was towering, and the first time the police drove along the bend, which merged rather sharply with the local road, they did not see anything amiss. The second police vehicle lost him too; it drove aimlessly until a call came in from dispatch. A local resident said she'd seen smoke ten minutes earlier as she was driving to pick up groceries.

They scoured the area. Visibility was poor, and the rain would not let up. There were no brake marks along the road and no visible signs that they could detect from their vehicles. Now there were three cruisers on scene. They parked, lights flashing like a carnival, and six officers began walking along the curling edge of the road. Up close like that you could more easily see the tire dent in the sodden grass, the split in the wall of feathery sumac that had opened and closed and now provided a shield hiding the woods beyond from view. Officer Latcham flicked on his flashlight and saw instantly the broken twigs and branches.

About ten feet farther on had lain the Falcon, trunk high in the air on a berm of pine needles and rocks, nose accordioned into the trunk of a midsize pine tree, shearing off the left door, crumpling the body. The car made a faint hissing noise as water from the radiator leaked and evaporated on the warm metal. Inside the car was a man, badly injured. It was suspected he had been driving in excess of eighty-five miles an hour as he took the curve. Later they discovered that his alcohol level was three times the legal limit. It took considerable time for the emergency vehicles to reach the site, and the paramedics had trouble accessing the injured party. He was still alive but not responsive as they strapped him onto the gurney and wheeled him toward the waiting ambulance. It was a twenty-minute drive to the nearest trauma unit. The man had serious intra-abdominal injuries.

They did everything in their power to save him, but they were not successful.

What she remembered best months later, when she was finally fully healed, was that when Zev came into the hospital room, the world seemed to slow down—not as though it were stuck or stuttering but as though it had found its own unique rhythm and was slipping into a groove it could sustain. Life was chaotic, and there was pain and anger, but with Zev there, regarding her with the vastness of his pale, oceanic eyes, it seemed she could survive it. "The baby? What happened to the baby?" she breathed in his ear.

"The baby is good." Zev put a cool hand onto her burning cheeks. Her mother brought over a damp washcloth, and he pulled it over Katie's forehead.

"We're going to have a baby," she said, incredulous, realizing she had already decided this was what she wanted.

One life for another. Why there had to be this blistering reckoning, she didn't know, and she wasn't sure how she would accept it. There was so much to figure out about her father, her past, but she wanted to look forward. She wanted to look toward Zev and their baby. The past was inextricably linked to the present—she understood that—but for now she wanted to think about building her own future.

Zev smiled, creases springing from eyes to mouth. "We're going to be a family, *yakirati.*"

"You'll have to teach me Hebrew," she whispered, spent.

"Precious," he said. "It means my precious."

Her body was broken in multiple places, her mind too weary and drugged up to think straight, but she'd held on; her life was not totally undone. She had not lost all agency, she thought, closing her eyes against the keen bite of her tears.

41

The leaves that fall were incredible: the brightest of yellows and oranges, red thrown in like splashes of blood. Katie turned off the highway at Winnisquam Lake, near Laconia. She passed Lake Kanasatka, and then, finally, after driving between two large ponds, she was in Moultonborough, a small town that lay beneath the White Mountain National Forest. The area was sparsely populated, the occasional wood-sided farmhouse and smaller suburban houses lining the roads. Number 89 Hartley Way came up on her right, and she pulled over.

There was an enormous yellow house with a sign jutting out from the roof: LULU's Dog Care, Grooming and Spa.

A large basket filled with muddy boots lay next to the front door. Dog toys were strewn over the painted floorboards of the porch. Two wicker rocking chairs looked as though they'd weathered severe winters, and an ashtray on a side table was filled with crushed cigarette filters. The front door had a sign tacked up on the top windowpane: "Back in ten!" The yellow paint on the side of the house was pale and peeling, stripped by the summer sun. Air conditioners hung from the windows.

Two crisp barks in the distance and a whistle. Katie stopped short.

At the back of the house, a meadow with soggy brown grass led to the edge of yet another pond. To the left was a collection of smaller houses, sheds that might have once belonged to a barn. Three people had their backs to her, looking out over the rippling water. One appeared to be a man, a giant, his broad back encased in a tan-colored Carhartt jacket with patches on the elbows. He must have been six five or even taller. His shoulders were vast, hunched against the wind. Next to him was a woman throwing something into the pond, a ball, maybe, or a stick. She appeared tiny in comparison, narrow and short, a child or perhaps a teenager. Her hair was cropped and blonde. Another woman was playing with a small yellow Labrador, a cloud of black curls bouncing around her head as she moved.

Katie pressed against the siding and caught her breath. Her nerves were live wires thrumming in her neck. It could only be Lulu. The man put his hands up to his face and let out a hoot. Three dogs emerged from the water, spraying droplets from their coats, causing everyone to step backward, laughing. The woman with the black curls hurled a ball, and the yellow Lab chased after it. She pushed the hair aside and called out, "Thatta boy!"

The blonde woman turned toward Katie and waved. She was older than she initially appeared, her hair more gray than blonde, her face lined like a piece of crumpled paper. The closer Katie got, the older she became. "Hi there," she said in a friendly, businesslike tone. "Can I help you?"

"I'm here to see Lulu. I'm a . . ." She didn't finish the sentence, but she didn't need to, because Lulu was staring at her, stock still.

"Katie," she said. "Holy fuck. You came."

"I thought we said today, didn't we? When we talked?"

"Yeah, yeah, I know. I just didn't think you'd actually turn up."

"All right, let's get these fellows dried off," the older lady said. There was sly curiosity in her eyes, but she pressed her lips together and didn't say more. When she headed toward the sheds, the dogs followed her.

"Give them dog food, and they'll follow you to the ends of the earth," said the giant.

"Trev, this is an old friend of mine. Katie Gregory," Lulu said. "This is Trevor. My husband."

They shook hands, and it was clear that Trevor knew exactly who Katie was. He crushed her hand in his as though to warn her to be careful with his wife. He'd have been the kind of boy who would hurt other kids by accident on the playground. Now he was a man who looked like he could knock you out with just a quick jab of his meaty fist, though he would never actually do it. His eyes, limpid and dark, settled on her. "Well, I'll never," he said. "Did not imagine her like this, Lu. Not one bit."

Lulu's face was more settled than when she was a child, her round cheeks flatter, her lips a little more compressed. In tight dark jeans, she was voluptuous in the way a model from the fifties would have been. When Lulu headed toward the house, Katie followed her. Now that she was here with her old friend, her breath slowed to a reasonable rhythm, and she could think more clearly. She'd never be able to make up for what had happened to Lulu, and she certainly didn't expect them to become friends again. But at the very least Katie could break into the silence, let her know that Lulu had not, in fact, lost her silvery voice; she had it still, and it rang in Katie's ears like a gong.

The back steps led straight into a large, cluttered kitchen with a potbellied stove in one corner and an enormous plank table with mismatched chairs crowded around it like passengers jostling to board a bus. Under the table was a frail dog that raised its head slightly as they entered and then put it down again on its paws, unimpressed.

"Like your hair," Lulu said, her back to Katie. She was at the sink, rinsing something. "You color it?"

Katie's hand reached automatically for her ponytail. "Highlights."

"Scandinavian," Lulu said. "Very ice princess. You didn't tell me you were expecting."

"I'm still kind of getting used to it myself."

"Oh yeah?" Lulu raised her dark eyebrows. "Well, it's sure hard to miss. When're you due?"

"February. I'm twenty-six weeks. Got a ways to go."

"Boy or girl?"

"We just found out. Girl," Katie said. She surprised herself by smiling widely. "That'll be a handful, huh? Serves me right."

"No kidding." Lulu reached up to get a couple of mugs from one of the cupboards and revealed a tattoo of what looked like a long black feather snaking up the left side of her back. "Trev wants kids, but I'm not so sure. Not everyone's destined that way, you know?"

"Yeah, well, I wasn't so sure either," Katie continued. "But I'm excited. I quit my job, and I'm starting my own business. Consulting with nonprofits on media outreach. Just getting going, but it's great." Her belly strained against her leggings, hard and taut. She wasn't yet fully mobile because of the injuries to her leg and foot, but each day she exploded with energy. The doctors had told her after four more months of physical therapy she could start running again.

"You with the guy? The father?"

Katie nodded and looked around.

"That makes a difference," Lulu said. "You need a village, right?"

Newspapers were piled high in one corner next to a stack of ancient-looking glossy magazines. The cabinets were honey-colored walnut from the seventies, the linoleum from that same era. The walls were entirely covered in postcards held up with tape.

Lulu saw her looking at them. "From the pet owners," she said. "They send their dogs cards when they board them here. You know, 'Frisky, we love you! We miss you so bad!' That type of thing. Feels like they're rubbing it in my face, their trips and stuff. Corsica and Barbados, when it's below zero up here." She was clanging around, picking things out of a drying rack and cleaning something. "Coffee okay? Or you want something cold?"

"You don't have to bother."

At this Lulu turned and put one hand on her hip. "You might as well sit down. I'm not gonna bite you."

Katie chose a chair by the window. Lulu was not at all as she had thought she'd be—neither the way she'd been that summer they were teenagers nor the broken, damaged, vulnerable woman she had been afraid her friend might have turned into. Instead, she was just an older version of the Lulu she had known. Unchanged, and yet also utterly unfamiliar.

"So. Here you are," Lulu said. "Now what?"

"I'm really glad you picked up. I mean, that you were willing to even listen, you know? Thank you."

"Yeah, well. You were persuasive. And your dad, I was sorry about that. The accident and all." Lulu scooped two spoonfuls of instant coffee into the mugs and filled them with boiling water. Taking a seat opposite Katie, she placed the mugs on the table. "You saw Jack again, huh? Boy, did I like him. I mean, *really* like him."

"I know," Katie said. "We were smitten." It felt as though a tornado were shoving them together, Lulu's breath on Katie's face and in her ears and hair.

"We kissed, you know. A couple of times. Well, only once, actually, the week before he left for camp." Lulu must have seen something on Katie's face, because she added, "To be honest, I kissed *him*, really. He didn't have much of a choice."

"Oh, okay," Katie mustered. So that must have been what had given Jack the courage to finally let Katie know that it was her he liked, not Lulu. "You know about the two of us, right? That we were sort of together, by the end?"

"I didn't really want to know. I always thought I could turn things around, that things would end up how I wanted if I just tried hard enough," Lulu said, picking at her cuticles.

"I should've just told you. I don't know why I didn't just tell you." Katie had been thinking about that for months now: Why had she been so afraid to tell her friend about the kiss? Why hadn't she been able to claim what she wanted? It seemed so simple now but so impossible then.

"There's lots of stuff we could've said and didn't," Lulu said. "You know, the boys in Blackbrooke were such assholes. I'd lost my virginity, earlier—right before summer break. This guy called Tim. A total lug."

This surprised Katie so much that she took an enormous gulp of her coffee, which scalded the roof of her mouth. All those weeks together, the countless late-night chats, the hours in the canoe and in the woods, and Lulu had never told her that she had already lost her virginity? It felt like a failing on Katie's part that Lulu hadn't trusted her or that she had been ashamed.

"You're awfully quiet," Lulu said. "Didn't you want to talk?"

"It's really hot," Katie said. "The coffee."

"A million times I thought of calling you. When I told people about your dad, I had no idea what was gonna happen. I just said it. I wasn't really trying to unburden my soul or anything. I knew it was pretty fucked up, but I liked your dad. He was a good guy, basically. Like, I know it wasn't right, but I wasn't intending to have him put in jail."

She paused and stared at Katie in a way that was unnervingly direct.

"Thank God for Trevor," she continued. "He's the one who brought me up here. Not that I love it in the middle of the freakin' wilderness, but I'm out a lot, moving around. My shrink says that's good for me." She took a sip from her mug. "Don't you want to ask me anything?"

"Brad, what happened with him?"

Lulu tilted her head, looking suddenly like a cat. Her eyes were a little wild, and her knee began tapping up and down. "What about him?"

"Is it true that—"

"Yes, if you mean, did we have sex. Who told you about him?"

Footsteps on the back stairs made them both turn their heads toward the door. Trevor came in, arms filled with firewood. He stamped his boots on the mat once, twice, then went over to the stove and dumped the wood on the ground. "Everything okay in here, girls?" he asked as though expecting them to be giggling over their drinks, swapping stories and secrets. But when he turned, still crouching, a look of concern crossed his face.

Lulu was shaking her head. "What happened with Brad, it was sort of an accident, nothing more. I was stupid; I let it go too far. And Jack's not totally reliable; you know that, right? He's kind of a pleaser type of guy, kind of weak."

"I, yeah . . . I think I made him into someone he's not, in my mind," Katie said. "I don't think we really knew each other at all."

"Well, me neither. Sometimes we only see what we want to see."

"Amazing, isn't it? We can be so sure, when we're kids, and we can be so wrong."

Lulu laughed, stretching out her long neck. For the first time that afternoon, Katie saw a glimpse of who she really was: still herself. She had not lost the ability to electrify when she connected, to make you feel right and solid, a better you.

It was hard to believe how much she had endured. "I read the transcripts of the trial," Katie said. "And that report, about what could be admitted at trial? I'm so sorry about what happened to you then. I mean, I had no idea. Your mother's boyfriends. I'm really sorry."

"Yeah. I was pretty good at talking without saying much," Lulu said, watching as her husband fussed with the wood. He got up, patted his hands together to rub off the wood dust, and then gave Lulu a peck on the cheek. "You don't have a cigarette, do you?" she asked Katie when he'd left again.

"No," Katie said, "sorry."

"That's what I figured, pregnant and all." Lulu's eyes were unblinking. She was still stunning, more so, even, than when they'd been teenagers. Although her skin had good color, there were bags under her eyes, but her weariness had something sensual to it.

"I quit," Katie said. "Smoking, I mean."

"You quit," Lulu repeated. "Did you ever really smoke in the first place?"

Her tone was so accusatory, as though she thought Katie was pretending to be someone she wasn't. "I'm not sure what you're getting at."

"You sound angry," Lulu said. She bit at the skin around her thumb. "You know, I stopped being angry at you so long ago."

"Angry about what?" Katie asked. "About Jack?"

"It's not what you did. You didn't *do* anything. But that doesn't mean it wasn't, you know, hard. Being your friend. And your parents never liked me," she said, "but I really, really wanted them to. I would have done anything to have them like me, love me, even. The way they loved you."

"They were my parents. Of course they loved me."

"Your mother, she felt sorry for me. She was nice that way. Your dad, he liked me one minute and then not the next. Hot and cold. I could never figure that out. And all I wanted was for him to look at me the way he looked at you. I was so excited when we were watching TV, and he, well . . . He asked me to get that lipstick I'd been wearing. He did that thing where he kind of crinkled his eyes, like he was going to tell a hilarious joke or thought you were funny or something? I loved that." Lulu mimicked a grin, and then her face fell. "Remember the red lipstick? He hadn't liked it at first, but then turns out he did."

Katie's stomach tightened. At the clubhouse, during the prize giving . . . she was remembering now. Hadn't her father—had he wiped the red off Lulu's lips? "Christ. I didn't realize. I just . . ."

"I was so happy—I figured it meant he thought I was pretty."

Katie stared at her, horrified. Her mind scrambled, then fixed on the fact of Lulu's bewildering vulnerability. She was not "pretty"; she was *beautiful*—didn't she know that?

"So I went and got another one from that bag we got at the dime store. You were sleeping, just totally out. He put it on me, and his hand

327

was trembling so much, like he was nervous. He was sweet with me, like *he* was the kid." She rubbed her lips together, remembering. A look crossed her face, and she seemed like a girl again, uncertain. "You know, Katie, I should tell you—I never said no. I could have said no, and he would have stopped. I know he would have stopped if I'd told him to."

Katie could barely breathe. She had been fast asleep, and *this* had happened. And Lulu still felt it was in some way her own fault. "You don't have to explain. It wasn't for you to say yes or no. You didn't do anything wrong, Lu."

"When he was convicted, that was a fucking shock if ever there was one. That the jury—all those people—they *believed* me."

"I believe you," Katie said, clamping her hands together in her lap to stop them from shaking. She had come to listen, and she was going to hear Lulu out, as awful as it was. "And I'm really sorry about it, all of it."

Lulu looked at her levelly, and there was no triumph in her eyes, no relief or gratitude. It was the same look she'd given Katie in the courtroom: stripped bare, untextured. "For a while, I thought it was right that your dad should be punished," Lulu said. "They sent me to this therapist . . . and she made me see it all differently. And I started to think he was a sicko—that being nice to me like that, it was all so he could get what he wanted, not because he actually liked me. She made me realize that it wasn't really about me at all."

"I get it," Katie said. She flexed her fingers and clenched them tight again. "Everything was always all about him. Right up until the very end. Kind of incredible."

Lulu's face fell. "I can't believe he's actually dead, Katie. I feel like it's my fault."

"Lu, no. Really. This is something I've thought long and hard about. My dad brought all of it on himself. Nothing made him get in that car." She paused. The violence of her anger was tempered by grief that the man she'd loved was gone, and she'd learned that she had to hold those two feelings inside her at once. "You know how much I loved you, right? I thought you were perfect—I wanted to *be* you. Good things happened too."

Lulu brought her hand up to her mouth again and pulled at the nail of her thumb with her teeth. "Mom told me a million times she wished you and I'd never met, but I don't," she said. "I didn't wish for that, not once."

Just a week after the accident, when Katie was still in the hospital, the *Boston Globe* had run a huge story on the way individual states handled the issue of consent, in particular the varied length of sentences that convicted rapists ended up serving. Her father was cited as having been given one of the longer sentences in the Northeast in the past decade, due to the age difference of thirty-one years between him and the victim. Anonymously, Lulu was quoted as saying, "I didn't even know it was rape till I told a grown-up." And then, as a side note, the article mentioned that shortly after his release, John Gregory had been killed while driving intoxicated.

After her mother showed her the clip, Katie had known Lulu would probably read it, and when she felt a little better, she'd tried calling her again. That time, the pall of a death hung over them as they stuttered into their receivers, and they had been more willing to sit with the silences. Now here they were, finally breathing the same air, and Katie had the sudden sensation of aging a year for every second that passed, as though she were morphing into an old woman, the same way the woman outside had shrunk and aged as she'd approached.

"Do you ever wonder about how things could have been different?" Katie asked as she got up to leave. "If we'd done just one thing differently that night? Like made one decision that would've changed everything?"

"I don't know," Lulu said, frowning. "I think I'd have ended up in the same place no matter what. But I guess it's different for you."

There was nothing Katie could say to that. In a way it *was* different for her. She had lost her way without doing anything. She'd always been convinced that she was to blame, and in a way she was, but not in the way she'd thought.

For years the Gregorys and Lulu had been like a series of interlocking concentric circles, all shifting and jostling against each other, and everywhere they turned led to the same place. It wasn't like that just for Lulu; it was like that for Katie too: there was no going back and straightening it all out, creating a beginning and an end, a path that led somewhere different. All she knew was that since her accident and her father's death, she saw the world in a different way, through a wider lens. Before, she'd been running so fast that the edges of her vision were blurred; now life was rendered in sharp detail, its crisp outlines sometimes nicking the tips of her fingers as she felt her way through. But it was a good kind of pain, one she was learning to bear.

As she drove back to the city, to the apartment in Bushwick that she shared with Zev (the one they'd finally decided on, because he could make a studio out of the enormous concrete block garage out back), she fiddled with the dial on the radio until she found a classic-rock station. She rested a hand on the mound of her belly. It would be the last time she saw Lulu, and that was all right. She rolled down the window, cranked up the music, and began to sing, quietly at first, then louder. Her voice was far from perfect, but she discovered that she knew all the words to the songs, and that felt good.

EPILOGUE

2024

The sea is calm after days of wind-whipped waves, and the turquoise waters are so clear she can see there are no rocks below, no hidden outcrops that will injure her. But the will it takes her to allow herself to fall is almost more than she can summon. She stands at the cliff's edge, her tanned toes curling over the rock, for a very long time. At first Zev encourages her, and then, seeing that she will do it—she *will* jump—he falls silent and watches.

Katie likes his eyes on her. He can't keep her safe, he can't help her jump, but he can watch her, and being seen in this way gives her the push she needs to launch her body forward and fall through space.

We have known each other almost a third of my life! she thinks as she kicks her feet and bursts through the surface, emerging into the air. Time seems immense; it is seconds and minutes and hours; it accumulates, heals, and hurts. Six months earlier, she turned thirty-two. She and Zev are celebrating their fourth wedding anniversary. Sasha is seven years old. It has only been a year since ovarian cancer killed her mother and two months since David had his second child. He lives near them in Brooklyn with his husband Markus, little Ella with the ginger curls, and a newborn named Cassius who rarely opens his pale hazel eyes. Her brother and his family come over often, the adults drinking red wine from oversize tumblers while their children make memories. Since Charlie died, Michel has already driven down from Montreal three times; these children are his only family—his chosen family. Their friends visit often: Tanisha and Radha and Frankie and many of Zev's old students. Soon Katie will stop traveling so much (she's gone two weeks out of four); she's selling her consulting business, which has taken off in recent years, and going back to school. Maybe she'll study to become a nurse. It took eight months for her leg to fully recover, and she came to love the people whose job it was to help her become whole again.

Up above Katie on the cliff, Sasha has joined her father. The Jamaican sun paints her long limbs with honey. They stand with their arms arched over their heads. Sasha's are impossibly delicate, covered in fine golden hairs. She rises on tiptoes and without waiting launches effortlessly into the air, head tucked under, white-blonde curls streaming behind her. When her fingertips break the ocean's surface, there is barely a ripple. Zev dives after her.

Katie's body rides along with the thrust of the water as he plunges in, and—bobbing up and down, watching their two sleek heads approach her, grinning—she thinks to herself: *Stop measuring everything. Just be.*

ACKNOWLEDGMENTS

I am so grateful for my agent, Erin Harris, whose enthusiasm, professionalism, and keen sense of story make great things happen (and she's a mensch, too!). I'm truly thankful for Jodi Warshaw's belief in this difficult story and her openness to my input, as well as the superb team at Lake Union.

A supportive, kind, and invested community makes all the difference to lonely writers. The staff, instructors, and students at GrubStreet in Boston have been crucial to my health and happiness for over a decade now. I could always count on Eve Bridburg's unwavering belief in me as a writer to keep me going. Eve and Chris Castellani helped with advice right when I needed it most—thank you both. Also, Chris took a chance on me when I was a teaching newbie and thus unwittingly helped me achieve one of my life goals. Huge thanks to Alexandria Marzano-Lesnevich, who went the extra mile for me.

I benefited immensely from many generous readers. Thank you, Kathleen Buckstaff, for your passionate advocacy and hours of conversation; it's largely because of you that this story was able to blossom. Kristi Perry listened and contributed enthusiastically as I regaled her with writing and publishing stories over many years—thank you for lovingly supporting me (even when you knew I was wrong) and for so much spot-on advice. Lynne Griffin and Lisa Borders, many thanks for your tough love and for sharing your astute understanding of narrative structure. I so appreciate Judy Sternlight's, Laura Chasen's, and Tiffany Yates Martin's sharp eyes and invaluable insights, which vastly improved this book. Thank you to Greta O'Marah for being my first real reader and for your relentlessly positive perspective; to Jennifer de Poyen for putting your poetic sensibilities to work; to Susan Howard for your infectious enthusiasm; to Francesca Nelson-Smith for your encouragement; and to Lil Weiner, Candice Reed, Dawn Tice, Kathy Sherbrooke, Polly Zetterberg, and Willow Humphrey for your thoughtful, invaluable commentary. Also, I'm grateful to Dr. Tracey Milligan, Natalie Wright, Ellen Rosenthal, and Max Wiley for helping me with research.

I'm astonished by the generosity of the many authors who carved out time to read this debut and offer their endorsements (many of whom I cold-called because I so admire their work): a huge thank-you to Carol Anshaw, Miranda Beverly-Whittemore, Robin Black, Jenna Blum, Tim Johnston, William Landay, Marybeth Mayhew Whalen, and Barbara Claypole White. What a literary community! I'm excited about paying it forward. Endless gratitude to the Virginia Center for the Creative Arts, the Vermont Studio Center, the Norman Mailer Writers Colony, and the Hemingway House for offering me beauty and quiet in which to work. I'd also like to thank the many agents and editors who took the time to read the book and respond so very kindly—it's because of dedicated book lovers like you that we are able to share our stories with the world.

I spend summers in an incredible community that shares some resemblance to Eagle Lake. I'd like to give a warm hug to everyone there for helping create such a unique, magical place in which I've always felt at home.

Kevin, I can't thank you enough; truly, words fail me.

A warm thank-you to my parents, Peter and Occu Schumann, who taught me about hard work and resilience—and also sometimes let me faff around reading and writing instead of dragging me along on hikes when I was a surly teenager. It matters to me that you are proud of what I do. Sheila O'Marah's unflagging interest in my work helped me shift my mind-set when it really mattered. Jay O'Callahan has been a model of how I'd like to live as a storyteller—with generosity, empathy, and deep listening skills. Thanks also to Peter and Svenja O'Marah, who suffered through my frequent tardiness and distraction with such good cheer.

Q&A WITH KATRIN SCHUMANN,
THE FORGOTTEN HOURS

Alexandria Marzano-Lesnevich is the award-winning author of The Fact of a Body: A Murder and a Memoir, *a book about how the story of one crime was constructed—but also about how we grapple with our own personal histories. It tackles questions on the nature of forgiveness and whether a single narrative can ever really contain something as definitive as the truth. Winner of the Chautauqua Prize, it was named one of the best books of the year by* Entertainment Weekly, *Audible.com,* Bustle, Book Riot, *the* Times of London, *and the* Guardian. *The recipient of fellowships from the National Endowment for the Arts, MacDowell, and Yaddo, as well as a Rona Jaffe Award, Marzano-Lesnevich lives in Portland, Maine, where she teaches at Bowdoin.*

AML: *The Forgotten Hours* feels almost astonishingly contemporary, raising questions of consent, power differentials in sex, and #MeToo. Yet, of course, you must have begun writing the book a long time ago! How long did you work on it, and how did the idea come to you?

KS: The characters were in my head for years before I found my way into this story. It took a while to work out how to unfold the narrative so that it felt honest and nuanced and conveyed the turmoil that these kinds of cases can cause. It was incredibly important to me that I do justice to this story, and it was a struggle at times. Once I found the voice and rhythm of the narrative, the structure fell into place, and the book began to take on a life of its own. That was when I started to have fun with it on a sentence-by-sentence level and when I felt I'd actually succeeded in writing the book I set out to write.

As for the idea, in some ways, Katie is a stand-in for me. I had two close friends become embroiled in legal proceedings around separate assault and consent issues—each on polar-opposite ends of the spectrum. I saw with my own eyes what happens to the accused and the accuser. I felt immense empathy for everyone involved—and it sent me into a total tailspin. I wanted to capture that confusion.

AML: Are you surprised to find the book so urgently relevant?

KS: The conundrums around sex and consent aren't new—it's a problem women have been trying to get to the bottom of for centuries, but no one really wanted to hear them out. It upsets our way of seeing the world. What's astonishing is that now, finally, it's becoming something both men and women can talk about, and people are actively listening.

There is such shame for girls and women around this topic, so much judgment, so many biases and assumptions. And a lot of well-meaning men have had their heads in the sand. The fact that my book is coming out now seems like a real gift, because it will get people of all ages thinking more deeply and talking more openly—and those are healing conversations.

AML: Part of what makes the book feel so real, I think, is how complex every character's actions and motivations are. John's not a simple villain—and Katie is forced to reexamine her feelings about

her former best friend, Lulu, and even her own mother, Charlie. Was the complexity of how the reader would view the characters something you were conscious of as you were writing?

KS: Yes, that's at the very heart of the book! A friend who suffered abuse once told me, "It's possible for people to be two things at once: kind and cruel." Of course, it works the other way around too: "good" people are not all good; they make mistakes.

We want to see the world as black and white and fit people into silos—it makes us feel as though we have some sort of control over what happens to us (and it informs the choices we make). But the truth is that life isn't like that. It's far more complicated. This is something I experienced myself, and I spent years feeling torn about my loyalties. When I was able to make better sense of that bewilderment, it was an enormous turning point for me.

AML: You've described feeling torn, and the relationships in this book feel so true to life in that way too—webs of conflicting loyalties, emotional entanglements, and histories. As a writer, I was struck by the high-wire act you did of pairing a complicated plot with intimate, nuanced portrayals of each of the characters. How did you approach that balance, and what books were inspirations to you along the way?

KS: I think the characters just felt really real to me. We all have different versions of history. We may share the same experiences, but we all feel them differently. So I took that idea and looked at it closely. I chose a single, limited point of view so that readers could form their own opinions about how "truth" is constructed. Also, a lot of editing and rewriting went into this book. It went through many drafts, and each time I thought deeply about human motivation and desire.

I tend to read very intensely and quite widely while I write, to remind myself of what writers can achieve and to figure out what my own goals are in terms of tone and story. Tim Johnston's novel *Descent* was inspiring, because I so admire the fast-moving story line and the beautiful writing. Same with Carol Anshaw's *Carry the One*, which does a stellar job of conveying her characters' complexities and growth. British writers like Tessa Hadley (*The Past*) manage to convey an interiority that never veers into melodrama. And then other books like *The Goldfinch*, by Donna Tartt, or *Beautiful Ruins*, by Jess Walter, remind me to have fun, to take risks. They inspire me to play more with the words and ideas and characters and not be so uptight. That's always a good reminder for us writers!

AML: It's interesting, too, that you've mentioned control in thinking about characters' motivations. Different characters in the book have different ways of trying to feel control over the complicated, difficult situations in which they suddenly find themselves. Katie's mother distances herself from her family, including from her own children, in a way that's very painful to Katie. Even Charlie's father, Katie's grandfather, Grumpy, separates himself. Yet Katie herself chooses a very different way of trying to regain her sense of control. She chooses not distance but kind of an extreme closeness to her father. She chooses to believe him absolutely. In a way she chooses him over everyone else, including even her best friend. It's only as her trust in her father's denials begins to crack that she starts to look into the case and revisit her memories and realize she may have been wrong. Did you know from the start of writing that you'd have her dig into the case?

KS: I knew that Katie had to go through a fact-finding mission that would release her from the constraints she's imposed on herself and allow her to live a more authentic and independent adult life. Even though she adopts this just-get-on-with-business approach, in the process she totally loses herself. The accusation and trial come at a pivotal moment for her—right when she's forming ideas about who she wants to be. As a consequence, she struggles to define herself and ends up making choices that are questionable. She's looking to adults to show her the way, and they fail her. Ultimately she's on a lonely journey.

What was hard for me to get right here in terms of storytelling is that she's an extremely reluctant truth seeker, and when she begins digging in to the case, she hopes (rather desperately) that it will help her reestablish a sense of safety and order. But the information doesn't give her greater control: quite the opposite. Of course, that doesn't mean it's not a necessary journey.

We all have different ways of coping with trauma. The thing is, we can't really grow up and heal until we figure out how to face the messy, painful stuff. Ignoring it doesn't make it go away. Bessel van der Kolk's nonfiction book *The Body Keeps the Score* helped me understand this, as did Roxana Robinson's incredible novel about PTSD, *Sparta*.

AML: Katie has this get-on-with-business approach you describe, yet of course she also has this unlikely romantic partner, Zev, who seems to have a much freer approach to life—one that ultimately seems to have a big influence on her, whether she consciously realizes it at the time or not. Why did you decide to give Katie and Zev almost the same age difference as John, Katie's father, and Lulu, Katie's best friend, whom John is convicted of raping?

KS: I wanted the reader to think about consent in a more nuanced way. The big age gap isn't the problem in and of itself. I thought it would be interesting to have Katie fall for a father figure who is nothing like her own father. It's as though her subconscious won't allow her to stop growing and learning. Also, for me, the sexual freedom that she feels with Zev is important because she finds it both threatening and liberating, and I think sex and intimacy are often complicated in that way.

AML: This connects to what I think is one of the central themes of the book: what we owe one another. Katie thinks, at one point, that there must be no greater sin than the choice her mother has made to distance herself from the family. But of course that's a question the events in the book force Katie—and the reader—to think about more deeply: Is she really understanding the size of that sin correctly? Isn't she ignoring another, greater sin? Is loyalty truly the highest value? What do we owe our loved ones?

KS: I could have written so much more about Charlie! I found her to be a fascinating, if opaque, character. As a mother, she's really caught between a rock and a hard place. She's an Englishwoman, mired in an old-fashioned "stiff upper lip" culture in which you don't whine and you don't do therapy. How can she protect her children best while also living her own life? She divorces John, even though she knows she's sacrificing Katie's love. I wanted the reader to wonder about her motivations and Katie's reaction. What happens when people can't talk? In what circumstances should parents hide grown-up truths from their children? Silence leads to all sorts of misconceptions and makes us feel very isolated.

Seeing our parents with clear eyes is exceptionally hard. It's almost impossible for us to know them fully as human beings, to disentangle ourselves from the emotional bonds that tie us together. They owe us and we owe them, and this can make for a toxic brew.

AML: It also leads to lots of confusion around loyalties. I was really struck by that with the relationship between Lulu and Katie. Katie immediately disbelieves her friend, taking her father's side, and a lot of the tension in the book comes from the increasingly complicated mental and emotional contortions she must perform to stay loyal to her father.

KS: We become deeply invested in believing that people are who we think they are. When we get it wrong, we see it as a reflection on ourselves, on our own failings, and this can be very disorienting. For Katie, it feels safer to disbelieve her friend and trust the man who raised her so lovingly. Also, I thought the best friend dynamic was especially intriguing, as there's an intensity and intimacy to those early friendships that's not entirely dissimilar to a sexual relationship. There's an enduring loyalty to them, too, and Katie has to struggle with that, because she's not allowed to feel loyalty toward both her father and her best friend.

I was also interested in exploring this dynamic through Katie's relationship with Jack, her first love. How much of her memory of him and what they shared is actually real? How does memory change reality? She's invested in believing Jack is the only person who really knows her and in the belief that through him she might be able to find herself again. These relationships we have as teenagers impact us for the rest of our lives.

AML: It's riveting to watch the changes in Katie's loyalty, the slow unspooling of her belief system. To what extent was that trajectory inspired by your personal experience?

KS: I know Katie, because her psychological journey was mine, and not just around issues related to this particular topic but around relationships in general. Being loyal was a trait I highly valued; it defined my way of seeing myself. As I've matured, I've had to reassess that. I strongly believe in values such as generosity, steadiness, and trustworthiness, but I've come to think that loyalty is misunderstood and overrated.

Some years ago, I heard Colum McCann talk about "radical empathy," and it really stuck with me. Radical empathy happens when we tell each other's stories, he says; it allows us to know each other in spite of our differences. All good, right? But blind empathy is often destructive and unearned. That's why writers like me spend years on our books: we're working hard to untangle and understand these human impulses.

I thought about this a lot over the years I taught writing in prisons. Every human being has a story, and there's power both in the telling and in the listening. And yet—where do right and wrong fit into the picture? Is there a limit to empathy and loyalty?

AML: What do you most hope readers take away from the experience of reading *The Forgotten Hours*?

KS: My mission is pretty simple: I want readers to see how this story might relate in various ways to their own lives and draw strength from it.

BOOK CLUB QUESTIONS

1. This book is set in two very different places at two pivotal times in Katie's life. In what ways do you think the two timelines contrast and play off each other in terms of theme? How do the style and tone of the past chapters set at Eagle Lake embody the notion of "forgotten hours"?

2. In every case in which a person is accused of wrongdoing, there are others caught in the middle who have divided loyalties: mothers, fathers, children, siblings, friends, lovers. Have you had this experience, and if so, in what way? How is this story different because it's told from the point of view of a "peripheral victim," rather than from the accuser's or accused's perspective?

3. After her family falls apart, Katie tries to reinvent herself, first in college and then in New York City. Do you think she succeeds? In what ways is her struggle to break free from the influence of her parents a normal process of maturation, and in what ways is it a product of her trauma?

4. The girls are mischievous teenagers, reveling in summertime freedom. How much do you think Katie is right in believing her behavior that night contributed to the choices Lulu made? Why does she blame herself?

5. Do you find Lulu to be a sympathetic character? What about John Gregory? Do you think it's possible to ever truly know someone?

6. As children, we often define ourselves in opposition to our best friends. Do you think Lulu is a good influence on Katie or a bad one? What about Katie's influence on Lulu? When they meet again at the end of the book, what insights do you gain about the dynamic between them when they were younger?

7. David, Katie's brother, seems to have a different relationship with his father than Katie does. Why do you think this is the case—does it have to do with gender or personality, or could it be something else?

8. Early on, we are told that Katie doesn't quite trust her feelings for Zev. Why do you think this is so? Why, and in what way, do her feelings for him change as she comes closer to understanding what really happened that night at the lake?

9. Does Zev "get" Katie? Why do you think he's drawn to her, and what does this say about him as a life partner? What do you think the author is saying about the different ways we try to make sense of our experiences?

10. The book explores Katie's first loves: her platonic love for her father and her romantic love for Jack. How do you think a woman's early experiences of love impact her ability to have a healthy sexual relationship as an adult? Where does Lulu fit into this picture?

11. Why is Katie so attached to Jack? In the end she says, "I don't think we really knew each other at all." Do you think she's right in this assessment? Have you ever had a similar experience?

12. John's defense team tries to portray Lulu as deeply troubled and unreliable, a highly controversial but common courtroom tactic. Do you think the morality or personal integrity of either the plaintiff or the defendant should be part of the equation when it comes to allegations/crimes of this nature?

13. Katie has always had a difficult relationship with her mother. By the end of the book, do you understand what has really been going on and why? Is there anything Charlie could have done differently?

14. Grumpy is an old-fashioned character, dearly loved and stoic. Did he fail his family by keeping quiet about what he knew? Do you think there's merit in having a stiff upper lip and just getting on with life? How did that approach harm or help Katie?

15. If there is a moral to this story, what do you think it is?

ABOUT THE AUTHOR

Katrin Schumann studied languages at Oxford and journalism at Stanford, and she is the author of several nonfiction books. She has been awarded fiction residencies from the Vermont Studio Center, the Norman Mailer Writers Colony, and the Virginia Center for the Creative Arts. Schumann teaches writing at GrubStreet in Boston and was an instructor in PEN's Prison Writing Program. She lives in Boston and Key West. For more information, visit www.katrinschumann.com.